Tallulah *Falls*

Tallulah Falls

Christine Fletcher

BLOOMSBURY

Published by Bloomsbury Publishing, New York, London, and Berlin
Distributed to the trade by Holtzbrinck Publishers

Library of Congress Cataloging-in-Publication Data
Fletcher, Christine.
Tallulah Falls / by Christine Fletcher.
p.   cm.
Summary: Having left her Orgeon home to meet a troubled friend in Florida,
high-school student Tallulah finds herself stranded in Tennessee and taken in
by the employees of a veterinary clinic.
ISBN-10: 1-58234-662-3 • ISBN-13: 978-1-58234-662-5
[1. Self-perception—Fiction. 2. Runaways—Fiction. 3. Veterinary hospitals—Fiction.
4. Manic-depressive illness—Fiction. 5. Mental illness—Fiction.]
I. Title.
PZ7.F62778Tal 2006   [Fic]—dc22   2005027869

First U.S. Edition 2006
Printed in the U.S.A.
2 4 6 8 10 9 7 5 3 1

Bloomsbury Publishing, Children's Books, U.S.A.
175 Fifth Avenue, New York, NY 10010

All papers used by Bloomsbury Publishing are natural, recyclable products
made from wood grown in well-managed forests. The manufacturing processes
conform to the environmental regulations of the country of origin.

For my dad
and in memory of my mother
with love

Chapter 1

The rain had been coming down for hours, yet every flash of lightning still made Tallulah jump. She was tired of jumping. She was tired. She'd been walking since morning in the chunky-heeled boots she'd brought instead of her Nikes, because the boots were adorable and the Nikes weren't, there wasn't room in her duffel for both, and besides, how could she have possibly foreseen she'd end up here? Wherever *here* was. A name for *here* was not on Tallulah's list of known facts.

What was on the list: She was soaked. Starving. Broke. Her feet hurt, and no matter how far she'd walked today, it wasn't nearly far enough.

At least the starving part was about to be fixed, as much as ninety-three cents could fix a hunger twenty-four hours old, give or take. Tallulah had forgotten her watch back in Oregon, so the time was also a guess. But it had already been full dark when she'd first glimpsed the truck stop sign, moon-sized and dim through the rain. Promising food. Coffee. Shelter. Since then, it seemed she'd spent half the night chasing it. Scrambling down muddy banks, tripping her way through ditches. Her elbow still ached where she'd hit it against an unseen post, but now, finally, the sign loomed, glaring yellow, practically overhead. The only thing remaining between her and it was the highway underpass.

In the small light spilling from the roadway above, Tallulah could see a little way inside. Walls of curved, corrugated metal, potholes half-filled with water. The underpass looked like the inside of a throat and smelled worse.

Lightning lit the air, an instant's strobe, blinding her. Tallulah began to count: one . . . Thunder cracked and boomed, rattling her heart inside her chest as though it was a penny in a can. She didn't wait for her vision to clear before leaping into the shelter of the underpass.

The afterimage of the lightning oozed in front of her, a greeny orange glow. From the highway overhead came the slice of car tires over wet asphalt: whoosh and gone, headed the way she had come. Nothing back there except a lot of empty road, staring cattle, and the motel room where she'd woken up this morning to find herself alone. Derek had disappeared, and with him not only her ride to Florida, but also her life's savings of three hundred fifty-four dollars and her brand-new black leather jacket.

Tallulah slid her feet forward uncertainly. Two steps lengthened into five. Eight. Now she could make out a pocked yellow sheen glimmering on the open road beyond the underpass: the reflection of the truck stop sign on wet asphalt. A few more steps, and she'd be sipping glorious coffee. If she mixed in enough creamers, maybe it would be almost like a meal. Tallulah focused on the yellow shimmer, shifted the duffel strap high onto her shoulder, and swung into a trot.

Immediately her toe caught on something. She lurched forward, windmilling her arms, and almost caught her balance but the duffel helicoptered off her arm and then she was falling. She landed hard, wrists-first, onto the asphalt. In the next instant she was on her feet and scuttling backward, recoiling against the dank metal wall.

It had groaned. Whatever she'd tripped over had groaned. And it had been solid-soft. No crinkling of plastic, no clang of metal. A body. A psychopath. A knife slicing toward her unseen. The air, sodden from the August storm, lay black and heavy as a hood over her face. Tallulah tried to stifle her gasping. She couldn't.

Run, she thought. Now.

Her muscles refused to move.

On her right, a rumble sounded. The rumble grew to a roar and in the glare of headlights the underpass sprang into sudden day: green and rust walls, black graffiti, and, within kicking distance of Tallulah's left foot, the body of a dog.

By the red burn of the car's taillights, Tallulah spotted her duffel. She lunged for it. Another moment and blackness swallowed her again, but she didn't care because it was only a dog, a dead dog, not a monster creeping to slit her throat. Once she was safe in Florida, in the bright sunshine, this would be just another story to tell Maeve. Maeve would probably think it was funny, once she got over being sad about the dog.

Another rumbling. A semi this time, so overwhelmingly loud that Tallulah shrank against the wall again and covered her ears. The underpass flared into light once more.

The dog had raised its head. It was staring at her, its eyes glowing phosphorous green.

Tallulah bolted. She stopped only when she'd reached the open road, the rain gushing down as though it had missed her, finding new paths down her face and neck and arms. Her legs shook so badly she had to bend over, hands braced on her thighs, to keep them from collapsing.

Just a dog. Just a dog. Still it took a long time for her breath to stop bucking, and her heart, and for the quaking in her muscles to subside. When she did finally raise her head, she saw towering above her, in yellow neon: SAM'S FOOD-COFFEE-PHONES. A reader board beneath scrolled the price of gas, alternating with the message: GOD BLESS AMERICA.

A short scramble up a muddy slope, and Tallulah was in the parking lot. Perhaps twenty feet away, on the other side of a plate glass window, an old man seated in a booth raised a hamburger to his mouth.

Tallulah had last eaten the night before, and then only half a slice of pepperoni pizza. She'd pulled listlessly at the cheese, waiting for Derek to notice she didn't have an appetite. Waiting for him to apologize for taking the wrong exit, for getting them lost in this godforsaken cow country. But Derek had ignored her through two cheeseburgers, a basket of fries, and two beers. Silent the entire time: Derek the wounded. She'd ordered beer, too, but the waitress had taken one look at her face and said, in that Tennessee drawl that sounded so kind until you deciphered the words, Nice try, honey. Come back in a few years.

This morning, setting out on foot from the motel, Tallulah had thought she was hungry. By late afternoon, after seven hours of walking and only three miles of rides, she figured she knew what it was to starve. Now, swaying in the rain, her guts felt endless and echoing, her muscles puddly as mush.

Forget coffee. Fries, crisp-hot and salty, burning her tongue. That's what she needed.

She was halfway across the parking lot when Maeve's swift-water voice floated through her head: *Not dead.*

It'll be dead soon, Tallulah thought. Tallulah didn't know a lot about dogs, but even she could see that.

I wonder how long it's been lying there.

I don't know, Tallulah thought back. Anyway, it's not like I can do anything about it.

You could go get it. You could get it help. Maeve's voice, soft, not pushing. Maeve never pushed. Maeve believed in self-determination. It was one of the reasons she and Tallulah were best friends.

"No," Tallulah said. No dogs. No detours. Maeve was expecting her in Orlando tomorrow. Instead, Tallulah was slogging around Tennessee with no money and no plan, with the notebooks Maeve desperately needed squashed in a duffel bag under three T-shirts, two cropped tanks, a bunch of cotton floral panties, one lycra thong, her second-best jeans, and huaraches bought on sale before Tallulah left Oregon, because every time Tallulah imagined Florida she imagined everyone wearing huaraches.

Florida. At this moment, Tallulah should have been eating hush puppies in South Carolina, with Orlando one easy day's drive away.

That morning, waking up alone in the motel room, she'd thought maybe Derek was getting a cup of coffee. Maybe a paper. She'd showered and dressed. Walked outside. The Honda Civic was gone. Still, she'd waited. She'd waited until checkout time, and when she went back in the room to gather her stuff she discovered her leather jacket was missing. That and all the cash in her wallet.

So maybe asking a guy she'd gone out with one time to drive her from Oregon to Florida hadn't been the smartest idea. But what else could she have done? Even the cheapest airfare would have taken more money than she had. Whereas Derek had a car and no job and he hated Portland. Plus, he still liked her.

It had been a good plan. It should have worked.

The arguments started before they even got to the Oregon border. They argued over which routes to take. They argued about who got to eat which snacks (Tallulah adamant that if she paid for it, it was hers; Derek, citing driver privilege, favored a more flexible approach). They argued about Derek smoking in the car, a right he held sacred, no matter how many times Tallulah explained that, having just managed to quit herself, him puffing away next to her for hours every day was driving her crazy.

Loudest of all, they argued over the sleeping arrangements. Derek took for granted that sharing a motel room included sharing the bed. Tallulah—having realized, by the end of the first day, that she couldn't stand Derek Hubner—insisted that one of them was sleeping on the floor, and it wasn't going to be her.

Getting lost in Tennessee was just the final straw.

Still, maybe she shouldn't have yelled in his face that he was a moron who couldn't even read a map. At least, not in the McDonald's. Most of the kids in line had snickered. Worse, so had the women.

Because after that, Derek had gone all broody and sulky. Instead of doubling back toward the interstate, he'd driven for miles in the opposite direction, the roads getting smaller, four-lane, then two, not answering when Tallulah told him to stop, to turn around, to PLEASE ask somebody for directions, until they came across the tiny motel and attached diner and the tavern across the road. By then it was so late she agreed to stop for the night but only if he promised to stop being such a jerk, and he said, Fine, just shut up for two seconds and pay for the room, will you? *Je*-sus.

After dinner Derek had gone to the tavern, where Tallulah couldn't follow. Hours later, she'd woken up to jostlings in the bed, beery breath in her face, and a hand massaging her hip. "Come on, baby, be a doll," she remembered Derek saying, just before his hand slipped and her knee jackknifed up in surprise. She remembered an explosive *oof*, the bed sinking down and springing up, and a thud on the floor. She'd propped herself on her elbows, squinting into the dark, and whispered, "Derek? Are you OK?" His only response had been a low groan. She distinctly remembered thinking, as she flopped back down and rolled over: Serves him right, the creep.

Trudging up the road in the rain, lost, soaking wet, and robbed blind, Tallulah still thought it served him right. In fact, if there was any justice at all, Derek would drive his stinky little Honda Civic off a cliff into a river, where alligators would tear him into tiny, unrecognizable pieces. Were there alligators in Tennessee? Tallulah didn't know. She decided there were, if only because she found the notion so soothing.

And yet she couldn't escape the feeling that if she were Maeve, none of this would have happened. If she were Maeve, she'd be in Florida already, feet up on a balcony railing, sipping a margarita.

If she were Maeve, she'd do something about that dog.

But she wasn't Maeve. She was Tallulah, and Tallulah was starving.

Tallulah sidled forward between a Bronco and a GMC Jimmy. The old man peered through the plate glass window, frowning, his burger suspended in both hands. He must have seen some movement, some shadow, but he hadn't spotted her yet.

I wonder if it's in a lot of pain.

Tallulah stopped.

I wonder how long it'll lie there before it dies.

Look, Tallulah thought. I'm doing the best . . .

Never mind, Maeve said, and sighed. *I'm sure you're doing the best you can.*

"Dammit," Tallulah said. The old man took another bite of burger. He had to bite twice. Probably getting the pickle. He batted a napkin at his mouth as he chewed. Tallulah watched until he nabbed the mustard spot in the crease of his lips and then, as if there was nothing more to wait for, she turned around.

It was worse going into the blackness a second time. Even knowing the dog was there, even knowing it was just a dog, when she felt her boot nudge into its side she gasped and started backward. Then, her hand pressed over her heart—in the dark, alone, its battering against her fingers was a tiny comfort—Tallulah took a deep breath and knelt down.

Now she could smell it: a stink of wet dog and dogshit and diesel.

What if it bites me?

This time, no answer came. But she hadn't come this far only to back down now. She forced her hand forward. Almost immediately she touched it: gritty wet fur clinging to the sides of her fingers. She prodded it once, ready to jerk away, half-expecting teeth to clamp into her wrist. But the dog didn't move. The flesh under the fur was cold. It felt like a wet sack of flour with bones.

She was too late. At least she could tell Maeve she'd tried. Good-bye, doggie. Hope you like doggie heaven.

The dog's ribs sprang up under her palm. Tallulah yelped and jolted backward, falling hard on her butt. From the blackness came a faint sigh of breath.

Goddammit all to hell.

She fumbled badly, picking it up. The dog hadn't seemed so big in the headlights, but she'd get an arm under one part and another would slip. It didn't struggle—it didn't move at all—but once it moaned, a deep hollow sound that seemed to scrape along her insides. Finally, she worked one arm under its chest and another under its belly. Her shoulders and thighs burned with the strain. The dog's head hung over her right arm, bobbing with each step, alternating in awkward rhythm with the duffel banging against her hip.

In the parking lot, Tallulah laid the dog down under the nearest lamppost. In the orange, rain-shimmery light it looked crumpled, like the jellyfish she and her older sister, Terri, used to find on the beach. She didn't know what kind it was—she'd never had a dog of her own—but it reminded her of a neighbor's mutt back in Portland. Some kind of retriever. Like that one, this dog was black, where its fur wasn't caked with mud. A glossy smear trembled along its side. Tallulah touched a finger to the smear, held the finger up to the light. Blood. The dog's breath came now in ratcheting gasps.

Tallulah stood up. Across the parking lot, an older couple

stood next to their pickup truck. They were staring at her. Tallulah began walking toward them.

"Excuse me," she called.

The woman popped into the truck like a mouse into its hole, but the man stood where he was. The shadow of a baseball cap obscured his eyes, but his mouth looked kind. The woman leaned across the front seat and rolled down the driver's side window. Under the cab light, her hair glowed an unnatural tangerine.

"Henry," she said. "Get in." The man ignored her.

"Hi," Tallulah said.

The man nodded. "'Evening," he said, his tone non-committal.

"I found a hurt dog." Tallulah pointed to where the dog lay under the light. The man looked, but said nothing.

"Henry, get in the car," the woman said.

"He needs help. I couldn't just leave him to die," said Tallulah.

Henry looked her over. His lips thinned a little. Tallulah glanced at the woman and blinked, startled by the mixture of disgust and outrage on the woman's face. She realized, for the first time, how she must look: hair plastered flat to her head, mud and blood all over her hands and probably her face. Her army surplus jacket didn't look like much on the best of days, but now it had dirt and dog hair and blood all over it, too. Well, there wasn't anything she could do about that now. She flicked the bangs off her forehead and lifted her chin.

"Where'd you find it?" he asked.

"Henry!" his wife hissed.

"Down there," Tallulah said. She jerked her head toward the underpass.

"Well," he murmured.

The wife leaned again across the truck's front seat and pointed a finger at Tallulah. "We have laws against panhandlers in this county, missy," she said.

"It's all right," Henry said to her. To Tallulah, he said, "It's out of our way some, but there's a vet a little ways up the road. I guess we can run you up there right quick."

"Great," Tallulah said. "That's great." She trotted back to the lamppost and, afraid Henry would change his mind, bundled the dog up so fast that by the time she got it to the truck its whole hind end had slipped under her arm, leaving her gripping it across the chest, like a child clutching an oversized doll.

Henry had lowered the tailgate and spread a tarp across the truck bed. He helped her lift the dog onto it. Tallulah noticed he peered at the dog closely, appearing satisfied only after it took another gasping breath. It did look just about dead. She hoped the vet could do something for it. She stepped back from the truck and wiped her palms on her jeans. "Thanks a lot," she said. "I really appreciate this."

"Now you hold on," Henry said. "I said we'd take you up to the vet's. You and the dog."

"No, I'm not . . . see, it's not my dog."

Henry's mouth hardened. "Well it ain't our dog neither and if you were thinking of dumping this mess on us then you get him out of my truck right now. We ain't got the money to fool with a dog what's not even ours."

The passenger side window began jerking down, *shul-shul-shul*.

"But I have to get to Florida," Tallulah said. "My best friend's in trouble, she needs me, but I got robbed and I don't even know where I am, I can't . . ." and then she broke off because if she kept talking she was going to burst into tears in front of this man and his horrible wife and after all she'd been through today she couldn't stand that, she just wouldn't be able to stand it.

"Henry!" the wife snapped. Henry reached into the truck bed and grabbed the dog by the front legs.

"No!" Tallulah said. "I'll go! OK? I'll go." She clambered up next to the dog. Henry muttered something, but he slammed the tailgate shut and got into the truck. Tallulah listened to his wife bitching him out through the closed cab window until the truck accelerated onto the road. Then the wind drowned out everything. She huddled with her back against the cab, which offered a little protection against the wind and rain.

The truck pulled off the highway onto an anonymous road. Tallulah sat up but she could see nothing beyond the black shapes of trees and brush on either side. She considered jumping, but Henry was hauling ass; she'd break a leg, if not her neck. After the fourth turn she lost track of the lefts and the rights and there was no way she'd get back to the truck stop now.

"Thanks a lot," Tallulah said to the dog. She nudged it with her foot. It didn't move. She said, "You bastard, you better not be dead. Hey! You hear me?"

There were buildings on this road, scattered here and there on either side, illuminated by lights in their parking lots or on their walls. Rock quarry headquarters. Machine shop. Roofing company. The truck slowed and swung into a gravel lot in front of a sprawling brick building. Henry got out, dropped the tailgate, pulled the dog off the tarp, and laid it on the ground. Tallulah climbed down. Her clothes had soaked through within a minute of the thunderstorm starting, and that had been hours ago. Despite the lingering heat of the day, her arms and legs had become chilled as stone, and shaking-tired.

"How do I get back to the highway?" Tallulah asked.

Henry clanged the tailgate shut. "Doc Poteet'll tell you," he said. When he opened the truck door, Tallulah glimpsed the back of his wife's head, livid in tangerine; then the door slammed, the cab light winked out. The tires threw gravel up as they spun away.

Chapter 2

She was standing in the rain again. Alone again. The dog hadn't moved since lifting its head in the underpass, so as a companion, it didn't count. The dog was a problem, was what the dog was. And it was about to become someone else's problem.

Tallulah slung the duffel strap diagonally across her chest, lifted the dog off the ground—exhausted as she was, it took two tries—and staggered with it to the front door of the building. Moths fluttered against the amber glass of a porch light, throwing leaping shadows over a sign on which someone had printed, in large block letters, RING FOR EMERGENCY. A red arrow pointed to a doorbell.

Tallulah extended a finger from under the dog's chest and jabbed the button. Somewhere inside the building a buzzer went off. Her arms trembled under the dog's weight. No one came to the door.

After the third jab her arms gave up. She dropped to one knee and, just as she clutched at the dog's head to keep it from thwacking onto the concrete, she heard the scrape and rattle of a chain bolt. The door jerked open.

A pair of wrinkled green cotton pants, the kind doctors wore, stood in the doorway. Tallulah followed them upward. They belonged to a skinny dark-haired guy a couple of years older than she was, she guessed; nineteen, maybe, or twenty. He wore a baggy matching green V-neck shirt and a bleary expression. He didn't seem surprised to find a soaking wet girl and an unconscious dog on his doorstep in the middle of the night. He leaned against the doorjamb, shifting his shoulder a little as if to get more comfortable, as if he might fall asleep where he stood.

Did the men in this state never speak? "Are you the vet?" Tallulah snapped.

He shook his head. "Naw," he rasped. He cleared his throat and for a second Tallulah was afraid he was about to hawk an oyster over her head. Instead, he asked, "You need the doctor?"

Tallulah stared at him.

"I guess you do," he said. He bent down and scooped the dog into his arms and stood up. He made it look easy, which Tallulah found vaguely annoying.

"Come on in," he said. "You ought to of called first, though. It's gonna take the doctor a little while to get here. He hit by a car or something?"

"Something," Tallulah said. She grabbed the doorjamb, pulled herself to her feet, and eased inside. The guy—Kyle, according to the name tag on his shirt—pushed the door closed with a foot. They were in a small lobby, dimly lit by one lamp on an end table. The air was sharp with disinfectant but mingled in it Tallulah thought she detected a faint, dark, welcoming scent.

"Is that coffee?" she blurted.

"Yeah," Kyle said. He'd already begun walking away, the dog in his arms.

"Could I have some?"

"Sure."

She followed him down a hallway into a tiny cluttered room. Back here the disinfectant odor was stronger and underneath, like silt in a pond, hung a musty animal smell. A bare metal table took up most of the room. Kyle laid the dog on it. Under the fluorescent light the dog looked wetter and more caved in. When it took a breath its neck arched and its lips pulled far back, exposing jagged white teeth. Kyle poked at its mouth and the blood smear on its side. He grunted and turned away.

"How bad is it?" Tallulah asked.

"Don't know, I ain't the doctor," Kyle replied. "Don't look good, though. No color to his gums. You wait here, I'll call Dr. Poteet. You want any milk or anything in your coffee?"

"Yes," Tallulah said. "And sugar. Lots." He left. She dropped the duffel on the floor, sank onto a stool in the corner of the room, leaned against the wall, and closed her eyes. Other than the rasping breaths of the dog, the building was silent.

She wasn't waiting around for the vet. Her mission was accomplished; the dog would get help. She would drink her coffee and find out from this Kyle person how to get back to the highway. And then she would start walking. Again.

The warmth of the room was comforting, the absence of rain blissful. If Kyle didn't come with that coffee soon she'd fall asleep.

"KYLE!"

Tallulah jerked upright. It was a man's voice and it had come booming from somewhere in the building and it sure didn't sound like some sweet animal-loving veterinarian. It sounded royally pissed. She scrambled off the stool and grabbed her duffel and ducked out of the room into the hallway.

"Kyle! Where in hell are you!" The door at the end of the hallway flung open and a man in a windbreaker and khaki coveralls and black rubber boots burst in. He took two long strides toward her before he saw her. He stopped short, his eyes narrowing, flicking to her shoes then up to her hair. Tallulah crossed her arms in an attempt to hide the filthy jacket.

"Help you?" the man asked.

"No," Tallulah said. "Yes. I mean, I'm lost. I took a wrong turn off the highway near the truck stop and I saw your light and thought maybe someone could tell me how to get back there?" No need to mention the dog. It might lead to questions which might lead to more delays and she couldn't afford that.

18

He studied her. He looked to be about fifty, a little older than Tallulah's parents, not yet in grandpa territory. She tried smiling but it felt fake and maybe he could tell, because he didn't smile back. His cheekbones and mouth were too wide for his face or else his nose and eyes were too small; whichever it was, he was not a good-looking man. From the way he'd come in yelling, she guessed he wasn't a good-tempered man, either. Surely he wasn't the vet.

"Hey, Dr. Poteet," Kyle's voice called behind her. "I was just calling you. She's got a dog in here needs looking at."

Heat washed up under Tallulah's skin. The man gave a little "hmph" and walked past her into the room.

"You know, I really need to get going," Tallulah said. "So if you could just give me directions . . ."

"Wherever you got to go can wait," Dr. Poteet said. "Right now you need to come in here and tell me what this is about."

The hell I do, Tallulah thought. But she couldn't very well leave, not without knowing which direction to take. She walked slowly back to the room, stopping just outside the door. Even from there the dog's stink reached her. It didn't seem to bother the vet. He stood on the far side of the table, bent low enough over the dog for Tallulah to see a thin spot in the graying blond hair on top of his head. He pressed a stethoscope to the dog's chest. Across the room Kyle leaned against a wall, his hands in his pockets.

"Look, doc . . ." Tallulah said. Poteet gestured at her sharply without looking up. She sighed and dropped the duffel with a thump onto the floor. He glared at her across the dog's body, took the stethoscope out of his ears, slung it across his neck, and straightened up.

"First thing," he said. "My name is Dr. Charles Poteet. You can call me Doctor or Dr. Poteet but 'Doc' is not a name and I don't answer to it. Second thing. You are about to explain to me in great detail how this dog does not in any way belong to you."

"How'd you know that?"

"Because I've been doing this longer than you've been alive. *Kyle!*" Tallulah jumped, but Kyle appeared used to being snapped at; he unfolded himself leisurely off the wall. "I used two surgery packs at Byer's tonight. Get them out of the truck and wash them and repack them for Jolene to autoclave in the morning. And hose the mud off the truck." As Kyle disappeared out the door, Poteet bellowed after him, "And don't forget the tires!"

After Kyle had left, Poteet began running his hands all over the dog's body, stopping here and there to press with his fingertips or to flex a joint. His hands were big, the knuckles like knots, the bones of his wrists sticking out like blocks of wood under cloth. Yet they had a way of knowing what to do. They reminded Tallulah of her daddy's hands. The way he'd shift a hammer in his palm and *bam,* another nail whacked straight and gone. Once, when she was five, he'd helped her drill holes for a table he was building. She was too little to hold the drill alone, so he'd wrapped his fingers over hers, guiding her aim, steadying her against the

20

noise and the vibrations that ran up her arms and chattered her teeth. Making her unafraid.

"Where're you from?" Poteet asked.

Tallulah thought back over the cities she and Derek had driven through the last four days. She picked one big enough and far enough away to be safely anonymous.

"Nashville," she said.

"That right?" Poteet raised his eyes to her face. She nodded. "No offense," he said, "but you sound like a Yankee."

Tallulah blushed again. "Yeah . . . no. I know. I'm from . . ." Oregon, she almost said, but what slipped out was, ". . . Nevada. Originally."

"That right? What part of Nevada, originally?"

"Elko." The lie flew off her tongue like she'd been saying it all her life. Although it was almost true. When she was seven, she'd lived in Elko for a week with her daddy.

"That near Vegas?" Poteet raised one of the dog's rear legs. The dog gave a gasping cry and Tallulah jumped. Other than the moan in the underpass, this was the first noise it had made. Poteet laid the leg down and stroked the dog's head, smoothing the curls of wet fur. The dog didn't respond. Its eyes were bugged and staring, but it didn't seem to see anything.

"Sort of. I'm not sure how far." Daddy had planned to take her to Las Vegas, to the Strip, to support her in style—she still remembered his mouth stretching wide, drawing the word out long, *st-i-i-i-le*—as a blackjack dealer. But before any of that could happen, her stepfather, John, had shown up and taken her back to Portland and she'd had to talk to a judge and after that Mom told Tallulah not to worry, the judge had made sure Daddy understood who had custody and who didn't, and Daddy understood it so well he'd signed a paper. What paper? Tallulah had asked. One that promises he'll never, ever take you from home again, Mom said. Tallulah's clearest memory of this was the shock on her mother's face when Tallulah shrieked, *"But I didn't mean it, I didn't mean it!"* and fell to the floor, sobbing.

That had been ten years ago. By now, as far as Tallulah knew, her daddy might be dead.

"I've been to Las Vegas three-four times," Poteet murmured. He was kneeling in front of the table, shining a narrow light in the dog's eyes. "Big conference there every year. Five, six thousand veterinarians from all over. Didn't make it this year, though. Just as well. I usually lose a pile of money."

He clicked the light off and stood up. He laid one hand gently, almost formally, on the dog's head, as though he were about to confer an honor. "Well, young lady from Elko, I'm going to be honest with you," he said. "This dog has, from worst to less worse, either a collapsed lung or bleeding in his chest. Maybe both. A probable concussion, a bunch of fractured ribs, and a busted pelvis. And that's just what I can see. Now, were he your dog, and if you wanted to, we could try. Although, even then . . ." He spread both hands, palms up, then let them come to rest on the edge of the table.

"He's not my dog," Tallulah said. "I just found him on the road."

Poteet nodded. "All right, then," he said. "Take a seat out in the lobby just a minute. Then we'll see if we can get you where you need to be." He left the room, leaving Tallulah and the dog alone. The dog's gasping had slowed. Poor doggie. Tallulah walked out into the hallway, where the smell was less intense.

Poteet seemed nice enough, once he'd stopped yelling. She bet he'd give her a ride to the truck stop, and if he wouldn't, surely Kyle would. An animal lover would be just the type to help a girl out of a jam.

She heard Poteet reenter the room and turned in the hallway to watch. He was holding a dark glass vial in the air and from it drawing an obnoxiously pink liquid into a syringe. Tallulah frowned and edged back into the doorway.

"What is that?" she asked.

Poteet continued filling the syringe. "I'm putting him to sleep."

"You're going to kill him?"

"How about you go on to the lobby."

"Wait," Tallulah said. "I didn't bring him here for this. Jesus, if I wanted him dead I would have left him where he was!"

Poteet glanced at her, the syringe a blunt pink torpedo in his hand. "Is this your dog?" he asked.

"No, but . . ."

"Are you going to adopt him? Take financial responsibility for him?"

"I dragged him off the road! I begged a total stranger to bring him here so now instead of being sort of lost I'm totally, completely lost but I did it anyway, I got him here, and for what? So you can kill him? What kind of a goddamn vet *are* you?"

Poteet put the syringe down. He rubbed his eyes with the fingers and thumb of one hand, then pinched the bridge of his nose and blinked. "What's your name?" he asked.

"What for?"

"Because if you're going to stand there and cuss me out in the middle of the damn night I need to know your name, that's what for."

"Tallulah."

"Tallulah." He said it slowly, his drawl making a kind of music of it: *Tah-LOOL-ah.* "Very nice. I compliment your parents."

Her parents had had nothing to do with it; it had been Maeve who'd named her Tallulah. But she wasn't about to start explaining Maeve to a guy with a bottle full of death on his counter.

Poteet leaned both hands on the table. "Tallulah, I need you to appreciate this dog's condition. He's hurt. He's hurt just about as bad as you can be hurt and still be breathing, and he's not doing real well with that. If this was your prize show dog and you had a million dollars, I wouldn't tell you any different."

"If I had a million dollars, the difference is you'd help him."

"If he was your dog and you wanted me to I would try. But . . ."

"But I don't have a million dollars. So he ends up dead."

"Forget I said anything about money. The point is . . ."

"The point is you're going to kill him because he doesn't come with a wallet stitched to his butt. That's how it works, right?"

Poteet pushed himself off the table. He wasn't tall, but the way he held himself he seemed to be looking straight down on top of her head. "The point *is*, this hospital does not have the time or the money to save every stray dog, cat, and possum that comes dragged in off the road." He looked away; when he faced her again, his voice was calmer. "You want me to take care of this dog. What I'm telling you is, the best way I can take care of him is to put him out of his pain. Now tell me you understand some small piece of that."

She looked at the dog. Its gasps were getting farther and farther apart, and yet it kept taking them. How could it keep fighting so hard, when every breath must tell it it was losing?

"He'll end the same, Tallulah," Poteet said. His voice was very gentle. "The only question is, how much do you think he should suffer before he gets there?"

He picked up the syringe.

"He wants to live," Tallulah said.

25

Poteet lifted the dog's front leg. "Wait in the lobby," he said.

Tallulah turned and ran down the hall. She thought there would be a sound, another dog cry of protest, but behind her all was silent. She yanked the front door open. The rain had stopped. Shadows of moths fluttered in the amber light at her feet.

Chapter 3

From around the corner of the building, Tallulah heard the sound of splashing water. She followed it and found Kyle in a carport, hosing off a large white truck with one hand, smoking a cigarette with the other. Blue lettering on the truck door read CLARK STATION VETERINARY SERVICES. Underneath, in smaller letters: QUALITY VETERINARY CARE SINCE 1984.

Kyle shook his head when she asked him for a ride. "Wish I could," he said. "But I ain't got a car. Have to borrow Dr. Poteet's truck, and can't do that with him on call for emergencies."

He gave her directions to the truck stop, though, even drew her a map on a clean paper napkin he found on the cab seat. "It ain't above four-five miles. It's just outside town, and Clark Station ain't that big." He drew an X for the truck stop, sketched a steaming cup of coffee below. "You oughta get a ride easy enough. Where you going?"

"Florida. Orlando."

Kyle took a drag on his cigarette, turned his head away

to blow out the smoke. Tallulah thought about asking him for one, then decided against it. She'd already quit once. She was pretty sure she couldn't quit twice.

"I hear Florida's nice. I ain't never been." Kyle picked up the hose again. "Good luck to you." He didn't ask what had happened to the dog.

A door opened along the back of the building. Tallulah took a step deeper into the shadow of the carport.

"KYLE!" Poteet thundered.

Kyle tossed the hose on the ground, dropped the cigarette, and stubbed it out with his toe.

"Does he always yell like that?" Tallulah asked.

"Not all the time." Kyle wiped his hands down the hips of his jeans. He tipped his head to one side, as if reconsidering. "Mostly."

"I'd quit," Tallulah said.

Kyle grinned. "Good thing you don't work for him, then," he said. "Take care of yourself." He headed toward the open door. When he was a silhouette against the light, Tallulah turned and trudged to the road.

Overhead, the clouds were tearing apart, revealing a three-quarter moon. Tallulah's feet hurt. Everything hurt. Every footfall sent a finger of pain prodding up from her knees, up her thighs, across the small of her back to her shoulders, and into the base of her skull, where it knuckled hard before giving way to the next.

As she walked, she considered what to tell Maeve about the dog. She could hardly admit she'd saved it, only to stand by and let it get killed anyway. Although surely that was better than leaving it in the underpass, helpless, in pain. Wasn't it?

She chewed her lip. It was sometimes hard to tell what Maeve would think. Tallulah had been wrong before.

She could say she didn't know what happened. That she'd left before she even saw the vet. Tallulah immediately rejected this idea. She and Maeve both believed in the truth above all else. That was what made their friendship different; that was what made it great.

So. She would tell Maeve she had tried to save the dog, but it had died. It was the truth.

True enough.

The wind kept whipping the ends of Tallulah's hair across her face. She should have gone to the stylist last month, but she'd just bought the leather jacket and had decided to put it off, and then Maeve disappeared, and after that, hair had been the least of Tallulah's worries. One night she and Maeve were drinking Thai coffees at a downtown restaurant; the next afternoon, no answer when Tallulah called Maeve's apartment. Or her cell phone. Not that night, not the next morning.

Then, five days later, Maeve's e-mail had arrived. *I'm in Orlando. I need my notebooks. I left a key taped underneath the doormat. Call this number when you get here. Hurry. Please.* Nothing else. No explanations. Replies to the e-mail went unanswered. The cell phone was never picked up.

So Tallulah did what any best friend would do. She

retrieved the notebooks, packed a duffel, and set out for Florida.

All of which meant that by now, half an inch of mouse-brown roots streaked the middle of her hair. It looked like a reverse skunk stripe, and fixing it was number one on Tallulah's list of Things to Do in Orlando. Maeve would loan her the money. After all, going platinum had been Maeve's idea. At first Tallulah had resisted, sure she would look washed out, she was so pale anyway, but Maeve said no, with Tallulah's hazel eyes and dark eyebrows it would work.

And it did. What's more, once she was a platinum blond Tallulah actually began *thinking* of herself as Tallulah. Up until then she'd considered the name one of Maeve's incomprehensible jokes, and she'd gone along with it only because she'd gotten tired of insisting her real name was Debbie. But once again, Maeve had been right. A Debbie could never look this sleek and startling. As a Tallulah, though, things would be different. As a Tallulah, even beautiful was possible.

Number two on the Orlando List: shopping. No more bulky sweaters made for nagging Oregon rain and gray Oregon cold. No, from now on it would be short skirts and sleeveless tops cropped to show off the tattoo above her right hip. Which meant, third: get in shape. Look at her. All she'd been doing was walking, and she felt ready to drop on the asphalt and die. She was only seventeen. The way she was dragging ass, she might as well be thirty.

Clouds drifted, shielding the moon. Tallulah had reached a long stretch of road between buildings; in this new dark, she slowed her pace. The wind picked up. From her right came a sudden wide rustling, as if an entire bleacher full of people had stood up without a word. Tallulah stopped. The back of her neck prickled; gooseflesh broke out across her arms. The moon reappeared, and under its cold light a field of corn rippled, silver-tipped and murmuring. Tallulah resumed walking.

Back to the plan. She'd noticed a couple of tables under an overhang outside the truck stop. She could crash there for the night. It would be miserable, but it wouldn't kill her and in the morning, she'd find somebody headed her way.

By this time tomorrow, she'd be in Orlando.

And then her real life would begin. She and Maeve would share an apartment with a balcony. And a pool. They'd drink margaritas and talk all night, same as they'd done in Portland, and Maeve would explain why she'd left Oregon and Tallulah would tell Maeve about Derek stranding her, and finding the dog, and the entire strange rest of it, whatever the rest of it would turn out to be. After all the stories Tallulah had heard about Maeve's travels, it would be sweet, finally, to have stories of her own to tell.

I can't believe it, Maeve would say. Did he really? Did you really?

You should have been there, Tallulah would say, and Maeve would laugh and toast her with another homemade margarita, not too sweet and so smooth you couldn't taste the tequila, which was exactly how Tallulah liked it.

She'd get a job that didn't interfere with afternoons at

the beach. Orlando, she assumed, had a beach. And the beach would have guys. Florida guys. Tan and lean and tall, with small cute asses. Like that guy at the vet clinic. Kyle. Only he was dark, and she preferred blonds. Blonds came pasty in Portland. It would be nice, for once, to go out with someone tan all over, instead of red arms, red faces, and fish-belly white everywhere else.

New city. New life. Away from the slow death that was summer school. Away from the endless, crazy-making arguments with Mom. *Where were you? No TV for a week. No Internet for a month. Borrow the car, after what you just pulled? No one in my family ever dropped out of high school and no daughter of mine . . .*

And then her older sister, Terri, sociology-major Terri, saying—in her reasonable, I'm-just-making-a-point voice, that made Tallulah itch to grab the nearest breakable object and throw it at her—*Formal didactic education just isn't some people's preferred learning style, Mom. If she can't do it, you shouldn't force her,* which sounded like she was taking Tallulah's side, except Tallulah didn't need a dictionary to know that Terri had just called her stupid.

Behind her, Tallulah heard the grumble of an engine. About time; this would be the first car to come along since she'd left the vet's. She bet it was Kyle after all. She pivoted to face the headlights, arm stuck out, thumb raised high.

But it was a car, not a truck. Slowing down, drawing alongside. A glittery green shield on the door. Tallulah yanked her arm down, but the rack of roof lights had already sprung to flashing life and the police cruiser swerved onto the shoulder ahead of her. Taillights threw a red wall in her face. She looked wildly left and right but before she could make up her mind to run, the driver's door clicked open. Under the cab light Tallulah caught glimpses of the deputy, thick wedges of pale skin and khaki that dissolved back into black as he got out. His boots crunched on the gravel.

He stopped about six feet from her. A circle of light sprang onto her body, eased up under her chin. In the flashlight's aura she could just make out the deputy's face, the solid bulges of cheeks and nose, the eyes black triangles under a rigid expanse of hat brim. The edges of him flickered crimson and blue from the cruiser's lights. He looked about as yielding as stacked bags of cement.

"Evening, miss," he said. "You live around here?"

Tallulah's breath skimmed in her throat like a stone on top of water. Unable to dive deep. "Pretty close," she managed to say.

"Where at?" The flashlight played over her army jacket, her duffel, her boots. Flicked over the side of her face.

Was hitchhiking illegal here? It was in Washington, Tallulah knew that much. Had he seen her with her thumb out? "Actually, I'm trying to get to Knoxville," she hazarded.

"You realize you're a ways from Knoxville, don't you?" the deputy said. "Were you gonna walk all night?"

"No, I . . ." She stopped, confused. Would walking all night sound better than sleeping on a truck stop bench? "I'm not sure. Maybe."

"Do you have any money?"

On that point she was certain. "All my money's gone," she said. "I got robbed."

"You don't have any money at all."

Ninety-three cents hardly counted. "No. Nothing."

"Stand up against the car, please," the deputy said. "Put your hands on the trunk for me."

"Why?" Tallulah asked, although she knew, but it couldn't be true, because this was not happening.

The deputy's hat brim lowered a fraction of an inch; his chest seemed to expand. "Just stand up against the car. Hands on the trunk. Leave the tote bag there."

She let the duffel slip off her shoulder onto the ground. She walked past the deputy and leaned over the cruiser and put her hands on the trunk. The weird thing was, she knew how to do this. All the crime dramas on TV. The reality cop shows. Mom loved them. Back when Tallulah could still joke with her mother, she'd tease that Mom secretly wanted to be one of those glamorous forensics chicks. Dressed in pinstripe gabardine, putting away the scumbags.

The deputy frisked her. His touch was impersonal and no-nonsense. When he was finished, he said, "No money and no place to stay means I'll take you in for vagrancy. Hands behind your back, please."

"What? What are you talking about, I haven't done anything!" Tallulah tried turning around, but the deputy placed a hand on her shoulder. It felt like a brick landing there. She glimpsed him reaching for his belt. Handcuffs. He was going to handcuff her.

"No, wait," Tallulah said. "I had money. I got robbed. I can tell you who did it, his name's Derek Hubner, he's driving a silver Honda Civic with Oregon plates, J-something-nine-something, nine-three, or no, nine-five . . ."

Metal hooked her right wrist and clicked. "You have the right . . ." the deputy said.

"No! You don't understand! *He* robbed *me*. Why don't you go find *him*? Why don't you go arrest *him*?"

"Yes ma'am, we'll sure look into that." His hand closed over her left wrist, lifted it off the trunk. Click. "Now, you have the right . . ."

"I have to get to Florida! It's a matter of life and death, my friend's in terrible trouble, she needs me and if I don't get there . . ."

"Thought you were headed to Knoxville," the deputy said. His hand on her head, guiding her into the cruiser's rear seat. It seemed she was staring down a tunnel with her future at the other end, and as she watched, the tunnel began to collapse, until with the thud of the car door it vanished entirely away.

Chapter 4

The he public defender seemed to think the whole thing was a joke.

"Nobody gets arrested for vagrancy anymore," she said, right after she'd shaken Tallulah's hand through the bars of the courthouse holding cell. "You're scheduled for General Sessions this morning. Plead guilty. The judge will let you off with a warning. Seeing as how you're destitute, we can probably even get him to waive the booking fee."

"And then what? I get to go?"

"Wherever you want," the p.d. said. She was a small, efficient-seeming woman with no eye for color. Someone ought to tell her nobody looks good in that shade of green, Tallulah thought distractedly. "As long as it's across the county line," the lawyer added. She patted the cell bars as though patting Tallulah's shoulder. "Relax. You'll be out of here by noon."

And Tallulah was. Later, she would remember only the broadest brushstrokes of the courtroom: a wall of windows soaring to a vaulted ceiling; the morning sun making a pale waste of the hanging lights; the spider veins laced across the judge's nose. She wouldn't remember any interchange of words, although there must have been some, because a few minutes later she was standing in the hallway with her p.d.

"That's it?" Tallulah said.

"All except for the court clerk," the lawyer said. She eyed Tallulah's army surplus jacket. "I guess you didn't get to clean up any last night at the jail. If you'd like to, the Ladies' is that way." She nodded down the reach of the hall. "Good luck to you."

The restroom was old-fashioned, just one toilet and a chipped porcelain sink. Tallulah didn't care. After one night in jail, she'd never appreciated so much the joy of peeing in private.

That done, she dabbed at the scrapes on her wrist and face with a wet paper towel, wincing at the sting. Clean of road grit, dog hair, and blood, her skin seemed colorless as ash. She didn't look like a best-friend-rescuer. More like a first-grader who'd been shoved down at recess. Tallulah flicked her bangs with her fingers until they fell like straw over her lashes. They were long enough, almost, to hide the scared in her eyes.

Outside, she started sweating halfway down the courthouse steps. By the time she reached the sidewalk, she could feel energy trickling out of her like the last drips of water from a hose. The air was spongy, rotten with damp. She'd thought Oregon was wet. But Oregon rain just spat on you.

It drizzled. It dripped like a leaky faucet that never got fixed, so you hardly noticed it after a while. Oregon didn't fling solid sheets of water and lightning bolts at you. And never, in Oregon, had it taken this much effort just to breathe.

She slid a piece of paper out of her back pocket and studied the directions the court clerk had scribbled out for her. Then she started walking.

After perhaps ten minutes, she became aware of a white pickup drifting alongside her. A lean tan arm hung across the open windowsill. Something about the driver's face—angular, with dark narrow eyes—seemed familiar, but she couldn't place it.

" 'Afternoon," the driver said.

"That's one opinion," Tallulah replied. She kept walking. With every step it felt as though a small, vicious dog was biting chunks out of her heels. If she could, she'd sit on the grass right over there, take off these horrible boots—what had possessed her to wear them on a road trip in August, just because they were adorable?—and not move for a week.

Except that Maeve was waiting. Tallulah had no time to waste on blisters. Or on any yahoo in a pickup truck, either.

The driver leaned out the window. "You want a ride?" he asked.

"Hell yes," Tallulah said.

She barely glanced at the blue writing on the pickup's doors, although that, too, seemed familiar. It wasn't until she was actually sliding onto the seat that it clicked.

"Kyle," she said.

"I was starting to think you'd forgot." He switched gears and accelerated up the street, just as another pickup behind them tapped its horn.

Tallulah hadn't forgotten. Thunder crashing overhead, the dank stink of the underpass. A black dog on a metal table, death purling pink into a syringe. The images seemed weirdly distant, though, as though she'd dreamed them. She laid her head on the seatback and closed her eyes.

"You have rotten timing," she said. "If you'd given me a ride last night, none of this would've happened." God, it felt so good to sit down on something cushioned. She stretched her legs out and sighed. "I need to go to the jail."

"I figured," Kyle said. "I saw you ain't got your tote bag back yet. They just get through with you in court?"

She turned to look at him. "You seem to know the routine pretty well," she said.

"I been through it once or twice."

"Yeah? What'd you do?"

Something he wasn't particularly sorry for, from the grin on his face. But all he said was, "Nothing much. I was just a kid." He shifted on the seat, pulled a pack of cigarettes from his back jeans pocket. "You mind if I roll down your window? I ain't supposed to smoke in the truck."

Tallulah had quit cold turkey the day Maeve had made it clear that, as long as Tallulah smoked, she had no chance of moving out of her parents' house and into Maeve's apartment. The last three months had been a nail-biting, caffeine-drinking, junk-food-scarfing battle—but she'd quit.

39

And stayed quit, even when the cravings felt like crazed bats rocketing around her insides. Like now. If Kyle lit up, stressed as she was, she might snatch the cigarette right out of his fingers. "I'd rather have the air conditioning," she said.

Kyle grunted and slid the pack back into his pocket. He closed his window and fiddled with the console. Cold air jetted over her. "That too much?" he asked.

"It's good," she said. "Thanks." She closed her eyes, rubbing sudden gooseflesh. Nothing out the window except fields and cows, anyway, and she'd seen enough of them yesterday to last her the rest of her life.

At the jail, Kyle offered to wait for her. "No sense you walking all over the county," he said. "I got a little while before I got to get the truck back." When she came out, duffel slung over her shoulder, she half-expected him to be gone. But there he was, leaning against the truck bed smoking. He stubbed the cigarette out when he saw her.

"Now where?" he asked.

"Orlando."

His boot toe paused on the cigarette. He slid her a long, sideways look.

"Guess not," she said. "The truck stop, then."

"Throw your tote bag behind the seat there. You still gonna hitch to Florida?"

"I don't have a choice, do I? Since you won't take me."

He didn't rise to the bait. As they pulled onto the highway, he snapped on the radio. She caught a snatch of violin and piano before he punched a button and the truck cab flooded with steel guitar. Tallulah recognized the song. It was one of her mom's favorites, sung by a woman whose voice rasped as though sorrow were sandpaper.

Tallulah sighed. She was free; she had her duffel and a ride, at least for the next couple of miles. Still, a nagging feeling chewed at her. She wished she could remember exactly what she'd said to Maeve's answering machine, during her one call from jail the night before.

All through the booking procedure she'd been flustered and disoriented, terrified of the out-of-sight sounds of slammed doors and the occasional raised voice, convinced that any moment she would be wrestled into an orange jumpsuit and shackles and thrown into a cell lit by one dangling bulb. By the time she was finally allowed to make her phone call, if the guard had said *Boo* to her she would have screamed. And then Maeve had not picked up. At the mumbling male voice—*"Leave a message"*—Tallulah had soared into a full-blown panic.

"I've been arrested," she'd wailed into the silent machine, imploring of the deputy, "Where am I? Where am I?" then repeating his inflections exactly, as if the words were a foreign language and the wrong pronunciation would render them unintelligible. What else had she said? Something about Derek, she remembered that much, although she'd barely begun describing his crimes when a beep sounded, then a click, then a silence even deeper than the one before.

"You don't listen so good, do you?" Kyle was saying.

"What?"

"I said I got to stop at the clinic first. It's just right here."

"Oh. OK." What must Maeve be thinking right now? What else *could* she think? She'd have no choice but to realize what Tallulah's family had, years ago—what everyone realized, if they only knew Tallulah long enough.

Tallulah screwed up everything.

She pressed the heels of her hands against her eyes. Then dragged her hands across her temples, pulling her hair back so hard it hurt.

"You got a headache?" Kyle asked.

"No."

"'Cause we got aspirin at the clinic."

She didn't answer. The pickup pulled into a gravel parking lot. In the dark and rain last night, Tallulah hadn't noticed the neat rectangle of grass in front of the veterinary hospital, or the blue and white sign in its center: CLARK STATION VETERINARY HOSPITAL. LARGE AND SMALL ANIMALS. Or the white clapboard of the second story, perched like a bonnet on the brick below. Kyle drove around the back of the hospital, past a barn and a complicated-looking array of pipe fencing, then pulled into the carport. He cut the engine and said, "Come on, I'll get you that aspirin."

"I don't need any."

"Yeah, OK, but there's air conditioning inside." He ducked his head and, fussing with a handful of receipts stuffed in a dashboard tray, mumbled, "It might be a little while."

Tallulah frowned. "How much of a 'little while'?"

42

Kyle shrugged.

"Dammit," Tallulah muttered. Already the heat was rising in the truck cab. "Oh, hell. All right."

The hallway, where Tallulah had first seen Poteet, was fresh and cool and smelled only faintly of disinfectant. Country music sounded somewhere to the left. Straight ahead was an open door, beyond which voices rose and fell. The lobby.

"Wait here a minute," Kyle said, and disappeared. Tallulah glanced around for a place to sit, but before she could find one, Poteet appeared in the doorway. Like the hospital, he looked different: instead of khaki coveralls, he wore a light blue button-down shirt, a yellow tie, and a white doctor's coat that reached halfway to his knees. Glancing at Tallulah, he said, "You don't shine a whole lot brighter by daylight. Come on with me." He strode up the hall. When Tallulah gaped after him, he barked, "Come on!"

There was no sign of Kyle. Not knowing what else to do, Tallulah trailed after Poteet. Passing through the room where the dog had died, Tallulah brushed her fingers along the edge of the metal table. No blood, no mud, no smell. Somehow she'd imagined the room would be permanently marked. *A dog died here.* Maybe a hundred dogs had, she realized. A thousand.

Poteet led her to what looked like a break room. Cabinets and a refrigerator and a sink, a table strewn with battered magazines. The music was louder here, the smells of coffee and disinfectant stronger. They brought back the aura of road weariness, of a gasping dog under fluorescent lights.

Poteet grabbed a mug off a shelf and poured coffee from a half-full carafe. "Want some?" he asked. Tallulah shook her head.

"I was just waiting for Kyle," she said, an instant before it occurred to her that maybe Poteet didn't care to have one of his employees driving strangers around in his truck. "I mean, I was just . . ."

"McLaren let you off," Poteet said.

"What?"

"Judge McLaren," he repeated. "I see you're out of jail."

"How'd you know I was in jail?"

Poteet snorted. "Because I was the one who called the sheriff."

Nobody gets arrested for vagrancy anymore.

"You what?" Tallulah said. "But . . ."

"You know when I first laid eyes on you I thought you'd been stabbed?" He picked a magazine up off the table, tossed it down again without looking at it. "Blood all over you. Then you say you're lost, which I believe, because if you're from Nashville, I'm a Mexican. Then . . ."

"You had no *right*!"

"Then, you pitch a fit over a dog and run out my door in the middle of the damn night." He took a long sip of coffee and shrugged. "I figured jail would keep you safe at least until morning."

He stood between her and the door they'd come through. But there was another door to her right, and she headed for it. Forget a ride. If she couldn't find Kyle, she'd

44

break the truck's window and get her stuff and get the hell out. She still had his map to the truck stop. And her own two feet. They hurt like sons of bitches, but they worked.

Behind her, Poteet said, "I wouldn't go in there. My technician's taking X-rays."

Tallulah stopped with her hand on the doorknob. A yellow sign with purple lettering hung at eye level: CAUTION: RADIATION.

"You're broke," Poteet continued. "Robbed, I believe you said. I'm short a kennel assistant. If you want, you can work for me a couple days. Cash under the table."

"I can't stay here. I've got to get to Florida."

"How? Hitching? You have any idea what kind of men pick up a girl like you? You think they'll give you a ride to Florida for nothing but your sweet smile?"

Blabbermouth Kyle. "I can take care of myself," Tallulah said. "In fact, if you hadn't called the cops on me, I'd be halfway to Orlando by now."

"If I hadn't called the cops on you, by now you'd likely be dead in a ditch."

"The hell I would. Anyway, that's my problem. Not yours."

"God knows that's the truth." He slung the remains of his coffee into the sink, brown streams swirling halfway up the side. "Well. If that's the way you want it." His voice sounded lighter somehow, rounded with what she suspected was relief. "I suppose I ought to have had Ruth ask you, it being her idea. Although I believe you're too stubborn even for

45

her. Anything you want before you go? A pop? Sandwich?" Tallulah opened her mouth to speak; he interrupted her. "Don't ask for money," he said.

"I was going to ask," Tallulah said, enunciating carefully, "if I could borrow your phone."

"Florida, I presume." She didn't answer. He frowned, then pointed to a phone on the wall. "Dial nine first," he said. "Do me a favor. Keep it short."

Tallulah pulled the e-mail with Maeve's phone number out of her pocket. As she dialed, she thought about asking Poteet to leave. Too late, the phone was ringing. She turned her back to him.

No hysteria this time. No panic. She would explain everything coolly, calmly. Maeve was not to worry. Tallulah had everything under control.

The answering machine again. Maeve must be screening her calls.

"Maeve! Maeve, pick up." Nothing. Where *was* she? "It all, it turned out OK. That whole jail thing." Tallulah managed an airy laugh. "It was so dumb, it was just one of those . . . So anyway, I'm leaving, and I'll . . ." She could feel Poteet staring; didn't he know not to listen to a private conversation? ". . . I'll get to Orlando just as soon as I can."

And then she remembered. What she'd said last night. *As soon as you can.*

"Are you . . . have you left? Are you on your way here? Because if you are, then . . . I mean, if you're not, stay there! Stay there, I'm on my way, I . . ."

A beep. Then silence. Tallulah lowered the receiver from her ear. After what seemed a long time, she hung it up.

"You told her to come get you." Poteet's voice was flat, as though reading a piece of junk mail aloud. Irritated that it had landed at his door. "I take it she's left already?"

Of course Maeve had left. After the message Tallulah had spewed onto her machine last night, she was probably halfway to Tennessee already. Tallulah focused on a chip in the wall paint. Pale green under tan. She pried at the edge with her thumbnail, flicked off a piece the size of an ant. "If you'd minded your own business," she said, without turning around, "none of this would have happened."

"From what I've seen so far," Poteet said, "I imagine it would have. Something like it, anyway."

He'd only just met her, and already he knew.

Chapter 5

I'm the head technician," the woman told Tallulah as she rummaged in a closet. "All that means is, I do the real work around here." Her name was Jolene; Poteet had introduced them before he disappeared to the front of the hospital. Jolene was heavy, her weight concentrated in front so that she walked with a sway in her back, as though braced against forces dragging her forward. Her face reminded Tallulah of a baby's fist, all tension under the dimples. "You ever work with critters before?" she asked over her shoulder. "Dog or cat of your own, anything like that?"

"No," Tallulah said. When it had been just the three of them, Mom and Tallulah and Terri, a pet had been out of the question. No time, no money. Then her stepfather, John, had arrived, and with him came allergies.

Jolene emerged from the closet, handing Tallulah a teal scrub top spattered with fuchsia puppies and orange kittens and a pair of solid teal pants. "Bathroom's over there," she said. "Hang on a second." She ducked into the cabinet again, held out a plastic garbage bag. "For your things," she added, nodding at Tallulah's shirt.

"Am I supposed to start right now?" Tallulah asked.

"You got someplace else to be?"

Tallulah had been trying to recall the road atlas in Derek's car. Specifically, the number of states between Tennessee and Florida. Three? Two? Whichever it was, it would take Maeve at least a day to get here. Maybe more. What was Tallulah supposed to do in the meantime? Sit on a truck stop bench in this heat, with no food, no water?

Cash under the table, Poteet had said. Having money in hand when Maeve got here might make Tallulah seem less of a complete failure. Besides, surely at some point these people would feed her.

The scrubs were too big. When Tallulah snugged up the drawstring on the pants, they ballooned like a genie's. They were lightweight as pajamas, though, almost too cool for the air conditioning, and so clean that Tallulah became freshly aware of the grit coating her skin. More damp paper towels, the back of her neck this time, her shoulders, her armpits. Then she shrugged on the scrub top and went out. She found Jolene in the next room, giving a silver tabby cat a pill. Country music poured from a radio on top of a cabinet. Unfortunately, it wasn't loud enough to drown out the yapping of a puppy in a nearby cage.

"This here's the treatment room," Jolene said, raising her voice over the yapping. The room was big, with metal cages along three walls and a raised white tub and equipment-strewn counter on the fourth. A small, white fuzzy dog pressed his nose against his kennel door and stared at Tallulah.

Pill-giving accomplished, Jolene rubbed the cat's ears and set it gently in a kennel. Then she gestured to Tallulah. "Come help me with your dog," she said.

"What dog?"

"The dog you brought in the other night. The one Dr. Poteet says you raised holy hell over." She pointed to a large bottom cage. "Ain't that him?"

Tallulah walked around the exam table. On the cage door hung an ID card printed in large blue letters: "STRAY H-B-L." In the cage was a black dog with white paws. She didn't remember white paws. And this dog, instead of flat out and gasping, was lying on his chest, those big white feet stretched out, his head resting on top.

"That's not him," Tallulah said.

"Dr. Poteet says it is," Jolene said. She reached past Tallulah and opened the kennel door. Tallulah started to squat down but the white fuzzball in the next kennel lunged at her, barking, and she jumped upright. Jolene made a noise that might have been a snicker. Tallulah knelt down again, farther away this time. The fuzzball growled, but stayed put.

The black dog gazed at her without interest. His coat curled around his neck, over his shoulders. She remembered Poteet petting the dog on the table. The wet curls springing up.

Under all that mud, he'd had white paws.

She swallowed hard against the sudden ache in her throat. "I don't understand," she said. "The vet was going to kill him. He had a whole thing of that pink stuff, I saw it."

"I don't know about that," Jolene said. "Kyle said Dr. Poteet stayed up most of the night with him. He still ain't out of the woods, but he's doing better." If this was better, Tallulah thought, the dog really must have been in bad shape. Patches of road rash on his legs and head, a skinned nose. Layers of wide blue bandage around his chest with a yellow tube peeking out.

"Hey, doggie," Tallulah said. The dog's eyes shifted up to her face. His lower lids sagged, two pink half-moons, as if he had a hangover. He raised his head a fraction of an inch, groaned, and eased over onto his side.

"Don't take it personally. He ain't about to jump up and celebrate just yet," Jolene said.

Tallulah reached forward and stroked the dog's shoulder. The curls were soft. Warm. She remembered the gritty, chill feel of his fur the night before, and shivered. When Maeve arrived, at least Tallulah could show her this: this warm, white-footed, easy-breathing dog. You saved a life, Maeve would say. You're a hero.

Jolene knelt next to Tallulah. She had two syringes in her hand. Tallulah was relieved to see no pink. Jolene fiddled with a bandage on the dog's leg. Narrow tubing ran from the bandage to a bag of clear fluid hanging above their heads. It looked just like the hospital fluid bags on TV. "What's H-B-L?" Tallulah asked.

"Hit by life," Jolene said. "We say that when they come in messed up and we don't know what happened. Though surely this one was smacked by a car." She set down the empty syringes, stroked the dog's head, then picked up a large striped towel. Working the towel under the dog's abdomen, she said, "We'll stand him up with this. Here." She handed Tallulah one end of the towel. "Lift when I say. He'll yelp some. His pelvis is broke in three places, and the painkiller don't kill it all."

The dog did yelp, piercingly, making Tallulah gasp and freeze until Jolene told her to keep going and get it over with. They shifted him out of the cage, Tallulah trying to be as gentle as she could, wincing every time one of the dog's hind feet bumped the linoleum.

"What are we doing?" she said, hoping that whatever it was, it would be over soon.

"I'll hold him," Jolene said, taking Tallulah's end of the towel. "See how he's peed in the kennel there? Take that pad out. New one's right there. Spread it open, yeah, that's good. OK, let's lift him back."

Once the dog was settled, Jolene said, "The critters stay clean. That's the first rule. If me or Dr. Poteet see anybody in a mess, you'll wish we hadn't." She grabbed a spray bottle and a roll of paper towels off the counter, then swung around to a nearby empty cage. "Pay attention," she said, "'cause I ain't got time to repeat myself. Open the door, get the critter out, put him in a clean cage. Blankets go in the wash basket. Then wipe the cage down good and I mean *good*. Make sure you get the corners."

The white dog was staring at Tallulah again. She stared back. It lifted its lip and growled.

"Maybe I should do something else. You know, filing. Or whatever," Tallulah said.

"Don't have files. Everything's been on computer past five years," Jolene said. She straightened up from the cage and ran the back of her hand over her temple, where dark blond strands had come loose from her single braid. "Anyway, Ruth handles everything up front. We need at least two people back here but the other girl up and quit, no notice, no nothing. Dr. Poteet ain't got nobody new hired and in the meantime I got sick critters coming out my ears." She stripped off her gloves, took the roll of paper towels out from under her arm, and handed it to Tallulah.

"Start with that one there," she said, pointing to the yapping puppy. When Tallulah hesitated, she said, "Don't tell me you're scared."

"I'm not *scared*," Tallulah said. The puppy bumbled forward, pressing its side into the kennel door and rolling its small eyes at her. "It's just . . . I've never . . ."

"Sweet Jesus," Jolene said. She opened the kennel door and scooped the puppy between one arm and a pillow of a breast. Immediately the puppy hushed. The silence was like cotton to Tallulah's ears. She worked her hands into the dishwashing gloves, then pulled the blanket out of the cage.

Behind it, a corner of the cage lay swamped in yellow diarrhea.

"Oh," she said. "No. No way."

Jolene set the puppy in a clean kennel. It instantly began yapping again. "What's the matter?" she said. "You got gloves on." When Tallulah didn't move, she made an exasperated noise, elbowed Tallulah aside, and began wiping out the cage herself.

"I cannot believe Ruth talked Dr. Poteet into this," she said. Her voice sounded echoey from inside the cage, swooping with the jerks of her arm. "Your Christian duty, she says. Can't let a poor girl come to harm. I been short-handed back here two weeks already; you'd think he'd of found it his Christian duty to get me some actual help. Instead I get some girl wandering up the road don't know how to do a lick of damn work." She banged the kennel door shut just as Poteet walked into the room.

His white coat was gone, replaced again by the khaki coveralls and boots. He wore a navy baseball cap, UT stitched in orange on the front. "Horse cut itself up at Cherokee Springs," he said to Jolene. "Bob Sholty's daughter's new hunter. Sholty doesn't know his ass end from a golf cart so somebody's got to come give me a hand."

"Somebody who?" Jolene snapped. "Kyle's shift don't start for another two hours and I still got all the afternoon treatments to do. Why can't the daughter help you?"

"Because my insurance company has fits when little girls get kicked in the head." Poteet looked at Tallulah.

Studied her, almost, as though finding her suddenly interesting. She glanced between him and Jolene, the disinfectant spray bottle suspended in her hand.

"Uh-uh," Jolene said. "If I have to do all the treatments *and* the dog-walking *and* the cleaning I'll be late picking up Tyler again. You know how much it costs every minute I'm late?"

"Can you hold a horse?" Poteet asked Tallulah.

"Yes," Tallulah said.

"The hell she can, she's scared of even that little puppy over there. I'll go, Dr. Poteet. She can stay here and help Ruth."

"Ruth doesn't need any help. And you have to be here in case an emergency comes in. That's what I hired a licensed technician for, not to go gallivanting around the country. Tallulah, take off those gloves and get some coveralls on and let's go."

Tallulah tore off the gloves. She had no idea how to hold a horse; her first and last time near one had been a pony ride at a fair when she was eight. But if going with Poteet was a chance to get out of this puppy-shitting, dog-lunging, slide-guitar-wailing room, no horse was going to stop her.

A tight-lipped Jolene handed Tallulah an old pair of coveralls. They were too short; every time Tallulah moved her shoulders they pinched her crotch. Two inches of teal scrubs showed below the hems. They'd been the previous assistant's, Jolene said, the one who'd up and quit.

Tallulah tugged the sides of the pants down. It didn't help. "Don't you have any others?"

"This ain't a department store," Jolene said, and turned away.

In the hallway, Poteet paused to stick his head into what looked like an office. "Ruth, I'm going to Cherokee Springs. Taylor Roach calls, you give him the cell number." He headed outside and Tallulah followed him. Immediately the heat clambered onto Tallulah's chest, like a steaming childhood monster from under a bed. Making itself comfortable, while the sweat condensed under her bangs.

Poteet drove with his window open, not seeming to mind the inrush of hot air battling the air conditioner. He wasn't talkative, which was OK with Tallulah. She adjusted an air vent so that it blew directly on her, stretched her legs as far as the coveralls would allow, and eased her heels out of her boots.

How, exactly, had she gotten here? Not that this was a new question; it seemed she spent half her life trying to figure out how she'd screwed up the other half. Her mother insisted it was because she didn't think things through. Not true. She always thought things through. Every disaster ever attributed to her had started as a plan. But from her grandparents' flooded bathroom when she was six, to wrecking her stepdad's Volvo when she was fourteen, to last year's shoplifting fiasco with her ex-friend Andrea—despite her plans, the results somehow were never what Tallulah expected. In fact, the only truly impulsive thing Tallulah had ever done was get into her daddy's car, her real daddy's, and driven with him to Elko. And you couldn't hold her accountable for that, she'd only been seven and besides, he was her father.

What happened? Every mess Tallulah had gotten into, that was the first question off everyone's lips, quickly followed by *Why?*

Tallulah was always clear on *what.* First A happened, then B happened, then C. Simple. The *why,* well, that was the plan, whatever the plan had been. The question that mattered, which no one ever asked, was *How? How* did A lead to B lead to C? That was what she could never figure out. How the harder she tried to make a thing happen, the more other things happened instead. Not until five months ago, when Tallulah met Maeve, had anyone ever been able to explain *how.*

She wished Maeve was here to explain this.

The truck turned off the road and began jouncing up a long gravel driveway. "We're here," Poteet said. "All you say is hello and nice to meet you. Then close your mouth and smile. I do all the talking on a farm call."

Tallulah shrugged; fine by her. They passed a painted wooden sign: CHEROKEE SPRINGS STABLES. BOARDING. TRAINING. LESSONS. off to the left, pasture rolled away down a hill; on the right, a gray horse trotted inside an arena, puffs of reddish dust rising under its hooves. The truck swung onto a dirt yard and coasted toward two long blue barns. Poteet parked near the end of one of them. "There's Bob Sholty," he said.

"The one who doesn't know his ass from a golf cart?"

Poteet grunted; whether he was amused or irritated, Tallulah couldn't tell. "You pay attention, at least," he said. "Open up my side of the VetPak. There's a green carry tray. Get it out and follow me." He swung himself out of the truck.

A storage unit took up the entire truck bed, *VetPak* emblazoned across its back. Tallulah opened the lid on Poteet's side and found a tray piled full of supplies and gadgets. It took both hands to lift it over the rim of the truck bed. Poteet was already walking away; she drifted after him, studying Sholty, a pale, paunchy man in pressed chinos and suede loafers, shoes that, even to Tallulah's unhorsey eye, looked completely out of place in a stable yard. Sholty nodded to Poteet and slapped him on the shoulder and said something Tallulah didn't catch. Without a glance at her, they walked around the back side of the barn.

When Poteet had said *daughter's horse,* Tallulah had imagined a pony, some small, shaggy, docile thing. The animal standing on the packed dirt was no pony. And it wasn't shaggy. Not anywhere. It gleamed, from the white stripe slanting down its nose to the brown of its slabbed flanks. Were all horses this big? They sure didn't look like it in the calendar pictures.

At their approach, the horse stamped a front foot in the dust. Tallulah could not take her eyes off the slide of muscles under its skin.

"'Afternoon, Miss Claudia," Poteet said to the girl holding the horse. He sounded more cheerful than she'd heard him so far; his voice was practically sunny. "How's your summer been?"

"Good," the girl answered. "You haven't met my new darling yet." Her voice was fluty and intense, with a drawl that rendered *good* into two syllables. She looked about twelve, tall for her age, with muscly arms. She also had a wide butt, a feature sadly emphasized by her stretch riding pants.

"I understand your new darling went and banged himself up some," Poteet said.

"Another horse kicked him in the paddock," Claudia said. "Dr. Poteet, what if it's the tendon? Angela Cranshaw's horse cut its tendon two years ago and never jumped again and . . ."

"Carelessness," Sholty said. "That's what caused it. I'll tell you what, if the horse is stove up because of this then the stable owner better have a good lawyer, that's all I can say."

"Now, it may not be all that bad." Poteet gestured casually at Tallulah. "Claudia, you let my assistant here hold your fine young man, and you tell me all about him while we take a look."

Claudia flicked her eyes over Tallulah and tightened her grip on the lead rope. "If you don't care, Dr. Poteet, I'd rather hold him. He's not a horse for an amateur."

Poteet shot Tallulah a barbed look. She widened her eyes, shrugged. *I didn't do anything.*

"All right, well, let's see how he does." Poteet eased around to the horse's left side. The horse snorted and tossed its head. "Whoa, son," Poteet said.

"Stand up. Stand up, Leopard, whoa!" Claudia said, yanking on the lead rope.

Leopard didn't whoa. Instead he rolled his eyes, showing new-moon slivers of white, and scuttled backward, dragging Claudia with him. He didn't seem to Tallulah to be particularly injured.

"Hey, now," Sholty said. He ran a hand over the back of his neck. "Hey, now. Make him mind, Claudia."

Poteet tried approaching from the other side and Leopard skittered sideways. Tallulah edged a step back. Maybe she did have NEVER SEEN A HORSE UP CLOSE tattooed on her forehead, but even so it was obvious to her who was in charge, and it sure as hell wasn't Claudia.

When all of the horse's hooves were on the ground, Poteet said, "Now, Claudia, if you let Tallulah here hold Leopard, it might be he'll settle down. And maybe we can find a nice little injection to smooth out the rough edges."

Tallulah let out a breath. Why hadn't he brought up drugs in the first place, instead of allowing all this jumping-around-and-dragging-people nonsense?

But Claudia was shaking her head. "Missy Thompson told me one of her horses got a sedative once and it had seizures."

"I don't know anything about Missy Thompson's horse," Poteet said, "but you've seen me use sedatives before and you know darned well there's never been any problem."

Sholty cleared his throat. "I hate to put it this way, Doc," he said, "but that's a twenty-two-thousand-dollar animal standing there. If we can't see eye to eye how to handle him, well, I hate to have called you out here for nothing. If you see what I mean."

Baffled, Tallulah stared at the horse. Twenty-two *thousand*?

Poteet pinched the top of his nose, squinting as though his head hurt. Then he shrugged. "All right, then, we'll do it the old-fashioned way. But I brought my crack horsewoman along to help, and that's what she's going to do. Tallulah, come over and hold this horse." His jovial tone slipped on *this horse,* but Tallulah seemed to be the only one who heard it. She glared at him, and met a pointed stare that knotted her stomach. By now, he'd figured out she knew less about horses than Bob Sholty. But he was in a corner; he had no choice but to use her.

She set the tray down and straightened up slowly. Leopard shook his head and skipped what looked like a little jig. Eager to haul her all over the barnyard, no doubt.

Wing it till you swing it. That's what Maeve always said. Fake it till you make it. For all these people know, you were *born* in a stable.

Tallulah stepped up to the horse's head and wrapped

her fingers around the lead rope just above Claudia's hand. Claudia hesitated. Then she let go. That small victory won, Tallulah turned her attention to the horse.

Leopard rolled one eye down at her, then over to the truck, where Poteet had gone. Now that no one was crowding him, his ears had come forward some. She'd noticed that when the rearing and leaping commenced, the ears went back. She'd watch the ears closely. The instant they flattened, she'd drop the rope and run.

Poteet ambled up on her right. Something in his pocket rattled with his steps. "Move over," he said in a low voice.

"What?"

"Move *over*," he repeated. "By me." Tallulah sidled next to the horse's left shoulder. "Don't ever stand directly in front of a horse unless you want to get killed," Poteet muttered. Apparently he didn't want the Sholtys hearing him give basic instructions to the person holding their twenty-two-thousand-dollar darling.

Poteet took the lead rope. He slipped the rattling thing out of his pocket, reached up past Tallulah, gripped the horse's upper lip, slipped on a shining loop of chain, and twisted. Tallulah blinked in surprise. She thought Leopard did, too. In less than a moment, with no fuss whatever, the horse's lip had been pinched up in the chain like a lady's waist in a corset. Leopard twisted his neck and shuffled his front feet. For the first time since they'd arrived, he seemed unsure of his place in the scheme of things.

"Take hold of this handle here and here, and hold the

lead rope along with it, like so," Poteet said. Tallulah placed her hands where he showed her. Immediately Leopard began wiggling his lip, exposing a set of enormous, flat, yellow teeth. Poteet grabbed the handle and twisted it back up and the wiggling stopped.

"*Tight,* now," he muttered. "This isn't a tennis racket you've got here. Look." He nodded at Leopard's face. The horse's eyelids had begun to droop; one ear sagged out to the side, then the other. "Endorphins," Poteet said. "The brain's own happy juice. No one knows why, but a twitch turns on the tap. He can wake up pretty quick, though, so watch out. Whatever happens, don't let go of that handle. Got it?"

She didn't, but she nodded anyway. Poteet picked up the tray and walked around to Leopard's rear. "Needs a couple stitches, Claudia, but it's not anywhere close to a tendon," he called. "Hang on up there. I'm about to put in the local." Local what? Tallulah wondered. Then a freight train smashed into her chest and she was soaring.

She landed butt-first just before the ground slammed up under her head. For a long, intense time it seemed she would not breathe again. Cirrus clouds, faint wisps against deep blue, drifted past her eyes. This is what it's like to die, she thought. Then the air rushed in, a great whooshing tide, and she sucked in all of it her chest could hold, disregarding the stabbing in her left side.

A shadow blotted out the clouds. It was Sholty's doughy face. He looked worried. Tallulah was oddly touched; he

63

didn't even know her. Then he vanished, and Poteet appeared in his place. Poteet did not look worried. He looked pissed.

"I told you not to stand directly in front of that horse," he said.

A boy in Tallulah's sixth-grade class had specialized in a form of torture called Super Atomic Wedgies. The borrowed coveralls were administering a Super Atomic to Tallulah right now. Tallulah struggled to form words with her lips. "Fuck you," she said.

Poteet grinned. "You're all right," he said. "Let's see you prove it. Get up."

He helped her stand. It wasn't until she was on her feet that she realized she was still holding the twitch. She opened her fingers and it fell to the ground with a sharp rattle, a final-sounding thud. Poteet brushed off her back and shoulders. Sholty hovered nearby. Two or three times he put out a hand as if to steady her, but each time stopped short of touching her. Tallulah wondered if he thought he was helping.

"Are you all right? Is she all right?" he kept asking.

Tallulah's chest felt numb, except for a place an inch below her left breast that hurt when she inhaled. A few feet away, Claudia's wide-load ass was bent over, one of Leopard's front hooves cupped in her hands. The horse appeared downright placid. Apparently attempted murder calmed his nerves.

"Looks like you're all of a piece," Poteet said. "Damn

good thing you kept hold of this." He picked up the twitch and ran a hand along the length of the handle. To no one in particular, he said, "You know these things are solid beech? I once saw a horse rear up, send one flying out of a man's hand. Hit a bystander in the head. Dropped him like a bullet."

Sholty cleared his throat. "Maybe you ought to sedate the horse," he said.

"I think it's best," Poteet said.

Tallulah trailed Poteet back to the truck. "I'm not holding that twitch thing again," she said. She was shaking; her voice sounded high and wavery in her ears.

"You won't have to."

"Then if it's OK with you, I'll just wait here."

"It is not OK with me." He opened the VetPak, put the twitch away, and rooted around in a drawer. "Someone's got to hold that shithead and it's not going to be Little Miss Lawyer's Daughter over there."

Tallulah pressed her hands against her thighs. They still shook. She tried to speak but the tremors rose in her throat, strangling her voice. He'll know you're afraid, she thought, and then: I don't care. I am afraid. I'm ready to piss my damn pants, if anyone wants to know.

She managed to say, in a voice just louder than a whisper, "That thing's a monster. It almost killed me, and I'm not going anywhere near it."

"Killed you my ass. All you got was a little bruised and a lot scared. Ask me sometime how many bones I've had broken." Poteet filled a syringe from a clear vial. "If you think you can hold that horse and make him mind, then do it. If not, you better fake it however you can. Just for God's sake don't stand in front of him this time."

"You can't make me."

"God help me, I don't have time for this." Poteet put the syringe in his pocket and slammed the VetPak closed. "You want to stay here, then stay. When we get back to the clinic get your stuff and hit the road. Go to Florida. Go anywhere you damn well want to. God knows it wasn't my idea to keep you."

He turned and walked away from the truck.

Chapter 6

It was easier walking up to the horse if she didn't look directly at it. When Tallulah arrived at Poteet's elbow, he didn't say anything; he merely handed her the lead rope. Tallulah stood well to Leopard's left side, gripping the rope so hard its stiff prickles bit into her palm. She smelled pungent sweat, but whether it was hers or the horse's she couldn't tell.

"I'm going to stick him in the neck," Poteet murmured. "If he jumps, you hold on. If he pivots, you pivot. Stay close at his side and he can't hurt you."

She nodded. Her throat was too tight with dread to speak. She could not stop shaking. Leopard flicked his ears back.

"When are you going to do it?" she asked desperately.

"Already done," he said, and stepped back.

A few minutes later the horse stood spraddle-legged and slack-lipped, head hanging almost to the ground. Poteet set to work. When the suturing was finished, Poteet helped Tallulah lift Leopard's head and showed her how to cradle the jaw on her forearms. It felt like a hairy sack of concrete. The weight of it settled into Tallulah's back, sending little lightning bolts of pain down her left side, while Poteet injected the horse a second time in the neck.

"That's the reversal drug. He'll be awake in about three minutes," Poteet said. "Claudia, come on and take your horse back." She did. Tallulah walked to the truck and got in. A few minutes later, Poteet joined her.

"Always clean up after a field call," he said as he started up the engine. He sounded annoyed. "I picked up all the gauze and suture wrappers this time, but don't forget next time."

Next time? Was he high? "You do know my ribs are broken," Tallulah said.

He snorted. "I doubt that."

"How do you know? I'm in pain all down my side, my . . ."

"Believe me, if you had broken ribs you wouldn't be sitting there so upright and righteous."

Sweat stung Tallulah's eyes; she rubbed them, then her forehead under her bangs. Her nose began to run. She sniffled, and wiped it on her wrist.

"Jesus Pete," Poteet muttered. Then, louder, he said, "There's paper napkins in the glove box." Tallulah opened the glove compartment and got a napkin and blew her nose.

"I'm sorry," Poteet said. "All right? I'm sorry. I didn't intend for you to get kicked." When Tallulah didn't answer, he reached over and snapped on the radio. Banjo and guitar bounded into the cab and he swore, punching buttons, muttering, "I've *told* Kyle . . ." The banjo disappeared, replaced by a violin.

Tallulah twisted the napkin in her hands. Outside her window, dense skirts of brush spooled past, an arching canopy of trees. After a few minutes, the truck swung onto a county highway and the landscape opened up. A mobile home sales lot, a church high on a lawn-blanketed hill, a mechanic's garage. A big roadside sign: REVIVAL SUNDAY AUG 3RD 7 PM. Blood red letters on white.

This place reminded her a little of the outskirts of Modesto. Farm country. When she was very small, her dad used to take her for drives there. It wasn't so much the way it looked—Modesto had been flatter, with only a fraction of the foliage, never this lushly green—but in its almost-familiar-yet-not-quite feel. As though it belonged to another world, where other rules might apply.

That summer, the summer of the evening drives, Tallulah—of course, she'd still been Debbie then—had been five. That was the summer Dad would get restless after dinner. Pace around the house. Fiddle with things. Then he'd tell Mom he needed to go to the store. Mom knew he wasn't going to the store, and Debbie and Terri knew, and they knew she knew. Still, Mom would say, Oh, good, because we need—and she'd name something, milk, margarine, anything. And she'd say, Take one of the girls. The first time, he took Terri, but she threatened to tell on him if he didn't buy her a Hello Kitty lunch box. After that, he took only Debbie.

He would go to the store first, leaving Debbie in the

car while he got whatever it was Mom had asked for, and whatever he'd told her he needed, batteries or cigarettes. That took all of five minutes. Then they'd drive out of town. Farm country. Long empty roads, fields like the ones flicking past Tallulah now. By then, it would be dark. They always went to the same place, a tiny wooden house with nothing else around it and light and music pouring out its windows. Daddy would get out of the truck, and once he was inside, Debbie would climb on the roof of the truck and watch the lights, and the moon, and listen to the crickets, and wait. It was warm outside, dry as dirt, and she was happy.

She remembered four drives clearly. Maybe there had been more. The last time, though, Daddy had stayed in the house longer than usual. Bored and chilled, Debbie climbed down and curled up on the front seat, pulling his sheepskin-lined denim jacket over herself. When she woke, Daddy was in the truck, and they were driving, but real slow. She sat up and looked out the window. The headlights looked the way her flashlight did when she and Terri played fort in their beds: a bubble of light, trapped.

"Hey, ladybug," Daddy said. She remembered his voice sounding thick, as though some of the fog had gotten in his throat. She could smell the whiskey on him. Usually she couldn't smell it, but that night she had. She already knew the difference between whiskey and beer; he'd given her sips of both at home, before Mom had poured out the bottles in the sink.

"Hey, Daddy," she said, and tried to squirm under his right elbow. She must have bumped him without meaning to, because the truck swung hard to the left and bucked and threw her headfirst into the dashboard. She tumbled to the floor under the glove compartment. The truck stopped. Her forehead hurt. She put a hand up to the sore and whimpered, but Daddy didn't seem to notice, so she climbed back onto the seat. Daddy was staring straight ahead. In the dim glow of the dashboard she saw his cheeks shivering with the rough idling of the engine. She wiped her eyes and waited.

Finally he said, "We got some tule fog here, no shit. Know how you can tell tule fog?"

"No. How?"

"You can't see through it!" He doubled up over the wheel, laughing, and although she didn't get it, she laughed, too. He said, "Ladybug, there's one thing you gotta know and don't ever forget about tule fog." She thought he was going to make another joke, but he turned to look at her and he was serious. His head rolled a little, as if his neck was too soft to hold it up. "Don't ever try to drive through tule fog with your brights on. Keep the beams on low. Got that?"

"Yes, Daddy."

"What did Daddy say?"

"Don't ever drive in toolee fog on brights."

He put out a hand and brushed the bangs back from her forehead. Even back then, Debbie hated her brown hair. It wasn't fair that Terri got to be blond, like him, when Debbie was his favorite.

71

"Roll down your window, ladybug, and stick your head out," he said. She did. The fog had a rotten smell, like the mud in the creek bed behind their house before the sun had baked it dry. "Look way down, at the road," he told her. "Is there a line?"

She leaned out the window. A little ahead, under the front tire, was a bit of white. She called this over her shoulder. Daddy backed the truck up, shifted gears, and pulled ahead, swinging to the left. Then he stopped again. Debbie hung out farther, grabbing the door with her hands and tucking her belly over them, thighs pressed against the armrest to keep from falling out. "I see it," she told him.

"Great. Great job, bug. You watch that line. If it goes under the truck, you yell. Can you do that?"

Of course she could. She only had to yell three times, twice when the line disappeared and once when it kept getting farther away. He hadn't said anything about that, but when she told him, he yanked the car to the right so hard she almost fell back inside.

When they got into town, he pulled the truck over. She peered around doubtfully. The fog blurred the houses, but still it didn't look like their street. It took her a minute to unfold herself from over the door. Her hands had gone numb where she'd lain on them, and there were deep grooves across both palms from the window crack in the door. Her hair and her shirt were dripping wet. She couldn't stop shivering. Daddy helped her out onto the sidewalk, then wrapped her in the denim jacket, and picked her up.

He swayed under her weight. She swayed along with him, nestling her face into the sheepskin collar, the whiskey tickly sharp in her nose. Unafraid, because she knew he wouldn't drop her.

Poteet snapped off the radio. Tallulah jumped a little, startled at the sudden movement.

"These are the rules," Poteet said. "If you're hateful to a client or a critter, you're out. I don't care how ornery they get. Understand?"

Tallulah closed her eyes.

"This isn't a game," Poteet continued. "It's a business. *My* business. I work hard and so does all my staff and because of that I run the best veterinary hospital in two counties."

For the first time since they got in the truck, Tallulah turned to look at him. His eyes were on the road, one hand on the wheel, thumb tapping. The other elbow crooked out the window. His snub-nosed face had the same expression her mom's did when she spoke to the women's groups, when she told the story about transforming herself from a Modesto grocery store clerk to a million-dollar real estate producer and a county commissioner. At the end of the story she always said, It's about choices and leaving behind what holds you back, and the women would turn to each other and nod and clap, and the expression on Mom's face said, You got that right. Of course, the first thing she'd left behind was Tallulah's father, but she never mentioned that part.

Poteet turned the radio back on. After a few minutes Tallulah asked, "Why didn't you kill that dog?"

"God knows," Poteet said. His voice was taut and flat, all the joviality from the stable gone. "He's old and a mutt besides. We'll have a hell of a time finding him a home."

Tallulah took a long, shuddering breath. Her side hurt. "Who's Ruth? Your wife?"

Poteet shot her a startled look. "No. My receptionist. Ruth has a big heart." He drummed his fingers on the steering wheel. "Bigger than her head, sometimes," he muttered.

Another few minutes and they were at the veterinary hospital. Walking inside was like diving into an unheated pool, a shock to the skin. Tallulah drew as deep a breath as she could without hurting her ribs, savoring the easy pull of cold, dry air. As she followed Poteet into the back hall, an older woman appeared in the office doorway. She was soft-shouldered, pillow-thick through the middle, with the most amazing old-lady hair Tallulah had ever seen: like a bubble of gold-tinted spiderweb, so lacy it seemed that if Tallulah stared hard enough, she might see through to the scalp underneath.

"Taylor Roach ever call?" Poteet asked.

"No," the woman said. "But Ellen's secretary came by again with those papers for you to sign." She tucked her chin, regarding Poteet over the top of her glasses. If she was bracing for a reaction, she got one; Poteet swept the baseball cap off his head and chucked it hard onto the counter, sending it skidding halfway down its length.

"What'd you tell her?" he said.

"Told her you weren't here. Same as last time. You want me to set up an appointment with your lawyer?"

Poteet wiped the back of his wrist across his forehead. "No," he said. He stepped over to the counter and picked up his hat. "Ellen sends that secretary again, you tell her I'm not selling. Not now. Not ever. You got that?"

"Told her that last week," the woman said, but Poteet was already striding down the hall. The woman looked over at Tallulah. "Ex-wife," she said, as if in answer to a question. She extended her hand; Tallulah took it.

"You're Tallulah," the woman said. "I'm Ruth. You did a kind thing, saving that dog. You thirsty?" She had what Maeve called sunrise eyes: the lower lids wide and perfectly straight, the uppers curved like bows. Under their pale blue scrutiny, Tallulah felt every streak of dust on her skin, every drying bead of sweat.

"Dying," Tallulah said.

"Thought so. You look parched. Let's get you a pop."

Kyle was seated in the break room, eating a hamburger and flipping through a magazine. He glanced up when they came in.

"Next time you complain you don't have any money, I'm gonna grab a pen and draw a big old hamburger right on your forehead," Ruth said to him. "With all you got going on, you need to be saving your money, not eating it. I told you, I can bring your supper. Make it when I make mine. It's no trouble."

Kyle squinched up one side of his face. Ruth said to Tallulah, "I've not raised two boys without knowing what that face means. You'd think I was asking to sew name tags in his underwear."

Startled, Tallulah choked back a laugh. Kyle shot her a look of outrage, dropped the remains of his hamburger in its container, and stood up. "'Scuse me," he said.

"Sit down, I'm going," Ruth said. She opened the refrigerator and handed Tallulah a soda. "When you're finished, just rinse out the can. Recycle, not trash. And then Jolene could use some help, if you don't care. Same for you, Kyle."

"Ain't my job to do evening cleaning," Kyle said.

Ruth had been almost out the door; at this, she walked back and planted herself next to Kyle's chair, one hand on the table, the other on her hip. "I didn't ask what your job is," she said. "I asked you to help Jolene who's been busting her butt all day by herself back in those wards."

Kyle glanced at Tallulah and rolled his eyes. She ducked her head a little, hiding a smile behind her fingers.

"Can I finish my supper at least?" he said to Ruth. "Or am I supposed to starve, too?"

Ruth *hmph*'d and straightened up. "I reckon you better finish. I'd hate for you to faint from hunger." She winked at Tallulah and walked out the door, just as Tallulah managed to gather her scattered thoughts into a question. She put down her soda and ran after her.

"Ruth. Ruth, wait."

Ruth turned.

"What about . . . I mean, then what?" Tallulah asked. "Later. Tonight. Do I go with him—with Poteet—or . . ."

Ruth laughed. "Dr. Poteet? God help us, no. You're staying with me." As she headed back up the hallway, she said, "And tell Jolene to find you another pair of coveralls. Those are too short."

Chapter 7

Tallulah dreamed of sinking in clear water, a stone bound to her chest. Above her, a scalloped blue sky. Just as she was sure no one would come for her, Maeve appeared, squinting into the water, her red hair and long nose made more crooked by the ripples. But she didn't see Tallulah. *I'm here,* Tallulah cried, reaching up; but the stone bore her down and water rushed in her mouth and Maeve was gone.

She woke flailing in a screech of bedsprings. A cat bounded off her chest as though she were a trampoline and disappeared into the dark of Ruth's living room, leaving Tallulah gasping, sitting up on the saggy mattress of the sofa bed.

She pressed a hand against the stabbing in her left rib and listened for sounds from Ruth's bedroom. Nothing. No strip of light springing to life beneath the closed door. She must not have made much noise, then.

Careful of the squeaky springs, Tallulah shimmied to the edge of the mattress. From the dark came the rustle of quick feet on carpet, a jingle of metal tags. Tallulah hesitated, then reached out a hand. Something cool and dry nudged her palm. "Good dog," she whispered. "Good Cowboy. Quiet, OK?"

She stood, felt fur brush against her leg. When she had her bearings, she aimed for where she remembered the windows to be. Small steps, her toes questing for obstacles, her hands fanned forward, waist-high. Her left pinky finger bumped into a hard corner, trailed over smooth plastic. The TV. By her right leg, the metal tags clinked.

Her hands found the drape. She fumbled along it until she located its edge, then pocketed herself between it and the window. The air conditioning hadn't made its way back here, and the air was still stale from afternoon sun. Other than crickets, the night was silent. The only light visible, from a neighbor's front porch, was too far away to illuminate anything. Not that there had been much to see, arriving in Ruth's Pontiac in the heavy gold of the evening. Ruth lived just off the county highway, only a few minutes from the veterinary hospital. Her doublewide trailer was one of only five or six houses on the road. A few lay close as gardens to each other; the rest were separated by pastures.

Tallulah hadn't hesitated taking Ruth up on her offer. After all that had happened to her in the last thirty-six hours, getting into a car with a woman she'd just met and driving off to an unknown destination seemed fairly mundane. Besides, Ruth had promised dinner. Tallulah's only meal that day had been a thin jail sandwich, ham and white bread, no mustard, which hadn't even carried her through the puppy diarrhea, let alone the Leopard episode.

Ruth had ushered Tallulah up the front porch, explaining, as she unlocked the door, about the cats. Cha-Cha and Merle and Tigger, she said, could go outside. But Tripod and Mrs. Jones were strictly indoors so if either of them made a dash to escape Tallulah should say "Shoo!" and wave them back. Tripod was easy to identify, as he was the one missing a front leg, but Mrs. Jones looked identical to Tigger, or maybe it was Merle. They were all some variation of stripy and anyway the anticipation of food, a shower, and sleeping on a mattress instead of a jail bench—even if it was only a sleeper sofa—kept Tallulah from paying full attention. Then there was the dog, a black-and-white shaggy thing that sat on Tallulah's foot, wiggling its tail and gazing full into her eyes.

"What does he want?" Tallulah asked nervously. She was still in the hospital scrubs, carrying her duffel and the bag of her own clothes. Ruth took the bag and disappeared down a short hallway.

"He's a border collie. Give him something to do," Ruth called. She came back into the living room and snapped her fingers. "Cowboy! Cat on the counter!" The dog launched itself off Tallulah's foot; a second later two cats rocketed out of the kitchen, the dog close behind.

"I set your things on the washing machine," Ruth said. "I expect about now you'd like a shower, though."

"I would," Tallulah said.

"Go on, then. We'll have chicken potpie for supper, if you don't care." *If you don't care,* Tallulah was realizing, meant *if you don't mind.* When it came to chicken potpie, she didn't mind at all.

Tallulah stayed in the shower longer than she knew she should, reluctantly turning off the water only when all the hot was gone. From her duffel she picked a pair of shorts and a tank top. No shoes. She had a blister on each heel the size of a quarter.

The chicken potpie was microwaved, not homemade as Tallulah had expected. But it tasted fine, the iced tea was delicious and there was plenty of it, and Ruth, when she asked Tallulah how she came to be walking alone and penniless miles from the interstate, proved to be a sympathetic listener. If she didn't quite agree that Derek deserved to drive his car off a cliff, she had no problem pronouncing him a First-Class Stinker. Tallulah liked the way she talked, the way her drawl went dry down to bone, as though a lifetime of cigarettes and practicality had smoked out all its limberness.

Not that Ruth smoked anymore. Quit, she declared. Three years ago, the same year she divorced her husband. Although unlike Derek, Ruth's husband had not been a First-Class Stinker.

"But I was," she said.

Once she'd hit fifty, Ruth had gotten—as she put it—prickly. Her husband had nothing to say that she cared to hear; a room with him in it felt squeezed. "Albert's a long-distance trucker," she explained. "He was gone most of the time anyway. I guess I just got to where I liked it better that way." When she'd asked him to move out, he'd gone amicably enough. "Lives just two roads over. Something blows up here, he'll swing by and fix it. And in thirty-six years, he's still not worn a shirt I haven't made." She bent toward Tallulah and said in a raspy whisper, as if imparting a secret: "Right arm's a half-inch longer than the left."

After dinner, Ruth insisted on washing the dishes. "You just relax," she kept saying. But relaxation seemed like a foreign country: someplace Tallulah had heard of, but couldn't imagine ever going to. She felt awkward sitting alone at the table. It was worse standing in the tiny kitchen. Her side ached. Her head ached. All she wanted to do was lie down and stop thinking. But first she had to know that Maeve was on her way.

"Could I use your phone?" she asked.

Both her hands in suds, Ruth pointed with her chin to a phone on the counter. "Help yourself. Or there's one in the bedroom, if you want some privacy."

Tallulah headed for the bedroom. Halfway there, she hesitated. Then turned around. "Where exactly am I?"

The answering machine picked up again, with its mumbling male voice. This time, though, Tallulah was ready. Clark Station, Tennessee, she dictated into the silence, then read off the addresses and phone numbers for both the veterinary hospital and Ruth's house. "I'll wait for you here. Is everything OK? It's hard not knowing . . . just, will you *call* me? OK?"

At the end, just before the machine cut her off, she added, "Hi, Michael."

She'd realized where Maeve was. Or, if not exactly where, at least with whom. Maeve had told her about Michael: friends since ninth grade, they shared poetry, an interest in all things pagan—Druidism on his side, the Goddess on hers— and a deep and abiding love for men. Maeve referred to him as her male soul and called him at three in the morning to discuss politics. Tallulah had spoken with him once on the phone. His voice had blurred like watercolors. He had been shy.

After she hung up she wandered into the living room, where Ruth was laying out bedsheets. Tallulah helped her pull out the sofa bed and make it up. "Remote's right here, if you want to watch TV," Ruth said. "Don't worry about the critters. The cats don't see much company, they probably won't show themselves. Except Tripod, he's a lover. That bathroom's yours. Best thing about a doublewide, two bathrooms. You need anything, just look in a drawer."

"This is nice. Thank you."

Ruth glanced around the room, straightened a crocheted doily on the end table. "All right, then," she said. " 'Night, hon." She walked toward her bedroom, Cowboy trotting low and quick behind her. Halfway there, though, he turned and came back, curling with a sigh next to Tallulah's duffel.

Once Ruth's bedroom door was closed, Tallulah shucked off her shorts and, wearing only the tank top, slipped between the sheets. She switched off the table lamp, and the yellow and country blue and fake wood grain of Ruth's living room vanished into a simple dark. It was quiet. Jail had been so noisy, even in the dead of night; she'd been put next to the drunk tank, and from the sounds it seemed like the party had just been moved, rather than broken up. Loud laughter, incoherent singing, things banging against the bars. The silence of Ruth's house seemed to have weight. Muffling and warm, like a second blanket.

The sofa bed's foam mattress was slightly crunchy, with a stale rubbery smell. The pillow was goosedown, though; Tallulah turned on her side, burrowing her face into its luxury. At its faint, cedar-closet scent, a wave of homesickness expanded from the middle of her chest down her sides, into the tips of her fingers, aching at the hinge of her jaw. Mom always stored the off-season linens in a cedar armoire in the upstairs hallway. Spring and fall, cotton and flannel; the scent always lingered through two washings, no less, no more.

Tallulah had planned to watch TV until the wee hours, if not all night. She never could sleep her first night in a new place. Yet she'd dropped off almost immediately and slept straight through. Until the cat, whichever one it was—Tripod or Merle or God-knows-who—had figured her for a cushion and woken her up.

Tallulah laid her cheek against the windowpane, expecting it to be cool. It wasn't. In Portland, no matter how hot it got during the day, it almost always cooled down at night. Here, the air conditioning had yet to turn off.

It must be this bad in Florida. Maybe worse. How was Maeve standing it? She'd grown up in Orlando, but she'd hated it, hated the heat most of all. It was one reason she'd left, she'd told Tallulah: to get out of the sun for a while.

Tallulah pushed the drape aside and slid her foot along the floor. Her big toe jabbed something furry. She heard a clash of tags and scuff of dog nails on shag carpet, and the fur disappeared. "Sorry, Cowboy," she whispered, at the same time gooseflesh rose across the backs of her arms. The dog had felt too much like the black dog in the underpass. Then Cowboy pressed himself against her, and she took comfort in the cool slip of his fur against her knee. He shadowed her back to the sofa bed.

"Shut your eyes, buddy," she said, and turned on the light.

The notebooks were still at the bottom of her duffel. Both spiral-bound, identical except for their covers: one purple, one green. If Derek had gone through her duffel—and from the thoroughness with which she'd been robbed, she knew he had—at least he'd left these where he'd found them.

Tallulah pulled out the green notebook and ran her hand over its worn, white-creased cover. Since retrieving them from Maeve's apartment, she hadn't opened them. For the past six days, she'd focused only on getting them to Florida.

The moment Tallulah had finished reading Maeve's e-mail, she'd gotten up from her desk and gone downstairs. After the Volvo incident, her mom and John had refused to buy her her own car; but Terri was home, and Terri had an old Subaru wagon. Tallulah stood in the kitchen, listening to the swell of Oprah's theme song coming from the family room, and over it, Terri's voice on the phone.

Better to ask for forgiveness than permission. Besides, she'd be gone an hour at the most. Tallulah went back upstairs, lifted Terri's keys off her dresser, and left out the back door.

Maeve's apartment building, like the apartments themselves, was squat and ugly. But Maeve had loved its 1920s quasi-Spanish look, unusual in siding-and-shingle Portland; the wrought iron letters spelling out its name, BELINDA, over dark yellow stucco; the common entry, all polished dark wood and red floral carpet, onto which the apartments' front doors opened. Most of all, though, she'd loved its flat and accessible roof.

In front of Maeve's door, Tallulah turned over the ridged green welcome mat. She peeled back the strip of duct tape in the upper corner, pried the key off its underside, and let herself in.

The first thing she saw was the red Superman cape Maeve had been making for her downstairs neighbor's grandson. It was draped over the arm of the couch, the sewing needle still attached by scarlet thread to the half-finished hem and jammed through a satin fold into the upholstery, as if just at that moment Maeve had gotten up to fetch something, scissors, or a cup of tea.

The quiet of the apartment was like a breath being

held. Tallulah found herself walking on the balls of her feet, easing around corners, reluctant to turn her back on the stereo, the orange crate of CD's, the boxes of books that Maeve had never unpacked, as if Maeve's belongings (why are they still here?) had swallowed Maeve and by some magic spit her out in Florida. In the bedroom (the bed sheets tossed and unmade, a white cotton nightgown crumpled at their foot) clothes and books lay strewn over the floor. Tallulah knew about the books; she'd helped Maeve find four of them in the county library. The rest Maeve had bought online. *Medical Records and the Law. Recordkeeping in Psychotherapy and Counseling. Medical Records: Getting Yours.* From the bottom of a pile, she extricated the notebooks.

These, too, she'd seen before. One night last month, Tallulah, buzzed on margaritas and unwilling to face the certain inquisition at home, had crashed on Maeve's couch. She'd woken at some dark hour to see Maeve, nightgown tawny in the glow of a streetlamp, sitting on the kitchen floor. Chin tilted up, eyes closed, her lips moving silently. A notebook open on her thigh. She was writing—she told Tallulah the next day—a book. A revolutionary book, telling people how to gain control of every scrap of personal information existing about them. Literally, how to set their records straight. Or wipe them clean. As she intended to do for herself.

People have lied about me, she told Tallulah. I thought I could ignore it. I can't.

But you can't write a book about it if you haven't done it yet, Tallulah pointed out.

I'm laying out my strategy, Maeve said. The rest will come.

Maeve had stayed up for three nights in a row, writing. The fourth day, she'd called a free law clinic run by the law school downtown. Tallulah had gone with her to the appointment.

Tell me how to get my medical records, Maeve had demanded of the little dark-haired student. Impatient. Tallulah had never seen Maeve impatient before. Then again, she'd never seen anyone go without sleep for four days.

Copies? the student had asked.

No. Not copies. The originals.

I don't think you can, the student had said. Why would you want to?

I want them destroyed, Maeve had said.

Tucking the notebooks under her arm, Tallulah explored the rest of the apartment. In the kitchen sink lay a plate and a buttery crumb-flaked knife. In the bathroom, the only thing missing was the toothbrush. Even Maeve's hairbrush was still on the shelf. Even her birth control pills.

Something must have happened. Some emergency. How it tied into the notebooks, Tallulah had no idea; at the time, though, she hadn't really cared. It wasn't for her to figure out. When, and if, Maeve wanted her to know—then she would know.

Leaving the silent apartment was a relief. As Tallulah

locked the door, she wondered if she should make some kind of arrangement for Maeve's stuff. Rent a truck, maybe. Put everything in storage.

But that would take time. And time was obviously something Maeve—and therefore Tallulah—didn't have.

Tallulah settled herself cross-legged on Ruth's sofa bed, the notebooks in her lap. In these pages somewhere had to be the reason Maeve had fled back to her hometown. Cowboy jumped up on the sofa next to her, circled once, and plopped down. Tallulah flipped open the green cover.

"Oh," she said, and picked up the Polaroid that lay on top of the first page.

The bluegrass festival. Tallulah and Maeve, arms around each other's shoulders, Tallulah grinning, Maeve laughing and leaning toward the camera, her eyes so wide that, even in the grainy film, their warm cherrywood color stood out. At the edge of the photo, part of a face. Tallulah remembered him: a thirty-something and his friend who'd struck up a conversation right after that photo was taken, and who had later bought Maeve and Tallulah beers. That sort of thing happened all the time with Maeve. Taken piece by piece, she was nothing special: her face was too wide, her nose too long, her eyes too small; true, her hair was spectacular, when it was brushed and flying free and not wound in hurried knots on top of her head, but still there was her size. Maeve was a big woman. All right. She was fat. Not sloppy huge, but still.

And yet you put it all together and let it loose in public

and heads turned. Not just men's, either. Everyone's. It was Maeve's energy, Tallulah thought, the joy that radiated from her like heat. Tallulah had felt it herself, the first time she'd ever seen her, in the tent at the motorcycle show five months before.

Tallulah ran her hand across her belly, feeling the whip-thin ridge of scar that angled crosswise below her navel.

The motorcycle show, Maeve, and the man-in-the-moon dagger.

Chapter 8

The morning of the motorcycle show, Tallulah Addy was still Debbie Badowski. Still a mousy brunette. She was still flunking her junior year of high school, and the only scar she possessed was the one on her right knee, from jumping off the garage roof when she was nine.

By the end of the day, she'd still be brunette (although that would change within the week) and still, of course, be flunking high school. But she'd been rechristened, her skin had been violated twice—once accidentally, once on purpose—and, for the first time since getting busted for shoplifting, eight months earlier, she had a best friend.

All she knew, that morning, was that she was going on a first date. Debbie had met Derek Hubner at the café where she worked as a barista. He'd come in and ordered a plain house coffee. No skinny wet half-caf cap, no grande quad macchiato with extra caramel, no venti extra-ice no-whip mocha frap. Just a regular dark roast. Not even room for cream. She'd given him crap about it—*We have a special name for customers like you. Clueless*—just to see what he'd do. He'd blushed, which hadn't exactly enchanted her; but when he'd asked if she was free the next day, she'd said yes. She'd been off probation (and the simultaneous Mom-and-John-imposed house arrest) for almost two months now, but her social life was still a cold dead beast, and she'd been waiting for something—or someone—to come revive it. Andrea Gilmore, Debbie's closest friend for the past year and a half, had dropped her completely. Wouldn't talk to her, wouldn't look at her when they passed in the hall. Worse, Andrea had spread a version of the shoplifting that cast herself as the wise all-seeing and Debbie as the reckless moron who'd gotten what she deserved. Debbie was left to choose between hanging with the stoners, the untouchables, or herself. Mostly, she chose herself.

She was lonely. Derek was interested. For now, it was enough.

It wasn't until she got into Derek's car, the next morning, that he told her they were going to a Harley show.

"Harley? As in motorcycles?" she asked.

"Yeah." He glanced at her. Dark blond hair falling in his eyes. "Cool by you?"

A motorcycle guy. He'd come pick her up after school on a big—red? silver? no—black bike. Right outside the main entrance. She'd run to meet him. Hop on and roar away in front of everyone. Ripped jeans. Black leather jacket. No fringe; fringe was tacky. But black boots for sure. Andrea Gilmore would pickle herself green with envy.

Things were looking up.

"Cool by me," Debbie said, and smiled at him. She kicked her sandals off and put her bare feet up on the dash.

What she hadn't envisioned were the two grubby Derek-friends who met them at the show. Or a morning spent trailing behind the three of them, from folding table to folding table under the canopies dotting the fairgrounds, every table strewn with greasy bits of metal that had to be passed around and discussed and compared with every other bit of greasy metal. She sure as hell hadn't envisioned rain. True, it was early March, but swear to God there hadn't been a single cloud that morning. Still, she'd lived in Portland since she was seven, she should have known the overcast would roll in and sure enough here it came, like a dog running to a whistle. Drizzle. Showers. More drizzle. Brief spats of hail to vary the monotony. And there she was in her jeans that showed the most skin and a bright yellow sleeveless baby-rib tee. Not even a hoodie for warmth.

"I'm cold," she said again.

"We need to check out that Fat Boy frame," the Derek-friend in the knit cap said. "Guy said he's not hanging around."

The Fat Boy frame, they informed her, was located in a pickup truck bed in the dirt parking lot behind the fairground lawn.

"But it's *raining*," Debbie said. "There's not even a canopy or anything over there. I'm freezing, Derek. I want to go inside." She pointed across the lawn to the main exhibition tent. For the past three hours she'd been listening to old-fogy music, Led Zeppelin and Aerosmith, blaring from its orange- and blue-striped flaps. She'd watched the people streaming in, then streaming out again, with balloons and hot dogs and popcorn and beer. They looked warm. They looked happy.

"It'll take like two seconds," Derek said. Tallulah hugged herself, glaring. The Derek-friends jostled each other and began walking away. "Then just wait here," he said, and trotted to catch up with them.

As soon as they were out of sight, she ran for the tent. The entry was jammed with people, a mist seeming to rise from their damp shoulders, as though drawn upward by the heaters suspended overhead. More people in leather and T-shirts and grease-stained denim choked the main aisle, milling around the booths. Smaller aisles led away in ragged lines to the sides. She ducked down the first of these, where the crowd was less and she could breathe easier.

She drifted past motorcycles, dozens of them, nail polish–bright in red or black or yellow, skirted in chrome. They leaned on their kickstands like rows of dancers resting, the men around them talking about Buells and Fat Boys, Softails and Electra Glides. As she wandered she detected the scent of popcorn rising above the base notes of sweat and pine shavings. Her stomach rumbled. She followed the warm butter smell past booths selling leather jackets and vests, halter tops and studded collars; helmets with chrome spikes jutting from their crowns; bumper stickers; T-shirts. IF YOU CAN READ THIS, THE BITCH FELL OFF. Then, just past the T-shirts, near the center of the tent, Debbie saw the daggers.

She'd owned a knife once. Her daddy had given it to her the week she'd lived with him in Elko. She'd loved the weight of it in her hand, the faded wear along the leather-wrapped handle, even the brown spots on the blade that Daddy claimed were bloodstains from a cougar he'd fought almost to the death and then nursed back to health and set free again. She loved the knife, even though she knew there had been no cougar, that the brown stains were only rust. When John had come to take her back to Portland, she'd hidden the knife in her schoolbag and then, at home, under her mattress, telling no one, not even Terri. She'd take it out to look at it, though, and one day Terri walked in and saw it and told Mom. Mom had searched Debbie's room, found the knife, and thrown it out.

Debbie worked her way over to the daggers. The crowd was especially thick here, but they were facing away, staring into the next booth. Curious, Debbie edged forward. In a gap between bodies she saw a curtain of red hair falling over a table edge almost to the floor, a hundred tangled shades of auburn and carrot and gold, blazing under the white light of studio lamps. The hair belonged to a woman, maybe twenty or so, lying facedown on a table. Her cheek rested on heavy pale arms; her slip dress lay in folds above her waist. A black sheet bunched from the small of her back to her upper thighs, veiling her buttocks from the crowd. Behind her, an older woman with blond-gray braids picked up what looked like a pen attached to a long thick cable. She dipped the pen's metal tip into a tiny pot of color, then lowered it until it disappeared behind the sheet. At the abrupt *bzzzz*, harsh as a yellow jacket, Debbie flinched. Murmurs and laughter rose from the watching crowd. Only the red-haired woman didn't move. In the heat and noise she seemed to float, like ice cream in coffee, like she was the only cool thing in the universe. The tattooist picked up a tissue, pressed it down, lifted. The tissue came away bloody. Debbie shuddered and turned away.

"Hi there," the salesman at the dagger booth said. He had a black handlebar mustache, a chapped lower lip. "Show you anything?"

Debbie tapped the glass of the display case. "That one," she said.

The salesman unlocked the case. "You've got good taste. That's a beauty."

LADIES DAGGER, the handwritten tag said. CARVED BONE HANDLE. With her fingertip, Debbie followed the intricate lines of a robed lady raising her eyes to a cluster of tiny, perfect stars. Over the lady, a man in the moon kept watch. The blade's double edges caught the escaped light of the tattoo parlor, compressing it into twin curving gleams that met in a point of silver. The whole dagger was just the length of Debbie's hand, from the base of her palm to the tip of her middle finger. She ached to pick it up, to feel the cool smooth tang, the weight of the handle balanced against the heft of the blade. A knife is part of your hand, her daddy had told her. It's part of you.

Debbie turned the tag over. A month's pay, plus tips.

Behind Debbie, a sudden crush of bodies pressed her forward over the display case. Her fingers curled around the dagger. She glanced up; the salesman's back was to her. Debbie twisted the dagger so it lay flat against the inside of her arm and slipped it, handle-first, down the front of her jeans. She flipped the hem of her shirt down over the knife blade and stepped back from the booth. Two women swirled into her place. Perfect. This was how it would have gone with Andrea in the music store, if only Andrea hadn't lost her nerve. Debbie turned away from the booth. The knife slipped—she puffed out her belly to trap it against her waistband—OK. Go. You're relaxed. Having a good time here with the Harleys. Don't walk too fas— no, get out of my way, please, oh *dammit*.

A small boy had darted in front of her, cutting off her escape. She forced a smile at him, at his mother. No, no hurry, nothing going on here. Just having a good time. . . . The mother caught her son's hand and pulled him along and Debbie stepped after them into the crowd. Ha! Wait until she showed Andrea—

Fingers seized her wrist and wrenched her around. The dagger blade scraped painfully across her belly button. She yelped and the salesman let go but before she could run, he'd stripped the purse off her shoulder and was rifling through it.

"Hey!" Debbie yelled. The salesman threw the purse at her. Without thinking, she bent forward to catch it and the dagger pricked the skin above her navel. She jerked upright.

"Where is it?" the salesman barked. Debbie pivoted but he lunged and grabbed her arm again.

"Let go!" She kicked at his shin and missed. He dragged her closer. She could smell cigarette ash in his sweat. The crowd had reformed around them, this new attraction, their bodies solid as the wall of an arena. Behind them, she glimpsed a blue uniform approaching.

From somewhere to her right, a woman shouted, *"Tallulah!"* Part of the arena wall jostled and stumbled and, in a torrent of white skirt, hair crackling from her temples, the redhead from the tattoo parlor shoved her way into the circle, an ocean liner plowing past rowboats. She strode up to the dagger salesman and bellowed, "GET YOUR HANDS OFF MY SISTER!"

Both Debbie and the salesman gaped at her.

"I send my sister to check out a knife for me and the next thing I know she's being *assaulted,*" the woman informed the crowd.

"What are you . . ." the salesman sputtered.

The redhead swirled toward him. "I was right over there, at the tattoo booth, getting a sword added to my Queen Mabh, I'd show you but it's on my butt, and I wanted Tallulah's opinion on that dagger to see if it would be a good gift for my aunt, *our* aunt, who's . . ."

The blue uniform had pushed his way to the front of

the crowd and stood, hands on his hips, gazing intently at the redhead. Over the woman's tirade, Debbie heard him say to the salesman, "Both of them, or just the one?"

"Her," the salesman said, jiggling Debbie's arm. Then, "I don't know. Both. The other one put her up to it."

The redhead bobbed close to Debbie. She radiated heat and nerves. A fine scrim of sweat shone on her face. She hissed, "Tallulah, will you just *give him the knife,* please?"

"Who the hell *are* you?" Debbie whispered.

"The person who's trying to save your ass," the woman said. "Unless you *want* to get strip-searched. I mean, just let me know."

"Dammit," Debbie muttered. She reached under her shirt with her free hand, grasped the dagger by the blade, and began sliding it out.

That was when everything seemed to slip into everything else. The salesman shouting, the dagger handle being twisted out of her grip. The sharp intake of breath from the redhead. The security officer's eyes suddenly going very round.

Curious, Debbie glanced down. The edges of her skin were welling up with blood. Her skin had never had edges before, not there, not on her stomach. *Cut. I've been cut.*

Her insides felt strangely still. She could hear gasps and exclamations, but they seemed to be from far away. Except the redhead's voice. That was very loud.

"You asshole, you are going to be *hugely* sorry for that! Our father is a *major* attorney in this town, and he . . ."

"It was an accident!" the salesman shouted. "She wouldn't let go, it wasn't . . ."

"My mother is running for county commissioner," Debbie said. Blood ran, merry as a creek, down her belly; on the waistband of her jeans, a flower of reddish black blossomed. She couldn't stop staring at it. "My mother is running for county commissioner," she repeated.

Someone said, "Watch out, she's going to faint," and a steady arm—it turned out to be the security officer's—propped Debbie up. He walked her to the first aid station, where another someone pressed the largest Band-Aid she'd ever seen onto her belly and told her to go to the emergency room for stitches, and, whether it was that or the redhead's bluff about having an attorney for a father, the end result was that Debbie and the redhead were only kicked out of the fairgrounds and not arrested.

The redhead—call me Maeve, she said—drove Debbie to the hospital. I'm Debbie, Debbie said, then she stopped talking because when she sat down in Maeve's car, the lips of the wound gaped open and the feeling of coming apart made her stomach do a slow, ominous back flip. She spent the rest of the ride, and the wait in the emergency room, concentrating on not throwing up.

The cut took seven stitches. While the doctor put them in, Maeve wrapped an arm around Debbie's shoulders and sang "Way Down Upon the Swanee River." She sang badly.

"Will I have a scar?" Debbie asked the doctor.

"Let me put it this way," the doctor said. "If you ever

get your navel pierced, it'll look like they missed the first time."

At the discharge window, Maeve slipped a credit card to the receptionist. Debbie protested, but not too much; she didn't have the money to pay, and if she handed a hospital bill to her mother, she might as well throw herself in front of a bus. There was no kind of story she could concoct that wouldn't break at least three of the rules on the contract her parents and the family therapist had made her sign in the wake of the shoplifting disaster.

"I'll pay you back," she told Maeve. By this time they were standing on the curb outside the emergency room's sliding double doors.

"Look, Tallulah," Maeve said. "My butt stings like hell. I didn't have breakfast. Since you got me kicked out of the motorcycle show, which by the way I've been looking forward to for weeks and weeks, marking each and every day off my calendar with my autographed Phish pencil, *and* since you got me tossed before I could vote for the best restored antique bike, I figure that, at the very least, you owe me lunch. There's a place two miles up the road that has marionberry shakes to die for."

Debbie considered her options. The security guard had made it clear that if she showed her thieving face inside the fairgrounds, he'd arrest her with pleasure, knife cut or no knife cut. Which meant she'd have to find Derek's car in the parking lot and wait there, in the rain, until he showed up. He was probably still pawing over every motorcycle part between here and Washington; he probably didn't even know she was gone.

Forget Derek.

So then what? Call home for a ride? Even if she was lucky enough to get Terri on the phone, her older sister would never let her live this down, plus odds were she'd tell Mom everything; which would leave Debbie, again, throwing herself in front of a bus.

"My name is Debbie," she said. "Not Tallulah."

Maeve was already walking toward the parking lot. At this, she did a high pirouette on her toes—impressive, given her size—and began walking backward.

"Debbies," Maeve said, "are short. Dark brown hair, dark brown eyes, big tits. You've got the tits, mostly, but you're not short enough. You've got Tallulah written all over you. And, oh, you should be blond."

"Interesting theory," Debbie said, drifting after her. "But my name's still Debbie."

"You really like being a Debbie?" Maeve said. "You're *enthralled* to be a Debbie?"

"I was named after my mother's aunt. It's a name. So what?"

"So change it to a name you adore. Everyone should have a name they adore."

"Did you change your name?"

"I did."

"What was it before?"

"Let's just say it didn't suit me." Maeve swept up to her

car, an olive green Monte Carlo. A '72, Maeve had informed her on the way here. At the time, Debbie hadn't paid much attention, given that her belly was falling open; now, though, she noticed that the car exuded an aura, like a mistress on a soap opera, of being expensively kept. Shiny, no dings, a California vanity plate: LUVLY1. Maeve called it by name, patted the hood. She unlocked the passenger door, then glided around to the other side. Instead of getting in, Debbie faced her across the car's gleaming roof.

"You're not really a motorcycle fanatic, are you?" Debbie asked.

Maeve grinned. She opened the driver's door, set a foot in the car. "I was driving past," she said. "I saw the sign. I thought it might be interesting."

"There are no autographed Phish pencils, are there?"

"There should be." Maeve's head disappeared. Debbie opened her own door and lowered herself into the seat. The stitches tugged a little, but held; no gaping-open, disemboweled feeling. Maeve started the engine, cranked her right arm over the back of the seat, and began backing out.

"Wait," Debbie said. "Is there really a lunch place two miles up the road?"

Maeve stopped the car. She turned to Debbie and raised her hand, four fingers straight at attention, thumb crossed over her palm.

"Tallulah, you can lay your life on one thing," Maeve said. "From this moment on, I will never lie to you. Especially about food."

And she never had. Other people claimed to be honest. Her sister, for example. Terri, the level-headed one. *You know how clumsy you are, you'd have cut your own fingers off,* she told Debbie after she'd snitched about her dad's knife. Or the shoplifting fiasco: *If everyone at school believes Andrea, maybe it's because they know she's not dumb enough to steal a DVD right in front of a security camera . . . no, I didn't say you're dumb. I'm just saying people think you're dumber than Andrea.*

I'm just being honest. That was Terri's motto. But Terri's was the kind of honesty that clobbered you and left you bleeding, wondering what the hell happened.

If she'd had a sister like Maeve, Debbie thought, a sister she could talk to—instead of Miss I'm-Telling-You-This-For-Your-Own-Good, who treated her like she couldn't tie her own shoes without messing it up—she'd be an entirely different person. Somebody better. Somebody like Maeve herself.

They'd talked all night that first night, on the flat roof of the Belinda. It was cold two stories up, the breeze biting deeper than it had on the ground. Debbie shivered and hugged her knees and drank in the odd sensation of sitting on a roof, unseen, while below her the white fluorescence of convenience stores and gas stations and corner markets lit the streets, car music blared then fell away, conversations rose and faded with footsteps on the sidewalk.

Maeve, though, acted like the roof was her personal living room. She'd climbed the access ladder with a bottle of wine tucked under one arm and a glass stuffed in each sweater pocket, then plopped herself down on the rough papery roof-stuff as easily as if it was carpet. She poured the wine—a Pinot Noir, she said, never heard of the winery, thought I'd give it a try—gave a glass to Debbie, then raised her own. "To the beginning of a great and permanent friendship," she said. Debbie laughed but clinked glasses with her.

While Maeve drank, Debbie sniffed. Cautious. She'd never had wine before. Beer was OK, she'd been drinking beer at parties since she was a freshman. Champagne she hated, and every New Year's, she refused the one glass she and Terri were allowed. Too bubbly, she'd complained. Bubbly is the whole point, Mom said. And it's sour, Debbie replied, to which Mom had rolled her eyes and said, You have to be open to new things, Debbie.

OK, then. Debbie tilted her glass, wet her upper lip, ran her tongue across. Rich acid tang. The inside of her mouth felt puckery. She glanced up to see Maeve grinning at her.

"It's good," Debbie said, and immediately wished she hadn't. *It's good* was something you said about lemonade. What did people say about wine? *Smoky notes and toasty overtones,* her stepdad always joked, no matter what Mom served. But that was John. Stepdad humor.

Better to change the subject. "So why'd you do it?" she asked. "Save my butt like that."

Maeve shrugged. "It needed saving. And I wanted to see if you took the dagger I would have."

"Did I?"

"The man in the moon? Of course. I picked it up when that bozo who grabbed it from you dropped it."

"He dropped it? You didn't give it back to him, did you?" Would Maeve let her have it, if Debbie told her how much she loved it?

No such luck. "With that cop standing right there? Of course I gave it back." Maeve set down her glass, stretching her legs out. "I almost wish I hadn't. That was one gorgeous knife."

"Yeah," Debbie said, and sighed.

The conversation settled into easy grooves. Where they were born. The places they'd lived. Debbie listed Modesto and Portland. Maeve described Orlando and Santa Cruz and Oakland, Albuquerque and Las Cruces and Missoula and finally, for only the past three weeks, Portland. She was twenty-one. She'd been on her own since she was sixteen.

"But what'd you do about school?" Debbie asked.

Maeve shrugged. "I managed. Anyway there's more to the world than school."

"Try telling that to my mother. It's become her mission in life. Making sure I graduate."

"I thought she was running for county commissioner."

"That too."

"Busy woman." Maeve laughed, then said, "I'm sorry. I don't know her. I shouldn't joke." She reached over, refilled Debbie's glass.

"She's not that bad," Debbie said, feeling a contrary need

to defend her mother to this stranger. "She's been through a lot. In general. And with me, and . . . everything."

"You?" In the aura of a nearby streetlight, Debbie could see Maeve struggling not to grin. "I mean, other than getting cut up with a knife that you were trying to steal and getting thrown out of a motorcycle show, what could you possibly have put your mother through?"

Debbie laughed and ducked her head, hiding her face behind her hand. "No, really," she said. "It's just that she's, you know, ambitious. Smart. My older sister's just like her. And I'm . . ." She shrugged, letting her voice trail off.

"Which? Not ambitious, or not smart?"

Debbie shrugged again. "I don't know. Neither. I mean, I know what I want, but . . ."

"Do you? What?"

Debbie took another sip. She held the wine in her mouth, feeling it warm, breathing its scent. Smoky notes. Toasty overtones. What did she want?

"You see?" Maeve sounded almost annoyed. Debbie was afraid for a moment she'd done something wrong, but Maeve continued, "It's just one more artificial thing they put on you. To help them categorize you."

Debbie stared at her.

"OK, look," Maeve said. "Take me. According to some people with lots of initials after their names, I'm bipolar." Maeve spread her arms wide, glancing right and left, as if appealing to a crowd. "I ask you. What *is* bipolar?"

"Some kind of brain thing, isn't it?"

Maeve's hands collapsed into her lap. Wrong answer, Tallulah guessed.

"It's *nothing*," Maeve said. "It's a label. That's what I'm telling you. It doesn't *mean* anything." She leaned forward, elbows on her knees. Her grin was gone; she seemed now entirely serious. "Look. People don't like it when they see other people moving differently through the world. They want to set it apart, away from themselves. So they put it in a box. Call it a name. It makes them feel safer."

Differently through the world. Debbie repeated the words to herself. She moved differently through the world. That's true, she thought. She just hadn't known how to say it.

"When you start believing the label," Maeve said, "that's when they have you. See what I'm saying?"

The wine seemed to have opened a tap in Debbie's veins; a warm flush flooded her limbs, as though her muscles were brand-new, aching to be tried. "What was the question?" she asked, and started laughing. Then Maeve was laughing and the two of them were howling for no reason, on an apartment roof two blocks off Hawthorne Boulevard, walking distance from the tattoo studio where a few hours earlier another yellow jacket had buzzed its way into the skin of Debbie's right hip.

Debbie set her glass down and leaned back on her arms, careful to move slowly, aware of the stitches, and the sting of the new tattoo. "My parents have a balcony," she said, "with a view of Mount Hood. Why is this better?"

"What's your dad like?"

"Stepdad. John. He's OK."

"What about your real dad?"

Debbie had a stock answer for people who asked about her real father: He left. People rarely pried further. He left. No story there. No interest. A few, undaunted, would ask if she kept in contact with him. No, she'd say. End of conversation.

"He stole me once," she told Maeve.

"No," Maeve said. "Tell me."

So she did. The whole story, from spotting him in the school parking lot ("I hadn't seen him in two years. Two *years*"), arriving in Elko, shopping for clothes (since all she had was what she'd worn to school, and the books in her book bag), eating banana pancakes at IHOP for dinner, to the afternoon, a little over a week later, that John showed up at Daddy's apartment.

Daddy had let him in. John packed Debbie's things into a grocery bag, set the bag in the car, then came back for her. He was gentle, as always, and kept saying he was sorry, even when he had her by the elbow and she kicked him four times as hard as she could in the shins. He was big and she was small, but that wasn't what finally defeated her. It was her daddy. Knock it off and get in the car, he said. Stop making such a goddamned racket.

So she'd let John put her in the front seat next to the grocery bag, and when Terri told Mom about the knife and Mom had found it and thrown it away, Debbie had gotten over it.

Debbie heard Maeve shifting, the scratching of her dress over the roof tiles. "Do you hate him?" Maeve asked. Her voice had gone high and breathy, like a little girl's.

A weight stirred in Debbie's chest. It reached thick fingers up her throat, fanned heat across the inside of her eyelids.

She'd never hated him. Not when he'd stood aside and let John take her away. Not when every birthday passed without a word. Not even when Terri informed her—unasked—that the papers he'd signed, after the Elko escapade, had terminated his parental rights. *Face it, Debbie. He gave us away. He didn't want us.* Yanking bobby pins until her elegant French twist fell in a blond mess around her shoulders. Terri had graduated high school that morning, salutatorian, a National Merit Scholar. No phone call. Not even a card. *He's nothing but a damn drunk,* Terri said. *It's better if you forget him. I have.*

But Debbie would never forget. She was his ladybug, and whatever he'd signed, they must have made him do it.

She shook her head, not trusting her voice. Maeve sighed. "I never hated my daddy either," she said. "Everyone thinks I should. But I don't." She'd been lying down; in one abrupt movement, she sat up again. "I used to wish he'd taken me with him. He took Brian, but not me."

"Where did they go?" Debbie asked.

"Dad came home early and caught them together. My stepmother and the neighbor." Her voice sank to a whisper.

"Daddy shot them. Then Brian. Then himself. Brian—my brother—he was only three."

"My God," Debbie said. She stared at Maeve's profile, the long nose, the high cheekbones. Frizzes of hair wafted around her face like an animate halo.

"They *insisted* that I hate him," Maeve said. "I never could, though." The tendrils of hair floated higher. Debbie reached out and touched her on the arm. Maeve's skin was chilly and smooth as marble. Maeve turned toward her, her face half-shadowed, half-luminous in moonlight. She raised her wineglass and smiled, a smile so sad Debbie knew Maeve understood every break in her heart. Because Maeve had breaks even worse in her own.

Yet she was the freest, most joyous person Debbie had ever met.

"To lost daddies," Maeve said. As they clinked glasses, Debbie knew, for the first time, exactly what she wanted.

She wanted to be like that.

At four that morning they stood side by side in Maeve's cramped bathroom, Maeve facing the mirror, Debbie with her back to it, her T-shirt hiked above her hip. Between the wine and the cold, the stinging of the tattoo had faded to a dull tingle. Maeve reached for the bandage. Debbie felt a ripping tug, the release of skin easing back.

"Ooh," Maeve said. Debbie craned to see in the mirror.

"Is it supposed to be all red like that?" she asked.

"It's gorgeous. Do you like it?"

In the tattoo studio, Debbie had flipped through page after page of flash art: roses, lightning bolts, bulldogs, and mermaids. She'd started getting nervous that nothing would be right but she didn't want to back down, she didn't want to appear afraid in front of this woman who was telling the tattoo artist and the receptionist a story about driving through Mexico in a VW bus that had caught on fire, laughing while she drew in the air with her hands the flames shooting out of the engine compartment, this woman who'd had guts enough to get her nipple pierced and *six* tattoos, the latest in a motorcycle tent in front of a crowd of strangers.

And yet Debbie couldn't choose just anything. It had to mean something. So that when somebody saw it, at school, for example, and they said, *Wow, Badowski. What does it mean?* she would say . . .

A snake coming out of a skull's empty eye. What was this crap? Debbie shut the book, reached across the counter for another one, and opened it at random. "What are these?" she asked. She slid the book toward the receptionist, a woman with cropped burgundy hair and cat-eye glasses who reluctantly shifted her gaze away from Maeve.

"Oh, the Chinese characters," the receptionist said, brightening. She read aloud the translations under each design. "Here's 'Love,' that's real popular. So is 'Good Fortune.' "

"I want this one," Debbie said. She pointed to the last character on the page.

Maeve stood on her tiptoes to see. " 'Truth,' " she read. "Really? Why not 'Love'?"

"The truth never changes," Debbie said. "See? A tattoo is forever. So is the truth."

Maeve frowned. "But so is love."

"Well . . . yeah. I guess," Debbie said, but Maeve was still frowning, staring at the characters. Just as Debbie was about to give in, to say, *You're right. Love is better,* the tattoo artist spoke up.

"Never thought about it like that. Tattoo's permanent. Truth's permanent. Something to think about, huh?" He jerked his chin at the receptionist. "You ever think about it like that?"

"Never," she said, and, seeing the sudden thoughtfulness on Maeve's face, Debbie felt oddly, wonderfully wise.

Now Truth lay etched just above her hip, bold and black, as straightforward as what it stood for, two inches high and an inch and a half across. Debbie had wanted it where it could be seen or hidden as she chose. No reason, for example, for Mom to know about it.

She swiveled, studying the tattoo in the mirror. "I love it. I absolutely adore it."

"That reminds me," Maeve said. "What's your last name?"

"Badowski. Not really, though. My stepfather adopted us when I was eight." Debbie still remembered her shock the first time someone called her by his name. As though

Badowski was the sticker and she the banana, a solid dumb thing. "My real dad's name is Addy."

"Go back to Addy," Maeve said. "It sounds better with Tallulah."

"I told you." Debbie eased her shirt back over the tattoo. "My name's not Tallulah."

"Trust me," Maeve said. "It is."

Chapter 9

Tallulah woke to kitchen sounds: bowls clattering, three shrill beeps of a microwave. She started to sit up, hitched her breath at the lancing pain in her side.

Carefully, she rolled upright. Sun struck her eyes and she squinted and raised a hand. She was sitting on a brown-checked sofa. Feet on gold shag carpet. An arm's-length away stood a coffee table topped with an enormous lace doily, three books of crossword puzzles, and, sitting square on the puzzles, a large, gray-striped, three-legged cat.

Ruth's. The veterinary hospital. Leopard. Tallulah groaned and rubbed her face.

Behind her, a dry Tennessee voice said, "Oh, good." Tallulah glanced around. Ruth was dressed already, same as yesterday: white stretch pants, blue-striped top open at the neck. Her gold lace hair flawless. "I hated to wake you," she said. "But we got to get moving. I washed your things, they're setting on the dryer."

By the time Tallulah came out of the bathroom in jeans and a scrub top—this one an orange and brown safari print that Ruth had laid out for her—Ruth had already finished eating. While Tallulah dug into her bowl of wheat flakes, she fussed, straightening this or that in the kitchen, rattling keys on the small table by the front door. Finally she stood, keys in hand and purse on her shoulder, waiting. Back politely turned, she gazed out the sliding glass door into her front yard. The clink of Tallulah's spoon seemed suddenly, obnoxiously loud. Tallulah gave up on breakfast. She carried her bowl into the kitchen, glancing at the rooster clock over the stove. Seven ten.

"What kind of mutant goes to the vet this early anyway?" she muttered. She hated being rushed in the morning. It made the whole day go off at crazy angles. It unsettled her stomach.

"Drop-offs for surgery," Ruth said. "Or sick ones that can't wait until later. Plus all the treatments need to get done before appointments start. Jolene's likely wondering where on earth you are." She opened the front door. "Watch Tripod, don't let him out. Shoo!"

Sure enough, there were already two cars in the gravel parking lot when they pulled in. Neither, though, was a Monte Carlo with LUVLY1 plates. Tallulah wished again she could remember how many states lay between Florida and Tennessee.

Jolene was in the treatment room drawing up shots out of a vial. She glanced up as Tallulah entered. "Looks like somebody has to learn how to get themselves up out of bed," she said, "and I know it ain't Ruth." She nodded toward the counter, where the disinfectant spray bottle and paper towels were laid out. Tallulah sighed, picked up the dishwashing gloves, and pulled them on.

So she had to clean up dog poop. It wouldn't kill her, and in two days—three at the most, she hoped—she would be in Orlando and all this would be yet another funny story to tell Maeve. Tallulah dumped out a litter pan, wrinkling her nose against the sharp ammonia stink of cat pee.

"Pick up the pace over there," Jolene called. "It's after eight already. Kennels are supposed to be done by seven thirty."

She helped Tallulah with the last of the cages. Tallulah noticed how the animals responded to the croon of Jolene's voice, the sureness of her touch. Even the growling white fuzzball seemed to trust Jolene, only grumbling once when she picked him up.

By the time they finished, new animals were already being brought back to the treatment room, some by Ruth, some by Poteet, each one complete with its own set of instructions. Catheter. Blood draw. Toenail trim. Tallulah's job, she soon discovered, was holding the creatures still for all these things. The other thing she discovered was that, while Jolene seemed to have infinite patience with animals, she had very little with Tallulah.

"Take hold up high or he'll whip right around and bite," Jolene told her. "No, like this." She rearranged Tallulah's grip, pushing it higher on a black kitten's neck, practically between its ears. The kitten's long hair tangled in Tallulah's fingers.

"This ain't no game," Jolene said. "Friend of mine over to Greeley Hill got bit bad by a cat, lost from here up to infection." She laid her right index finger across the slender, livid-wrinkled knuckle of the left. Tallulah was still picturing this vanished digit when Jolene picked up a syringe and stuck the needle in the kitten's skin. The kitten squalled and lunged forward. Its fur slipped, like wet silk, from Tallulah's grasp. Jolene had to drop the syringe and grab the animal to keep it from leaping off the table.

"I told you to hold on," she said. "When someone says hold on, you hold *on*."

"I was," Tallulah said, staring at the kitten. "It's so tiny. How could it get away like that?"

"That's why you got to hold on," Jolene said.

That was the way the entire morning went. And if Jolene was persnickety, Poteet was downright exacting.

"Re-grip that leg, the vein's not standing up. No, that's not it . . . thumb across *here*, then roll out."

"I can't see a thing in this ear if you keep letting him swing his head around like that. Where's Jolene? Fine, OK, look. Put one hand *there*. . . ."

Jolene again: "Don't *never* throw needles in the trash, even if they got caps on, needles go in the sharps box, syringes in the trash unless they've got blood in 'em, if they got blood in 'em they go in biohazard. Microscope slides and scalpels go in sharps, ear swabs in the trash. . . ."

Tallulah had never done work so physically demanding. She'd had no idea how muscular animals were under their fur, or that holding them involved strength not just in the arms but in the whole body, or that she'd have to be precise, on top of it. Jolene corrected her half a dozen times with each patient—the way she leaned over an animal on the table, the way she carried a cat, or even how she walked a dog on a leash—nothing she did was right, and when a Rottweiler, whose head she was supposed to be holding, moved and Poteet snapped at her, she had to bite back really, really bad words because the dog weighed as much as she did and if it wanted to move what the hell did he think she could do about it? She blew air out through her lips then hugged the dog up tight, the way Jolene had shown her. Poteet clicked his penlight on and shone it again in the dog's eye. This time, by some grace of God, or the poisonous thoughts Tallulah directed at its head, the dog stayed still.

When Poteet slipped the penlight back into his pocket, Tallulah asked, "How far is it from Orlando to here?"

"By car?" Poteet lifted the Rottweiler's lip and peered underneath. "Day, day and a half." He let the lip fall and stood up.

Tallulah calculated in her head. She'd first called Maeve the night before last. If Maeve left the next morning, presuming she'd checked her messages and knew exactly where Tallulah was, then . . . today, sometime, the Monte Carlo would come roaring up the highway. Maybe in just a few hours, Maeve would burst through the hospital's front door in a blast of steamy air and gauzy cotton, larger than life and twice as loud, demanding the whereabouts of her,

Tallulah, best friend *extraordinaire*. They'd hug and cry, then leave nothing behind them but a cloud of dust, saying, Seeya.

Dammit, she forgot to bring her duffel. This is what happened when she got rushed. Well, it wouldn't take long to stop by Ruth's and retrieve it. Maeve would like Ruth. Maybe they'd stay a half hour, drink some iced tea.

"I understand you made some calls from Ruth's last night," Poteet was saying.

"Just one," Tallulah said.

Poteet took the Rottweiler's leash from her and wrapped it around his hand. "Don't go running up Ruth's phone bill," he said. "You need to make any more calls, do it from here. Keep it short. And only on a break or after hours. Understand?" Tallulah nodded. He started walking out of the treatment room, the Rottweiler dancing at his side. Then he stopped and turned back.

"How's that rib doing?" he asked.

Tallulah touched her side. "It still hurts," she said, then, reluctantly, "Not too bad."

"I knew it wasn't broken," he said, and walked away.

The morning passed in increments of animals and hurried directions. Hold this here. Run get that. Well then, ask Jolene where it is. Hurry! One saving grace: That morning Ruth, learning of Tallulah's blisters and limited choice of shoes, had dug out a pair of ancient sneakers that had once belonged to her daughter. They were a little big, but compared to the boots they were heaven.

With every crackle of the intercom, Tallulah expected to hear Ruth's voice saying, *There's some redheaded girl here says she knows Tallulah.* Instead: *Bring up the Williams dog. We got a mess in the lobby needs mopping. Mr. Goodhew's on the phone, wants to know how Buster's doing.*

At twelve fifteen, Tallulah was washing out litter pans when she heard footsteps approaching. Jolene stuck her head around the corner and said, "If you're about done, take a break for dinner." Lunch was dinner here, and dinner supper, which still confused Tallulah every time she heard it; but as long as it meant food and a chance to sit down, she didn't care what they called it. She dropped the litter pan she was holding, washed her hands, and followed Jolene to the break room.

Ruth was already seated at the table, a thermos, a paper bag, and two paper plates in front of her. Kyle wasn't there. He'd told Tallulah, while they were cleaning cages the evening before, that if anybody—Ruth, Poteet, or Jolene—caught him at the hospital before his shift started at four, he'd invariably be given a job to do. "They'd work me twenty-four / seven if they could get away with it," he said, "especially now we're short-staffed." Jolene had snorted at this. "I don't hear you complaining about the overtime on your paycheck," she'd said.

Ruth nodded at the cabinets over the sink. "Grab you a glass off that shelf there," she told Tallulah, "and I'll pour you some iced tea. You like chicken salad?"

"I guess," Tallulah said. She couldn't remember having

ever had it, but she hoped it was unlike tuna salad, with its simultaneous chewiness and sliminess. She selected a Road Runner glass and brought it to the table. Ruth set a sandwich on one of the paper plates and slid it over to her. It looked promising: thick, with ruffles of lettuce hanging out the sides and a red moon-edge of tomato. She was just fitting her fingers around it when the scrape of a lighter made her glance up.

Across from her, Jolene held the lighter to a cigarette—a Marlboro, Tallulah recognized it—pursed between her lips. The flame broadened and yellowed, Jolene's thumb let go, the flame went out, and as Tallulah watched Jolene take the first deep drag, her chest felt as though it had eyes. Watching that other chest, aching for the hit.

"How many times has he told you not to smoke in here?" Ruth said.

Jolene's lips *whuffed*; she turned aside, a peremptory pivot of her head, and blew out the smoke. "He lets Kyle smoke upstairs," she said.

"You know that's because there's no oxygen tanks upstairs."

"There ain't no oxygen down here closer than surgery, and that's three rooms away." Jolene rested one elbow on a crossed arm. Wrinkles zagged like creek beds between her collarbones and the tops of her breasts; the Sun, Fun, and Nicotine look, Maeve had called it, back when she was pointing out examples to Tallulah, trying to persuade her to quit.

Tallulah had always pictured her nicotine cravings as weasels: sneaky, bite-y creatures, a dozen at least, scurrying frantically around her head. Maybe it was the Marlboro—Tallulah's old brand—or maybe it was the sound of each deep drag, but for whatever reason, the weasels went crazy. She bit into the sandwich. Food, she'd discovered, was the only thing that calmed the beasts. The chicken salad, fortunately, was chunky and flavorful, nothing like tuna, with thick slices of cheddar laid over the tomato. The weasels pulled their claws a tiny bit out of her chest.

"I heard Ellen's secretary was here again yesterday," Jolene said. "Dr. Poteet say yet if he's gonna sell Kasmir?"

Ruth's mouth was full of sandwich; she swallowed hard, took a sip of tea. "You know he won't. He and Ellen have owned that horse fifty-fifty for ten years. Now all of a sudden she has to own all of him?" She shook her head. "Doesn't make any sense."

"Maybe it's because she's married again. You ever think of that?"

"Been remarried a year. Hasn't bothered her before now."

Jolene tilted her chair back, snugging the crossed arm tight up under her breasts. The wrinkles in her chest deepened. "Maybe her new husband just plain doesn't like it, his wife owning a horse with her ex-husband. Maybe he figures it's time they all moved on."

"Ellen tell you that?"

Jolene let her chair down with a thump. "You think because she's my boy's godmother, she tells me everything.

123

All I know is, if Ellen wants it, Dr. Poteet's gonna make damn sure she won't get it. He's gonna make her fight every step of the way—" She broke off, lowering her cigarette underneath the table just as Poteet poked his head into the kitchen.

"Ruth, Mr. Castleberry's ready to go," Poteet said. "Jolene, bring Arabella up front. And put that thing out before you blow up my hospital." A flash of white-coated arm, and he disappeared up the hall.

Ruth sighed and wrapped her sandwich back up in its foil. "Be nice to have one day this week where I can finish my lunch. Guess it won't be today. Tallulah, when you're finished go ahead set this and the thermos in the fridge, will you?" Her mouth full, Tallulah nodded.

As soon as Ruth had left, Jolene pulled her empty chair closer and set her feet on it. "Arabella's the redbone hound in Ward One," she said. "Leash is on the run gate. She won't give you no trouble."

"Poteet told you to do it," Tallulah said.

"And now I'm telling you." Jolene crushed out her cigarette and flipped open one of the magazines scattered on the table. When Tallulah took another bite of sandwich, Jolene gave her a sidelong glare.

"I'm eating. I'm hungry," Tallulah said around a mouthful of chicken.

Jolene smacked the magazine shut. "You might be Ruth's bright idea, but you answer to me. If I tell you to do something, you better get your panhandling fanny up off

124

that chair and do it. Ruth or no Ruth, I'll toss you out so fast you'll have road rash on your ass." She picked up the magazine again and snapped it open. "Maybe then Dr. Poteet'll hire somebody can do some actual work around here."

Tallulah opened her mouth, ready to say something loud. But then a thought came to her, as it had in the underpass, in Maeve's voice: After today, none of this will matter.

She put down her sandwich and went to get the dog.

Arabella was rangy and long-legged and, except for the gray on her muzzle, the exact color of paprika. All of her seemed to sag: her ears dangled halfway to her chest, her lower eyelids were limp pouches, and her belly, when she struggled to her feet, hung below hollow flanks like water in a trash bag, in a way Tallulah vaguely sensed was not quite right. Only her thrashing tail seemed resilient. Tallulah was wary; but the dog stood still while she fastened the leash, then waddled alongside amiably enough, panting.

Tallulah found Ruth stapling paperwork in a hallway off the reception area. Ruth nodded her head at a doorway and said, "Go on through that exam room to the lobby. Hold your breath."

Tallulah swung open the door to the room and immediately took a step back. She covered her nose and mouth with a hand.

"What died?" she said.

"Loren Castleberry," Ruth said. "Only he's not dead yet."

The room looked clean. But it smelled as though

someone had taken the worst of the jail odors—urine and vomit and sweat—mixed them, and left them to age in a vat of alcohol. As Tallulah wrinkled her nose she caught the unmistakable bluntness of whiskey: sour, as though exuded through unwashed pores, broader and less sharp than she remembered, but like enough to call up a flash of arms holding her, warm sheepskin against her cheek, the check and sway of steps carrying her home. The last time Daddy ever carried her. That night she and Terri crouched in their beds, hands over their ears to shut out the yelling. The next morning he was gone, and she'd been left behind.

"Close the door behind you," Ruth said. "No sense letting that stink loose everywhere."

"Can't you use air freshener or something?" Tallulah said.

"We tried that once. Made it smell like a gutter drunk wearing a corsage."

Tallulah took a breath and held it for the four steps it took her to cross the room and emerge in the lobby. Arabella padded behind her.

For such a big smell, Loren Castleberry was surprisingly little. At first, Tallulah guessed him to be seventy or so; a few feet closer, she changed her mind. It might just be the way his skin fell in slack folds off his cheekbones, like fabric thrown over a frame, and how his ears stood out from his head, as if straining away from the smell, that made him look old. He might be no more than fifty. The buckshot scatter of stubble, thick over his chin and sparse on the sides, was an indeterminate light color, maybe blond, maybe gray. Yellow polyester slacks hung from his hips and bagged toward the floor. Their front was mottled with stains. Unwilling to get any closer, Tallulah stopped. Arabella lumbered forward until she was straining against the leash, her tail spinning in circles.

Poteet leaned on the reception counter, his back, swathed in a lab coat, inclined to one side like a melting alp. He was telling a long jokey story, it sounded like, from the way he bent forward and chuckled and waved one hand in the air. Castleberry stood with hands folded in front of him. His eyes wandered around the room, the walls, the floor, like a pair of kids exploring a field. Then they found Arabella and fixed themselves on her and didn't move. Poteet finished his story and laughed at his own punch line. Still without taking his eyes off his dog, Castleberry's head snapped down and up and he grinned.

Poteet looked over his shoulder and spotted Tallulah. He unfolded himself from the counter, took Arabella from her, and led the dog to Castleberry. Castleberry held the dog's leash between thumb and forefinger, as though it were a flower he didn't know what to do with. He mumbled something Tallulah couldn't catch.

"You bet we will, Loren," Poteet said. Castleberry blinked hard and bobbed his head again and raised one hand as if in farewell. The hand looked too large for him.

As soon as he was gone, Ruth came into the lobby. "I wish you'd keep him in the exam room," she said. "Anybody come in while he's here, they're liable to walk right on out again."

"If I stayed in that room one more minute, I was going to pass out, and Loren and I had things to discuss," Poteet said. "I don't care if he could knock a buzzard off a carcass. He's in a rough patch right now with that dog. Anybody thinks he doesn't deserve the same consideration they do, they're welcome to go elsewhere." He glanced behind him at Tallulah. "Finish your dinner?"

"No," Tallulah said.

"Then finish it later. I want you out in the barn this afternoon."

"What for?" Tallulah asked, but Poteet had already walked past Ruth into the office.

"You ready?" said a voice behind her. Tallulah turned to see Kyle leaning against the counter by the back door. In place of the green scrubs, he wore age-faded jeans and a white V-neck T-shirt. Bits of what looked like grass clung to one sleeve.

"What for?" Tallulah asked again.

"He ain't told you?"

Tallulah shook her head. Kyle shrugged, then jerked his head toward the door. "Guess you'll find out. Come on. I ain't got all day."

Chapter 10

Uh-uh," Tallulah said. "I don't do horses. Not anymore."

Compared to the blue sauna of unsheltered day, the barn was marginally cooler. It smelled good in here, too, earthy, like the black rich dirt in Mom's garden beds mixed with warm grass. But that was a horse hanging its ugly, boxy head over the stall door, which meant that if Tallulah had a choice between staying here and wiping up puppy diarrhea, she'd skip right back to the kennels and slip on the gloves.

From inside the stall, Kyle said, "Dr. Poteet said for me to teach you some stuff. So you don't go getting yourself killed like yesterday." As he led the horse out, Tallulah scuttled back through the barn doors. Back into the open, where she could run if she had to.

In the dimness of the barn, she'd thought the horse was white. As it ambled into the sun, she saw it was white with age, the salt of its face shading into a washed-out brown. Its back sagged between shoulders and hips, like her stepfather's hammock at the end of summer. Kyle walked the horse to a pipe corral between the barn and an uneven patch of grass. Tying the lead rope to the corral fence, he said, "Name's Pickles. His folks brought him here then skipped town. Dr. Poteet keeps saying he's gonna find a home for him, but there ain't too many people want a stove-up old lawnmower they can't even ride."

Whatever momentary interest Tallulah had in the horse died a few minutes later, a hot, bored, wretched death. Kyle launched into a horsey lecture: near and off sides, the rules of approach, of haltering, of tying, the signals of ears and head and tail. Pickles flopped his own ears until they were horizontal, slumped his weight on one hip, and went to sleep. Tallulah wished she could join him. When Kyle bent over and started fiddling with Pickles's leg, she shaded her eyes and peered over the horse's swayed back to the highway.

Where was Maeve?

Maybe she hadn't left Orlando yet. Maybe—Tallulah chewed her lower lip—maybe Maeve couldn't come for her. Worse yet, maybe she could—but had decided not to.

No. Maeve wouldn't leave her here.

"I ain't planning on standing in the sun all day saying everything twice and three times," Kyle said. Tallulah blinked, startled to see that Kyle was no longer bent over beside the horse but standing next to it, one arm thrown across its craggy rump.

"When you showed up, before," Tallulah said. "After I got out of court. That wasn't a coincidence, was it?"

She was gratified to see his neck turn an interesting shade of cherry bronze.

"Ruth just asked me to see if you was around," he said. He ran the flat of his hand down the horse's hip, flicking free a shower of dead hair.

"And offer me a ride. And bring me back here."

"You want to leave, you can. Ain't nobody stopping you. Though if your friend's coming, seems like you ought to stay put."

"Do all of you always tell each other everything?"

He grinned. He was good-looking, in an angular kind of way. Lean, with muscle that looked like it came from out-side work rather than a gym. He looked like he would know what was wrong with things and how to fix them. Too bad he wasn't blond. But big points for the tan.

"You're a stranger," he said. "Town this small, that makes you news."

"What I am is tired," Tallulah said. She yawned again and started to stretch, cutting short at the jab in her ribs where she'd gotten kicked. "And hungry. I didn't get to fin-ish my lunch."

"Yeah, well, it ain't like I want to be out here playing teacher. I got my own stuff to do."

"Go do it, then. I won't tell."

He eyed her a moment; then his mouth twisted up in a crooked smile. "Naw. You get yourself tromped on again, Dr. Poteet'll bust my ass." He slipped something out of his back pocket and held it toward her. It was a metal hook, small and blunt-tipped. "Tell you what, though. Pick out a foot and we'll call it a day."

She stared at the hook. "Do what?"

"What I just showed you."

She had no idea what he'd just showed her, but apparently picking out a foot was more involved than just choosing her favorite. *The left one, with the little bit of white, that's adorable.*

"Can't we just pretend I did?" she said.

He ignored this. "The back foot," he said. "That one there." Tallulah sighed and took the hook from him and sidled up to the horse's rump. Its thigh was three times as big around as her head. She wasn't sleepy now. Her stomach felt as though half a dozen hands were inside, groping for an exit.

"I've never done anything like this before," she said, hardly knowing as she said it whether she meant horses, or setting out across the country in a Honda Civic, or being discarded like a piece of litter among strangers in a state she hadn't given one thought to since memorizing its capitol in eighth grade. *I'm two thousand miles from home,* she thought, *and nobody between there and here knows who I am. Or cares. Except Maeve, and right now I don't even know where Maeve is.*

"Me either when I first come here," Kyle said. "But it ain't hard. Jolene taught me, mostly."

Puzzled, Tallulah looked at him, then at the soft green hills, the fields stretching away behind the hospital. "Didn't you grow up with horses?"

"Me? Hell, no. Horses are expensive, one. Two, I ain't never had the interest."

"But you work here."

"Three, I work here 'cause it's better than McDonald's and I get the apartment over the hospital free."

"So that's what that is," she said, then, "No wonder they keep catching you before your shift. I figured you just hung around because you didn't have anything else to do."

"I got plenty to do. You still ain't getting out of cleaning that foot."

Tallulah studied the horse's gray-flecked hide. She'd been this close to Leopard and she'd never even seen him move. *Bam.* Blue sky. No air. At the memory, her armpits were a sudden glut of sweat.

Wing it till you swing it. Fake it till you make it.

Maeve, you better be on your way. I don't know how much more I can fake.

Tallulah took a breath and bent over, her fingers brushing the dusty hair. *Hey, horsie. Don't hurt me.* She reached down and, not knowing what else to do, tapped the side of the hoof with a fingertip. Pickles's tail flicked around her ears, but the foot didn't move.

A brown hand snaked past her face and grabbed the back of Pickles's leg. "Pick it up!" Kyle commanded. Tallulah was about to snap that she didn't know how, when the horse's ankle sagged forward and she realized he wasn't talking to her. Kyle leaned in. His shoulder pressed hard against hers and she caught a deep whiff of him, sun-hot skin and sweat, the sweetness of hay. With a short grunt of effort he hauled up the foot and placed it in her hand. Its heaviness startled her and she almost dropped it, so she let go the hoof pick and wrapped both hands around its cool curved surface and then she was staring at the bottom of a horse's foot. It was packed flat with hay and wood shavings and something she suspected was horseshit.

Kyle helped her hoist the leg higher and slide the hoof onto her thigh, then he held the pick out to her. Tallulah let go with her right hand just long enough to snatch it from his fingers. He talked her through scraping out the foot. It was disgusting and it smelled. Once Pickles tried to kick his hoof out of her grasp; her body was yanked forward but she hung on, her own feet firm on the ground, teeth set grim in her bottom lip. She wasn't going to get knocked down again, at least not by some grayfaced nag. Dammit, there had to be limits.

When she was finally done and able to straighten up, dizziness rose like a cloud of bees into her head.

Dimly, she felt Kyle's hand gripping her arm. "You OK?" he asked. "You need to sit down?" She shook her head. The bees cleared, the dizziness was gone. Kyle let go and turned away to untie Pickles's lead rope.

"Guess we're done," he said. "You want to take him on back?"

"Not especially."

He made her do it anyway. When the horse was finally unhaltered and Tallulah had shimmied, relieved, out of his stall, Kyle said, "You did pretty good. Main thing you got to remember is, stay close." He made a fist and drew it back. Then drove it at her, stopping just short of her chin. She jerked her head away, staring.

Then he stepped close enough that the air between them took on the prickly heat of an Indian burn, the kind she and Terri used to inflict on each other's arms in the summertime. This time he held his fist less than an inch from her cheek. He pushed it forward, until his knuckles just brushed her skin. "Closer you get, less they can hurt you," he said. "No leverage. See?"

He had possibly the darkest eyes she'd ever seen. Here, in the barn, they looked pure black. Intense.

"Yeah," she said. "I see."

He dropped the fist, took the halter from her, and hung it on a nail. "If they ask," he said, "tell 'em I left. Otherwise they'll just think up something else for me to do." He nodded to her. It seemed old-fashioned, almost gentlemanly, like something out of a movie her mother would watch. "See you later." He jogged to the hospital, to an outside flight of stairs that led from the carport to a second-story door. He took the stairs two at a time.

Tallulah watched him until he disappeared inside. Had he just flirted with her? She'd never been the type of girl guys flirted with. Maeve, when asked, had only remarked that not being flirted with by high school guys showed future promise. At the time, Tallulah had been too embarrassed to admit she didn't understand what Maeve meant.

Not that it mattered. Tomorrow Kyle would still be cleaning kennels, and she'd be gone.

Tallulah strolled out to the highway. Shading her eyes, she scanned both directions. Nothing. Heat billowed up from the blacktop, burned its way through the soles of the old sneakers. Tallulah didn't shift her feet to ease them. She didn't move.

A car was coming over the hill.

Even after she saw that it was blue, not green, and a pickup truck, not a sedan, Tallulah stayed where she was. The driver, a short, dark-haired woman, waved to her as she passed.

Tallulah lowered her hand from her eyes and trudged back to the hospital.

Chapter 11

The next day, Saturday, was a half-day. They'd be running start to finish, Ruth told Tallulah on the drive over. No breaks. Although, she went on, Saturdays were less crazy now than they used to be six, seven years ago, back before the two factories that had employed most of the county packed up and went overseas. Now plenty of their clients worked six days a week, holding down two jobs to replace the one they'd lost.

Still, Ruth said, by the end of a Saturday, you know you been working.

They arrived at seven a.m. to find four cars lined up in the parking lot, their owners milling by the front door, or sitting with their driver's side windows cranked open to the cool air.

No Monte Carlo.

Worry began nibbling at the edges of Tallulah's brain. Last night, she'd resisted the temptation to call Maeve again, sure that come morning, she'd be slinging her duffel into LUVLY1 and waving good-bye.

Maeve would be here if she could. Of that, Tallulah was sure. Which could only mean that something had happened to her.

It wasn't until hours later, as Tallulah helped Jolene wrestle a massively obese Labrador into the bathtub, that it occurred to her that even if something had happened to Maeve, it didn't necessarily have to be a tragedy. A flat tire. An overheated engine. LUVLY1 was old; a million things might go kablooie under its acre of hood. As soon as the place closed at noon, Tallulah decided, she would call again. With luck, she'd get Michael. She no longer hoped Maeve would answer. She wanted Maeve to be on the road.

After this, Tallulah was almost as confident in Maeve's arrival as she'd been the day before.

She was also as tired as she'd been the day before. Ruth hadn't exaggerated: the work never stopped, the pace never slowed. At eleven-fifty, Tallulah trundled the mop bucket up front yet again. Tallulah didn't know much about dogs, but she knew they were supposed to be housebroken. Either this was a myth, or coming to a veterinary hospital made them lose all control, because this was the fourth time Ruth had called her over the intercom to mop up dog pee. The latest puddle was in the exam room hall. Both exam rooms were full, their doors closed. Tallulah heard Poteet's voice booming from one. Six clipboards, each one representing a patient waiting to be seen, were stacked on the back counter next to Jolene, who sat staring into the microscope.

Tallulah tapped the top clipboard with her finger. "I thought Poteet closes at twelve on Saturdays."

Without looking up, Jolene said, "That's *Dr.* Poteet. He hears you calling him just Poteet, he'll pin your ears back. As far as when we close, all you need to know is you work until we say stop working."

Ruth came into the back hall and slipped another clipboard at the bottom of the stack. "I should have told you, but truth is, honey, Saturdays we close when there isn't anybody left in the lobby."

"But we'll be here all day," Tallulah said.

"It's been known to happen," Ruth said.

At two-forty-five, Poteet left on a farm call. Tallulah had just finished cleaning the wards for the second time—at least the yapping puppy with the intestinal waterworks had dried up and gone home, for which she was grateful—when Ruth called her up front for a final mopping of the exam rooms and lobby.

As Tallulah pushed the bucket past the office, Jolene appeared in the doorway, purse slung over one shoulder, sunglasses on top of her head.

"I hear this girl's gonna be gone by Monday," Jolene called over her shoulder to Ruth. "That right?"

Tallulah straightened up. "This girl's right here, and she sure as hell hopes so," she said, at the same time Ruth called back, "You go on have a nice weekend, Jolene. Tell Tyler if he gets in another fight with that neighbor girl, Aunt Ruth's not going to throw him a party for his birthday."

Jolene laughed. "That child," she said. "He gets that from his daddy."

As soon as the door closed after her, Ruth said, "Tallulah! You like burgers?"

"Yeah, sure," Tallulah said. "Burger King, if there's one around here." Thank God. All she'd had to eat since breakfast were two molasses cookies, snuck from a batch brought in by a client and dunked in the dark hot water Jolene called coffee.

"We don't truck with that trash. I'll call Kyle on the cell phone, tell him to get us some dinner."

Fifteen minutes later Tallulah was done. She rolled the mop bucket back to the ward and emptied it into a floor drain, stashed the bucket and mop in the janitor's closet, then headed to the office. Surely there'd be a phone in there she could use.

Hang in there, she imagined Michael saying in his soft blurring voice. *She left yesterday. She'll be there soon.*

Tallulah was in the back hallway, a few steps from the office door, when she heard Kyle say " 'Scuse me," behind her. Tallulah stepped aside, stumbling over a case of cat food someone had left on the floor. Kyle carried three Styrofoam containers stacked atop each other, crowned with a cardboard cup holder containing three giant-sized soft drinks. Underneath, clutched in his fingers, dangled a white paper bag. He had to feel ahead with his feet to navigate into the office. Tallulah followed him.

"Bless your heart, you're gonna drop every bit of that," Ruth said.

"No I ain't," Kyle said.

"Where's . . ." Ruth looked up, saw Tallulah. "There you are. Clear some space on the desk, honey, and pull us up a couple chairs."

"Dr. Poteet said I could use the phone, and . . ."

"He told me when you're done and you're not done yet. There's flower beds up front need planting. But first eat your dinner. You're pale enough to spook the dead."

Ruth doled out the containers and drinks, paper napkins and ketchup packets. Tallulah found a stool next to a filing cabinet and lugged it to the far side of the desk, next to the window. Then she rolled in the receptionist's chair from the lobby. By the time she'd navigated the chair over the tangle of computer cables, Kyle was sitting on the stool, emptying ketchup packets, one after another, into a glossy red mountain next to his onion rings.

Tallulah bit the corner of her lip. The only place left for the chair was next to a big wooden bookshelf that blocked half the window. But the stool had a clear view—just in case an olive green sedan came cruising up the highway.

"Here, Kyle, you can have the chair," she said. "I'll sit there."

Kyle glanced at the chair and shook his head. "I'm all right," he said. He selected an onion ring, swiped the top off the ketchup mountain, and stuffed the ring in his mouth.

This gentleman thing was getting to be a pain in the ass. Tallulah picked up the one unopened container and walked around the desk. Startled, Kyle looked up at her, just as she pivoted and sat down next to him. There was barely room for one butt-cheek, but it was enough. Kyle, his mouth full, made an inarticulate sound of protest; before he could do anything else, she scooched her hip hard against his, making him grab the desk edge to keep from falling. He tried shoving back, but he had a skinny ass and her own feet were braced firm.

"Honest to Pete, you two are worse than a couple third-graders," Ruth said.

Tallulah scooched again, but this time he didn't budge. He smelled like all the good bits of the barn: warm grass, the dust of horses. He must have been out with Pickles earlier. She popped open the box. The onion rings were wider across than her palm, the burger so big she had to lift it with both hands. Real Cheddar cheese, ranch dressing. She closed her eyes and sighed and chewed.

"Jake's makes the best burger in east Tennessee," Ruth said. "You want, though, we can give yours to the dogs and Kyle'll go to Burger King for you."

"Over my dead body," Tallulah said, at the same time Kyle grumbled, "Hell I will."

Tallulah bumped him with her shoulder. "You would. If I asked you nice."

Kyle snorted. "That'd be a change." But when Tallulah reached past him for a napkin, he handed one to her.

"Thank you," she said, then, bumping him again, added, "See, I can be sweet." He was chewing and didn't answer; but he pushed back, just a little, so that his arm pressed against her shoulder and stayed there. Even under the air conditioning, it was too hot to be so close. But she didn't move away. He felt nice. Solid.

Ruth began asking Kyle about his errands, whom he'd seen in Gardner's feed store, who'd said what about whom. Tallulah ate and watched the highway. In five minutes, not a single car passed by. Bored, she studied the orchids on the windowsill: five pots of tall, delicate blooms, white and yellow and pink, arrayed on arching stems.

Maybe if she didn't stare at the road, Maeve would appear. Tallulah shifted on the seat, jostling Kyle's arm—he jostled back, almost spilling her drink—and surveyed the wall behind Ruth.

It resembled the side of a badly shingled house, crammed as it was with documents, photographs, and tattered slips of paper. Her eyes slid uninterested over Poteet's diploma. Then stopped on the framed photo next to it. A dark horse jumping a fence, ridden by a girl of twelve or thirteen. The girl wore a helmet and high black boots and a fierce expression like she intended to eat the fence alive. Next to that was another framed photograph of the same girl, a year or two older, Tallulah guessed, astride what looked like the same horse. The girl was beaming in this picture; affixed to the horse's bridle was a bright red rosette and ribbon. An identical rosette hung from the corner of the frame, its ruffles faded to an unsavory tomato.

"Tallulah," Ruth said.

Tallulah started. "Huh?"

"I asked how's Diesel doing today."

"Who's Diesel?"

Ruth frowned at her. Kyle cleared his throat, leaning away so that their arms no longer touched. "Your dog," he said.

Tallulah craned her neck around to stare at him. "You named him Diesel?"

"Yeah, well, he's black, and when you brought him in that's what he smelled like." Kyle picked at a bacon crumb on his napkin and put it in his mouth. "You found him, though. Call him whatever you want."

"Diesel's fine," she said. "I guess."

"Now that we got that straight," Ruth said. She picked up a napkin and wiped her fingers, each one separately, wrap-scrub-scrub, her pale blue eyes intent on Tallulah. "He still on all those pain meds?"

Tallulah blinked. How was she supposed to know? Jolene administered all the medications. Anyway it wasn't like, these past two days, she'd had a lot of extra thought to spare for the dog.

Kyle's elbow dug into her ribs. She yipped and jabbed back at him, but he twisted on the seat, hands up in self-defense. Grinning, he said to Ruth, "Dr. Poteet says he's gonna keep him on the painkillers another couple weeks. But he's walking on his own already."

"Right. He's walking," Tallulah said. She remembered now: two gimpy steps with his back feet. He'd been slung up in the towel at the time, but still Jolene had been delighted.

"Bless his heart, that dog's a trouper," Ruth said. She dropped her napkin in her burger box and snapped the lid shut. "Well, if you two are done fooling around, then Kyle, get those flats out of the barn and set 'em up front. Tallulah, help me clear this away."

"Yes, ma'am," Kyle said. He unfolded himself off the stool, his knee bumping against Tallulah's. Still grinning, he nodded to her—that same old-fashioned gesture—and left.

As she carried the trash out to the Dumpster, Tallulah wondered how Kyle spent his time off. A town this tiny probably didn't even have a mall, and Kyle had said he didn't have a car. Tallulah tried to imagine his days. She couldn't. If she lived here, she'd go crazy in a week.

Once the table was clean, Ruth said, "Well, let's get those flowers in. We've managed to get stuck in the hottest part of the day, but if we take it slow, we ought to be all right." She walked out of the office into the lobby.

"Ruth," Tallulah said.

Ruth turned around. The lobby lights had been turned off; with the windows behind her, her face was cast in shadow, impossible to read.

"I really need to make that phone call," Tallulah said. "Two minutes. Please."

"You did good today," Ruth said, and then: "All right. Go on."

Tallulah made herself wait until she heard the front door deadbolt snap open. Then she pulled the phone toward her. One-four-oh-seven-eight-nine-four-oh-two, on and on, her fingers punching the keys. By now the litany of numbers called up its own tight-winding anxiety. Come on, Michael. Answer your phone for once.

Ringing. The answering machine always picked up on the second ring. Third ring. Fourth. She closed her eyes, motionless, not breathing. Waiting for the click. Waiting for a live voice, Michael's voice, telling her that Maeve was on her way, that everything was going to be all right.

Click.

"Michael!" she said.

Three tones, escalating in pitch. Then a voice. Not Michael's.

"The number you have dialed is no longer in service, or has been . . ."

Tallulah slammed the receiver down as though it had crept over her ear with tarantula legs.

Obviously she'd dialed the wrong number. She'd dialed wrong because she thought she knew the number when she didn't; you'd think she'd have learned by now not to trust herself with numbers, she mixed them up all the time, half the time she couldn't even remember her own, let alone some huge long-distance one. Tallulah fished in her scrubs pocket for the slip of paper and smoothed it on the desk. She took a breath, deep enough to raise a ghost of pain where Leopard's hoof had struck. Then dialed again, gripping the receiver as if the strength in her fingers could force the signal along the wire to the correct house, the correct phone, where Michael waited to tell her that Maeve was coming to rescue her.

"The number you have dialed is no longer in service, or has been . . ."

The tips of her fingers went cold. She stabbed the phone lever down and dialed again.

The fifth time she reached the recording she dropped the receiver onto the desk but she could still hear the voice so she fumbled it back into its cradle.

Maeve was gone. Not on her way to rescue Tallulah. Gone. As certain as she'd been that Maeve was coming for her, now she was certain of this.

She was alone.

Tallulah sank forward onto the desk. Her chest filled in a great wrenching gasp and then released itself and wrenched and released itself again.

I'm alone. That was the one thought in her head: *I'm alone.*

After a while she became aware of someone else in the room. She lifted her head. It felt huge, heavy, as if filled with concrete. She'd gotten snot on the August 22 box of Ruth's desk calendar. The thirteenth through the sixteenth were darkened, wavy damp from tears. Tallulah shifted her eyes sideways, saw Poteet's khaki leg next to the desk. His hand reached for the slip of paper with Michael's number. Before he could pick it up, Tallulah snatched it. She crumpled it and shoved it in her pocket.

"Your friend?" Poteet asked. Instead of answering, Tallulah laid her head back down. She heard Poteet leave, heard him say something to Ruth outside. Then both of them were in the office. Ruth lay her hands on Tallulah's shoulders.

"Worst thing is to coop yourself up, honey." Tallulah sensed Ruth bending forward, trying to see Tallulah's face. "You don't let yourself see nothing but four walls and soon enough you've got four walls built in your head and then you're flat convinced there's no way out. Come on, now."

She allowed Ruth to stand her up, but when Ruth would have helped her as though she were crippled—one arm around her, the other hand cupping her elbow—Tallulah curved her body away. Outside, Diesel lay on the concrete walkway in the shade. He thumped his tail when he saw her.

Easy for you, she thought. If you've got four legs and fur, everyone loves you. The rest of us can eat shit and die. The throb in her throat became a high keening ache. She bit her lip hard. She wouldn't cry anymore. Not here. She'd already made enough of a fool of herself in front of these strangers.

Poteet was talking again, she thought to Ruth. Then she heard her name.

"What?" she asked.

"I said you're coming with me. Hurry up."

On the walkway lay the flats of flowering plants, dozens of them, summer-bright, cheerful as rainbows. She could refuse to go. She knew Poteet wouldn't insist. He'd never wanted her here to begin with, had barely spoken to her since she'd arrived. She could stay here, all the long blazing afternoon, digging one hole after another while Ruth filled every empty space with chatter, leaving Tallulah no room alone with her fear and grief.

The truck would be quiet and cool. And she would be moving. It didn't matter where. Just so long as road rolled away beneath her, Tallulah could make believe she was going somewhere.

She crossed the parking lot to the truck and got in.

Chapter 12

I meant to tell you," Poteet said. "You did real well the other day. With that horse."

They were sitting in the corner booth of a roadside diner, waiting for Poteet's lunch to arrive. Tallulah rubbed the sides of her fingers against her thumbs. She'd washed twice with the hose in the truck's VetPak, making the water as hot as she could stand it, but her hands were still greasy.

She slid out of the booth. "I'm going to the restroom," she said.

"It's lanolin," Poteet said. "It's good for the skin."

"It stinks," she said.

The illusion of going somewhere hadn't lasted long. Ten minutes on the road. Then they were out of the truck and she was carrying the green tray again, this time following Poteet across somebody's front yard to a pen containing a wobbling, bloodstained sheep. Neighbor's damn German shepherd, the sheep's owner had said. Tonight I'll be waiting up with the shotgun. While he described how he planned to display the carcass of the dog on his neighbor's porch,

Poteet took the sheep's jaw, laid its head back along its flank, and folded it up easy as a letter until its rump was on the ground, back vertical and all four legs sticking out in the air, like a table stood on one end. Then he made Tallulah hold it that way while he cleaned and stitched the wounds. For forty minutes she'd stood hunched over, a foreleg gripped in each hand, the sheep's head banging into her stomach, all two hundred greasy pounds of it pressing against her knees and its smell, like a wet wool sweater dipped in compost, flooding her nose. When Poteet finally told her to let it go, her back had seized up like a rusty chain. She'd had to hang onto a fence post and straighten up one inch at a time.

Back in the truck, Poteet had asked her if she was hungry. No, she'd said. Well, I didn't have any nice Ruth to buy *me* dinner, he'd said, and he'd pulled off the road in front of this tiny box of a building, with its two low glary windows and a rope of steam drifting from a roof vent into the brilliant burden of sky.

The restroom's cracked wall sink was too low, and her back too sore, for Tallulah to bend over. She stood upright and squirted half a teaspoon of pink pearlescent soap into her palm and began scrubbing.

When they'd first arrived, Poteet had ushered her to the booth, waving to calls of "Doc!" and shaking hands and slapping shoulders, pausing to speak to a booth of older women by the window. Now, going back to the table alone, Tallulah was conscious of the other customers' stares. She didn't look at anyone. Slipping back into the booth she saw, next to the plastic vase with its dyed red daisy, a full glass of cola.

"Figured you'd got to be thirsty," Poteet said.

Tallulah pulled the paper cap off the straw and drank until the rasp in her throat smoothed out. Then she slid her butt forward on the seat, settled her shoulders against the backrest, and wove her fingers together loosely over the yellow Formica. Poteet crossed his arms on the table and gazed out the window. He cleared his throat.

A waitress approached, coffeepot in one hand, a massive white china plate in the other. "Here you go," she said. She side-dipped, knees bent, and slid the plate in front of Poteet. "I see you got a helper with you today," she said, her voice fluting high on the *help*, as if she were addressing a six-year-old.

"Got to have a hand now and again with these wild critters," Poteet said. He sat back to make room for the plate. "You'd know about that, being such a wild critter yourself and all." He winked at the waitress and grinned. The waitress yelped a laugh and spanked his hand; he shook out his fingers, grimacing in mock pain, and she laughed again. Tallulah narrowed her eyes. The waitress had to be at least as old as her mother. Poteet was an ugly man who not ten minutes ago had been hosing sheep shit off his boots. What did they think they were doing?

The waitress turned to Tallulah. "Sure you don't want anything?" she asked. Tallulah didn't need to look up to know the woman was taking in her inch of mouse-brown roots, the bits of dirty wool clinging to her scrub top, the polish flaking off her nails. No doubt the waitress would include these details when she told how she'd seen that homeless Yankee girl, the one Dr. Poteet was helping, bless his heart.

"Yeah, I'm sure," Tallulah said.

"You let me know you change your mind," the waitress said.

"Thank you, Jean," Poteet said. He rotated his plate an inch, then pulled the toothpick out of half his sandwich and picked it up. "Any thought what you're going to do now?" he asked.

"Go to Disneyland," Tallulah said. "Oh, that's right. I have no money and no car. I can't."

Poteet grunted; he was in the middle of a bite. After he'd swallowed, he said, "I suppose you can stay on here. You've got two days of work in; make it two weeks and you'll have, what—four hundred or so. I don't suppose Ruth would mind putting you up a little longer."

"You mean since this was her idea in the first place."

He took another bite of sandwich. Tallulah looked out the window. Poteet cleared his throat again. Then he said, "Maybe it's time you called your folks."

"Maybe it's not."

"You don't think—"

"I'm not calling home."

She'd planned to. When she was safe in Florida, with Maeve. As it was, she'd clean puppy crap the rest of her life before admitting to her mother that she'd gotten herself stranded in the middle of nowhere.

Anybody could have seen this was going to happen.

Debra, you just don't think.

But I did, Tallulah answered. I had a plan. It should have worked.

Shoulda woulda coulda. Delivered in a weary monotone, anytime Tallulah tried to explain the *how*.

"It just seems to me," Poteet said, "that maybe you ought to go home."

"Why do you care?"

He stabbed a forkful of coleslaw and raised it to his mouth. Then lowered it again. "Ruth went to an awful lot of trouble to keep you off the road. She'll be sorry to see you back on it."

"I didn't ask her to butt in. Or you either. If you hadn't called the cops—"

"None of this would have happened, yes, I know." He bounced the fork on his finger, sending bits of coleslaw onto his sandwich. "Even if you get to Florida," he said, "how do you plan to find this friend of yours? You thought about that?"

"No. I haven't. I haven't thought about anything, so why don't you just leave me the hell alone!" She pushed the table hard, lurching out of the booth, and saw Poteet grab for his mug. Around her, the undercurrent of conversation faltered. She ran for the door, head down against the pressure of their stares. Someone backed hastily out of her way.

Outside, the heat closed over her like a sweating hand, making the tears on her face feel oddly cooler and wetter. She stumbled between Poteet's truck and the pickup next to it and sat on the ground, her back against the rear bumper. Her sobs sounded harsh and idiotic in her ears, but she didn't try to stop them, not even when footsteps approached over the gravel. Poteet's khaki legs appeared next to her. The boot toes scuffed back, the legs bent. Without turning, she could see his arms braced on the tops of his knees, hands wrapped in a double fist.

"I just don't understand," Tallulah said. Her voice rose and broke over the strangling in her throat. "I don't understand how I messed up so *bad*." She wiped the back of her hand across her eyes. "No. I know how. I'm the stupidest person on the face of the earth. That's how." The fields across the highway were green blurs, the passing cars blue and red streaks. "And you want me to call my mother. You don't know. Everytime something happens she's like, 'What did Debbie do *now*?' Even when it's not my fault, she won't believe me. '*Now* what have you done? How much are you going to cost us *this* time?'" Snot was running down her upper lip. Of course. Gross stupid Debbie. Poteet's boots shifted; a white paper napkin appeared in his hand. She hesitated, then took it.

"I guarantee you she's not thinking about blame," Poteet said.

"Believe me. She is." The napkin was already sodden and gray. Tallulah ran the edge of it through her fingers.

"She practically threw me out. She's glad"—Tallulah drew a deep, hitching breath—"she's glad I'm gone." Inside her chest felt empty. Aching. As though someone had carved it clean of her heart.

Footsteps scraped close by. Between the trucks, a door latch clicked open.

"We'd best get going," Poteet said. He stood up and held out a hand. After a moment, Tallulah took it. He pulled her to her feet. Out of the truck's shadow, the glare of the sun spiked through her head.

Poteet was getting in the truck. "Aren't you going to finish your lunch?" Tallulah asked.

"Does it look like it?" Poteet said. His jaw was stubbed forward, making his nose appear even blunter, his lips scanter.

Instead of heading down the highway, back to the hospital, Poteet cut over on a side road. A few minutes of pastures and brush, then they emerged onto regular streets, with the densest collection of buildings Tallulah had seen yet. The courthouse had been surrounded on three sides by open lawn and oak and maple trees, the veterinary hospital was flanked by fields; but here, for a length of two blocks, storefronts lay jammed together with no shade except what they provided each other, and no landscaping except flower boxes and telephone poles. Most were two-storied, some only one: red brick, yellow brick, white siding; plain-fronted, awninged, porched. A drug store, a real estate office. Two attorneys and a flower shop. It took less than a minute to roll past them all. At the end of the second block, Poteet pulled the truck onto a patch of rough asphalt that lay between the last building and a single set of railroad tracks. He sat, one hand draped on the wheel, the other arm crooked over the windowsill.

"What are you—" Tallulah began, but Poteet interrupted her.

"I had a daughter," he said. "My wife and I. My ex-wife."

He turned the fan off. Except for the idle of the engine, the cab fell quiet. It became muggy almost as fast, smells of dust and hot asphalt leaking in with the heat.

"She was a firecracker," Poteet said. "Not afraid of anything. Certainly not me." He was staring out the window. Nothing there that Tallulah could see, just the railroad tracks and empty fields beyond. "She used to sneak out after curfew. You ever have a curfew?"

"Unfortunately," Tallulah said.

He glanced at her then. "Snuck out, didn't you?" When Tallulah didn't answer right away, he snorted. "Hell, I did. Everyone does."

"Yeah," Tallulah said.

"One night she snuck out. Came into town here with her friends. One of them had the bright idea of jumping the freight train. I went down to the trainyard later. Long way to jump. Little thing like she was, she'd have to have wings to jump that far. I think they dared her. They swore they didn't. But Emily never turned down a dare."

The photographs in the office. The girl's slim fierce body.

"Did she—" Tallulah began, but Poteet interrupted her.

"She died instantly. Fell under the wheels. She was fourteen. She was the bravest person I ever knew."

Poteet took his foot off the brake. The truck rolled backward into the road, bumping over potholes. "I don't pretend to know what-all you're dealing with," he said. He turned to see behind, right arm over the seat back. As he shifted gears, he looked her in the face; a moment only, just enough for Tallulah to see the flatness in his eyes. "You've got guts, I'll give you that much. But you better go on home. Whatever mess you're in. Go on home."

For the rest of the ride back to the hospital, neither of them said anything.

Chapter 13

Tallulah stayed on. She didn't know what else to do.

Besides, she argued to herself, just because Michael's number was disconnected didn't mean that Maeve had disappeared. Surely she'd gotten Tallulah's messages. She could still be on her way to Clark Station. It was just a matter of time.

Three days passed. Every morning, Tallulah woke up in Ruth's saggy sofa bed with Cowboy's cold smeary nose wedged between her earlobe and her neck. At the veterinary hospital, she cleaned kennels and scrubbed litter pans and mopped floors. Every night, back at the doublewide, she ate Ruth's dinners, watched game shows on Ruth's TV, and waited for Ruth's phone to ring.

Which it did. A lot. Tallulah always expected it to be Maeve. It never was. Still, she recognized the conversations; Mom got these kinds of calls all the time. Arranging meetings of the realtors' association. Organizing get-out-the-vote rallies. Ruth's sounded like church activities, mostly, and some kind of club. Gardening, maybe. The calls always ended with Ruth saying, Try me again next time or Next month I ought to be able to handle that or Thanks for thinking of me, but—

Tuesday night, as Ruth was settling herself back on the sofa after the second call of the evening, Tallulah said, "You should go."

Ruth had picked up her crossword puzzle; at this, she put it down again. "Go where?"

"Wherever that lady just invited you."

"How do you know that was a lady? Maybe that was my boyfriend."

"Then your boyfriend's got a problem. Unless you don't care that he's hot for the deacon."

Ruth hooted. "If I ever do get a boyfriend, I'll have to take my calls in the bedroom where you can't hear."

I'm not going to be here *that* long, Tallulah almost said, realizing just in time it might sound insulting. Instead she said, "I understand, though. If you don't want to leave me alone."

Ruth chuckled and clicked her ballpoint. "Seems to me a girl who's roaming the countryside by her lonesome doesn't need a babysitter." She filled in a word. Then laid the puzzle down again. "That's not what you meant," she said slowly. "You think I don't trust you in my house."

Tallulah shrugged. One of the game show contestants guessed an R. There were five R's. The contestant pumped her fists in the air, but her whoops of elation cut out in the middle, muted. Tallulah glanced over to see Ruth aiming the remote at the TV but staring at her.

"You must think I'm soft or stupid, one," Ruth said. She dropped the remote onto her puzzle and smacked both onto the coffee table. "I raised three babies mostly on my own. You think I let just anybody into my home? God's gracious light, girl." She picked up her empty iced tea glass and went to the kitchen.

Bewildered, Tallulah sat on the couch a moment; then she got up and followed. Ruth was lifting a half-gallon of Rocky Road out of the freezer. Tallulah crossed to the cabinet and took down two bowls.

"People do what they are," Ruth said. "Most would've passed that dog by. You had enough problems on your plate to choke a goat, but you still went out of your way to help him." Elbow jacked high, she dug out a scoop of ice cream. "Just because I let you sleep on my sofa, don't swell your head thinking I plan my life around you. I'm not going to that meeting because I'm tired and my feet hurt, and listening to Carlie Anderson go on about the Hospitality Committee is enough to make my ears bleed. Go on get us that marshmallow sauce from the fridge."

Tallulah set the bottle on the counter. When Ruth reached for it, though, she didn't let go.

"I didn't do it because of the dog," Tallulah said. "I only did it because my friend would have wanted me to." She pushed the bottle toward Ruth. "If that makes a difference."

"It does not." Ruth sucked a smear of ice cream off her knuckle, then popped off the bottle lid. "Come on. Let's see if the lady from Arkansas won herself the car."

Instead of watching the game shows, though, Ruth pulled out her photo albums. After Tallulah had perused twenty pages of grandchildren, she dug in her duffel for the Polaroid of herself and Maeve. Not one for polite glances, Ruth studied the photo. "She as much of a live wire as she looks?" she asked. The approval in her tone was good as an invitation, and in response to her questions—one after another, gentle, never prying—Tallulah found herself explaining everything that had happened in the past five months, from the man-in-the-moon dagger to Michael's disconnected phone three days before. Talking to Ruth, it was easy to believe—to insist, even—that the next day, Wednesday, Maeve would surely arrive.

But the next day passed, and Maeve still didn't come, and Tallulah's last, fraying strand of hope finally and quietly snapped. She could no longer fool herself. Maeve wasn't going to charge over the hill, like the cavalry, to rescue her. After a week in Tennessee, Tallulah was truly alone.

And, for the first time, alone in Ruth's house. Wednesday night church services, Ruth explained, which even aching feet wouldn't keep her from. Tallulah declined her invitation, opting instead to stay behind with Cowboy and the cats and a microwaved lasagna. As soon as the Pontiac was out of earshot, Tallulah poured her glass of lemonade down the sink and snagged herself a Rolling Rock from the stash in the refrigerator door.

She had to saw through the lasagna with the side of her fork. The ground beef was dry, the red sauce metallic-tasting.

It leaked watery pink across the plate, reminding Tallulah of her mother's early pastas, before she'd discovered fancy cookbooks. Somewhere between the first Modesto apartment, when Mom had thrown Daddy out, and the third, before Mom married John, the stacks of cans in the cupboard had changed to heaps of plastic bags in the refrigerator crisper. After the wedding, at the new house in Portland, Mom bought only whatever produce she couldn't grow in the raised beds out back. By that time her lasagnas had become Nancy Badowski originals, almost unrecognizable as lasagna: tender and green, thick with homemade pesto and artichoke hearts, slices of eggplant, chunks of tomato.

The house in Portland was where Mom started saying how much she loved to cook. She'd never liked it before. Tallulah knew, because Mom had said that, too.

"You girls need to start learning how to do this," she'd said, when Tallulah—still Debbie, then—was six and Terri was eight. "I'm tired of being the only one around here who can put a meal on the table." So Debbie had learned to measure the water and open the box and Terri to thaw the hamburger and turn on the burner and stir, and three nights a week they cooked and their mother did the dishes.

They were in the third Modesto apartment when Mom bought the first fancy cookbook. She'd met John the week before. With John she was interested in cooking, unlike before him, when it was just the necessary process by which she and Debbie and Terri stayed fed. Debbie sat at the kitchen table picking at a rip in the red-and-white checked vinyl tablecloth, making it bigger, and watched Mom make dinner for John: yellow apron over one of her good shorty skirts, in pantyhose feet and no shoes, her ash blond hair caught in a clip at the back of her head, leaning forward from the hips to taste from the spoon's edge. At the time, Debbie had wondered if this was how Mom had cooked for Daddy. She couldn't remember. When she'd asked Terri, Terri told her not to talk retarded.

After they moved to Portland, the dinner parties began. At first, they were for the people John worked with; later, for whomever Mom needed to shmooze for her campaigns: PTA, education board, county commissioner. They were rarely big affairs; *intimate*, Mom said, or *cozy*, which if she was writing one of her real estate ads would mean *small*. Mom cooked, Terri made the salad, Debbie set the table. It became a ritual, one that, when she was younger, Debbie had adored. Mom taught her about colors and seasons. She taught her how to arrange flowers in a centerpiece; that the crystal candleholders went best with the lace tablecloth, pewter with the linen; how bright or dim to set the lighting. Most important, how to step back and take it all in, and—if the effect was too fussy, too polished—how to go back and change one thing. Just one, Mom said. People will notice, even if they don't see it.

By the time Debbie was twelve, though, setting the table had begun to feel like a monkey trick: see what my little girl did! Mom coaxed, then nagged. Then insisted.

Debbie tried to explain. "I'm tired of it," she said. "It's old."

"Then try something new," Mom answered, and went to her bedroom to shower and change.

Debbie chose a clean terra-cotta pot from Mom's garden shed, brought it into the kitchen, and went rummaging in the vegetable drawer. When she turned the pot upside down and set a head of lettuce on it, Terri looked up from peeling cucumbers. "What are you doing?" she asked.

"Something new," Debbie said, and headed into the back garden with shears.

Daisies for hair. Olives for eyes. The cut end of a cucumber, swiped off Terri's cutting board, for the nose. Everything attached with straight pins from Mom's sewing kit. Finally, one of John's ties draped around the pot and secured with a safety pin, because Debbie didn't know how to tie a real knot. She placed her creation precisely between the two silver candlesticks and stepped back.

Perfect.

After that, Mom hadn't asked her to set any more tables.

Tallulah finished the lasagna and washed it down with the Rolling Rock. The beer made her blood a surge of warm bubbles, down her arms, her thighs. She set the plate on the floor—Ruth disapproved of table food for the animals, poor Cowboy never got a thing—and, while the dog and two of the more assertive cats worked it over, she picked up Maeve's notebooks.

The evening she'd retrieved them from Maeve's apartment, on what turned out to be her own last evening in Portland, she hadn't gotten home until after seven. After leaving the Belinda she'd swung by Art World, where Maeve had worked off and on as a sketch model, to see if they'd heard from her. They hadn't. By that time it was well into rush hour, the traffic from the east side to the West Hills one giant hair ball. It had taken her half an hour just to fight her way across the Marquam Bridge.

When she entered the kitchen, Mom looked up from the table. No house showings tonight, apparently; she'd taken off her makeup and skimmed her ash blond hair flat under a headband. Without lipstick and mascara and clean bright necklines, she looked sallow, the skin under her eyes pouching out like dabs of clay molded with a thumb.

"Nice to see you," she said.

Tallulah slung her purse—vintage Mexican, its saddle-bag leather cracked and handpainted, completely unlike the sleek shining things her mom and sister carried—onto a peg hook by the back door. The kitchen was warm, and smelled of brownies.

"Not that I suppose you care," Mom said, "but John had to leave work early so Terri could take his car to her appointment. He thought you might get home in time for him to make his meeting, but it seems that was too much to hope for."

"Maybe John could have dropped Terri off," Tallulah

said. "You know, like in the olden days, when people were deprived of three cars to a family."

"Maybe if you'd asked her permission and promised to pick her up, that might have worked." The table was covered with stacks of Kinko's boxes and sheets of mailing labels. Tallulah edged around it, aiming for the pan of brownies. Mom had won the primary in May; now she was gunning for the general election in November, barely three months away. But Tallulah had no intention of being drafted as a campaign drudge. Not tonight. "I presume you made it to your class this afternoon," Mom said. "You did, didn't you?"

Class. Geometry, which Tallulah had flunked two years in a row. Summer school was her last chance, and there had been a quiz this afternoon. "Yes," Tallulah said, then, at her mother's flat stare, she added, "I mean, I was going to, but—"

Mom had shimmied the top off one of the boxes; she smacked it down on the table. "For God's sake, Debra, how many times do we have to go through this?"

Tallulah abandoned the brownies. She tucked Maeve's notebooks higher under her arm and headed for the stairs. Mom pushed her chair back. "You stay right there," she said and flashed her patented, Nancy-Badowski-I-Will-Hold-The-County-Accountable five-finger point, cocoa blush nails aimed at Tallulah's chest.

The door between the living room and kitchen swung

open and Terri came in. "So, she finally shows up. Is my car still in one piece?"

"It's been three years since the accident, Terrier, why don't you give it a rest?" Tallulah said.

"Because I saw the Volvo after you got done with it, that's why. The image is seared into my brain." Terri held out a hand. "Just give me my keys, will you?" Tallulah tossed them across the table. Terri caught them, pocketed them, and sat down next to Mom. Terri had their mother's face: wide across the cheekbones, rounded at the chin. Looking at the three of them always gave Tallulah the odd feeling of being cobbled together from spare parts.

"The contract specifically states . . ." Mom began.

Lord, here we go.

". . . that this summer you would make up the classes you flunked so you can graduate on time next year. Now it's almost September . . ."

"I know, but—"

". . . and here you are skipping classes. If you flunk geometry again, your father and I are done. Do you understand? No TV. No Internet. No job. No allowance. No more money for all those beat-up things you buy with that friend of yours."

"They're *vintage*. Will you listen?"

"Vintage, excuse me." Mom lifted the top copy out of the open Kinko's box. She'd designed the campaign flier herself; in it, a navy-suited Mom, full color and beaming, shook hands with a man in a flannel shirt and jeans. NANCY BADOWSKI, the flier read. GETTING THE JOB DONE.

"Maeve's gone," Tallulah said. She knew better than to say *in trouble* or *emergency*; words like that would raise any number of her mother's red flags, and besides, Mom would insist on details, which Tallulah didn't have. "She left for Florida. She forgot something in her apartment and she asked me to get it for her."

Her mom folded the flier and closed it with a mailing label, smoothing it with her thumb. "And that had to be done tonight."

"Yes. All right?"

"Actually, no. It's not all right. The contract specifically . . ."

"Look, Maeve needed me to do this. I'm sorry it went against the all-holy contract—"

"If you're going to get sarcastic, then spare me your explanations," Mom said. "And if that girl's gone, then frankly, I'm relieved. Terri, will you fold this batch, please? Thanks." She got up and carried her coffee mug to the counter. Tallulah stared after her.

"I thought you liked Maeve," she said.

"Debbie, even you have to admit it was odd that a twenty-four-year-old woman . . ."

"Twenty-*one*. Maeve is twenty-*one*."

" . . . spent her time hanging around with a seventeen-year-old girl. I did some reading on the Internet about this bipolar business . . ."

"Bipolar? Who's bipolar?" Terri said.

" . . . and I suppose we're lucky the worst thing she

seems to have talked you into is that ridiculous tattoo. A tattoo which, by the way, is going to cost at least two thousand dollars to have removed." Mom lifted the top off the coffee carafe, peered inside, then refilled her mug.

"Why don't you say the rest of it?" Tallulah said. "You think it's *odd* that she hung out with a seventeen-year-old idiot who's flunking out of high school. That's what you really mean, right?"

Terri raised her two hands in a T. "Wait a minute, time-out," she said. "Your friend's bipolar? I just had a class on this. What—"

"Can it, Terrier," Tallulah snapped, at the same time Mom said, "Terri, please." She rattled the carafe back into the coffeemaker. "I'm not getting into this tonight. If you want to take it up with the therapist Tuesday that's fine, but in the meantime maybe you want to think about what he asked you last week. About why you choose unreliable friends."

"That's not what he said, he said you weren't supportive of the friends I have which is *exactly* what Maeve—"

"I said take it up with the therapist. Not with me. Not now. I don't have the time. God knows I don't have the energy." She began to turn away from the counter, mug in hand.

"Fine. Go get yourself elected. Maybe when you have the whole county to order around you won't be such a bitch to me."

An explosion cracked across Tallulah's cheek and her head snapped sideways. Tears flooded her eyes. She hadn't even seen her mother's hand move. Blinking, she pressed her fingertips to the side of her face, wincing at the sore spot below her temple. When she looked up, John was standing behind Mom, his arms crossed over hers, his hands clasping hers to her sweatshirt. The coffee mug lay in pieces on the floor, shards of white in a dark lake flung from oven to table.

"Debra, apologize," John said.

"Me? You don't even know what this is about. She—"

"You raised your voice first. I heard you. You know the contract, now apologize."

Seeing the rightness in his face, the *reasonableness,* while her cheek still throbbed made something inside come free and raging and Tallulah welcomed it, she stoked it like a bonfire. Leaning forward from the hips, she yelled, "All I know, *John,* is you're not my father. So why don't you just shut the hell up?"

"For God's sake, Debbie, are you eight years old again or what?" Terri said.

"No. She's right." Mom shrugged John's arms off. "If John was your father, then maybe you'd have inherited some sliver of common sense. Some shred of consideration—"

"Nancy, don't," John said. He laid his hand on her arm. She jerked it away.

"—but you, no, you're your father's daughter. All the way through. And you're determined to bang your head against the same stupid"—she caught her breath—was she

171

crying?—"*stupid* walls. Well, I'm sick of that game." She dragged the headband loose and ran her fingers through her hair. "I have nothing else left," she said. "I'm done. If you stay, Debra, you'll abide by the rules of this house . . ."

Her voice was steady. She wasn't crying. Of course not. Mom never cried.

". . . or you'll get out. Think hard."

"I don't have to think," Tallulah said.

"I suppose not. You never do." Mom glanced down at the shattered mug, at the black lake of coffee, and pressed her palm against her forehead. "We'll discuss it tomorrow," she said. "I don't want to see you again tonight."

Or ever. Tallulah heard it in the weariness of her voice. Plain as if she'd spoken the words.

She'd stayed awake most of the night, coming up with the plan. At three, the house long since slipped into a dead quiet, she was ready.

In the kitchen, her packed duffel slung over her shoulder, she'd searched the corkboard for the stack of notes. Six or seven of them, all different dates, all stabbed on one pin: *Derek called. Pls call back. Derek called* again—*pls call!!* The last one, in Terri's handwriting: *Debbie, either call this guy and put him out of his misery or next time I'm telling him you died.*

Why is he doing this? she'd asked Maeve. I disappeared on him. You'd think he'd take the hint.

You're a mystery, Maeve had said. He's dying to know what he missed.

Tallulah took down the notes, riffled through them.

Then crossed her fingers and dialed the number. Come on, Derek. Mystery calling. Be home.

He was home.

After she hung up, she wrote a note of her own on the grocery list pad. She put the note on the kitchen table and set her keys and cell phone on top.

No going back.

Tallulah drained the Rolling Rock and got up from Ruth's table. On her way to the kitchen she picked the plate up off the floor, Cowboy and three cats trotting after her, necks craned upward, sniffing for more handouts. Tallulah set the plate in the sink and got herself another beer. Then she went back to the table, sat down, opened the green notebook, and read again the lines on the first page.

I am Maeve Anaïs MacRae.

I renounce the culture of What and I reclaim the culture of Who.

This is my Manifesto and my Purpose.

Broad red ink strokes, Maeve's large slanted loops dominating the center of the page. On the other side, nothing but blurred spots where the ink had soaked through.

Wherever Maeve was, whatever was happening to her, the key lay in these lines. Tallulah knew it. But she didn't understand it. She stared at the handwriting, traced it with her finger. *Tell me what you mean. Tell me what I'm supposed to do.*

Maybe Maeve didn't mean for anyone else to understand. Or maybe Tallulah was just too dumb to see it. The way she'd been too dumb to get these notebooks to Florida in the first place.

If you had a sliver of common sense . . .

Tears blurred the writing into a red haze. So she'd changed her name and dyed her hair. It still came out the same: How much is Debbie going to cost us *this* time?

Except this time, Maeve was paying. Tallulah just didn't know what.

She could still hitchhike to Florida. Starting right now, if she wanted to. Tonight. And then what? She still had no idea where in Orlando Michael lived. She didn't even know what his last name was. In the past five nights she'd searched through both notebooks, and not a clue.

Maybe Poteet was right. Maybe she should call home. John would come get her, the same way he'd gotten her in Elko. It was too late in the summer to catch up with her classes, which meant she wouldn't graduate on time. Mom would be pissed. There would be a new contract, hammered out with the family therapist, which Tallulah would have to sign. And Maeve's notebooks? Tallulah would tuck them in the drawer with her other souvenirs, the Mickey Mouse ears from Disneyland, the stubs of concert tickets.

She wouldn't be Tallulah anymore, not to anyone. Not even to herself.

A car pulled into the driveway. Tallulah grabbed the Rolling Rock bottles and the notebooks. By the time Ruth's steps sounded on the front porch, the bottles were at the bottom of the trash, the notebooks were in her duffel, and she was on the sofa watching *Jeopardy*. Cowboy lay sprawled beside her, his head in her lap.

"You get supper all right?" Ruth asked, as she came in the door. Cowboy bounded off the sofa and hit the floor, tags jangling.

"Fine. Thank you," Tallulah said, not taking her eyes off the screen. "How was church?"

She nodded as Ruth talked, grinned when Ruth laughed. All the while thinking, I'm not going to quit. Not until I know for sure I can't find Maeve. I have to go to Florida. I have to try.

"Want some more lemonade?" Ruth called from the kitchen.

"Love some," Tallulah answered.

Payday was a week from Friday. Ten days. By then, she had to have a plan.

Chapter 14

Tallulah had gotten fast enough with the morning cleaning that, afterward, Jolene started sending her up front to help Poteet in the exam rooms. From comments Jolene dropped to Ruth, Tallulah suspected that Jolene regarded this as an infliction on Poteet, rather than a kindness; her way to make the point—as complaining so far hadn't—that Jolene needed an assistant, and Tallulah wasn't it.

Tallulah didn't care what her motives were. Helping Poteet sure beat scrubbing litter pans, and if Jolene's spite freed Tallulah from the drudgery of endless kennel cleaning, then Tallulah was all for it.

Training for her new responsibilities was, of course, not part of Jolene's agenda. Ruth knew a lot of the job; but between answering the phone and checking clients in and out, she couldn't spare much time for teaching. It was from Kyle that Tallulah learned how to prepare vaccines; how to take an animal's temperature; how to clean the rooms between patients. He explained the boxes of test kits stacked in the refrigerator, and when Dr. Poteet was likely to call for each:

leukemia virus for sick cats and new kittens, heartworm for almost every dog that walked in, immunity failure for newborn foals. Mostly he helped her out in the late afternoon, when he showed up for his shift. But often, too, at odd times of the day, Tallulah would turn around in the back hall to find him quietly assuming some task. He'd give her a pointer or two, identify some obscure instrument, or answer a question. Then he'd disappear again.

Once, he walked back from the reception area with a margarine tub and handed it to her. Curious, Tallulah flipped off the lid.

"Aarghl," she said, thrusting the container back at him. He laughed.

"Sorry," he said. "Around here you don't want to open nothing without being under a ventilation fan first." He reached up under the overhead cabinets and flipped on the fan. Over the whir of the motor, he said, "I'll show you how to set up a fecal."

"And that would be what, exactly?"

"Test for worms."

"Great," Tallulah said. "Another simply marvelous thing to do with shit."

But she did it. She even stirred the crap in the special solution with the little wooden stick, just like Kyle showed her. The more she knew how to do, she figured, the more likely it was that Poteet would let her stay up front.

Especially since it became obvious Poteet needed the help. August, Ruth explained to Tallulah, was their busiest month. Appointments ran back-to-back all day, and every day six or eight additional people walked in demanding to be seen without one. But while Jolene and Ruth rushed, and fussed, and looked harried, the pace didn't bother Tallulah. If anything, it helped her concentrate. It had been the same at her coffee barista job, and one of the reasons management had kept her on, despite her habit of making fun of customer's drink orders. After only a month on the job, she'd come to the conclusion that the more complicated the drink, the bigger the jerk ordering it; and since she never could repeat back "grande half-caf no-fat no-whip extra-hot mocha one shot hazelnut" in anything approaching the required, customer-is-always-right tone of voice, by the time she'd left Portland she'd earned a bucketful of complaints and one written reprimand.

Most days they managed half an hour for lunch. Tallulah would get Diesel—now that he was walking and his chest tube was out, he'd been moved to a regular run in the dog ward—and lead him to the break room. He'd choose a spot and settle down, always close enough to Tallulah's chair that she could slip bits of her lunch to him when Ruth wasn't looking. Ruth's dinners might be either microwaved or take-out, but her lunches were excellent: an egg salad sandwich on Monday, a BLT on Tuesday, peanut butter and strawberry jam on Wednesday, the sandwiches always accompanied by two large sugar cookies and a thermos of iced tea.

On Friday, just before the lunch break, Poteet caught

Jolene and Ruth in the back hall thrashing out details for the next day's annual hospital picnic. All week, Ruth had been making lists, drawing diagrams of tables, and sending Kyle on errands; now, she and Jolene were deep in discussion about potato salad, instead of helping two clients at the reception counter.

"For God's sake, Ruth, it's going to be exactly the same as the past ten summers, now leave it alone," Poteet said. He picked up a piece of paper off the counter. "What's this picture of a tent for? Who needs a damn tent?"

"It's an awning, and we're renting it." Ruth plucked the paper out of his fingers. "They're saying thunderstorms tomorrow and we can't cram eighteen people not counting the little ones into that two-room shack you call a house."

"If they're saying thunderstorms it's bound to be clear. You've lived your whole life in this state, don't you know that yet?"

"I know what a soggy hamburger tastes like and I don't aim to repeat the experience. You don't want the awning, fine with me. You can stand out in the rain by yourself." Ruth headed up front, taking the paper with her. A moment later, she poked her head around the corner of the hallway. "Mr. Castleberry's come in," she said. "He doesn't have an appointment. Should I tell him to come back later?"

"Do that and he'll sit in the lobby and stink up the whole place," Jolene said.

"Go get your tent," Poteet said. "Ruth, put Mr. Castleberry in a room. Arabella with him?"

"Yes sir. You want us to wait until you're through with him?"

"No, go on. Tallulah can give me a hand if I need it."

Ruth and Jolene left. Poteet disappeared into the exam room with Castleberry. At first Tallulah sat on a stool in the middle of the hallway; but after a few minutes, when nothing looked like it was going to happen, she got up and went to the break room. Might as well eat; she was starving.

She'd barely unwrapped the foil from the leftover fried chicken—last night's dinner had been from Popeye's—when Poteet yelled for her over the intercom. As soon as she arrived in the hallway, he barked, "Stay where you're needed. Don't make me chase you all over the damn hospital. You know those radiographs we took last week on the Castleberry dog?" Tallulah didn't, but she nodded. "Bring them up here," Poteet said.

Radiographs were filed in the big manila envelopes, she remembered that much. She found Arabella's, brought it up to the exam room, and handed it to Poteet. Then she sat back down on the stool, listening to the rumble of voices drifting through the closed door. Castleberry she could barely hear, but Poteet seemed to be getting irritated, his voice coming more and more clearly into the hallway.

". . . have to be out for about fifteen minutes for the biopsy. Well, yes, it's anesthesia, but Loren . . . Loren, it's the biopsy that's going to . . ."

A murmur rose, a humming of bees, angry.

"Then there's no damn point, Loren. It's the biopsy that

tells us is it worth doing or is she dead before we start. . . . Hell, that's not what I meant, I meant . . ."

A door opened. Shuffling footsteps and the click of dog nails heading into the lobby.

"Dammit, Loren, wait." A pause, then Poteet yanked open the door into the hallway and strode past Tallulah. Without looking at her, he said, "Mop that room."

Tallulah went to the ward and got the mop bucket. On her way back, she stopped by Diesel's run. He was used to getting out at noon; no reason he should have to wait just because Castleberry couldn't remember to make an appointment. When she opened the gate, the dog picked up his head and yawned.

"Come on, goofball. Lunchtime," she said. She helped him get up; he was improving, but still it took him a few moments to hitch everything into place. Once he was on his feet, she scratched the little hollow at the base of his throat. Diesel thump-thumped his back foot in happy response. Kick-starting his motorcycle, Kyle called it.

Diesel limped one step behind her through the ward, his eyes straight ahead, ignoring the other dogs' barking. On the way out Tallulah grabbed a clean fleece blanket from the closet.

Back in the hallway, she spread the blanket in an open space underneath the counter, between two banks of cabinets. As soon as Diesel was settled, Tallulah slung her mop over the exam room floor, left to right to left, backing her way across the room. The whiskey smell seemed stronger today. Flashes of warm sheepskin again, the safety of being held. And an unsettled sensation, high in her chest, of excitement and grief mingled. A feeling of being out of place.

She was just closing the door when Poteet came back into the hallway. "What's that dog doing here?" he asked.

"He's not bothering anybody."

"That wasn't the question. Put him back."

Tallulah sighed and slapped her leg. Diesel thumped his tail, but otherwise refused to move. She had to crawl under the counter and pull him out. As she was helping him up, she asked, "What's Castleberry's problem, anyway?"

"Loren or Arabella?"

"Him. Loren."

Poteet tugged a lab form from one of the counter trays and began filling it out. "His problem's the fact that no one's seen him sober in fifteen years. His dog's problem is she's got a mass in her belly."

"A mass, like what? Cancer?"

"A mass isn't always cancer. Only way to find out is to get a piece of it. Either open her up on the surgery table or send her to the university for an ultrasound and biopsy. Doesn't matter, because Loren refuses to consider anything involving anesthesia. Convinced Arabella'll die." His pen made raw scoring sounds on the paper. "Of course, she'll die for sure if we don't do anything. But Loren was a stubborn son-of-a-buck when he was sober. Drunk, he's hopeless."

"That's sad," Tallulah said.

"What is?"

"Him," she said again, waving a hand vaguely in the direction of the lobby. "Drunk and poor and all he's got is a dog. It's sad."

Poteet stopped writing. He tilted his head to look at her; his expression was half-amused, half-irritated. "What gave you the idea Loren Castleberry is poor? Or alone in the world, for that matter?"

"I looked at him."

Poteet walked to the back door. "Come on out here a minute," he said.

Tallulah and Diesel both followed him onto the back porch. Poteet raised his arm and pointed left, over the fields that rolled back from the hospital in yellow green waves.

"You see that line of trees? Just this side of the water tower?" Tallulah nodded. Poteet swung to the right. "Now. See over there, that road where that pickup is right now?"

Tallulah stepped forward to see around him, shading her eyes. "Where?"

"The red pickup, going up that road. See that?"

"Oh. Yeah, OK."

"Loren Castleberry owns everything between those trees and that road. There's more, but you can't see it from here."

Tallulah dropped her hand. "You're making fun of me."

"No, I am not. Loren could buy me out and most of the other businesses in this town—save Wal-Mart—and he'd never feel it. As my daddy used to say, he's in high cotton.

And he's got a wife and three grown children and a passel of grandbabies and one great-grandbaby and he can't stand a single one of them. Ten years ago he got himself a redbone pup and put a refrigerator and hot plate in the barn and that's where he lives. He's got his drink and his dog and all the peace he can stomach. His wife's got a big house all to herself and the use of his money. Plus the sympathy of the family and the whole county besides."

"But why—"

"Don't bother asking." Poteet waved Tallulah back inside and closed the door. "And don't feel sorry for him. He's made his choices, same as everybody else. Now get that dog out of here."

In the break room, Diesel settled himself carefully under Tallulah's chair. Then he thrust his head forward to stare at her, one toffee-colored eye just visible under the edge of the seat. When Tallulah gave him a dog biscuit, he took it politely, almost distantly, with the air of a stranger asked to hold someone's coat. Only a lengthening drip of saliva from his lower lip betrayed any personal interest. Tallulah sat down. From under the chair came the sharp crack of breaking biscuit, followed by crunching, and a series of small smacks.

The microwave dinged. Tallulah took out her chicken, retrieved the thermos of iced tea from the refrigerator, and sat down. Beneath her chair, Diesel whined. She tore off a strip of chicken and dropped it to him.

What kind of person would leave his family for a dog?

Nobody would. She bet it was a made-up story; juicy gossip, spread by people who didn't have anything better to do. Probably the truth was Castleberry's wife kicked him out. And he didn't move away because he couldn't bear to leave his kids. He'd wanted to stay close to them, even if he couldn't give up drinking for them.

The unsettled feeling came back. The Elko feeling. Joy at being with her daddy; chest-busting pride that he'd picked her instead of Terri. The excitement of a new place. The grocery store was different from the one at home. So was TV during the day. Wal-Mart and TV at night were the same. There had been only one banana pancake dinner, the first night; after that, she ate mac'n'cheese by herself in Daddy's apartment, because when he'd asked her what she liked to eat, that's what she told him. He'd filled up a whole grocery cart with mac'n'cheese. And Coke. The living room smelled like sour milk, but the bedroom smelled like him, whiskey and worn clothes, like the night he'd carried her home; so she sat on his bed and watched TV and waited for his key in the door. She never remembered going to sleep. Every morning when she woke up, stiff and achy on top of the bedspread, Daddy would be snoring on the couch. She'd make mac'n'cheese for breakfast and watch TV and wait for him to wake up.

The fifth morning when he woke up he found her crying. "What's the matter with you?" he asked.

"I miss Mommy," she told him. Knowing as soon as she said it, she'd made a mistake. "No I don't," she added hastily. "I don't, I didn't mean it."

Two days later, John was knocking on Daddy's door.

Her first night back home, Mom had made a cake to celebrate. Tallulah still remembered the warmth of the kitchen from baking, the air so heavy with the scent of devil's food it made her stomach growl. Mom had given her the bowl and scraper to lick. Terri had gotten stuck with the mixing paddles, even though she'd complained those were for babies.

Her mother's kitchen. The coffeemaker carafe that was never entirely empty, the corkboard shaggy with notes in her mother's slim, neat handwriting. The secretary desk in the corner niche that served as Mom's office, where Tallulah had written the note in green felt-tip pen telling them she was leaving.

Maeve's in Florida. That's where I'll be. She'd almost written *Love.* Then decided not to. Instead she'd just signed, *Debra.* So that her mother would know she was serious. That she wasn't coming back.

For the first time, she wondered if Mom had cried when she read it. The last time Tallulah had seen Mom cry was the morning after Daddy had left. Would she have cried this time? Sitting at the kitchen table, her face lowered into her hands, Tallulah's note raw as a sore on the red and white tablecloth, no *Love,* nothing?

Tallulah shoved her chair away from the table and got

186

up. Twelve thirty here. Nine thirty in Oregon. No one would be home. She paused at the phone on the wall. No. Not here. Anyone could walk in. But the office had a door that closed. It would take only a minute to leave a message.

Jolene was back already; Tallulah could hear her in the treatment room, talking to someone over the blast of the radio. Poteet, probably, getting ready to start the day's surgeries. She ducked down the hall to the office and eased the door closed. Leaning over Ruth's desk, she tapped in the numbers of home.

Ringing. What should she say? Everything's fine. Don't worry. I'll call you soon.

The receiver clicked. "Badowskis'," Terri said.

Tallulah froze.

Terri's voice sharpened. "Hello? Who is this?"

"Tallulah!" Jolene yelled from the hallway. "Where you at? *Tallulah!*" On the other end of the phone, Terri sucked in her breath. "Debbie? Is that you?"

Tallulah slammed the phone down just as Jolene swung open the office door, Diesel yawning on a leash next to her. When he saw Tallulah he wagged his tail leisurely, like an old person waving.

"Did you leave this dog loose?" Jolene demanded.

Terri worked in the mornings. What was she doing home? "I was only gone for a minute," Tallulah said.

"Long enough for him to steal my dinner. Now I don't have nothing to eat and we got six surgeries to get through yet."

187

"You can have my chicken. I ate hardly any of it."

"Yeah, well, he got the rest."

"What's going on?" Poteet said from the hallway.

Jolene pointed at Tallulah, "She left her damn dog loose in the kitchen. Ate my hot dog and a mess of fried chicken. Guess we get to see if any of them bones puncture his insides." She tugged sharply on the leash. "Come on, dog." As she passed Poteet she said, "If you don't get me some decent help I swear to *God* I'm going to quit. See if that little girl in there can take your X-rays and run all your lab work and do all your damn anesthesia!" Until her voice faded down the hallway, Poteet's gaze seemed locked somewhere above Tallulah's head. After the door to the treatment room slammed, his eyes traveled slowly down to her face.

"Will it hurt him?" Tallulah asked. "The chicken bones?"

"What were you doing in here?"

She walked to the door, but Poteet didn't move out of her way. "Excuse me," she said.

Debbie, is that you? Terri's tone: angry, accusing.

She didn't look at Poteet. She didn't have to; she knew what she'd see. An expression in his eyes like Jolene's. Like Mom's, that last night. Cold. Contemptuous. *I don't want to see you anymore.*

"Please," she whispered. Poteet stepped aside. She fled into the hallway.

Chapter 15

Cast-iron stomach," was all Jolene muttered the next morning, when Tallulah asked how Diesel was. He seemed fine, too, scarfing down the bland diet of cottage cheese and rice Poteet had prescribed for him, plus the three biscuits Tallulah smuggled into his bowl.

During a sleepless night on Ruth's sofa, Tallulah had decided not to call home again. Not yet. Today was Saturday; six more days and she'd have her pay. Another day after that and she'd be in Florida. Much better to call from Florida. She still couldn't figure out how to explain Tennessee. It was better not to try.

Jolene's mood was as cantankerous as the day before; she'd been late again picking up her son, and that morning she'd picked a fight with Poteet, insisting that if he was going to make her work overtime, he could just damn well pay the extra day care. Now, except for Poteet's stone-faced orders and Jolene's sardonic Yes *sir*'s, they were barely speaking. Of the two of them, though, Tallulah preferred Poteet, and once the cleaning was done, she was glad to escape to the exam rooms. Already clipboards were stacked like an untidy deck of cards on the back hall counter. Poteet appeared in the hallway only to get things: a vial of medication, the otoscope, Tallulah. An exam room door would open, he would take one long stride to the counter or the refrigerator or a shelf, reach and grab and disappear back into the room. He reminded her of an octopus she'd seen once on a nature show, whipping tentacles from its rock crevice to snare its prey, then recoiling into shadows.

In the middle of the morning, Poteet emerged from an exam room with a tiny orange kitten cradled against his shoulder. He jerked his head at Tallulah and started down the hallway. She trotted after him.

"Leukemia test," he said, once they were in the treatment room. He handed the kitten to her. She scruffed up high on its neck and tried to lay it on its side, the way Kyle had showed her, but she couldn't get all its scuffling little feet off the table. Poteet helped her.

She hated holding the little kittens. Their veins were blue threads, barely as wide as six of Tallulah's hairs; next to them, the needles seemed huge, a violation. Tallulah squinched up her face in anticipation. Sure enough, the instant Poteet slipped the needle in, the kitten arched its back, sucked down a double lungful of air, and screeched. Tallulah squeezed her eyes shut until Poteet let go of the leg and the screaming stopped. Immediately Tallulah clamped a finger over the needle puncture to keep it from bleeding. The kitten writhed and scratched her, raising tiny rags of skin across the back of her hand.

"Good," Poteet murmured. Tallulah stared at him. Aside from his remark in the diner, this was the first praise he'd ever offered. He took the kitten and nodded at the syringe of blood on the table. "Give that to Jolene. If it's negative, pull up an FVRCP and get a flea treatment. Oh, and there's a fecal sample in the lab, start that running too. You remember what an FVRCP is?"

"Yes."

"Good. Snap to it." As Poteet walked away the kitten squirreled itself backward on his shoulder and stared at Tallulah, its head bobbing with Poteet's stride, the trauma already forgotten.

By one thirty, only two clients remained in the lobby. Ruth's head popped around the corner of the hallway. She gestured to Tallulah.

"Bring the mop bucket on up," she said. "Soon as the last client's in a room, start mopping the lobby. That way anyone comes in'll get the idea we're done for the day and we might get this picnic started before sundown."

At two o'clock the front door was locked. Tallulah was in the ward putting the mop bucket away when Kyle came up behind her.

"Come on, " he said. "Let's go."

"Go where?"

"Picnic, where else?" Kyle said.

"I thought I was going with Ruth."

"She's still gotta do the books. You want to, though, you could wait for her. I bet Jolene could find some dog poop for you to clean up somewhere."

In the hallway, Kyle stopped so abruptly she stepped on his heel. "Ow! Watch where you're going, girl." Then he reached back and laid a hand on her arm. "Wait," he whispered.

Tallulah could hear Poteet walking through the lobby. He wouldn't be able to see them unless he turned right, down the exam room hallway. Kyle's fingers tensed on her wrist, and Tallulah pressed close behind him, making herself small. She felt a sudden thrill, as if they were committing some kind of crime rather than just sneaking out of work.

Poteet's footsteps headed into the office. "Ruth," he called.

"Now!" Kyle hissed. He pulled her arm; they darted past the office doorway and out the back door, rocketing down the porch steps. By the time they got to the bottom, they were both laughing. "Wait here, I'll be right back," Kyle said. He ran through the carport and up the flight of stairs leading to his apartment.

Tallulah looked around. There was something oddly familiar about the air. The light had seemed to change color. Not dim, exactly. Tinted, as though someone had covered the sky with a dull green glass.

The night she'd found Diesel. Hitchhiking through the storm. Tallulah looked straight up. Sure enough, the sun had disappeared behind a mass of thunderheads. The heat had become even more oppressive, and wind drove a spattering of rain into her face. She turned to see Kyle trotting down the stairs, two jackets slung over his arm, one nylon, the other leather.

"I hope Jolene got that awning," she said, as he handed her the leather jacket. She slipped it on. The shoulders sagged over her upper arms, the sleeves hooded her fingertips. "Nice," she said. "Can I keep it?"

"No. Come on." She followed him across the back lot, to a metal shed behind the barn. He opened the door and gestured inside.

"No way," she said.

He grinned at her. "You ain't chicken, are you?"

"Of course I'm not chicken."

He went into the shed and backed the motorcycle out. It was a little one, red and chrome. It didn't appear to have much of a backseat. "Ain't you ever rode a motorcycle before?" he asked. "I thought you met that friend of yours, what's-her-name, at a Harley show."

"Her name is Maeve and yes, I did, but—"

"Wait, I almost forgot," he said. He went back into the shed and came out with a helmet. "Put this on," he said, holding it out to her.

"What about you?"

"Don't wear 'em. Can't feel the wind like you ought. Wait, give me that back." He turned the helmet upside down, swept a hand inside it. "No spiders," he said. He helped her with it, threading the chin strap through the rings, snugging it up. "All set," he said.

With the helmet faceplate closed, her head felt twice its size and wobbly. Kyle got on the bike. At his gesture, she lifted her right leg over and hitched herself onto the seat behind him. There were foot pegs, but no handholds, not even a sissy bar to lean back against. "What do I hold on to?" she yelled through the faceplate.

"Either hang on to me, or . . ." Kyle called over his shoulder.

"Or what?"

"Sit up real, real straight."

"And fall off. No thanks." She put her hands lightly on either side of his waist, barely touching him. The bike leapt to life underneath her. She swayed backward; in a surge of panic, she slid her arms around him, clasping her hands in front.

"Don't you dare think this means anything!" she yelled in his ear.

He turned his head. He was laughing. "Don't worry, I won't hold you to nothing," he yelled back. "Look!" Following his nod, Tallulah glanced back at the carport. Poteet, for once in neither coveralls nor white coat, his tie loosened, was coming down the porch steps. He saw them and waved. Tallulah braved letting go with one hand and waved back.

"Looks like he might make it to his own party," Kyle shouted. He accelerated the motorcycle up the driveway past the hospital, then stopped in the front parking lot. A car had pulled up to the building. Kyle jerked his head at

Tallulah: Get off. She did, tottering a little from the weight of the helmet. Kyle switched off the engine, swung off the bike, and walked over to the car, where a young man and a girl holding a squirming baby were getting out.

"Need something?" Kyle called. Tallulah fumbled with the chin strap. She couldn't get it loose, so she settled for pushing up the faceplate.

The girl came around the front of the car. Before the baby, her figure had probably been cute. Now she was low-slung through the belly and starting on a double chin. The baby wore a pink tank top, a diaper, and nothing else.

"There's a cat been hit on the road up by State Bank," she said.

"Your cat?" Kyle asked.

"No. But it's layin' out there and it'll get hit again if someone don't go get it. It ain't above three miles, just up by the bank."

"Westbound side," the man said. He wore a black Jack Daniels baseball cap that he pushed back on his head, giving Tallulah a glimpse of too-big blue eyes in a round face before he pulled it down low again.

The baby began to make little huffing noises. The girl fished in her shorts pocket, emerged with a pacifier, and stuck it in the baby's mouth.

Kyle swung his head around, looked past Tallulah. He seemed to be considering. He turned to face the couple again. "Vet's gone," he said. "But Dr. Bodean over to Greeley Hill, he's open till three. You could bring it there."

"She just told you," the man said. "It ain't our cat."

The baby spit out the pacifier. It bounced on the gravel. The girl didn't seem to notice. "While we're standing here the poor thing's layin' out in this heat dyin'," she said. "Somebody has to go get it."

Tallulah walked over to the pacifier, picked it up, and gave it to the girl. The baby stared at Tallulah, an intense baby-stare, open-mouthed, rapt. The baby had blue eyes, too. From behind the building, she could hear the truck engine shifting into gear.

"Ain't nobody here but me and I ain't got a car," Kyle said. "Look, whyn't you call the Humane Society? They'll . . ."

"Screw that," the man said. He gestured to the girl. "Come on, Jessie. They don't give a shit, they ain't gonna help." They got back in the car. As they pulled out, Tallulah could see the baby fussing on her mother's lap. The girl stuck the pacifier back in the baby's mouth.

Poteet's truck lumbered up the drive. As it came even with the motorcycle, he leaned out the window. "Everything all right?" he called.

"Just somebody needed directions," Kyle said.

"Must be my lucky day," Poteet said. "Ruth called me back in the hospital but turns out she just forgot to get paper plates. You think you-all could swing by Wal-Mart?" He looked tired, the skin under his eyes sagging; but he was smiling, rare for him when no clients were around.

"Sure," Kyle said.

Poteet fished a twenty out of his wallet, handed it to

Kyle. "Good. Then I can go home and get the grill going. Most years," he told Tallulah, "I get called to some emergency or other and poor Ruth ends up running the whole show. Last year I didn't get home until the whole dang party was over. Be nice if this year turns out different." He raised a hand; Tallulah waved back. As the truck surged onto the highway, she said, "What are we going to do about the cat?"

"That road ain't much out of our way," Kyle said. "If there really is a cat, I got my cell phone. I'll call the Humane Society, they'll come get it."

"Seems like there's a lot of run-over animals around here," Tallulah said.

Kyle shrugged one shoulder. "This is only the second one since you been here, counting Diesel. Last month once we got two in a night." He swung onto the seat, gestured for her to follow. "Come on, girl. Daylight's burning."

He gave her no warning before gunning the motorcycle onto the highway. Tallulah lurched backward, yelped, and clenched her arms tighter around Kyle's waist. Lightning flashed off to the left. As if waiting for this signal, the thunderheads burst. In seconds her jeans were soaked through. She screamed again, this time to hear her voice tear away in the wind, and then she began to laugh. It occurred to her that she hadn't laughed, really laughed, since she'd last seen Maeve. She missed laughing. It felt good.

Kyle also felt good. He had a very nice waist, slim and muscly. Might as well enjoy it, she thought, and snuggled a little closer. As they raced along she turned her head from side to side, partly to take in the scenery whipping past, partly to keep the rain from spattering full onto the faceplate.

They had just come around an exhilarating sweep of a curve when the bike abruptly slowed. Tallulah jolted forward, bumping the side of her helmet against Kyle's neck.

"What is it?" she yelled. She didn't want to waste any part of this ride going slow.

"Accident," he yelled back. "Looks like it just happened." He drove the bike forward at a trotting pace. Tallulah unclasped her hands from around his waist and sat up straight, trying to see over his shoulder.

Ahead of them, a pickup truck stood crossways over both lanes of the highway. The driver, a man, was still in it; as Tallulah watched, he raised his hand to his head, slowly, as if dazed. The motorcycle's headlight picked out a heavy shimmer on the asphalt, heavier than the rain. Broken glass.

Kyle stopped the bike on the shoulder. Tallulah scrambled off, yanking at the chin strap on her helmet. This time it came loose. She pulled off the helmet and laid it on the ground. Kyle ran to the pickup driver. "You all right?" she heard him yell. She couldn't hear the man's answer, but she saw him nod his head.

With the motorcycle engine cut, she could hear a horn blaring. It wasn't from the pickup; it was from the car the pickup must have hit, about fifty feet ahead. She jogged along the shoulder, squinting through the rain. The car's front end dipped down into the ditch at the side of the road.

Its mangled rear end tilted up, one rear wheel off the ground. Between the pickup and the car lay two lumps, one large, one small. Both were dark and still. The horn blared on without stopping. Like a mad kitten with bottomless lungs. Tallulah began to run.

Ten feet from the larger lump, she stumbled to a halt. It was the girl from the parking lot. Rain mixed with the blood on her face and ran into her hair and over her torn lower lip where her teeth should have been. The girl didn't blink. She didn't move. She only lay there with the rain streaming over her open eyes.

Don't look, Tallulah heard her mother say. Sweetheart, don't look. But Tallulah's gaze was locked on the girl's, she couldn't break away, the girl staring as though waiting for Tallulah to do something, as though she could wait all day, all week, all year because when you're dead you don't care about time anymore.

Tallulah's heel caught and she fell backward. She landed hard, gasping. She hadn't even realized she'd moved but she must have, she'd backed all the way to the shoulder of the road. The car horn still blared. Why wasn't somebody stopping it? She got to her feet. Where were the police? Where were the people who knew what to do?

Jesus. The baby. Where was the baby?

Kyle was still with the driver of the truck. Tallulah shouted, but he didn't hear her. She turned and ran to the car. She barely registered the smaller lump, the calico cat sprawled on the asphalt.

The man sat crumpled over the steering wheel, his Jack Daniels cap skewed sideways on his head. Blood trickled down his neck. Tallulah couldn't see his face. She yanked at the door handle, but the whole side of the car was warped and the door wouldn't open. She banged on the glass with the palm of her hand.

"Are you all right?" she yelled. "Hey! Are you all right?" The man didn't move. Tallulah ran, skidding around the front bumper to the other side. The passenger door hung open. No baby in the front seat, not under the dash, not between the seats. She wiped her hair out of her eyes, then, shaking, she laid her hand against the man's neck. She'd taken CPR last year. Think, Tallulah! Where's the pulse? She couldn't remember. She didn't know. The man's flesh was clammy, not cold, nothing could be cold in the muggy rain, but the skin dented under her touch and at the thought he might be dead, too, she snatched her fingers away.

He might be alive. You can't just leave him; you have to get him out of here.

I can't.

You have to. There isn't anyone else.

She braced her knees on the passenger seat and grabbed his shirt and pulled. But he was wedged tight between the rippled door and the steering wheel and when his sleeve tore away in her hand, she sobbed in frustration.

"I'm sorry!" she yelled. "I'm sorry!" Then she backed out and began searching for the baby.

She found it—her, she found her, she learned later that

it was a girl—in tall grass on the far side of the ditch. Not at the bottom, thank God, because down there shot a fast-moving stream two inches deep. Deep enough to drown an eight-month-old. Tallulah saw the diaper first, a triangle of white against the rain-darkened grass. She scrambled across the ditch and fell on her knees at the baby's side. The baby lay like a doll tossed facedown in the grass.

Don't be dead, she prayed. Please, God, don't be dead. The pink tank top was jammed up under the baby's armpits. Rain drummed over the tiny bare back. Tallulah stared at the baby's chest. Breathe. Come on. She counted her own breaths. Sucking the air in hard, as if she could will the baby to join her. One, two. Two-and-a-half. Three.

The baby didn't breathe.

"Goddammit," she sobbed, "don't make me do this," but the baby didn't breathe, and didn't breathe, for another two of her own breaths, and then she had no choice. She reached down, spreading her hands to make a safety net of fingers, and—*careful, careful!*—she turned the baby over. It sank into the grass, a pink and white comma. The baby's eyes were half-open, its lips were slack and gray. Frantic, Tallulah pressed her fingers to the baby's chest. Nothing. She pressed harder. A flutter. She felt it again and then she was sure.

She lifted the baby and straightened out its comma-shape (Oh, God, please don't be broken, don't let me be hurting you) so that the small gray face turned up to the sky. Then she clamped her mouth over the tiny nose and lips and she blew, just a puff, she remembered that much from the CPR class, just a puff because babies are little and you can hurt their lungs.

She had no idea how long she was there, only that the flutter under her fingers never faltered, not once, and that with every puff the baby's chest lifted and fell, lifted and fell. Then a small forest of legs in yellow slickers and black boots surrounded her and a man pulled her, gently but with no room for nonsense, out of the way. She tried to stand but she couldn't feel her feet and almost fell. Someone caught her. She was glad to see it was Kyle.

One of the yellow-slicker men placed a mask over the baby's face. "Little puffs," she yelled. They had to listen, it was important. "Little puffs!"

We know, someone said, and someone else said, Get her back, son; but she wouldn't leave until she saw them carry the baby away on a stretcher, with the man giving little puffs running alongside. There were two ambulances and a lot of sheriff's cars with the blue lights going and a slew of people crawling over the mangled car like ants on a dead thing.

"I need to sit down," she said. Somehow she expected Kyle to argue, and if he did she would simply collapse and let him deal with her limp body. But all he said was, "Yeah, I expect you do," and he helped her into the field next to the ditch. He sat with her and put his arms around her and held her until she stopped shaking.

. . .

By the time they got to Poteet's, the storm had long passed, and it was late enough in the afternoon that the cicadas were in full song. The first time Tallulah had heard the bugs, she'd thought the power lines over Ruth's trailer were overloading. Now, in the aftermath of the accident, their unearthly rattles filled her with a sense of disconnect. The very air felt unstable.

She got off the motorcycle, staggering a little on the sloping gravel of Poteet's driveway. Her knees felt treacherous, not her own. When she pulled off the helmet she could hear the party, on the other side of the carport, laughter and voices raised in teasing, smells of charred meat and grill smoke. Tallulah thought of the dead girl, the blood and rain, the tarp thrown over her on the asphalt, and she thought, in a sudden rage, How dare they have fun. Then she remembered. They didn't know.

"I ain't gonna say nothing about them showing up at Dr. Poteet's," Kyle said. He meant the couple in the accident. He'd said the same thing in the emergency room, after the ICU nurse reassured them that the baby was alive and breathing on her own. He said it now like he had then, as if he'd thrown a pebble and was waiting for a noise to see if it hit. Then, Tallulah hadn't answered.

Now she said, "We should have sent Poteet to get that cat."

Kyle strode toward her and grasped her upper arm and pushed her stumbling down the driveway, away from the house. "Don't you say that," he said.

Tallulah wrenched her arm out of his grip. "I *will* say it. I should have told that deputy when he was taking our statements. I heard them; they think that guy stopped in the middle of the road for no reason. They said he might be charged with something. That girl's *dead*, Kyle!"

"She was standing in front of a car in the middle of the goddamned highway in the rain. What the hell did she think would happen?" Kyle glanced back at the house, then tried to push her another step down the driveway. Tallulah shoved him away from her with both hands. He leaned forward, jabbing a finger at her. "Nobody told them to park in the middle of the road like that. Nobody told her to go walking in front of the car. Or leave the door hanging open so the baby'd fly out. Should have had a baby seat anyway. What were they doing, little baby like that and no baby seat? Huh?"

Tallulah said nothing. He stared at her then kicked the ground, a vicious dig with his boot that sent gravel flying. "If people decide to be stupid, that ain't my fault," he said.

Tallulah turned away. Poteet's lawn—a deep blue green, smooth as carpet—ranged over the entire top of the hill. Six greenhouses stood in short rows catty-corner to each other. Through the clear ripply wall of the nearest one, she could see the shadows of flowers, a hazy sword of leaf. Behind her, she heard Kyle walking away.

"Wait," she said.

He let her walk ahead of him over the narrow flagstone path that ran between the carport and the house. On the other side, another broad, grassy hill sloped down to a lake. Near the water were the awnings: two, not one, a picnic table under each, twenty or so people sitting or milling, talking and eating and laughing. Tallulah recognized only Poteet and Ruth and Jolene.

Poteet was standing next to an enormous black grill, wearing jeans, a dark red Hawaiian shirt with white flowers, and the UT baseball cap. When he saw them, he waved a spatula over his head. "Ta-a-arnation, Kyle, where in hell are my paper plates!" he yelled. "Where you two been? Smooching in the barn?" Laughter erupted from the crowd. Someone yelled something from one of the picnic tables. She didn't catch it, but Kyle ducked his head and ran a hand over the back of his neck.

"Ruth was about to send the sheriff after you," Poteet said. "Hard as that rain was coming down a little while ago, she thought you was two smears on the road."

Tallulah shuddered.

"There was an accident," Kyle said. "Highway this side of Exeter Road. Not us, though," he added hurriedly.

Poteet shaded his eyes and looked them up and down. "And what's Tallulah's excuse? Abducted by the aliens, I bet."

"Better give 'em a minute, let 'em get their stories straight," someone said.

"I ain't fooling," Kyle said. "Pickup smashed into a car. There was a little baby would've died but for Tallulah. She gave it CPR and saved its life."

People pressed around them. "Where was it?" "Whose baby?" "Anyone else hurt?"

"The woman died," Kyle said. "Man's got two busted legs at least."

A petite blond woman Tallulah didn't know pushed her way to the front. "Who was it, Kyle? Did they say?" she asked. Her face was grave, but her eyes were avid. Eager for gossip. Tallulah glanced around the circle enclosing her. All their eyes were the same. Except Poteet's.

He wasn't looking at them. He wasn't looking at anything. His face seemed as brittle as a teacup Tallulah had once seen in an antique store. The salesman had held it up to the window so that Tallulah's mother could admire the light seeping through the crazed eggshell porcelain. The cup had looked as though it might shatter at a tap, or a wrong word spoken aloud.

She died instantly. She was the bravest person I ever knew.

"Never saw them before," Kyle said.

How had Poteet found out his daughter was dead? A phone call in the middle of the night, a deputy at his door?

Tallulah felt Kyle's eyes on her. The air seemed suddenly fragile. She shook her head.

"I never saw them before either," she said.

They were made to sit at one of the tables. Iced tea was poured for Tallulah, a beer for Kyle. Kyle did all the talking. When he got to the part about finding Tallulah kneeling on the bank of the ditch, with her mouth over the baby's, Jolene pulled a stout blond toddler onto her lap and hugged him, rocking, her face buried in his hair. The child whimpered; she murmured in his ear, and he hushed.

They asked her questions. She didn't want to talk about it. The desperate minutes in the ditch were sacred, like nothing she'd ever possessed. The baby's flesh belonged to her. She did not want to spread it out for these strangers to finger, step on, examine.

"Bless your heart," they murmured. "Bless your heart." The women touched her shoulders, her elbows, her back. The men nodded at her. She noticed the gray edges receding from Poteet's face. A girl dead in an accident, she thought. Somebody's daughter. The cicadas overhead suddenly became very loud; the inside of her skull buzzed with them. Her vision blurred.

"Watch it, she's gonna faint!" Hands under her shoulders, her head.

"Sit forward, honey." Ruth's voice. "Head between your knees. That's it." More hands rubbed her back. A glass of iced tea appeared, hovering over the grass; someone had snaked it under her knees. She wondered how they thought she was going to drink it upside down.

The dizzy spell passed, and she sat up. People wandered away to get more food, or discipline their children, or talk in their own small circles. Kyle went to toss a football with Jolene's husband—a jovial, crew-cutted man—down by the lakeshore. Ruth and Jolene sat chatting with the blond woman, who turned out to be the wife of Poteet's accountant. From time to time, Ruth smiled at Tallulah and dropped tidbits on her plate: another dollop of potato salad, a cookie. When Tallulah was full, she pushed her plate away and sipped her iced tea and watched a group of children playing tag on a level stretch of lawn. There were five of them, all between the ages of six and ten, except for one tiny girl with mouse brown hair who looked to be about three. When the children scattered and ran, shrieking, the mousy-haired girl raised her arms and danced in a circle. The boy who was It walked up behind her and leaned down and tapped her shoulder. "You're It!" he yelled.

At the utter astonishment on the girl's face, Tallulah burst out sobbing.

Chapter 16

The women gathered around her again, murmuring and soothing. "I'm all right," Tallulah said, her voice hiccupy with tears. She waved a hand in front of her face. "Really. I'm all right."

Next to her, a beer bottle thudded down on the scarred wood of the table. Poteet swung his leg over the bench and sat astride it. "You haven't seen my orchids yet," he said. "Come on, I'll give you the tour."

"Poor girl just saved a baby," Ruth said. "Leave her a bit, can't you?"

"Nonsense. Best thing for her."

Tallulah stood up. In the past half hour the conversation at the table had drifted from speculation about the accident, to rose pruning, to breast-feeding, and she'd heard all she could take on all three subjects.

Instead of going straight up the hill to the greenhouses, though, Poteet led Tallulah down to the lake. He didn't say anything and Tallulah was grateful. An absence of words suited her.

The lakeshore cupped inward, cradling the water like the palm of a hand. Tallulah stood on the bank, a sloping three-foot wall of rocks, and watched the waves lap beneath her feet. The water was dark, almost black, glistening silver where the sun hit it. It wasn't as smooth as she would have imagined.

As if he'd overheard her thinking, Poteet said, "Wind's kicking up a chop."

"I didn't know you lived on a lake."

"No reason you should," he said, and then added, "It's artificial."

"Oh." Clouds scudded toward them. They looked like marching columns, charcoal at the bottom, their humped tops blinding white.

"We meant to get a boat ourselves," Poteet said. "Go out on the lake of a Sunday." A plastic ball swirling with color bounced toward them, three children hard after it. Poteet bent down and scooped the ball up and tossed it to the boy bringing up the rear. The kid flubbed the catch but got it off the ground and began running in the opposite direction. The other children yelped and scrambled after him.

Poteet turned and began walking up the hill. Tallulah followed him. A little way ahead, Jolene was bending over one of the coolers, her son hanging onto her knee. Tallulah had never seen her out of hospital scrubs. She was wearing a sleeveless denim blouse and shorts; her hair, freed from its usual braids, broke in dark blond wavelets almost down to her waist. She fished out a piece of ice and gave it to her

son, giggling at his attempts to hold it, catching it—
whoopsie!—when it slipped. She had the same absorbed,
cheerful manner with him that she did with her patients,
only merrier, the dimples in her cheeks deeper. Seeing
those dimples made Tallulah wonder, again, how someone
so soft with little helpless things could be such a crab to her
co-workers.

Jolene straightened up. Poteet waved to her. In an instant both laughter and dimples disappeared, replaced by
the grim-eyed flintiness she'd shown him all day. She picked
up her son and turned her back.

Poteet sighed. "Ruth's after me to make nice," he said.
"I suppose I ought to."

Surprised, Tallulah looked at him. She'd never heard
him sound like this—rueful, almost—and he'd sure never
talked about any of the staff, at least not to her. She glanced
again at Jolene, facing away from them with her weight on
one hip, the leg underneath as unyielding as a tree trunk.
Even her back radiated resentment. "Why?" she asked.

Poteet made an aggravated noise in his throat. "Because
Jolene's got a bug up her butt. Because somebody has to.
Ruth likes to say our staff's like family. Sometimes it's too
damn much like family, if you ask me." He took off his baseball cap and scratched over one ear. "But Jolene's the best
technician I've ever had. And I'm the boss. So it falls to me, I
guess." He paused, as if considering; Tallulah stopped with
him. "Ah, hell," he said. He snugged the baseball cap back on
and started again up the hill. "It can wait until Monday."

Jolene's husband sprinted in front of them. Poteet stopped short and barred Tallulah's way with his arm, as though he'd hit the brakes in a car; an automatic gesture, unselfconscious. Jolene's husband lunged high, fingered a soaring football out of the air, took two long, stumbling strides, then trotted in a half-circle, football held overhead. From the table where the women sat came a spatter of applause; Jolene whistled. He waved to her, grinned at Poteet. "'Scuse me," he said, panting. He pivoted, bellowing, "Heads up, Kyle!"

Poteet gestured Tallulah onward, his hand on her back. Tallulah watched as the football sailed over Kyle's head and thudded to the ground behind him. He didn't seem to see it; he was staring at her and Poteet.

As they walked up the hill, Tallulah studied Poteet's house. Ruth had called it a two-room shack, and certainly, compared to the white-columned, red-roofed mansions directly across the lake, that description didn't seem far off. The house was tiny, shingled in brown, and, except for its white window frames, almost invisible against its backdrop of fir trees. Its only touch of distinction was the wide brick chimney rising from the back of the house.

It'll do as a summer home, Tallulah could hear her mother saying. If there were no children. But the location is premium, of course, and you can always build bigger.

But Tallulah liked it. The house seemed somehow self-reliant.

On the flagstone path curving toward the carport, they

met a man coming the other direction. He was older, large, taller than Poteet and bigger around. He wore loose trousers and the ubiquitous baseball cap; his was bright green, with a John Deere logo.

"Ronald," Poteet said, surprise evident in his voice.

"'Afternoon, Charles," the man said. "Sorry to bother you at your house, but I figured better here than at work. Hope you don't mind."

"Not at all," Poteet said. He gestured down the hill. "Summer barbeque for the clinic. You're welcome to join us, you'll know some of the people." His eyes flicked across the man's face, the carport, the trees. "Ah . . . Ellen with you?"

"No, she's at home. As I say, I hate to take you from your party, but if you can spare a minute . . ."

"Sure, sure."

"No point beating around the bush, Charles. Ellen wants to buy out your half of Kasmir."

Poteet dragged his cap off again; Tallulah edged slightly away, in case he was going to chuck it, but he only slapped it against his thigh.

"I've been through this already," Poteet said. "I told Ellen's secretary and now I'll tell you and maybe one of you will get through to Ellen herself. I'm not selling."

"Well, the difficulty is, Charles, we are."

Poteet cocked his head slightly to one side, as if he hadn't heard. "I don't—"

"Farm up in Ohio called us. They've had their eye on Kasmir some time now. Truth is, they want him pretty bad."

"Ellen wouldn't sell Kasmir." It was a flat statement. The man didn't reply; he just sucked in the left corner of his mouth, as if working an invisible lollipop, and regarded Poteet from under the brim of his cap.

"Why?" Poteet's voice was harsh. The man blinked.

"Not sure that's any of your business. We contacted these people, that's all, and they're interested, and we decided to sell him."

"Contacted them? You just said they called you."

The man chuckled, waved a hand. "All this horse stuff is new to me, you know that. In any case, Charles, they want the horse and we want to sell. Except we can't, of course, until you sell us your half first. Of course, now that you know, you can simply sign the bill of sale as co-owner and we'll split the proceeds fifty-fifty."

"Name your price."

"Beg your pardon?"

"I'll buy him. If Ellen doesn't want him anymore, I'll buy him. Name your price."

The man shook his head. "You couldn't afford him, Charles. Not what these Ohio people are paying. And—to be absolutely honest . . ." he paused, working the invisible lollipop. "Well, I'm sorry to say it, but Ellen doesn't want you to have him."

The brittle expression slipped back over Poteet's face. When he spoke, it took Tallulah a moment to realize he was talking to her. "Take Mr. Hewitt on down to the barbecue, will you?" he said. "Get him a beer from the cooler."

"Charles—" the man said, but Poteet strode past him into the carport. The man started to follow; then he slipped his hands into his trouser pockets and shrugged. He turned to Tallulah. "Say, you know Jolene? Works at the clinic with Dr. Poteet there."

"Yeah," Tallulah said.

"Would you do me the favor of giving her a message? Would you let her know my wife, Ellen, wants to talk to her? Just tell her Ellen. She'll know."

Tallulah nodded.

" 'Preciate it," he said. "Enjoy the party."

She watched the man drive away. Then went looking for Poteet. She couldn't find him.

Chapter 17

Sunday afternoon, Ruth took Tallulah grocery shopping. Tallulah was reluctant. Every time she went out in this town, people stared, and she was tired of it.

In the Food Lion she stayed a half step behind Ruth, arms crossed, her gaze fixed on the Froot Loops and Pop-Tarts. So when the first woman nodded hello to her, she missed it. Ruth had to touch her arm to get her attention for the introductions.

It went that way all afternoon: the grocery store, the Wal-Mart, the gas station. Ruth had lived all her life in this town; she knew Everyone. And Everyone shook Tallulah's hand and called her by name and said, Hello, good to know you, how're you liking Clark Station? One or two phrased it, You're liking Clark Station better *now*, I *hope*, with an amused squint at the corners of their eyes, as though the circumstances of her arrival, the arrest, jail, were nothing more than an in-joke to which they were privy. Others, by not mentioning it, seemed to convey that the whole business was an unfortunate misunderstanding, best soon forgotten. A few of the women shook their heads and said, Bless your heart, child. As if she'd been lost to the wolves and brought home.

It was the rescue that had changed things, of course. Everyone wanted to know about the accident, about finding the baby in the ditch, about the CPR. Tallulah still didn't want to discuss that. Not with strangers. If Maeve were here, Tallulah would have delved into every detail, the terrifying, soul-lifting brush of the baby's cheek against hers, the fluttering of the tiny heart under her fingers, the way time had pulled itself out thin, like the old-fashioned taffy at the Rose Festival back home. But Maeve wasn't here.

Tallulah had called the hospital that morning to see how the baby was doing. Through some network of neighbors and friends, Ruth had discovered the baby's name. *Crystal-Amber,* Tallulah had murmured to herself as she'd looked up the hospital's number. *Crystal-Amber,* she'd said to the receptionist. No, I'm not a relative. The brisk voice on the other end told her only that Crystal-Amber was stable and out of ICU; the same information, it turned out, that was in the morning paper. But when Tallulah relayed it to curious strangers, they digested it solemnly, as though they hadn't heard it before. Then came an invariable, informal moment of silence, broken only by a close-mouthed Mmm-mm-mm. Tallulah understood, without being told, that this was for the mother.

One woman leaned forward and laid her hand on Tallulah's bare arm and said, God meant for that child to live. He

217

put you in her way on purpose. That was when Tallulah began to understand how her standing in the town had changed, and by what measure. The realization made her feel as if she were staring in a mirror, wondering which of her was real.

In the few silences that fell between them in the Pontiac, Tallulah considered telling Ruth about the couple coming to the veterinary hospital, about the cat hit on the road. But then she remembered Kyle—*what were they doing, little baby like that and no baby seat?*—and the brittleness on Poteet's face, and she felt herself baffled, tangled up in the *how*.

Sunday nights Ruth cooked a real supper. She was just laying the raw breaded steaks in the skillet when Kyle knocked on the door. Ruth made a show of twisting his arm to stay and eat, but from the practiced way he set himself a place and pulled up a chair, Tallulah guessed he mooched pretty often.

There was certainly enough food for three, what with potato salad and cornbread and sautéed greens accompanying the chicken-fried steak. Tallulah drank three glasses of iced tea; it did more to push back the muggy heat than the air conditioner chugging crankily in Ruth's kitchen window.

At first their conversation followed the same lines as it had in town that morning: Crystal-Amber, Crystal-Amber's mother, her father, the accident. Tallulah was sick of the subject. She glanced at Kyle fiddling his fork through his greens. He'd probably gotten it ten times worse than she had. And now Ruth was pumping him for more details.

When Ruth paused for breath, Tallulah jumped in with the first topic that popped into her head.

"So what's this thing with Dr. Poteet's horse?" she said.

Caught between two equally engaging subjects of gossip, Ruth paused, fork halfway to her mouth.

"I didn't even know Dr. Poteet had a horse," Kyle said. He leaned forward on his elbows, the fork dangling from his fingers.

The distraction worked. Ruth chewed thoughtfully. "Well, they used to breed them, you know. Dr. Poteet and Ellen. Ellen and Emily—that was his daughter," she said in an aside to Tallulah, who nodded, "they showed those horses all over, over to Nashville, South Carolina, North Carolina, and I don't know where all. Kasmir, though, he was the best. He was special."

Kyle picked a bit of steak off his plate, leaned down to give it to Cowboy. Ruth noticed—Ruth noticed everything—but she continued her story. "Emily's pictures in the office, those are all her and Kasmir. She and her folks used to fight something fierce over him. Kasmir was a stallion, and Dr. Poteet said he was too dangerous for her to ride."

"But she did ride him," Tallulah said.

"Emily did what she wanted," Ruth said. "When she was killed, Lord, that was a terrible time. Kyle, there's another steak in that pan."

"Yes ma'am." Kyle got up, headed to the kitchen.

"Then Ellen left," Ruth said, "and Dr. Poteet let her take the house, the land, all the critters. Except Kasmir. He's the only one they still own together. Ellen fought him on it at the time, but Dr. Poteet just wouldn't let go of that horse."

Kyle sat back down. Cowboy laid his chin on Kyle's thigh. Ruth frowned, but before she could say anything, Kyle asked, "If he's so crazy about the horse, how come she has it? Seems he'd of kept it himself."

"Where? The hospital barn's no place for a stallion and there's no room at the lake, even if he hadn't put up all those greenhouses. Besides, Ellen's the one breeds him and shows him. Dr. Poteet doesn't have time for that."

"Does he ride him?" Tallulah asked.

"Never did have time, even before. Now he only sees Kasmir once a year or so. Gives him his vaccines, looks him over." Ruth pushed back her chair and began stacking plates. "I think he just wants to hang on to something Emily loved, even if it's just to have his name on it."

Ruth and Tallulah cleared the table. Kyle made a show of helping, then wandered into the living room.

"This your friend?" he asked. Tallulah looked up to see him holding the Polaroid of her and Maeve. She must have left it on the coffee table after showing it to Ruth.

"Give me that," she said. She tried to swipe it from him, but Kyle shifted the photograph to his other hand, out of her reach. When Tallulah grabbed for it again, he swung it overhead. He was tall, at least half a head taller than she was, and from the airy smirk on his face he was expecting her to jump for it. Instead she dove her hands into his exposed flank and tickled him, not stopping even after he'd dropped the Polaroid, not until he grabbed both her wrists and held her at arms' length away from him, snorting laughter. He let go when Ruth came around the corner into the living room. She bent and picked up the photograph.

"Pretty, isn't she?" Ruth said.

"The redhead?" Kyle shrugged. "I've seen prettier."

"For your information," Tallulah said, snatching the Polaroid from Ruth, "Maeve had guys *begging* her to go out with them. They thought she was gorgeous."

"Too fat for me," he said. Ruth *tsk*'d and swatted at his shoulder.

Cretin. Tallulah slipped the photograph back into her duffel, zipping it shut as loudly, and emphatically, as she could. What did he know, anyway? Small-town hick like him, probably the closest thing he'd ever had to a girlfriend was a porn video.

"Kitchen's too small for more than one person in this heat," Ruth said. "Kyle, take Tallulah on up the hill. Show her the graveyard while it's still light."

As soon as they were outside, Tallulah said, "I don't want to see any graveyard. I'm going down to the creek." She'd discovered the little birch-lined creek the other day. It was pretty, and the coolest place outdoors she'd found yet in this state.

Kyle grinned at her. "Scared?"

"No, I'm not *scared*. I just bet it's cooler down by the creek."

"It ain't," Kyle said. He led her through Ruth's yard to

the cow pasture beyond, ducked through the fence, then held the strands of barbed wire apart for her. As Tallulah followed Kyle across the corner of the pasture, she kept one nervous eye on the cows. But they lay under a stand of trees at the far end, seemingly uncaring about the intrusion. The far bigger threat was cow pies. She picked her way carefully through the grass.

At the far fence line, Kyle had to hunt a bit through brush tangled in the wire. Beyond the fence, the ground rose into a heavily wooded hill. A narrow trail disappeared among the trees.

"Ruth said there's rattlesnakes," Tallulah said.

"Don't go stomping under any bushes and they won't bother you," Kyle said. "Here's the gate." The gate was nothing more than four strands of wire stretched between a couple of two-by-fours; he folded it back, and, when they were both through, closed it with a loop of smooth wire passed over a stationary post. He set off up the trail. Tallulah sighed and trudged after him, trying to step where he stepped, alert to any rustlings in the carpeting of leaves. The light wasn't dim, exactly, but with all the trees and vines and brush she probably wouldn't see a snake even if she looked right at it. Ruth said their colors and speckles made them look like nothing more than a row of pebbles on dirt. As she walked, Tallulah studied the ground so intently that when Kyle stopped she ran into his back.

"So where is this place?" she asked. What were you supposed to say about a graveyard? Boy, would you look at the carving on that headstone. What a thrill, now let's leave.

Kyle stepped to the side. "Right here," he said.

She looked past him. There were no headstones. Not even a little fence showing where the borders of the cemetery lay. There was nothing but a clearing, really not more than a widening of the trail, perhaps twenty feet across at most. Straight ahead lay a parked car.

A very old car, by the still-graceful arc of its tailfins. Any other grace it may have possessed had long since vanished. Along with its wheels and doors. And seats, Tallulah saw as she edged up to it. The car was sunk so deeply in the ground that drifts of pine needles and leaves stretched uninterrupted between the floorboards and the embracing earth. The paint job might have been blue once. Or green.

"Fifty-two Merc coupe," Kyle said. "That over there's a forty-seven Buick. And a fifty-five DeSoto. That one used to be pink. It's faded now but still, you can tell."

A dozen cars lay in the clearing, randomly scattered as if thrown by a raging giant. Under the surrounding pines and birch and dogwood, Tallulah could make out the shapes of at least two dozen more.

"This is the graveyard?" she asked.

"Uh-huh." Kyle's voice floated out of the open DeSoto window. His entire upper body hung inside the car; he appeared to be fiddling with something on the dash. "Couldn't remember if I checked the glove compartment on that one," he said when he emerged. "I thought I'd got 'em all, but it's been a while since I been up here." He brushed at a line of dirt on his T-shirt, smearing it.

"What are they doing here? Whose are they?" Tallulah asked.

"The guy what owns all this property. The hill, and pastures, and the land Ruth's trailer's on. He has the used car lot a little ways up the highway. His papaw started it after World War II. Any cars too old or busted up to sell, they just drug 'em up here to rot."

"Do they still do that?"

"Naw. Youngest car up here's that sixty-four Ford Galaxie behind the Nash over there. Come look at this Studebaker. Hood ornament looks just like a little airplane."

They wandered uphill, drifting a slow zigzag from car to car. Tallulah ran her fingers across their pitted hoods, the mildewed sticky vinyl of their seats. They'd been shiny once. Now the chrome was blind and dull with grit, clouded as a cataract in an eye.

She leaned over the driver's door of a yellow convertible, through the open space where its ragtop used to be, and caught herself—dark-rooted, white blond hair, pale oval of a face—in the rearview mirror. She struck what she imagined was a fifties pose: head tilted, lips plumped and parted, eyelids half-closed and swooning. An unknown but outrageously beautiful actress, cruising up Hollywood Boulevard to the audition that would make her a star. She tossed her head. Her hair, limp from humidity, flapped against her cheek; her bangs tangled into her eyebrows. She flicked them loose, stuck out her tongue at the mirror, and pushed herself off the car.

The last vehicle at the top of the clearing was a '39 International Harvester pickup. What little paint it still had bristled between lakes of rust. Looking at it, and the spill of ruined cars below, Tallulah became aware for the first time of the peculiar silence. It was more than the quiet of woods; it was like being in a room full of dead things that couldn't see her and yet knew she was there and hated her because she was warm and she breathed.

A shudder rippled up her belly. "We need to leave," she said. "Right now."

Kyle took her hand. His fingers were lean and hard. She clutched at them, then, embarrassed, loosened her grip.

"Come on up top of the hill," he said.

The crest of the hill was a broad curve of earth, covered with tall, dry grass and scattered with bushes and small pines, all shorter than she, as if once upon a time the car dealer's papaw had inflicted a clear-cut here.

Kyle led her to an outcropping of boulders on the far side of the crest. He clambered onto them, selected one, and sat down. Tallulah chose a broad rock a little lower than his. The stone was rough and warm on the backs of her legs. She was wearing denim shorts that had once belonged to Ruth's daughter. Two sizes too big, but they were comfortable, and the sensation of free and unencumbered legs was worth the bagging in the butt. She'd been careful not to walk in front of Kyle.

Above her, Kyle sighed. "All we need now's some beer and we'd be about perfect," he said.

"Uh-huh," Tallulah said, although she'd rather have a margarita. How many times had she and Maeve shared margaritas on the roof of the Belinda? Ghosts wouldn't scare Maeve. She probably would've talked to them, made them her friends, found out their names and how they'd died. Then invited them all over for a party.

On the other hand, Maeve had never saved anyone's life. This thought was so new, Tallulah had to turn it over and around in her mind to get the full shape and weight of it.

"First time I was in the graveyard I got so spooked Ruth thought I'd got snakebit," Kyle said. "She said my face was that white. Since then, they don't bother me none. Now they're just hunks of scrap."

He reached into his shirt pocket and pulled out a mostly empty pack of cigarettes. He tapped one out for himself, then held the pack down to her. Tallulah hesitated.

It wasn't like Maeve would ever know. And anyway, Tallulah thought with irritation, so what if she did? Let Maeve go through what Tallulah had. Just one day of it. Then see if she still believed smoking was the end of the damn world.

Tallulah pinched a cigarette between finger and thumb and slid it free. The last niggling of Maeve's voice died with the lovely, throat-searing rush. She let the smoke out, watched it drift and tear apart.

"I've been thinking," Kyle said. "You know what you oughta do?" She heard him shift forward on the rock. "You oughta train for a EMT. I heard one of them talking at the accident. He said with most people that baby would've died. He said they'd of panicked and not known what to do."

"An EMT? You mean like a paramedic?"

"EMT's like the first step. Paramedic trains a whole extra year. It's good work. Good money."

Tallulah took another drag, tapped the ash on a rock. "You really think I could do that?" she said. "Save people's lives?"

Kyle's voice was casual as a shrug. "You did once already," he said.

"I guess I did." The memory of the baby's flesh on hers was like a ghost's touch. Invisible, slightly chill.

The daylight was settling into its long, subtle fade. Hills ranged to the horizon, line after line of them, like soldiers in a ragged formation, hazy in the late, muggy light, shading from green to blue to a purple gray that dissolved into the sky as she watched.

She and Maeve had had hills to look at, too, but theirs were studded with lights, and instead of this lancing quiet they'd had to raise their voices over the hum of traffic, people talking on the street below, sirens and horns and barking dogs.

She knew she would never have that again. The kind of friendship that made her feel bigger than herself, as if between the two of them, she and Maeve, they could do anything, be anything. Nobody could be like them. Nobody could touch them.

She was alone again, and small.

Only somehow, she wasn't.

"I never thought I'd be in a place like this," she said. "Not in a million years."

"Where? Tennessee?" Kyle asked.

"Yeah." Tallulah scootched her butt, easing a spot where the rock dug in. "No. I don't know. Everything." She held out a hand and studied it. The flesh of her fingertips just under the nails still felt raw and new, as though startled by their sudden exposure to the world. Work had broken two nails, and her polish—gorgeous, a burgundy so deep it was almost black—had chipped so badly that two nights ago Tallulah had borrowed Ruth's manicure kit and scrubbed away the remainder. Then she'd picked up the clippers and chopped back the rest. She hadn't had bare nails since she was thirteen.

Sitting on a rooftop with Maeve. Feeling bigger than life. But what had she done, really? Gotten a tattoo. Drunk some margaritas. Talked a lot.

Tallulah stubbed out her half-finished cigarette and flicked the butt down the hillside.

"Want another?" Kyle asked. The cigarette pack floated into the side of her vision. She forced herself to shake her head. The flick of the lighter almost made her change her mind. She already regretted the butt tumbling down the cliff.

Strong, she thought. You're strong.

"Moon's rising," Kyle said.

It was just a sliver, a paring-knife glimmer, without enough light to penetrate the shadows.

After a moment, Kyle said, "Know what I want to do?" Without waiting for her to answer, he said, "Firefighter." His voice was low, almost shy. She twisted her head around to look at him again, and was surprised to find it too dark to see his face clearly. The ember of his cigarette flared.

"I thought maybe you wanted to be a vet or something," she said.

"Me? Naw. I can't take that much school. I like the critters and all. But I don't want to be fifty and still be jumping every time Poteet yells. By that time I could be fire chief somewhere, have my own crew. Yeah." He paused for another drag. "That'd be cool."

"That is cool."

"You think so?"

"Yeah. I do."

Kyle sat up straight. "I been volunteering with the county for a year already," he said. "I got my name on a list with the state but they ain't got no openings yet. When they do my crew chief says he'll put in a good word for me. He thinks I got a chance." He didn't look at her as he talked; he was staring off over her head. "Wanted to be a firefighter since I was four years old. Saw my first engine go down the street, sirens screaming, everyone pulling over. My ma, she followed the engine so I could see them put out the fire. Made up my mind right then. Never saw anything since to make me change it."

He stood up. Tallulah looked over her shoulder in time to see the ember of his cigarette fall end over end to the ground. He stubbed it out with his toe.

"We better go," Kyle said. "Ruth'll be worrying." He held out a hand. She took it and got to her feet.

At the top of the hill, it had been deep dusk. Back in the trees, it was already night. Tallulah took smaller and smaller steps, then stopped altogether. The highway underpass had been dark, too, but that at least had been a nice paved road, not this treacherous slope covered in leaves that slid underfoot, hiding rattlesnakes and ghost cars and God knew what.

Kyle's steps had been receding ahead of her; now they stopped, paused, and came back, scuffing an easy rhythm through the pine needles. She could just make out his lanky shape, a little lighter than the black of the trees.

"I ain't met a woman yet could see in the dark," he said. "Here, take my hand."

"I can see better than you," she said. "I just don't know the way."

"Oooh, pardon me, Miss X-ray Vision. You won't have no trouble getting down, then. See you at Ruth's." Footsteps scuffed away.

"Goddammit, Kyle, wait!" she yelled.

"What's wrong, Miss X-ray Vision? Can't see the trail?" he called. Reedy laughter came from a little to her left. Then leaves crackled just ahead, then silence. What was he doing, hiding? Planning to scare her, no doubt. In a sudden, glorious rage, she whooped her best war cry, the one that in third grade had never failed to make Tommy Sota pee his pants, and charged headlong down the hill.

A black bulk of something loomed in front of her; she threw out her hands, caught at thin pointed metal. Rear fins. She stumbled over the car's bumper and hung on it, panting. Scuffling in the trees to her right. Trying to lure her out of the clearing? Ha! He only wished she was that stupid. She set off again at a choppy trot, straight down. Keep to the beaten path. Only the path wasn't very beaten; her feet slipped every other step, sending her bobbing from side to side like one of those wobbly toys she and Terri used to play with before they wised up to Barbies.

A series of cracking snaps sounded straight ahead, as though something was plowing through a dry bush. She tried to dodge aside, but her foot caught, and with a sinking feeling of déjà vu (*why am I always tripping in this place!*), she fell to earth.

The earth grunted and writhed when she landed on it. It smelled like cigarettes. She rolled off. The edge of something dug into her ribs, and she swore.

"Someone's gonna wash your mouth out with soap, you keep that up," said Kyle's voice from the ground next to her.

She scraped up a handful of leaves and threw them blindly.

"You trip me," Kyle said, "you land on me, you bust my

ribs and stomp my privates, and now you're cussing and throwing dirt in my eyes. You like me, just say so."

"You got it," she said. She scooped up another gob of leaves, a double handful this time, and threw them. The showery sound they made when they hit filled her with satisfaction.

But either Kyle could still see better than she could, or his ability to aim by sound was more accurate, because the leaves he threw caught her square in the face. She yelped and spat, and he started laughing. She growled and bent forward to rake up an armful of forest floor. She heard him scrambling to his feet.

"Uh-uh," she said, and threw herself forward.

She managed to bring him down, but by then she was laughing uncontrollably and her arms gave up. Kyle was laughing, too, but it didn't seem to affect his muscles the way it did hers because in less than a minute she lay on her back in the dirt, him on top, his hands pinning her wrists to the ground. She kicked upward. He dodged his hips to one side and she missed, but with him off balance, she managed to squirm a hand free.

"Wait, wait," Kyle gasped. He let her other wrist go and she felt his body retreat from hers. He grabbed her hands again, but this time he stood and pulled her, still giggling, up with him. She could smell the cigarettes on his skin, but his face was a black blur, nothing more. She wondered if he could see her. She stuck her tongue out.

"That's nice," he said. "Didn't your mama tell you your face would stick that way?"

The cigarette tang grew stronger and warmer. His breath nuzzled along her cheek, lifting the tiny hairs.

"You know that picture of your friend, when I said I'd seen prettier?" Kyle whispered. "I meant you."

His lips were soft. And, she realized with embarrassment, smoother than her own.

The kiss broke. They stood forehead to forehead; when he blinked, his eyelashes crumpled against her eyebrow.

"Worked out good, her not coming," Kyle said.

"Who?"

"Your friend."

"You think that's a *good* thing?" Tallulah backed away, but Kyle's hands slid from her shoulder blades, collaring her biceps.

"Seems to me it is. Seems like maybe you thought so, too, couple seconds ago."

"Yeah, well, let me enlighten you." Tallulah twisted her arms until his grip gave way. "The only reason I'm still here is the money. And the minute I get it I'll be leaving so fast, you won't see me through my dust." She took off downhill, bumping his chest hard as she passed. The ground flattened out under her feet; she trotted forward and her knee slammed into a fence post. "Ow! Dammit," she hissed.

"Wait, I'll get the gate," Kyle said.

But she'd already found the post with the loop of

smooth wire. She wrenched the wire free. The gate sagged; she pulled it just enough to slip through, then dropped it.

"Wait a minute," Kyle said. She heard him wrestling with the post and wire. "Wait!" The pasture was full dark but the light from Ruth's back porch shone like a beacon. Tallulah ran for it. She heard Kyle swear sharply under his breath. Good. She hoped the barbed wire had cut him. She jogged as fast as she dared for being unable to see the ground. Or the cows. If she so much as stepped in cow shit, he'd be sorry.

On the back porch, Cowboy shot out as soon as she jerked open the door. He bounced twice at her feet, sniffing, then scrambled down the porch steps and disappeared. She thought about calling him, but she saw something moving quick in the pasture and she slipped inside, closed the door and locked it. The trailer still smelled of steak. Over the TV in the living room, Ruth called, "That you, Tallulah?"

"It's me," she said. Footsteps on the back porch. Kyle appeared in the back door window. He rattled the doorknob and looked at her and said something. *Let me in.*

"Kyle with you?" Ruth said.

Tallulah raised her hand, middle finger high. "He went home," she said loudly. She reached up and flicked the door's curtains closed. She half-expected him to knock, but he didn't. After a moment she walked into the living room. Ruth was seated on the couch, a glass of iced tea in her hand.

"Cowboy ran outside," Tallulah said.

"I've raised both boys and dogs," Ruth said, "and when they get it into their heads to roam of a night, it's no use yelling after them. How'd you like the graveyard?"

"Splendiferous," Tallulah said.

Monday morning, Jolene greeted Tallulah with, "I got so many treatments to do, you better walk the dogs. Clean the kennels after. And if that makes you late getting up front to help him with appointments, then he can just do everything his own damn self."

Tallulah guessed that Poteet hadn't made nice yet. Fine with her. Compared to kennel cleaning, dog walking hardly qualified as work, which meant that she hardly ever got to do it.

She took Diesel out first. Once on the patch of grass across from the barn, she slipped the leash off his neck and let him wander. Two weeks after the underpass, he still had, as Poteet put it, a hitch in his git-along, but he didn't need help getting up anymore. And the chicken bones he'd eaten hadn't caused any problems, to Tallulah's huge relief. Diesel flopped onto the grass, rolled onto his back, and writhed side-to-side, white paws in the air. What must it be like, Tallulah wondered, to be able to give yourself over so completely to a moment? It was a gift Maeve had, one that Tallulah had always envied.

The early sun was comfortably warm across her shoulders. She yawned. Diesel rolled to his feet and shook himself; his head popped up, and the broad flaps of his ears tipped forward. Tallulah turned around, shading her eyes.

Kyle was coming toward them, negotiating his way around the dog turds hidden in the grass. He held one hand behind his back, which didn't help his balance any.

"What do you want?" she asked.

He looked up. His dark eyes were solemn. " 'Morning," he said. He pulled the hand from behind his back and held a bunch of flowers out to her.

They were just wildflowers, the same ones Tallulah had seen choking the ditches, dotting unmowed strips of grass. But Kyle's bouquet held two dozen at least, with three, four, five . . . eight different kinds of blooms, all in the bright loudmouthed colors she loved.

"Oh," Tallulah said. She reached out and took them. It took both hands to hold them all.

"I know they ain't much," Kyle said.

"No, they're gorgeous. They're . . ." Tallulah held them up to her face, inhaled deep. Woodsy green scent, a flare of spice. No one had ever given her flowers before. A sudden pressure rose in her chest; she blinked and swallowed hard, to keep it from pushing up into her throat.

"I like you," Kyle said. He'd leaned over to play with

Diesel's ears; she couldn't see his face, but the upper edge of his cheekbone flared red. "I liked you since I first saw you sitting on the doorstep with a half-dead dog in your arms." He glanced up at her. "You like the movies?"

How could she ever have thought blue-eyed blonds were attractive? Blue eyes showed you everything. No mystery.

"Yeah. Absolutely," she said.

"Then let's go."

She blinked. "Now?"

"Tonight. I'm off Mondays."

From the treatment room window, Jolene's voice cut across the yard. "Tallulah, you still out there?"

"Christ, hide those," Kyle said.

"Why? She can't see from there."

Kyle picked the leash up off the grass and slipped it on Diesel. "Look, do me a favor, OK? They find out I gave you those, I ain't never gonna hear the end of it. And don't say nothing about the movies."

"I think Ruth's going to notice I'm not sitting on the couch watching *Wheel of Fortune* with her."

"Tell her I'm taking you out with my friends. Tell her I'm fixing you up with my brother. Or all damn day it's gonna be," he twisted his voice high, " 'Oh, Kyle likes Tallulah. When you two getting married?' " At the disgusted look on his face, she started laughing. "I'm serious," he said. "Don't say nothing. All right?"

Tallulah lifted the flowers toward him. "Then where do I say I got these from?"

"Tell 'em you picked 'em," he said, and headed for the barn.

On a top shelf in the break room, Tallulah found a dusty green vase. She rinsed it out, Diesel panting at her feet, and was rummaging through drawers when Jolene walked in, humming under her breath. When she saw Diesel, the humming quit abruptly as if someone had punched a Stop button in her head.

"After what that dog did the other day, you'd think you'd keep him out of here," Jolene said. She reached a broad bronzed arm past Tallulah to set her coffee mug in the sink. Then paused halfway. Her voice sharp with suspicion, she said, "Where'd you get that mess of flowers?"

"Somebody gave them to me. Is there any aspirin?"

"Who gave them to you? When?"

"Just now, when I was walking Diesel. I don't know who."

Jolene poked among the blooms. "These are fresh cut," she said.

"That's why I want the aspirin," Tallulah said. "Put one in the water, the flowers keep longer." Her mom had taught her that.

"You're saying somebody walked up out of the blue and handed *you* a bunch of flowers for no reason at all."

"I'm sure he had some reason," Tallulah said. She opened another drawer. Aha. A bottle. She rolled it to read the label. Ibuprofen. Close enough.

"Exactly what did this 'he' look like? What car did he drive?"

"I didn't see the car." Tallulah flipped off the bottle cap, shook a tablet into her hand, and dropped it into the vase. "It was an old guy. He had on overalls and a T-shirt and a baseball cap."

Jolene gave an impatient *huh*. "That could be half the men in this county."

I know, Tallulah thought. She lowered the stems carefully into the water.

"You don't remember *anything* else about this man?"

Tallulah lifted her eyes to the cabinets, head tilted to one side, as if concentrating; then, in a tone of pleased conviction, she said, "The baseball cap was red."

When Jolene didn't answer, Tallulah glanced up. Jolene's puzzled expression had changed; now she looked like she could happily wring Tallulah's neck. "You must think," Jolene said, "we are all of us dumber than rocks. I know where you got those flowers."

Tallulah's face froze. Had Jolene seen her and Kyle from the back window after all?

"I got work to do," Jolene went on, "and I'm busting my ass to do it, and as sorry as you are, I don't need you wasting half the damn day in the field next door picking a bunch of damn weeds. You hear me?"

She hadn't seen. Tallulah grinned at her. "Okey-dokey," she said. She carried the vase to the table.

"And get that mutt out of here right now."

Tallulah fussed with the stems. Make sure all the blooms

240

face out, her mother had told her. Make sure none of the little ones get squashed. See how pretty?

All day she found excuses to cut through the break room. At lunch, she ate her ham and cheese sandwich and admired the bouquet while Jolene and Ruth argued about where she'd gotten it. Ruth was sure some relative of Crystal-Amber's had brought it; Jolene remained convinced Tallulah had skipped work to gather it herself. If either of them thought of Kyle, they didn't say so.

The afternoon was hectic. Solid back-to-back appointments. But the clients had changed; where before they'd acted friendly, if noncommittal, now everyone wanted to talk to her. Are you the— Did you really— Isn't that something, they said, one after the other. To escape, all Tallulah had to do was mention Dr. Poteet (Excuse me, I think he needs me), which meant she received steady doses of admiration with few prying questions. By the end of the day, she was so wrapped in a warm glow even Poteet noticed.

"Pretty full of yourself, aren't you?" he said, examining the vaccines Tallulah handed him. "That's a basset hound in there, you know. Not a cat." He handed the vials back to her.

"Oh. Sorry," Tallulah said. She turned to the refrigerator to get the correct vaccines, but he stopped her.

"Why don't you go on and help Jolene," he said. "This is the last one, I can do for myself."

But Tallulah felt too good to scour kennels while listening to Jolene's nasty comments about her flowers, her work ethic, and her general character. So she snuck into the break room, grabbed the vase, and slipped into the laundry.

The laundry was tucked in a corner of the storeroom behind floor-to-ceiling shelves of pet food. It wasn't a convenient location—a complaint Tallulah had heard Jolene make more than once—but it was quiet. Even the dogs' barking barely penetrated back here. Best of all, there was a continuous mountain of blankets and towels that had to be sorted, loaded, moved, and folded. In the laundry, Tallulah could take ten minutes to relax and think, and not even Jolene could say she was shirking.

Dust motes danced silver in the light from the window. The air was sleepy-warm, pleasant with the smells of soap and corncobby dog kibble. Tallulah sat on the floor, her back against the wall, out of sight of the door should anyone come in. She hugged her knees and gazed at the flowers on the washing machine.

Even her date for the sophomore spring dance—the last dance she'd gone to, since she'd been barred from social activities most of her junior year, thanks to shoplifting that stupid DVD—hadn't brought her a corsage. She'd met him only that night. He was a friend of Andrea's boyfriend, Sean, a last-minute fix-up. *He's blond,* Andrea had promised. *You'll love him.*

He'd shown up at her house empty-handed and already stoned, wearing a glow-in-the-dark skeleton T-shirt and baggy pants and a tie made of red crepe paper around his neck. Tallulah was thankful her mother had been called out to show a house, that Terri was upstairs with headphones on and hadn't heard the doorbell.

"That's not a tuxedo," she'd said, staring at him from the open front door.

"Sean said Andrea said you wouldn't care," he said.

Skeleton-Shirt didn't dance and didn't talk. He did seem to think he would score—misinformation from Sean, no doubt—and as soon as he realized that kissing was as far as Debbie was prepared to go with a guy who looked like a Halloween kid on steroids, he'd disappeared. Andrea and an irritated Sean had had to drive her home. Getting in early had gained her no points with her mother, though, not after Mom had found Debbie's plum-colored, double-layered georgette dress stuffed in the clothes hamper, still reeking of marijuana from Skeleton-Shirt's car. "But I didn't even smoke any," Debbie had protested, and it was the truth, she hadn't, but the thing about her mother was—the thing that had changed between them—in every situation involving Debbie, her mother always decided to believe the worst.

It occurred to Tallulah that the incident at the spring dance made Derek the *second* guy to strand her someplace. Good job, T. Batting a thousand here.

But Kyle was different. She could talk to him. He made her laugh. She liked the way his eyes glinted and got narrow, so all you could see was the dark, with sparks in it, when he was being a smart-ass.

From behind the partition, the door banged open. Tallulah lunged to her feet and grabbed a towel out of the basket just as Poteet's head appeared around the corner.

"You seen Kyle?" he said.

"He's not here," Tallulah said, trying to sound in full possession of her breath.

"I can see that much," Poteet snapped. His head disappeared.

"I mean he's not *here* here," Tallulah called after him. "It's his day off." She heard a smack against the partition; on impulse, she hurried after him. "Can I do anything?" she asked. Poteet jerked around and fixed her with a look so foul-tempered that she hung in it, unbreathing, the towel suspended in her hands.

"I've got to leave right damn now to see a colic and the truck's not stocked. Jolene in the treatment room?"

"I can stock the truck."

He narrowed his eyes at her, as if this was a lie. Which it essentially was. Kyle had shown her the VetPak only once, and that had been ten days ago. At the time, Tallulah had still been watching for Maeve in every car coming up the road, and she hadn't paid attention.

"Make sure there's stomach tubes and the pump and at least two gallons of mineral oil," Poteet said. "Hurry up." He pivoted and reached the door in three strides, white coat billowing back from his knees. Tallulah threw the towel back into the basket and caught the door on its back swing. Poteet headed left down the hallway to his office and slammed the door shut. Tallulah knew it took him only a couple of minutes to change from white coat to khaki coveralls. The door to the carport lay to the right. For a bare moment, Tallulah hesitated. Then she ran left, past Poteet's office to the employee lockers.

By the time Poteet came striding into the carport, Tallulah was lifting the second gallon of mineral oil into the VetPak. Fortunately, somebody with organizational skills— probably not Poteet, certainly not Kyle, she guessed Jolene— had marked each drawer and shelf in the unit with label tape, white letters on bright blue: EMASCULATOR; SUTURE; SURGICAL PACKS; BANDAGING. Thank God the only supplies the truck had needed were things she could identify, cotton and tape, syringes and needles. A metal cylindrical object occupied the slot labeled STOMACH PUMP. She hoped it was the right thing and not some other weird horse tool put there by accident. She couldn't tell a stomach pump from an emasculator, or any other piece of equipment for that matter, and if she got it wrong she was screwed.

Poteet strode up to the open VetPak and brushed her aside. She stood by as he inspected, ready to run for anything he found missing. Instead he thudded the VetPak closed. As he walked around to the driver's side, Tallulah made a grab for the passenger door. By the time Poteet was in the truck, she had her seat belt fastened and her hands were folded in her lap.

"What the hell are you doing?" Poteet asked.

"You said it was an emergency. I'll help," Tallulah said.

"If I wanted any goddamned help I would've said so. Get out."

"You needed help with Leopard."

"I needed help with Leopard because my only other options were a twelve-year-old girl or her lawyer father who knows less about horses even than you. Besides you're not dressed for—" He broke off, staring at the coveralls she'd snatched out of Jolene's locker. "I don't suppose," he said, "you've ever heard the saying 'out of the frying pan, into the fire'?" Tallulah shook her head. "I didn't think so. It means if you come along, you'll be sorry." His hand paused on the ignition key.

Tallulah turned and fixed her eyes straight ahead.

"Don't come crying later," Poteet said, and turned the key.

246

Chapter 19

Tallulah had heard enough about colic from Jolene and Kyle to know it meant a horse with a painful belly. Everyone, both staff and clients, treated colic like a huge emergency—even rescheduling appointments, if necessary, so Poteet could drop everything and go—but so far no one had explained exactly how a stomachache could be so dire.

At the moment, though, Tallulah was glad it was. Field calls could take an hour, sometimes more, which meant by the time they got back, the kennel cleaning would be done.

She wondered if Jolene would be late again picking up her son. A splinter of guilt pierced her good mood. Tallulah had played peekaboo with Tyler at the picnic, while Jolene and Ruth had packed away the food. He had the same round, dimple-starred face as his mother, the same blue gray eyes. He squinched his eyes shut when he laughed.

Tallulah worried a hangnail with her teeth. This will be the last time, she told herself. No more skipping out. Besides, if Jolene actually got to go home on time, maybe she'd lighten up a little.

This field call was the farthest yet. Almost twenty minutes passed before the truck pulled off the road. The driveway skirted the biggest lawn Tallulah had ever seen: bigger than the one surrounding the courthouse, bigger than the football field at her high school. The grass sprawled in a vast arc, and if it was grand, well, it had to be to match the house. Brick, three stories. White columns sectioning an expanse of front porch. Tallulah thought of Leopard, the Sholtys' twenty-two-thousand-dollar darling. What kind of sleek, deadly horses must these people own?

The front door of the house opened and a woman, stout in jeans and an untucked oxford shirt, stepped onto the porch. She waved with an abrupt, urgent choppiness. Poteet raised a hand in reply, but he didn't slow down. He turned the truck off the driveway onto a narrow, rutted gravel path. In her side mirror, Tallulah saw the woman hasten down the porch steps and trot after them, and even through the dusty haze of the truck's wake, Tallulah noted the awkward jouncing of her gait. Not someone used to running. Tallulah felt a prickle of apprehension and pushed herself upright on the seat. Ahead lay a small red stable and a gray-haired man leading a horse in a ragged circle.

Before they got out of the truck, Poteet said, "You're here, so you'll help. But say one word and by God you'll be walking back. Understand?"

He didn't wait for an answer. By the time she joined him by the driver's side VetPak, he was already arranging needles and syringes and glass drug vials in the green carry tray. "Get that bucket and put three-four inches of water in it," he told her. "Bring it and the stomach tube and the pump and the mineral oil and go stand over by that fence post. Don't bring anything to me until I tell you."

She dragged her eyes off the horse and filled the bucket from the VetPak's water hose and carried it and the rest of the equipment to the fence. She set the bucket and the gallon jug of oil on the ground and the stomach pump—she hoped it was the stomach pump—in the bucket. She didn't know where to put the stomach tube. Made of clear plastic and thicker than her thumb, it didn't seem like something that should get dirty, and it was too big to cram in the bucket with the pump. She finally looped its coils over one arm and gripped them with her other hand, as if it might leap away and escape sidewinding over the packed red dirt of the stable yard.

The woman had caught up to Poteet. Between her gasps for breath, Tallulah could catch the words, Fine last night. The woman kept repeating it in a shrill, rising inflection, emphasis on the Fine, as if by saying it enough times the horse would revert back to its former Fine state.

It was a long way from Fine now, even Tallulah could see that. Dirt caked its coat, making it impossible to tell what color it was. Where the sweat dripped from its sides and the undercurve of its belly, the dirt had slicked into mud that matched the mud under the horse's hooves. The rest of the stable yard was dry. It hadn't rained since the thunderstorm the day of the party, two days ago. How much sweat did it take to churn a circle of dirt into mud?

Poteet motioned to the man leading the horse. They stopped walking. Immediately the horse kicked upward, a short, choppy punt with its hind foot toward the underside of its belly. Its tail wrung in a circle and it struck the ground twice, hard, with a front hoof. As restless as it was, though, it didn't seem to notice any of them, not even when Poteet laid a stethoscope onto its side.

Then it began moving in such a peculiar way, Tallulah couldn't tell what it was trying to do. Its head was held fast by the halter rope, but its neck seemed somehow to get longer, narrower, like honey dropping out of a bottle.

"She's going down," said the man holding the rope. His voice was high with strain, but resigned, as if the horse was a force of nature and he helpless to control her. He was right, Tallulah realized; the horse's neck was stretching because her shoulders were sinking toward the ground. The horse's hind feet began to step in place, right then left, urgently, like a child needing to pee. Then she set them both on the ground and crouched, the bulges of her thigh muscles visible even under the dirt-stiff coat. Her neck had become impossibly long, as if most of its length had lain concealed in her shoulders, like fishing line on a reel.

Poteet slung the stethoscope back around his neck and stepped to the mare's head. "Let me get in there," he said. The man gave him the lead rope and stepped aside. Poteet grabbed the halter just under the mare's eyes and hauled the sagging head up.

"Hyah!" Poteet cried. "Get up there! Get up!" The mare's legs, halfway to collapsing, jerked and trembled. "Tallulah!"

Tallulah started.

"Get over here!"

She dropped the stomach tube in the dirt and trotted forward. "What do I—"

"Smack her rump. Hurry up!"

Tallulah edged close to the mare. She could make out every rank, sweat-soaked curlicue of its coat, every shake and quiver of its muscles. The horse was a mountain of wet flesh about to topple. Onto her. She raised her hand, slapped the tremoring rump, then scuttled back to safety. The horse sank another two inches.

"Damn it, *hard!*" Poteet yelled.

She seized her lower lip between her teeth and danced in close again, high on her toes, ready to leap out of the way. As if from a long distance, she could hear the cries of the man and the woman, Hyah, hyah, last night she was *fine,* get up, Sunny, stand up! Tallulah lifted both arms, squeezed her eyes shut, and swung, levering from the hips. The smack was loud and sharp; her elbows jarred painfully. The mare jumped forward a half-step.

"Do it again," Poteet barked. He swiveled to the mare's side, keeping his left arm straight to hold her head. With his right hand, palm open, he walloped a tremendous cracking underhand up under the horse's ribs. "Get up!"

Soaked in adrenaline and panic, Tallulah yelled "Hyah!" and struck the mare again on the rump. Under this double assault the mare snorted and lunged; pressing his advantage, Poteet half-led, half-dragged her forward. One step, two, and she was staggering once more in the rut of her circle.

"Go get the twitch," Poteet said. Tallulah ran to the truck, grabbed the heavy, smooth wood shank with its circle of chain, the same one that she'd held on Leopard just before he kicked her across the stable yard. She tried not to think about that. She caught up with Poteet and the mare again on the far side of the circle. She held the twitch out to him, but he shook his head.

"Hold on to it," he said. "If she starts to go down again, use the handle, beat her rear if you have to. Next time will be worse and you won't be able to keep her up with your fists." He motioned to the man. "Take her head. Keep her moving. How many times has she been down?"

"Two. We got her up as quick as we could—"

"I'm sure you did. Tallulah! Bring that tray over and give me two cc's of xylazine."

Tallulah pulled bottles out of the tray, scanned their labels, put them back. Zyla-*what*? What if she picked the wrong drug and killed the horse by accident?

"I don't see it," she said.

"X-Y-L-A-Z-I-N-E," Poteet rattled off.

She found it, fumbled the bottle, almost dropped it. Idiot, her mind hissed, but a more practical voice broke in: It's just a horse with a bellyache. It must look worse than it is.

"Where's that drug?" Poteet called. He made her show the bottle to him before he accepted the syringe. "Good. Give it here. Four cc's of flunixin."

She pulled up the dose, double-checking the label and the black numbered line on the syringe barrel. She was doing all right. It was going to be all right. Keeping pace alongside the mare as she walked, Poteet injected both drugs into the horse's neck, then handed the empty blood-spotted syringes to Tallulah. She jogged back to the truck with them. Needles in the sharps container, syringes in the biohazard bag. She tore off a paper towel from the roll hanging on the underside of the VetPak's cover and wiped the smears of blood from her fingertips.

After a few minutes, the mare's stagger became wide and halting. Her legs angled out like tent ropes; she seemed about to tip over onto her nose. She swung around to nip at her own flank and tottered sideways. The man danced frantically to keep up. He sawed at the rope, yanking ineffectually at the halter.

"Jeezum crow," he said. "Jeezum crow."

"You're doing fine, just hold her there," Poteet said to him. He'd gone to the truck himself and now approached the mare with a length of thick rope. He tied one end around the mare's neck, ran the rest down along her side, looped it around a hind foot, then brought the free end

253

back to her neck, taking up the slack until the mare's hind foot scraped forward along the ground.

He motioned Tallulah close and handed the end of the rope to her. "Hold this," he said. "Keep tension on it. Make sure she doesn't kick me, now." He walked back to the tray and pulled on a clear plastic glove with a sleeve that reached to his shoulder. With his other hand he squeezed lubricating jelly from a tube over his gloved fingers. Tallulah wondered, until she saw him pull the mare's tail aside. She grimaced and looked at the muddy ground. The mare shuddered and groaned, shifting her weight on her hind feet. After a couple of minutes, Poteet let go of the tail and stepped away. He shucked the feces-smeared sleeve inside out and tossed it onto the ground near the tray, then took the rope from Tallulah and released the mare's hind foot. When he untied the knot at her neck, he laid his palm on the quivering flat of the muscle and stroked her gently, twice. He opened his mouth to speak, but the man forestalled him.

"Whatever you need to do, Doc," the man said. "Whatever you need to do, you just tell us. We'll—"

"Your horse has a volvulus, Mr. Lawler," Poteet said. "A twist in the gut."

"Whatever you need to do, do it," the man repeated. "Money's no object so long as we have a chance."

"Then we need to send her to the university, to the specialists there. She needs surgery and she needs it now. Do you have a horse trailer?"

"Surgery?" the man said.

"Yes, at the veterinary school in Knoxville. When a colicking horse gets down and rolls it can cause the gut to twist and I think that's—"

"I know about that," the man said. "Even you and your girl had trouble keeping her on her feet. And it was only me here, before."

"Those shots look like they've done something," the woman said. "Why don't we just give her more and see?"

"Your horse has a twist in her gut," Poteet said. Tallulah could sense the impatience building in him, like thunderheads. "Drugs can't reach in there and undo the twist. She needs a surgeon and she needs one now." He gestured at the mare. Sweat still dripped from her flanks. As they watched, she lifted a front hoof and dug laboriously into the mangled ground.

"What kind of money would that run?" the man asked.

"David," the woman said. Her voice drew out on the last syllable; Tallulah couldn't tell if it was a pleading tone, or a warning one.

"Several thousand," Poteet said. "Could be more."

The woman turned and walked back to the house, her heels striking hard against the gravel. The man didn't look after her, but his chin crumpled for an instant, like a baby's. The mare's tail wrung and lashed against the backs of her thighs. "I'd hate to put her through a surgery," the man said. "She's been through hell already."

"Most of them do well. Most of them live."

"It's not the money."

Poteet looked away then. "No, of course not." The mare swayed and shook between them. "Do you need me to arrange for after?" he asked. "I can have my girl at the office call someone for you."

"No. No, there's a fella up the road with a backhoe." The man reached out and patted the top of the mare's neck. She made no response, not even a flick of an ear. "You'd better get on," he said.

Poteet walked back to the truck. Unsure of what had just been decided, Tallulah started to follow. But then the man spoke up and she stopped, trapped.

"Crackerjack mare," he said. "Not so pretty, but a real corker. She's only eight." He combed the mare's mane with his fingers. "Last night she was just as fine as she could be."

I'm sure she'll be OK, Tallulah almost said, but Poteet was already back. She stared at the two syringes gripped in his hand. They were big, over a foot long from plunger to needle, and filled with bright pink. As soon as Tallulah saw the pink, she knew what the man's decision had been. She frowned. The horse maybe could be saved, Poteet had said so. What were they doing?

"I'll have you step back, Mr. Lawler, if you don't mind," Poteet said. "Tallulah here will hold the mare. That's not a job you want."

It's not a job I want, either, she thought, but Mr. Lawler thrust the lead rope at her and she had no choice but to take it.

The first night at the veterinary hospital. A black dog

gasping on a metal table. Since then, Tallulah had seen the pink fluid only one other time. She'd walked into the treatment room to see Jolene cradling an emaciated white cat, Poteet leaning over it, syringe in hand. A few seconds later the cat lay unmoving in Jolene's arms, staring straight ahead, its eyes dilated to a glassy black.

"How long will it take?" Tallulah had asked. "Already over," Poteet said.

Just like that. Alive, then not.

Later she'd asked Jolene, "How long did it take you to get used to . . . to that?"

"I've been a veterinary technician for twelve years," Jolene had said. "The day I get used to it is the day I quit. Anybody gets used to it has no heart left."

Poteet slipped one of the syringes into his pocket. It was so long the plunger jutted next to his hip, like a bulky gray antenna. He twisted the needle off the other syringe, kept it in his hand, and gave the syringe to Tallulah. The width of it took up half her palm.

"Give that to me when I ask for it," he said. "When I tell you to get back, go stand over by the fence. Understand?" Not waiting for an answer, he dug his thumb into the groove of the mare's neck. The needle, a gleam of bare metal, hung poised for an instant against the dirt-stained hair. Then the mare flinched and the needle disappeared, swallowed under the skin, with only the hub remaining above. Its opening looked like a tiny, smooth-walled mouth. Poteet grabbed the syringe out of Tallulah's hand, twisted it onto the needle hub, and began pushing the plunger. Pink disappeared into the vein. When the syringe was empty, he tossed it behind him. Before it hit the ground, he had the second one out of his pocket. A moment later it, too, was tossed aside empty. It landed on the dirt with a hollow clatter.

He took the halter rope from Tallulah and elbowed her aside. "Get back," he said.

Tallulah looked at the mare's neck. The needle hub was gone. Only a thin line of blood showed where it had been.

The mare's hindquarters began to sway, not like before, but with an increasing arc, like a playground swing being pushed harder at each pass.

"I said get *back*," Poteet said. He pushed Tallulah's shoulder. She staggered, a sprawling lurch, and at the sudden movement the mare flung up her head. Her left eye—the eye that Tallulah could see—flew open, and, for the first time since they'd arrived, the mare was looking outward, not in, her eye wild and white-rimmed, pinning Tallulah where she stood with a crackling mixture of fear and surprise.

Then the life went out of it. That was the only way Tallulah could think to describe it later. The eye did not move, or blink; it simply flicked into vacancy, leaving a window of fluid and tissue empty as a shed skin.

The mare fell. Not all at once, but as if in pieces. The hind legs went first, skidding as though the ground had been yanked from under them. Her body twisted in midair, throwing her forelegs high and to the side, and when she crashed to the earth the shock of it ran up through Tallu-lah's knees but the mare was not done, the neck was still arching through the air, driven toward the earth by the dead weight of the head. Poteet scrambled backward, his arms hauling, taking up slack on the lead rope and then the mare lay entirely still, her head suspended by the rope in Poteet's hands, the empty eye a bare inch from the ground. Poteet took one step forward. The eye settled into the mud.

Poteet knelt over the mare and unbuckled the halter. He lifted her head by the forelock and slipped the halter off, stood up and coiled the lead rope neatly in one hand. As he walked past Tallulah, he said, "Pick up those syringes."

Poteet and the man talked. Tallulah could not hear what they said. Their words were a buzz, a hum one tone lower than the flies. She picked up the syringes but couldn't find the needle; perhaps Poteet had put it in his pocket. She dumped the syringes and the discarded plastic sleeve into the tray. It seemed no matter where she faced, the dead mare hovered at the edge of her view. The woman came back up the path, sniffling, clutching a folded sheet. Tallu-lah helped her spread it over the body. They anchored the corners with rocks and broken bricks. A yellow dog slunk forward, head down and sniffing. The woman shooed it away. Afterwards, the woman wanted to tell Tallulah about the horse's virtues, through small quick sobs and a hand-kerchief held to her upper lip, but Tallulah pretended not to hear her and turned away. It was worse, now that the body was covered. The bland white hillocks reminded her first of the tarp thrown over the dead girl, and then of Maeve when Tallulah had first seen her, draped under the sheet on the tattooist's table, the shape of her betrayed by the drifting of the fabric. You weren't supposed to know what was underneath, and yet you knew exactly.

In the truck, driving away, Poteet said, "Did you see, as soon as I said 'surgery' it was all over. Too bad, that was a nice mare. Next time get the hell out of the way. Last thing the animal needs is to get startled like that. You were lucky it went smooth, or you would've gotten clobbered."

Tallulah looked out the window. The rounded hills were suddenly of no comfort and she fixed her eyes on the dashboard instead. "That was smooth?" she asked.

"As smooth as it gets when you drop an animal that weighs half a ton."

Tallulah thought of the mare's open dead eye, and shuddered. "I don't understand how you can just kill something like that," she said.

Poteet's voice took on an edge. "You think it's better to die slow? In agony?" He shook his head. "This way's painless. And quick. They don't know what hits them."

Wrong, Tallulah thought. The mare had known. Her wild, rolling eye had said it: Someone's killing me.

And then Tallulah realized: She thought it was me.

Chapter 20

It wasn't Tallulah's intention to break into Kyle's apartment. Not at first.

Riding back in the truck with Poteet, her insides felt shrill as whistles. Images of the dying horse and the dead girl mixed together in her head until the mare's eye became the girl's. Shocked wide open, empty as a window. Over a twisted gut. A cat in the road. Don't pull over, it'll just take a second. Mommy will be right back.

She needed Maeve to explain how these things happened. Then maybe Tallulah could believe it was Fate. Or God. Or the Goddess or Buddha, or Zeus, or Jesus. Whoever. Anyone, anything but what she suspected: This was how life was. You had a mother. You had a father. Then you didn't. Too bad, so sad.

She couldn't go back to Ruth's. Not yet. The thought of being hemmed in within the confines of the doublewide was unbearable. Ruth would listen, she would pat Tallulah's hand. She would tell Tallulah everything was all right, which was the one thing Tallulah was certain was a lie.

Kyle on the hill last night. That had been real. She needed real. Just for a little while. Then she would be able to stand it.

But Poteet drove past the hospital. "That was it," Tallulah said, craning her head around to look.

"It's past six thirty," he said. "Ruth'll be home already."

She did manage to persuade him to drop her at the intersection of Ruth's road and the highway, rather than drive her all the way to the doublewide. She made a show of marching up the road, at the same time watching to see if he'd turn back toward the hospital. He didn't. The pickup truck continued straight on. Home to Greeley Hill. As soon as he was out of sight, she trotted back to the highway and began walking.

Driving to the hospital in Ruth's long-bodied Pontiac had seemed to take no time at all, and the hills had been the gentlest of inclines. Walking, the highway climbed and curved and fell away, so that the hospital always seemed to be just out of sight. And where had these mountains come from? Sweat ran in creeks down her face, her back. She unzipped Jolene's baggy coveralls all the way down to her navel and flapped the hem of the scrub top underneath to move some air around on her skin. It was her first day in Tennessee all over again, that terrible long afternoon before the thunderstorm hit, the heat like a vise, crushing her in its jaws.

Just as she reached the hospital's shaded walkway, a wave of lightheadedness washed over her. She stumbled to the wall, crossed her forearms against its warm brick, and laid her forehead down until the dizziness passed. Then she shuffled around to the carport and banged on the hospital's back door. No answer. The front door, the windows. Nothing. It wasn't until her third circuit around the building that she noticed the shed was open and Kyle's motorcycle was gone. It hadn't even occurred to her that he might not be here. He'd said he was off tonight. He was supposed to take her to the movies.

Well, wherever he was, he had to come back soon.

Tallulah climbed the stairs that led to his apartment and set herself down to wait. But the landing was full in the sun. She was already slick with sweat, gritty with dust, and now thirst crackled over the back of her throat like fire in a box.

If she'd gone to the doublewide first, she could have showered and changed her clothes, then told Ruth she was going for a walk. The way she was now, Kyle would probably take one look at her and say, Get on the bike, I'll take you back to Ruth's.

Don't you want to see a movie? she'd ask.

I can't go. I forgot I told my ma I'd wash her car.

Maybe later? she'd ask.

Yeah, maybe, he'd say.

Yeah, right.

Tallulah stood up to go. That was when she noticed the window over the stairs. Actually not the window, so much, but the opening between the bottom sash and the sill. A four-inch gap, dark behind a rusty screen.

263

The window was situated about shoulder height, a foot or so from the landing's edge. Tallulah stood on her toes on the top stair and leaned sideways, gripping the windowsill with her fingertips. She tipped her chin up to see inside. The screen smelled metallic, high-pitched as a whine. Beyond it, she could just make out a sliver of chrome. A sink faucet.

Her first thought was, Someone could break in this way.

Her second thought was, If I don't get some water, I'll never make it back to Ruth's. I could be having heatstroke right now. I could be dying.

Stubby metal flanges secured the screen to the window frame. She tried to pry one off. It didn't budge. She fit a thumbnail into the screw slot and twisted. Her nail cracked into the quick with a flash of pain so intense her knees gave way. She stumbled backward onto the landing and sat down hard.

There were tools in the barn. She descended the stairs, her throbbing thumb in her mouth, and retrieved a hammer from its cobwebby wall stud. Back at the window, two good *whams* freed the flange from the screen. Once the bottom was loose, it took only a minute and a couple whaps of the hammer to jiggle the screen out completely.

"Take that," she said. She dropped the screen and the hammer on the landing and pushed the window sash up.

It took her three tries to hoist herself onto the sill. Once there, her arms shook so badly that, halfway in, her torso hanging over the sink, she knew that if she tried lifting her knee to the sill she'd fall backward onto the stairs and that's where they'd find her, her neck snapped in two.

With one great heave, she hoisted her knee up and launched herself, hands outstretched, toward the counter. The open flap of her coveralls caught on the faucet. She wrenched around in midair. The counter slid away beneath her, her back scraped down a solid edge of something, and she hit the floor, her shoulder crunching painfully. She lay panting, wondering if the wet on her back was sweat or blood. She would rest a minute and find out. It was hot in here. But dim. Dim was good.

After a few moments, she was able to push herself to her feet. The scrapy thing turned out to be the refrigerator door handle. A few feet away, at the junction of carpet and the kitchen linoleum, a large brown tabby with green eyes studied her.

"I don't suppose you know where the glasses are," Tallulah said. The cat yawned, curling its tongue elaborately. Tallulah turned the faucet full on cold and went looking.

After the second glass of water, pulled in long swallows while leaning her elbows on the counter, her shakes had subsided to mild tremors. She ran a hand across her back. No blood.

Kyle kept a pretty clean kitchen for a guy. Only a couple of stains on the counter, no decaying food bits. She opened the refrigerator. An almost empty liter bottle of generic cola, half a package of white bread, margarine, a jar of strawberry preserves. She took out the preserves and twisted off the top and dug out a swath with her index finger. Cold, sweet-tart. She took another swath, careful to use a different, dry finger—it was only polite—and put the jar back next to a partly empty six-pack of beer.

Tallulah filled her glass a third time and wandered out of the kitchen. The cat trilled and drifted next to her, its tail curved high.

The apartment was a one-room studio. Beige carpets. White walls. Poteet obviously hadn't invested in a decorator. Against one wall was an unmade bed, twin-size, tumbled white sheets, no blankets, no headboard. At its foot stood a small television on a plastic crate; on the wall overhead, a poster of a red racing car, NASCAR emblazoned across the bottom. Jeans and socks and a couple of T-shirts were strewn on the floor. Neither jockey shorts nor boxers visible. Could be good or bad.

A torn blue armchair in one corner; in the other, a piece of plywood on two sawhorses. Papers littered the plywood's surface. Algebra problems, scribbled in blue ballpoint pen, with drawings of flames in the margins. Next to the papers a large paperback book lay open. Tallulah turned the cover over. GET YOUR GED! STUDY GUIDE: MATHEMATICS. She laid the book back the way it was.

The air conditioner was in the window over the makeshift desk. Tallulah reached up and turned it on. She still felt sweltering, shaky. Maybe she should sit down. Five minutes, that's all.

The armchair smelled of salt and cigarettes. She tucked

her feet under her and picked a handful of magazines up off the floor. *Performance Cycle*. She flipped to the next one. *Stock Car World*. The cat jumped onto the chair arm and from there to the back. It arranged itself neatly, tucking bits underneath, and began to purr. Tallulah settled her head just below its paws. The blast from the air conditioner raised goose pimples along her thighs. Five minutes. Then she'd leave.

"Hey!"

"What," Tallulah mumbled. Her eyelids stuck together. Had she closed them?

"I could ask *you* what." Kyle's voice. Tallulah blinked and sat forward in the chair. Kyle stood in the open doorway, the sun low and directly behind him. She couldn't see the expression on his face. She unfolded her legs and tried to stand up, but she couldn't feel her feet and ended up plopping back onto the cushion.

"Hi," she said. "I was, I was hot." There was some other reason she was here, something important. She couldn't think what it was.

"Everybody's hot. They don't go breaking into other people's houses." Kyle shut the door, and now she could see his face. His mouth was compressed into a tight triangle. He held the hammer in one hand. "You're lucky I didn't call the cops when I saw my screen busted out."

"No, I mean . . ." It had seemed so clear, before. "I was waiting for you. Outside. And I got thirsty, and woozy . . . I thought I had heatstroke. So I, I came in."

"I guess you did," Kyle said. "Though you wasn't so woozy when you was bashing up my screen." He tossed the hammer onto the bed and crossed over to the desk. He stuffed the math papers into the book, closed it, and turned it front cover down. "I don't suppose, while you was walking back and forth to the barn getting that hammer, you noticed the water faucet and hose down in the carport."

"What ho—" she began, and then remembered. The hose Kyle used to wash down the truck, coiled outside the hospital's back door. "Oh. That hose," she said. She tried a giggle but it caught in her throat and she coughed instead.

Kyle slipped her a sideways look of—disgust? contempt?— and walked into the kitchen. Tallulah again became acutely aware of the baggy coveralls, the scum of dried sweat covering her skin. Now not only would he think her a pig, but a psycho, too. Breaking into his home. For all he knew she'd rifled through his stuff. She would never be able to explain it, because if someone had done this to her, she'd never believe a word they said. Never.

She put her hands on the chair arms and pushed herself upright. This time her feet held her. She walked to the door, careful not to look at him as she passed. The cat trailed after her, mewing.

"Now where are you going?" Kyle asked. He was standing behind the open refrigerator door, digging into the jar of strawberry preserves with a spoon. She was suddenly glad she'd switched fingers on the second dip. It was a small thing to get right, but it was something.

"Back to Ruth's," she said.

"You went to an awful lot of trouble getting in to be leaving already," he said. He put the spoon in his mouth, pulled it back out upside down.

"Look, I'm sorry," she said. "All I could think about was water, and I forgot about the hose. Anyway, you shouldn't leave your window open like that. If I could break in, anyone could."

Kyle grinned. "Good thing for Dr. Poteet all you wanted was water. You could've cleaned him out."

"And taken what? Some dirty towels and a sick cat?"

Kyle laughed, and something in Tallulah lifted. Maybe it would be all right.

Kyle shut the refrigerator and clattered the dirty spoon in the sink. "So how come you was waiting on me?"

"I don't know, I just . . ." She remembered the mare, but suddenly that event seemed too big, too vague to put into words. "Nothing. I should go back to Ruth's."

"Why?"

Tallulah ran a hand through her hair. It felt like a skirt of damp string. "Gee, I don't know. A shower. A change of clothes."

"There's a shower here," he said. "We could eat after, if you want. I ain't had supper yet."

She grinned. Snarky as she was, he still wanted to go out with her. "I don't have any clean clothes here," she said. "It'll take me, like, two minutes at Ruth's."

"And in that two minutes she'll make me eat, and

I won't be hungry anymore, so she'll make you eat, and we'll end up watching *Wheel of Fortune* talking about Jolene and Dr. Poteet and clients all night long." He stepped out of the kitchen and crossed to a small chest of drawers on the other side of the desk. He pulled out a pair of scrubs and tossed them to her.

"Bathroom's right there," he said, pointing. "Come on downstairs when you're done." He left through a door at the far end of the apartment. Tallulah heard his feet thumping down an inside staircase.

The bathroom was tiny, and not as clean as the kitchen, but still it wasn't bad. Six out of ten, with a half-point for effort. Tallulah locked the door, turned the shower on, and shucked out of her clothes. She didn't wait for the water to warm up before getting in.

Basic white soap in the shower caddy. Basic baby shampoo, clear gold, no scent. A disposable razor. Kyle was a basic kind of guy. Except for the crème rinse. Tallulah examined the bottle. Hibiscus flower extract. For a glossy shine. She thought of his smooth, seal brown hair and smiled. So he was a little vain, after all. She tilted her head backward under the water and closed her eyes.

Chapter 21

Sure you don't want no more?" Kyle extended the white carton toward Tallulah. She wrinkled her nose. Kyle closed the carton and set it in the plastic bag with the others, then laid back, hands folded under his head. Tallulah rolled onto her side and gazed out at the lake, the little of it she could see in the dark: moonlight on the water, like shards of china on black marble. They lay on a grassy beachlet sheltered by pines and a fall of boulders, just big enough for the two of them and four cartons of bad Chinese takeout.

While they'd eaten, Tallulah had told Kyle about the mare. In the dark of the trees, awash in smells of sweet and sour pork and beef chow mein, it sounded slightly unreal: the sweat-churned mud, the dull thwack of the mare's body under her fists, the wild eye flicking out of existence.

"Sounds to me like you moved too sudden and spooked her," Kyle said. "Dr. Poteet was right. Close as you was, you could of gotten the snot clobbered out of you."

Tallulah fell silent. She'd failed to convey the spark that had flared between her and the horse; as far as Kyle was concerned, she might have been a bit of paper blowing past. Maeve, she knew, would have understood instantly.

"You been thinking what you're gonna do?" Kyle asked.

"About what? That EMT stuff?"

He shook his head, waved a hand toward the lake. "That's like, way in the future stuff. Naw, I mean now."

Tallulah shrugged. "I don't know. I was going to go to Florida, to find my friend, but . . ." But you're scared, her mind finished for her. Well, maybe she was. She was no closer to a plan than she'd been three days ago, and the thought of being alone again, in a strange city, no idea where to find Maeve, no idea even where to start—anybody would be scared.

Anybody, of course, but Maeve herself.

Kyle extended his fist straight up in the air, thumb extended, and squinted one eye shut, as if trying to blot out the moon. "Think you might stick around?" he asked. His tone almost too casual.

"Here?" She laughed.

"Dr. Poteet'd hire you. I mean, for good."

He was serious. Tallulah sat up. It was so quiet here; no car noise, not even a scrap of TV from the houses hidden beyond the trees. She shivered and rubbed her arms. "Payday's Friday," she finally said.

"So?"

"So I've got four hundred dollars coming. As soon as I have it, I figure whatever crap I just wiped up is the last crap I ever wipe."

It didn't occur to her until after she said this that Kyle's job was largely cleaning shit, too. But he didn't seem insulted. He simply asked, "You gonna go home then, or what?" When Tallulah didn't answer, he said, "Don't you miss 'em?"

"Sometimes," she said, then, "Yeah. But I don't know. Maybe it's better for me to be on my own." And maybe it's better for them, too, she thought. Then, to her own utter surprise, she said, "Sometimes I think about going to find my daddy."

"Oh yeah? Where's he at?"

"Elko," Tallulah said. "Nevada. At least he was when I was seven." All these years she'd waited for him. What was some paper he'd signed, compared to his ladybug? But just like Mom had predicted, he'd never come back.

Why couldn't she go to him?

"I tried living with my dad after the divorce," Kyle said. "That lasted all of two months. He sent me back to my ma."

"Do you see him a lot?"

"Sometimes. Not much since he got married again. His new wife's an anklebiter. No bigger'n a Chihuahua. Mean as one, too."

Married again.

The thought hit her like a slap in the face. All these years she'd pictured her daddy where she'd seen him last, in the tiny Elko apartment. Alone. Somehow, it had never occurred to her that he might be married, living in some big house with some new wife and . . .

And children. Other children. Little Terri's, with Daddy's thick blond hair and straight nose.

No. He couldn't have, she thought; at the same time some logical part of her brain said, Of course he did. That's why he never came back. Or called. Or sent one single lousy birthday card. He was too busy keeping track of his other kids' birthdays.

Kids smarter, prettier, better than you.

"Not that living with my ma was a piece of cake," Kyle was saying. "I dunno how many times I walked out with her throwing pans and shit and yelling, Don't come back. I'd stay with my brother a couple days. Then I'd go back and she'd cry and cook me supper. The last time, though, she threw the stew pot. Bashed me right on the ear."

Startled, Tallulah glanced down at him. As dark as it was, she could barely see his high cheekbone, lit silver against the black of the lake. Then the cheek rounded, and she caught the glint of teeth. He was grinning.

"That's not funny," she said.

"It didn't do no damage," he said. "Sooner or later, though, one of us was gonna get hurt, and since I never threw nothing at her, I figured it was time to go." He sat up, legs crossed Indian-style. Tallulah could see the shine of his eyes in the moonlight, steady on her own.

"That's what we oughta do," he said. "Let's go."

"What are you talking about?"

"What you just said. Nevada."

"But I didn't . . . I mean . . ." She saw herself knocking

on a strange door, watched as a younger version of Terri opened it. Worse: a younger version of *herself.* Another ladybug. . . . Tallulah squeezed her eyes shut, as if blackness could blot out the picture. "Look," she said, "it was just something I said, it's not—"

"My brother'll sell me his car. We've been talking about it, anyway. He says he wants my bike and five hundred bucks, but I bet he'll take three. Couple two-three weeks, I could have the money. The car ain't pretty but the engine's practically new. It'll get us there."

"Get who where? Us who?"

"You and me, that's who. Ain't you been listening?"

"What makes you think I want to go anywhere with you?" she blurted.

"You like me," Kyle said. "I like you." He shrugged: *What more do you want?*

Even more than the nonchalance in his voice, it was the shrug that irritated her. "You haven't even taken me on a date yet," she said, "and you want to go to Nevada with me?"

He gestured around him. "What do you call this?"

"This? I call this sitting on the dirt with sucky Chinese food. What about that movie you promised?"

"You're the one broke into my apartment to seduce me. Doesn't seem like you're too hung up on formalities."

Tallulah swung at him, missed, and almost landed on a carton of food. "I did not break into your apartment to *seduce* you!" She scrambled to her feet. "And anyway, look. Look at this!"

He stood up, glanced around. "What?"

"This! Fighting! Every time we're together more than five minutes, we fight. I wouldn't go to the *store* with you, let alone across the goddamn country!"

"This ain't a fight." He was grinning again. "Ain't nothing broke. Ain't no one crying."

"Yeah, well, the last time I fought with a guy I ended up dumped. OK? I'm not about to get stranded by another one in some other godforsaken boonieville."

"You know I wouldn't do nothing like that," Kyle said.

"No, I don't know. That's the whole point. *I don't know you.*"

His voice hardened. "All right. Forget it. It was just an idea."

"Yeah, well, it was a stupid idea."

"I said forget it."

"I will."

He rummaged in a back pocket. Tallulah heard the crinkle of a cigarette pack. Don't you dare offer me one, she thought. Flare of a lighter; more crinkles as the pack was slipped back into the pocket. Fine. I didn't want one anyway.

"So is it true?" he asked.

"Is what true?"

"Dr. Poteet likes you."

"*Likes* me? What do you mean, *likes* me?"

"Likes you. You know." He hung his thumbs in his jeans pockets, the cigarette glowing near one hip. "You heard Ruth the other night. Daughter's dead, wife's gone. Lives all alone with a bunch of damn flowers. Here he is a vet, and he ain't even got a dog." He took a short, hard drag, blew it out. "Seems like don't nothing go deep with him."

"So what?"

"So now all of a sudden he takes in some girl? Does all this stuff for her?"

"Hiring me was Ruth's idea. Not his."

"He's the damn boss. He don't do what she says." Kyle glanced sideways, into the trees. "You sleeping with him?" he asked.

Tallulah picked up a carton off the ground and threw it. She heard it hit—she was already striding away, across the clearing—and hoped it was the sweet and sour pork. Something sticky, that would stain. She began to run but then she was in the brush surrounding the clearing, branches grabbing at her legs. Where was the path? She flogged to the left, yelping as something sharp nicked across her wrist.

"That ain't the way back," Kyle said.

Tallulah thrashed her way out of the brush. "He must be fifty. Sixty. If his daughter hadn't gotten herself killed, she'd be older than me. God!"

"He's only forty-something. Not that old. Not for some girls. I wouldn't blame you or nothing. He's educated. He's got money."

The scratch on the inside of her wrist stung; she lifted it to her mouth, tasted blood. "You're a pervert just for think-ing it," she said.

"Just so you know," Kyle said. "I ain't stupid." Tallulah opened her mouth to retort, thinking he was accusing her again; but then he said, "I'm gonna get my GED."

The breath and the anger both went out of her, all at once.

"Anyway," he said, and turned away toward the lake. Tallulah crossed the few feet between them and laid her hands on his shoulders. He shrugged, but not hard enough to shake her off. She reached around, took the cigarette from his fingers, and pulled herself a long, satisfying lungful. Then she slipped in front of him, arms sliding around his waist like snakes, rocking him just enough so that the moon lit his face full on. She wanted to see how his eyes looked when she kissed him.

Afterward, she laid her head in the hollow between his neck and his shoulder. His arms tightened, warm across her back. Tallulah gazed out at the lake. Moon on the water, china-sharp, shifting.

"I have to go to Florida," she said. "I have to find my friend. Maybe something happened to her. You'd do the same thing, if she was your friend."

His hands drifted across her back. "If it was you, I would," he said.

She tilted her head back to see into his face. "Do I go deep with you?"

He nodded. "Yeah. You do," he said, and bent to kiss her again. When they broke apart, he said, "Way they been running my ass, they owe me time off. If Dr. Poteet'll give me tomorrow night then I'll take you to the movies." He took a last drag on the cigarette, ground it out with his boot toe. "Come on. We better get you back before Ruth calls the cops out on you."

Which, Tallulah found out the next day, had very nearly happened. Ruth barely looked at her and spoke less, saying only Good morning and Here's your dinner. Jolene showed no such restraint, ripping her up one side and down the other for skipping out—her words, as if Tallulah had gone to a picnic, instead of a field call in which the patient ended up dead—on the evening cleaning. Then Poteet asked if she thought he enjoyed getting phone calls from frantic receptionists in the middle of the night regarding the whereabouts of wayward kennel girls. Kyle, who as far as Tallulah knew was the only person in Tennessee who still approved of her, was of course nowhere to be seen.

By late in the afternoon, Tallulah had had enough. When Jolene got involved in an X-ray procedure, Tallulah took her chance. "I'll start walking the dogs," she called cheerily, then escaped, hustling herself out of earshot before Jolene—weighted down in a lead apron, lead neck shield, and lead gloves, both hands occupied with the patient on the X-ray table—could gather her wits enough to object. Tallulah leashed Diesel and hustled him outside, heading for the barn. Sometimes Kyle worked on his motorcycle there, using Poteet's tools. She still didn't know if he'd gotten the night off, if he was taking her out.

He wasn't there. She hovered in the barn doorway,

disappointed. Pickles hung his head over his stall door and whickered to her. She walked over, patted his nose. Diesel flopped down next to her. The heat and silence pressed, heavy as water, against her skin. The barn smelled like old wood and dust and the insides of grass, the tough, jointed stalks Tallulah had chewed for their sweetness when she was a little girl in Modesto.

She heard a car engine rumbling close. Clients sometimes parked their cars next to the barn when the front lot was full. As she listened, the engine grew louder, idled, then quit.

She sighed and tugged lightly on Diesel's leash. "Come on, buddy. He's not here. No use roasting to death." Diesel hauled himself to his feet and lumbered after her. Outside, Tallulah squinted her eyes almost shut against the sun, aiming for the dark shadow of the hospital's back door. Behind her, a car door clicked open. She glanced over her shoulder. Then turned around. There was Ruth's blue Pontiac, and next to it, at the end of the row, an olive green sedan. Tallulah's heart thudded hard. She began walking toward the car, to see the license plate, but before she took two steps farther, a pale red-haired woman got out of the car and faced her. She held the car door open between them, as though it were a shield.

"Hello," Maeve said.

Chapter 22

Maeve's hair was short. Chopped and wildly uneven, as though she'd taken scissors to it without using a mirror. Strands and shoots coiled out from her skull like electrified copper. Her eyes were hidden behind sunglasses.

"It's wonderful to see you," she said.

Tallulah took a stunned step toward the car. Maeve did not move to meet her. With an odd ducking motion, she dragged the sunglasses off her face. The skin around her eyes was sickly pale, half-moons underneath dark as bruises. "Your hair's growing out," she said. Her voice was tentative, as if addressing a barely remembered cousin at a wedding. Red lines strained across the white of her knuckles where they gripped the car door. Her breathing was shallow and quick. Like Diesel's on the exam table.

"Oh my God, Maeve," Tallulah said, and ran to her.

She draped Maeve's arm over her neck and bent forward, taking Maeve's weight onto her own shoulders.

"Come on. The hospital's right over there," Tallulah said.

Maeve laughed, a breathless, rueful laugh. "What is it

they say? It's not the heat, it's the humidity. . . . I'd forgotten. It was just like this in Florida. You need gills to breathe, not lungs."

In the back hallway, Tallulah could hear the bustlings in the exam rooms, the murmur of people in the lobby, a man's voice telling his dog to Sit. *Sit.* SIT. The office was empty. Tallulah steered Maeve toward it.

"My word," Tallulah heard Ruth say from the reception counter. Then Ruth was in the office with them, helping Tallulah get Maeve to a chair.

"I'm all right," Maeve kept saying. "Really. I'm OK. I'm just tired. And hot."

"Sit awhile in the cool," Ruth said. "Tallulah, run get that thermos of iced tea."

Tallulah ran, returning in less than a minute. Maeve drank the way Tallulah had in Kyle's apartment, both hands on the glass, her breath small explosions between draughts. After downing the second glass, she seemed to relax a bit.

Ruth had left the office; now she bustled back in with an ice pack, the flat bricklike kind that came in the shipments of vaccines, and a damp towel. "Better?" she asked.

"Much. Thank you." Maeve looked around the office, at the pots on the windowsill. "What pretty orchids," she said.

"Ruth, Maeve MacRae," Tallulah said. "Maeve, this is Ruth. I've been staying with her."

Ruth wrapped the ice pack in the damp towel and handed it to Maeve. "You have any headache? Dizziness?" Maeve shook her head. "Let's hope you don't have heatstroke, then. Scorcher of a day like this, what have you been doing? Walking?"

"The air conditioning's broken in my car. I never had it fixed," Maeve said. She laid the wrapped ice pack against the back of her neck and closed her eyes.

"Was *I* going to Florida in August, fixing the air conditioning would be the first thing I'd have done," Ruth said.

For the first time, the dryness in her tone annoyed Tallulah. Since when was this any of her business? "It was an emergency," Tallulah said. "There was no time."

Maeve opened her eyes. "What was an emergency?"

"Going to Florida," Tallulah said.

"No it wasn't. I'd been planning it for a month." Maeve ran the ice pack to the hollow at the front of her throat, then up to her temple. Tallulah stared at her. *You never told me,* she almost said; but she could feel Ruth's eyes on her, and kept quiet.

"Tallulah, why don't you and your friend go on," Ruth said. She fished in her purse for her keys, began working one off the ring. "State she's in, she ought not to sit around here waiting for you to get off work. Go on home and she can rest a bit. There's only an hour left in the day, anyway."

"Jolene's going to be pissed," Tallulah said; but she took the key.

"Kyle'll help Jolene. Or I will, one."

As they were leaving, Tallulah turned to say something to Ruth. She never did remember what, later, because at the clouded expression on her face, Tallulah turned back toward

283

Maeve and looked at her, too, not with the eyes of a best friend, who noticed only the shock of razored hair, but as a stranger might. She saw a heavy, exhausted woman, whose hands trembled, whose eyes wandered around the room like Loren Castleberry's on a bad day, whose long paisley skirt was almost as wrinkled and stained as Castleberry's slacks. Grease smudges, as though Maeve had worked under LUVLY1 at some point, and something else—was that ketchup? Lord, let it not be blood—were smeared across her blue cotton shirt.

But, Tallulah reminded herself, she herself had looked worse her first twenty-four hours in Tennessee. And there was no telling what Maeve had been through.

Looking inside LUVLY1, though, she got rattled again. True, the car had never been neat; since Tallulah had known Maeve, it had been strewn with library books and newspapers and CD's, in varying proportions depending on Maeve's interests at the moment. But it had never been littered with trash. The rear foot wells were ankle-high with crumpled fast-food bags, empty potato chip bags, and soda cans, as though Maeve had eaten all her meals driving and tossed the garbage behind her. Or dropped it underfoot; every time Tallulah stepped on the gas, a nest of Twinkie wrappers crackled. Since when did Maeve eat Twinkies? Or any junk food, for that matter? On the back seat lay a tangle of maps, open and piled; another map, torn almost completely down one side, tented crazily across the passenger dashboard. The car smelled of overheated vinyl, sour food, parched cotton, and sweat. The same odors as Maeve herself, only stronger.

She's been on the road, Tallulah told herself. She remembered how fast the garbage had piled up in Derek's Honda, even though he'd insisted on keeping it clean, yelling every time Tallulah tossed an empty juice carton into the backseat.

It was scorching in the Monte Carlo, the steering wheel almost too hot to touch. Maeve lapsed into a drowsy silence, so Tallulah did almost all the talking. As she drove, she told Maeve about Derek. About tripping over Diesel in the underpass. About Poteet. Maeve nodded, said, Oh my God, and You're kidding. But at the most exciting part—Tallulah scrambling to her feet, blind in the dark, terrified of who or what was in the underpass with her—Maeve's gaze slipped away out the window.

A minute later, Tallulah pulled the Monte Carlo into the doublewide's carport.

"This is your place?" Maeve said in a bemused tone.

"Mine? No. Ruth's. I told you. I've been staying with her."

"That old woman? With the yellow hair?"

"She's not *that* old," Tallulah said, unlocking the front door of the doublewide. "Get back, Tripod. Scat! Come in quick before they run out."

"How many are there?"

"Four, I think. Or five. I still can't tell."

Once inside, Maeve drifted around the living room, brushing her fingers over the back of Ruth's blue velour recliner, the brown-checked sofa, the series of painted wooden butterflies affixed to the wall. She passed by Tallulah's duffel without seeming to see it, or her own notebooks, the green and purple covers visible under the half-open zipper.

Tallulah followed her. "Maeve, what's been happening?" she asked. "Where have you been?"

"Please. Later." Maeve lifted her arms from her sides, gazed down at herself. "I'm a mess."

"I'm sorry. You're right, I shouldn't have . . . the bathroom's right there. Is there a suitcase in the car?"

"The trunk."

"I'll get it for you. There's clean towels in the hall cabinet."

Tallulah waited until she heard the water jetting into the tub, then grabbed Maeve's keys and headed outside. Swung open LUVLY1's trunk and, for perhaps a full minute, could only stare.

It looked as though someone had set off a bomb in a closet. A full closet. A sleeve here, a pant leg there, a jungle of a hundred different fabrics tangled together. Tallulah groped to the bottom of the pile, to the right, to the left. No suitcase. It was as though Maeve had simply picked up armfuls of clothing—jeans, dresses, underwear, shoes, jackets—and thrown them in. Many still sported tags in collars and sleeves and waistbands, from stores whose names Tallulah didn't recognize. Maeve was capable of no-holds-barred shopping sprees—she'd gone on one in Portland, just before

286

she disappeared—but a black suede vest studded with rhinestone lariats? A red spike-heeled sandal? That had been in Maeve's size, at least. The lace camisole, though, was a size ten. The fake snake leather pants, a six. But if the clothes were someone else's—which they had to be, there was no other explanation—then whose?

As much as Tallulah tried, she could come up with no explanation for this.

In the meantime, though, Maeve needed something to wear. Tallulah rummaged until she found something she recognized: a long yellow skirt, a favorite of Maeve's from Portland, clean and only moderately rumpled. It took a few more minutes to unearth a white T-shirt and bra and panties that appeared to be Maeve's size.

She carried the clothes into the doublewide, intending to lay them on the washing machine, across the hall from the bathroom. But the bathroom door was open. From the hallway, Tallulah could see the mirror over the sink; its edges were obscured by steam, but the center had been swiped clear. Maeve stood at the counter, her back to Tallulah. Tallulah stopped, shocked not so much at Maeve's nakedness as by her size. Or lack of it. Maeve wasn't a size ten yet, nowhere near; but the rolls over her waist had thinned and sagged, and the flesh along the backs of her arms hung loose. From the pale, rippled expanse of Maeve's right buttock, a tattooed queen glared at Tallulah. The queen was robed in blue and green; from under her crown, red hair flared like a mantle. She was seated on a gold throne, a scepter in one hand. A sword lay under her feet. The entire design was so large it would take both of Tallulah's hands to cover it. It was the most beautiful tattoo she had ever seen.

"Queen Mabh," Maeve said. "She led her armies into battle. They said she could run faster than horses. That she brought thirty men a night to her bed." In the mirror, Tallulah met Maeve's eyes. Wet half-curls and ragged spikes, dark as cherry wood, boiled up from her scalp; drops fell from them, skimming tracks down her back.

From the carport came the slam of a door. "That's Ruth," Tallulah said.

"Then I guess you better give me those clothes." Maeve held out a hand. After she swung the bathroom door shut, Tallulah stared at its dark surface a moment, as if something more—some explanation—might yet come. Then she went to help Ruth with whatever she'd brought for supper.

Styrofoam boxes, a flat of sodas. Jake's again. And Kyle again. Poteet must have given him the night off, because he showed up just after they sat down, pulling up a chair and helping himself to half of Tallulah's onion rings, no asking permission, just grabbing. Like two kisses gave him some kind of right.

Tallulah didn't want him there. It was bad enough that Ruth was there, but it was her house, Tallulah could hardly ask her to leave.

"Tallulah says you're from Florida," Ruth said, once the boxes were open and the sodas passed around. "Do you-all have family there?"

"Not anymore." Maeve shoved her chair back, got up. "Thank you," she said, gesturing at her cheeseburger, which she hadn't touched. "I'm not hungry. You want it?" she asked Kyle.

"If you don't." He pulled the Styrofoam box from her place to his.

"Do you want to lie down?" Tallulah asked.

"No," Maeve said. She walked around the room, the same way she had when she'd first arrived, seemingly aimless, and yet unable to stop, to rest. "Do you like living in a trailer?" she asked Ruth abruptly.

A V, like the tension in a bird's wing, drew down between Ruth's penciled brows. "Suits me well enough," she said. Tallulah winced at the coldness of her tone. No, wait, she wanted to say. If you knew Maeve, you'd know. This is just the way she is.

Only it wasn't. Maeve was different, and it wasn't just her hair or her weight. The Maeve Tallulah had known shone. She laughed. She talked easily, intimately, to people she'd just met. By now, Maeve and Ruth should be gossiping like fiends.

"So now you got your papers," Kyle said to Maeve, "you heading on back to Florida?"

"Papers?" Maeve asked.

"The notebooks," Tallulah said, looking at Kyle in surprise. Early on, during one of the evenings Ruth had made him help clean kennels, she'd told him about the notebooks, explaining how she'd ended up here. But he hadn't expressed any curiosity about them, and she didn't think he'd even remembered.

"What I don't get," Kyle said, talking around a mouthful of cheeseburger, "is if you needed them papers so bad, how come you forgot 'em."

"What are you talking about?" Tallulah said sharply.

Kyle shrugged. "Just seems to me if they was that important, she'd of brought 'em with her," he said. "Instead of making you chase all across the country."

"There's things I didn't want certain people to see," Maeve said. She shook her head a little as she walked. Tallulah knew that gesture; but there wasn't enough hair, anymore, to ripple down Maeve's back. "People in Florida. They don't know Tallulah. The notebooks were safer with her."

"People in Florida? What people?" Tallulah asked. So Maeve hadn't forgotten the notebooks in Portland after all. Had she said she'd forgotten them, in her e-mail? Or had Tallulah just assumed that she had, the way Tallulah had assumed that Maeve's disappearance had been brought about by some emergency?

"My family," Maeve said.

"You just said you ain't got family," Kyle said.

Maeve gave a short laugh and turned to Tallulah. "You didn't mention him," she said, jerking her chin at Kyle. "Your knight in shining armor."

"No, it's not . . . he's not . . ." Tallulah began. Then stopped, when she realized they were all staring at her: Maeve, Ruth, Kyle.

"Not what?" Kyle said. "I'm not what?" He'd been leaning back in his chair, arms crossed. Now he let the chair thump to the floor, and he stood up. "Thanks for supper," he said to Ruth. Then, to Tallulah, "I'll see you tomorrow." He hovered, as though waiting for her to answer. Tallulah dragged an onion ring through the ketchup on her plate, drew an arrow, blurred it into a solid square. She didn't look up until she heard the front door slam.

Ruth began clearing the plates. Tallulah knew she should offer to help; but one more minute cooped up between this odd, jarring Maeve and a silent, pensive Ruth and she'd go crazy. Away from here, once they were by themselves, surely Maeve would explain everything.

"I'm going to show Maeve the graveyard," she said.

Ruth was crushing Styrofoam boxes into the garbage. "Watch out for snakes," she said, without turning around.

On the back porch, Tallulah paused. "Wait here," she said. She brushed past Maeve into the doublewide, grabbed her duffel, and trotted back outside.

"This way," she told Maeve, heading for the pasture. Cowboy bounded ahead of them. As though being outside had lifted some constraint, Maeve began to talk: the heat in Florida, the heat here, the storms, the humidity. Tallulah led the way up the wooded hill, Maeve panting behind her. They came to the car graveyard, but Tallulah didn't slow down to explore or explain. She no longer felt the glimmer of a roaring past here; the cars were simply hunks of rusty metal, sticky crumbled foam, cracked glass hazed in dirt. To her surprise, Maeve seemed hardly to notice them. At the crest of the hill, Tallulah clambered onto the rocks and sat down, the duffel beside her. Maeve again refused to sit. Instead, she paced a tight short line at the top of the outcrop.

"Michael was an angel," she said. Emphatically, as if Tallulah had expressed an opinion otherwise, as if they'd been talking about Michael at all. "Anything I needed, anything I wanted, he would get it or do it or be it. And beautiful as a god. I swear if it wasn't . . ."

Maeve had always been a talker. She talked constantly and fast, her hands dancing, a hundred expressions flitting across her face in as many moments. But Tallulah had marked a difference here, too, and now it came to her what it was: Maeve's words leaped out of her like water out of a hose, as though hundreds of gallons, thousands, thronged behind, shoving. Before, she talked as though if only she talked fast enough, she could encompass the world; now, she talked as though she simply could not stop. As though a pressure had built up inside that had no other relief.

But for all Maeve's talking so far, Tallulah still couldn't piece together what had happened. If only they could tally their experiences—*at that time I was here, where were you, what were you doing?*—then, she was sure, everything would slip into place.

"What happened in Orlando?" she asked, when Maeve paused for breath. "Are you going back?"

"Do you know I made it there in three days?" Maeve said.

"From Portland?"

"Of course from Portland. That's where you saw me last, wasn't it?" A hint of sarcasm in her tone. Tallulah frowned. Of the two of them, she was the sarcastic one, not Maeve. But she was being dense, and Maeve was tired. Tallulah routinely got sarcastic with far less provocation.

"It took me and Derek three days just to get to Kansas," Tallulah said.

"You slept." Maeve's statement was so bald that Tallulah blinked, confused. She looked again at the bruiselike half-moons under Maeve's eyes, and this time she realized what they meant. She'd seen them before, back in Portland, the time Maeve stayed up three nights in a row pouring her thoughts into the notebooks. Maeve had acted a little like this then, too. Rattled. Impatient.

"Have you been sleeping?" Tallulah asked.

"I needed noise. It was too quiet. Michael didn't even have a television, did you know that?" Maeve's voice rose in accusation. "What kind of idiot doesn't have a television? What was I supposed to do?"

And she was off again. Each sentence made sense, but when Tallulah tried to grasp where Maeve was going, the larger sense slipped away from her. And yet there was a logic. She could feel it, just out of reach. If she just listened, if she concentrated hard enough, she would understand.

"It's over, now," Maeve said. "There's nothing I can do. It's over."

"But . . . the notebooks," Tallulah said. She zipped open

the duffel, reached inside. "See? I did bring them. You can go back to Florida, you can—"

"Go back to Florida?" Maeve stopped pacing; she looked down at Tallulah and if Tallulah didn't know better, she'd think the expression on Maeve's face was contempt. "It's too late. Even you must realize that."

Too late. "Because of me," Tallulah said. The jewel colors of the notebooks blurred through a sudden welling of tears. "Was it? Because of me? Because I tried, Maeve, it was just that when Derek—"

"You have no idea what they can do. How they can poison everyone against you."

Tallulah scrambled to her feet. "But your friends still love you. I still love you. Michael—"

"Michael turned against me." Maeve was facing away from Tallulah, looking out over the ridge to the mountains beyond. Her hair radiated from her skull like a shorn sun. "He called them. He told them where I was. When I begged him not to."

"Told who?"

"My parents." Maeve turned. She was crying, rubbing the heel of her hand under one eye. "And then he kicked me out. He cut off his phone so I couldn't even call him. . . ."

"But . . ." The feeling of disconnect was back, stronger now. As though Maeve's words had taken on different meanings from the ones Tallulah knew. "You don't have parents. Your parents are . . ." *Dead.* Go on, say it. Maeve's family, all dead. Maeve had told her the stories, up on the roof of the Belinda. It seemed a long time ago, now. "Maeve, listen to me. It doesn't matter."

"I thought I could live as if their lies were nothing. I can't. They've poisoned everything." She exhaled, a long, shuddering breath. "I have to go."

She means it, Tallulah thought. She's going to leave, and I don't even understand why. She waited for the hurt and was surprised to feel only an ache. Blunted, like lifting a heavy pack onto her shoulder after she'd laid it down awhile to rest. The groove had already been worn.

"I'll help you," she said. "Whatever you need." Feeling like the worst hypocrite in the world. Like a fool. *Look what you've done already,* her mind jeered.

"I can't go back to that trailer," Maeve said. "It smells of dead flesh and grease. That woman, you saw the way she looked at me. And all those cats. Maybe they already know I'm here."

"Who? The cats?" Tallulah asked, a split second before she realized this had not been what Maeve meant. Maeve shot a startled glance at her. Then she laughed. A real laugh, her cherrywood eyes wide open and delighted. "God, I've missed you," she said, and for an instant it seemed she was entirely *there,* like the Maeve Tallulah had always known. She pointed at Tallulah's duffel. "Is that all you have? Or is there more in the trailer? I'll wait for you in the car if there is."

It took Tallulah a moment to understand. "But I'm not going with you," she said. Take it back, she thought, half-panicked. Then she remembered the cool damp of the baby's lips against her own. Just a scrap of recollection; but her breath caught. She shook her head. "I just . . . I can't."

Maeve's eyes narrowed. "Don't be stupid. What did you think, I came all this way just to say good-bye?"

"You're my best friend," Tallulah said. "I'll help you. But . . ." How could she explain, when she didn't understand herself? "It's just that . . . stuff's happened to me. You see? I've been through things."

"Things?" Maeve's voice, which less than a minute before had scraped low with despair, rose up sharply. "Stuff? What stuff? What things? I swear to God, Tallulah, a three-year-old has a better vocabulary than you do."

"No, I—" Tallulah broke off, looked away. She couldn't meet Maeve's eyes, not with that look in them. That contempt. She rubbed the inside of her arm, then shrugged. "I guess things have—I guess I've changed."

"What's changed since you left all those messages on Michael's answering machine? *Come save me, oh oh oh, I'm in such terrible trouble, oh hurry hurry!* Like someone about to be boiled in goddamned boiling oil."

"You got my messages? You got them and you didn't call me? My God, Maeve, I was in *jail!*"

"Oh, please." Maeve gestured toward the graveyard. "One night in the slammer, then little mamacita down there stuffing you like a turkey, letting you sleep on her couch. Look. Was that you begging me on all those messages to come get you, or wasn't it?"

"It was. I did. But that was—"

"So get your stuff so we can get the hell out of here. How much money do you have?"

It was coming at her too fast. Too much. Tallulah shook her head, trying to sort through what Maeve had said, trying to hold on to her own thoughts. They slipped away like eels, leaving her with scraps and bits that didn't fit together.

"Con-cen-trate, Tallulah." Maeve drew her words out, as though speaking to a child. "How . . . much . . . money . . . do . . . you . . . have?"

"None," Tallulah said. "I don't have any."

"You took off across the United States with no money."

"I told you about Derek, I—"

"Yeah, I heard. Well, let me tell you something. I didn't have to come to God-knows-where, Tennessee, just because my friend, who was supposed to be helping *me*, got herself stranded high and dry. Why? Why is my friend high and dry? Because she picked her ex-boyfriend as the most reliable mode of transportation across the goddamn country. Just a thought, Tallulah, OK? A suggestion? Next time, take a plane. Michael was like, what was she thinking? I mean, the second I met you I knew you weren't the reincarnated Einstein, but I bet not even your mother thought you'd be that stupid."

Tallulah clenched a fold of jeans in one fist. "I thought of a plane. I did." Her voice shook and a tiny part of her was glad, thinking, She'll stop, when she sees how much she's hurting me. "But at the last minute like that, I didn't have enough money and Derek—"

"That hillbilly down there." Maeve began pacing again. "He's what's changed. Right?"

Tallulah gaped at her. "He's not— No! Kyle has nothing to do with it, Maeve, *listen* to me!"

"I knew it. God, you are such a liar. You couldn't tell the truth if it was stenciled on your forehead." Maeve peered at Tallulah from under the shade of a hand. The setting sun washed her skin a pinkish gold, lit her freckles to copper.

"Maeve, I was trying to get to Orlando. I was. The only reason I'm here is because of the dog, and I only went back for him because I knew if I left him there to die you'd be upset. That's what started this whole mess. And then things just . . . happened. I don't know how."

"Go on," Maeve said. She didn't sound angry. She didn't sound like anything anymore, except tired. "Go to your hillbilly trash. You're too weak to help me." She turned away, facing out over the ridge.

"I tried," Tallulah repeated doggedly. *Sometimes, Debra, trying isn't good enough,* her mother had old her once, *and this is one of those times.* But now—like then—it was the only thing left for Tallulah to say.

"Don't feel bad," Maeve said. She spoke quietly, without looking at Tallulah. "Do you think you're the first person to jump ship on me? You're not. Do you think you're special? You're not. So don't think you are."

298

"I saved a baby's life," Tallulah said.

Still Maeve didn't look at her. At first she acted like she hadn't heard. And then she shrugged.

"You shouldn't have," she said.

Tallulah didn't remember turning around. It seemed as though someone picked her up and set her on the far side of the crest of the hill and she was running, the grass whipping her thighs, the dark edge of the trees and the graveyard just ahead.

"You should have let it die in peace," Maeve called after her. "It would have been one less agony in the world."

Chapter 23

The dead mare came to Tallulah. A riffing of hooves, staccato raps like accusations. Poteet was shining a light in her face so that the seams of her eyelids glowed red orange. Why did you kill her? Poteet asked. His face a black mask behind the light. The dead hooves grew louder, insistent, beating out a rhythm that Tallulah could almost understand.

Then the mare was beneath her and bucking and Tallulah was sitting up—she knew she was sitting up, but the clatter of hooves still roared and her heart stampeded with the hooves. She thought, Stop it, you're awake, and then Cowboy barked and she knew she was. She groaned and rubbed the heels of her hands into her shut eyes until red lightning ran all up and down the insides of her eyelids. The knocking erupted again. When she opened her eyes, the sun flared into them from the window above Ruth's TV.

Ruth came into the room, slippers flapping, tying her blue terry robe. She crossed behind the sofa and opened the door.

" 'Morning, Ruth," a man said.

"I guess it is," she said. "Get back, Cowboy."

"Sorry to wake you-all up so early. 'Morning, there." He raised his voice. Tallulah peered over the back of the sofa. She nodded to the man—Ruth's neighbor, he and his wife had once brought over a peach cobbler—and the thought came, with no particular urgency, It's something about Maeve.

Tallulah kicked off the sheets, fumbled for her scrub bottoms and yanked them on.

"It would have been along your back line," the man was saying when she stumbled around the corner of the sofa.

"I tell you what, if I'm asleep at the Second Coming, Jesus Himself will have to dump me out of bed." Ruth turned to Tallulah. "Mr. Johnson wants to know did we hear anything in the pasture last night."

"Who? Who was it?" Tallulah said.

Mr. Johnson grunted. "Not who, what. Cows. Scattered all over the g.d. road."

"Cows?" Tallulah said.

"The missus and me figure it must've been kids," Mr. Johnson said to Ruth. "She heard a car and got up to look and there was headlights in the pasture. I bet they got spooked out of their fun because the pasture ain't too tore up, but they didn't bother about the gate."

Tallulah slipped behind Mr. Johnson onto the front porch. It was true. Cows, all over the road, on the side of the road, wandering up the road. A gray speckled cow was nosing one of Ruth's camellia bushes.

She trotted down the porch steps and across the swath of grass that separated Ruth's yard from the pasture. Dew soaked her bare feet and the hems of her scrub pants. The wide metal gate at the front of the pasture hung open. Hoof prints had obliterated whatever tire tracks might have been there, but at the edge of the road, she found a thin sweeping curve of mud, tread-shaped and laced with torn grass, aimed at the highway.

Last night, when Ruth had come home from Wednesday night church, Tallulah had been lying on the sofa bed, the lights turned out, sheets pulled under her chin and her eyes closed. She heard the sudden check in Ruth's movements, the low clacking of keys laid down on the entry table, the sharp jingle of Cowboy's tags and Ruth's shush. A cat mewed. A floorboard near the sofa creaked and a moment later something brushed Tallulah's forehead. Her closed eyelids jerked in surprise. Whispery dry skin, the hint of a fingernail. The back of Ruth's hand. Mom used to check for fever the exact same way, when Tallulah was small. The gesture seemed so overwhelmingly kind, so warm and sane, that Tallulah was tempted to sit up and pour the whole mess from her own shoulders into Ruth's soft and practical lap.

The hand lifted. Ruth's footsteps receded into the kitchen; Tallulah swung her feet to the floor, ready to follow. Then she heard a cabinet door creak open. A rustling of plastic, a sudden clink of glass. Tallulah froze.

Earlier, she'd helped herself to two more Rolling Rocks.

She'd been so upset, she'd thought the alcohol would calm her, but it had only gotten her more confused, more jumbled. She'd been careful to hide the bottles in the trash . . . but Ruth knew. Of course Ruth knew. Cheeks flaming, Tallulah eased herself back down, listening as Ruth rinsed out the empty bottles, as she placed them, faintly chinking, in the recycle bag.

Finally, after what seemed an eternity of puttering, Ruth went to bed. Tallulah pressed her head deep into the goosedown pillow, pulled the sheet over her head. But she couldn't stop replaying the conversation on the hill.

She hadn't understood Maeve. That was the only explanation. From the first, Maeve had been trying to tell her something, and when she couldn't make Tallulah understand, she'd gotten upset. Tallulah tried to remember exactly what they'd said, to find the key in Maeve's words, her lashing moods. The contempt on her face when she'd looked at Tallulah. The horrible things she'd said, at the end.

Outside, an engine had roared to life. LUVLY1. Tallulah lurched upright, her heart pounding. Cowboy gave one short, sharp bark; she put a hand on his muzzle. "It's all right," she kept saying, listening as the engine backed out of the driveway, as it receded, then flared, then receded again. And vanished. Tallulah waited for its return, but nothing sounded except the crickets, and, much later, a yowling cat-fight. She didn't remember falling asleep.

No use now going back to bed. She showered and dressed, and by the time she padded out to the kitchen barefoot, her wet hair slicked back, the Johnsons and three or four other neighbors were gathered on Ruth's porch, speculating who might have left the gate open. The owner of the pasture came walking up in overalls and a disheveled comb-over, complaining bitterly about the cattle's owner, who was nowhere to be found, while Cowboy started a whirlwind fight with the dog next door over the right to herd the cows up and down the road.

Ruth came into the kitchen and poured Tallulah a cup of coffee. "I notice your friend didn't stay," she said, setting the mug on the counter.

"No," Tallulah said. She stirred in a spoonful of sugar, keeping her eyes on the dark eddy in her cup.

"Coming back?"

"I don't think so," Tallulah said. She shook her head. "No."

Maeve was gone. Tallulah was alone. But the thought didn't scare her. Not like before. No, what bothered her was the fact that, underneath her sorrow, and her grief, and her worry for Maeve, she was . . . relieved.

What kind of friend are you? Tallulah laid her forehead in her hand. A terrible one. I'm sorry, Maeve.

Ruth cleared her throat. "We'll let her be, then. Just in case any of them," she waved her mug in the direction of the porch, "ask where that Monte Carlo got to during the night."

"Thanks," Tallulah said. She waited for Ruth to say something about the stolen beer. *You were right. I shouldn't have trusted you in my house.* But Ruth only sipped her coffee in silence.

Tallulah lifted her own mug. Then set it down.

"Ruth," she said.

"Mm?"

"Do you want me to take out the recycling?"

Ruth's sunrise eyes widened, a flash of surprise. She didn't smile, but the grimness around her mouth softened. "Bag's not full," she said; then, as if considering, "Reckon it'll get full before Monday pickup?"

"No," Tallulah said.

Ruth nodded. "Good enough. Leave it, then." She glanced at Tallulah's mug. "Better drink that. Seems you might need it." She headed out to the porch. Tallulah ate a handful of Frosted Mini-Wheats dry out of the box, then put on her shoes and walked outside.

"I'll see you at work," she told Ruth.

"It's only six o'clock," Ruth said. "You got an hour before you got to be there."

Tallulah skirted wide around the tail end of a red cow. "I'll get started early," she called. "Make it up to Jolene." As she'd hoped, Ruth had no good answer to this argument.

She walked and dog-trotted, rubbed alert by early morning air. Compared to the other evening, it seemed to take no time to reach the hospital. The carport was empty. Good, Poteet hadn't arrived yet. She climbed the stairs to Kyle's apartment and gave the door a sharp double knock with both sets of knuckles.

Kyle opened the door. She'd gotten him out of bed; his hair was tousled and his eyes slanted, half-open. He was wearing jeans and nothing else. Tan all over, she saw. Then she thought, I'll be seeing the rest pretty soon. She felt a burn climbing her cheeks; her eyes flicked away from his bare chest, then back again, before she settled her gaze on his left shoulder.

"I've decided," she said. "You could come with me. If you want to."

He crossed his arms and leaned against the doorjamb. He looked exactly as he had when he'd opened the door of the hospital to her and Diesel, that first night in the storm: thinking her over, and not in a hurry about it.

"I could come with you if I want to," he repeated.

"Yes," Tallulah said. She pushed her hair behind her ears, suddenly uncertain. This wasn't going the way she'd imagined. Kyle stared at her, expressionless; then he rolled his eyes and pushed himself upright. "Do you *want* me to go with you?" he said.

"I'm asking, aren't I?"

"A person likes to know is all."

"Well? Are you coming or not?"

"I ain't said no." He eased a step back from the door. Lacing her fingers behind her back, Tallulah slipped sideways past him into the apartment.

It was messier than before: more strewn clothes on the floor, dishes and glasses stacked beside the sink. On the bed the cat regarded her from deep within a pile of sheets.

"What'd you do last night that I wasn't invited to?" Tallulah asked. "Have a party?"

"I might have invited you, except for that friend of yours. Where's she at?"

"She left." It was getting easier to say. Kyle's arms came around her from behind; she turned in their circle, and he gathered her in. She laid her head on his shoulder, listened to him breathe, to the pulse in his throat. "She wanted me to go with her," Tallulah said.

He shifted, his muscles tensing. "Yeah?" he said. "How come you didn't?"

"I don't know. Things got . . . I don't know. I can't explain."

Kyle leaned back a little, tilted her chin up. "I bet this is why," he said, and kissed her. His breath was stale and at first she minded, but he kissed sweet, very sweet, and she gave herself over to it and then it didn't matter.

Was this why? Maeve had thought so.

She broke the kiss and shimmied out of his arms. He reached for her but she drifted into the kitchen and opened the refrigerator. Still practically empty. Didn't he ever go shopping?

"So when do you want to leave?" she said.

"Damn, girl. We got to decide that now?" He pulled her back close to him. She let go of the refrigerator door and it swung shut, wafting cold air across her legs. He tried to kiss her again but Tallulah pushed him away.

"We don't have time for that," she said.

He grinned. "Sure we do." His hand brushed across her hip. "Unless you got something special in mind."

She edged away from him, irritated. She wasn't supposed to be irritated. She was supposed to be happy. Excited. It's because he's not taking this seriously, she thought. "What I have in mind," she said, "is making a plan. We're going, right? We might as well figure out when."

Kyle sighed. He walked over to the dresser, opened a drawer, and pulled out a T-shirt. "All right," he said. "Tomorrow."

Tallulah laughed. "You're nuts."

"Tomorrow's Friday. Payday. What else we got to wait for?"

"Don't you have to give notice?"

"People give notice around here, Poteet treats 'em like shit until they leave. Guy before me left a note on the door. I figure that's notice enough."

"I thought you liked Poteet."

"He's all right. Those women, though. Like a herd of monster trucks. And I'm the beater car they jump on." He bent down, hooked a wrinkled pair of jeans up off the floor, and rummaged in the back pocket. He pulled out a pack of cigarettes, held it out to her. She shook her head.

"What about the five hundred?" she asked.

"What?"

"The money for the car. The other night you said you wouldn't have the five hundred for a couple of weeks."

"Oh, that." He shrugged. "Don't worry about it."

"You have enough for the car and the trip and everything? We have to eat, remember."

"You ain't the only one knows shit around here. I said don't worry about it." He unzipped his jeans and jabbed the hem of his T-shirt inside. Tallulah stood up and walked past him to the bathroom.

"Hey," he said. She tried to slam the door but he stuck his foot in the way. He grabbed the door's edge and wedged his shoulder in. She could see half his face, one eye. "Don't be mad," he said. "I didn't mean it like that. It's just, it's sudden. You know?"

She let go of the door. He swung it back and reached out a hand as if to brush her bangs out of her eyes. She jerked her head away from his fingers.

"If it's so sudden maybe we ought to forget it," Tallulah said.

"I'm gonna borrow the money from my ma," he said. "OK? I wasn't gonna tell you but now you know. So don't worry. Besides." He lifted his hand again; this time she let him skim her bangs back. He traced the top curve of her ear, ran a finger down her neck. "When you're in love with a person, you just do it," he said.

A sharp thud from downstairs made them both jump. "Kyle? You up there?" Jolene called.

"Son of a *bitch*. What time is it?" Kyle muttered. He strode to the desk and picked up his watch. There was a clock radio on the floor by his bed; it read six forty-eight.

"She's early," Tallulah whispered.

"I know she's early, but she's here, ain't she?" Kyle yanked open the door that led to the inside stairway. "What do you want?" he yelled.

"Well, good morning to you, too," Jolene yelled back. She sounded close enough to touch; Tallulah wondered if she was actually on the stairs. "You know where the new can of coffee is? It's not in the cupboard where it's supposed to be." Fainter, as if coming from the room below, another woman was saying something. Tallulah couldn't make out the words, but it didn't sound like Ruth.

"Christ almighty," Kyle muttered. He yelled, "I ain't seen it, I don't know where it is, I ain't touched it!" He slammed the door shut. "It's like living with my mother and sisters all over again. You know Jolene actually come in here once when I wasn't here? Claimed she was looking for the truck keys. Just an excuse for her to snoop in my business." He rattled the watch onto his wrist and snatched his wallet off the desk. "You better go down the outside way." He put a hand on her arm, as though to steer her to the door, but Tallulah resisted.

"Come by at noon," she said. "We can go get lunch somewhere."

He dropped his hand. "I can't. Come on, you better go."

"Why not?"

"Because I can't. I got stuff to do."

"Like what? Car stuff?"

"Yeah, car stuff." He ran one hand up under her hair and

pulled her close and kissed her again. "You better go," he said again.

The sun wasn't yet high enough to spill over onto the outside landing, and the coolness of the early morning still lingered. Tallulah raised her arms high overhead and stretched, rising onto her toes.

Kyle had said he loved her. She tasted his words in her mind. It was like running her tongue over a new flavor of ice cream. Shivery.

She'd made the right decision, not going with Maeve. Definitely the right decision.

"'Morning," Poteet called. Tallulah yanked down her arms. He was looking up at her from the carport below.

"I was just looking for Kyle," Tallulah said. She started down the stairs.

"Uh-huh." Poteet glanced toward the barn. "Where's Ruth? I didn't see her car."

"I walked."

Poteet raised his eyebrows. "Industrious," he said. He ushered her ahead of him through the carport. Just as Tallulah reached for the back door, though, it swung open toward her and a woman stepped through, almost colliding with her. Tallulah stumbled backward and tripped over Poteet's shoe. He grunted and grabbed her arm to keep her from falling.

The woman was fortyish, her features long and smooth as a greyhound's, her curly blond hair pulled back into a ponytail. She held a large manila envelope in one hand; she shifted it in front of her body, crossing both arms over it, as though afraid someone would snatch it away. "You're supposed to be on a field call," she said to Poteet.

Behind her, Jolene's head bobbed out the doorway. "What's—" The expression on her face changed instantly from curiosity to alarm. "Oh, shit," she muttered.

"'Morning, Ellen," Poteet said. "I was indeed on a field call. I finished early." His voice was easy, but his eyes were intent on his ex-wife's face. He nodded at the envelope. "Let me guess. A signed bill of sale for Kasmir. Did you use my signature stamp? Or did Jolene do a bit of forgery?"

Ellen's tone rose an impatient notch. "For Heaven's sake, Charles, I'm not stealing him. There's a certified check on your desk. And don't take this out on Jolene. All she did was—"

"Jolene's done enough, I'm sure. I don't need the details." His face took on the hard, brittle cast Tallulah had seen at the picnic. He extended a hand—*give me.* Ellen ignored it. Gently, slowly, as though reaching for a skittish dog, he pried a corner of the envelope away from Ellen's body. Ellen stepped back, twisting, and the envelope flicked out of Poteet's hand.

It was a subtle collapse, his face. Nothing so dramatic as dropped porcelain. A crumpling around his mouth, a sagging at the corners of his eyes. As though strings had been cut.

"Ronald doesn't want me handling a stallion," Ellen

312

said, "not even Kasmir. It's too dangerous, you know that. We can't take the chance. And once the baby comes . . ."

Baby? Tallulah's gaze shot to Ellen's midsection. There, behind the envelope, a hint of curve.

"Honestly, I thought you knew," Ellen said. Her words rattling fast now. "I thought everybody knew. Jolene knows, and so I . . ."

From the front of the building came a hammering series of knocks, a muffled *halloo*. Poteet didn't move. His gaze was fixed on the envelope, but he didn't seem to be seeing it. "Get that, Jolene," he said.

Jolene disappeared. Tallulah heard the front door open, a sudden bustling, a loud voice, slurred, reedy.

"Tell Ronald congratulations," Poteet said.

"Charles, I . . ."

Jolene stepped onto the back porch. "Dr. Poteet," she said, "Loren Castleberry's here with Arabella and . . ."

Poteet exploded then. "Goddamn it, put him in a god-damn room and tell him to *wait*!"

"Dr. Poteet, he says Arabella's dead," Jolene said.

Chapter 24

They bustled Arabella to the treatment room, Jolene and Tallulah carrying one side of the stretcher and Poteet the other, the dog flat on her side between. Even with Poteet pronouncing her alive, the way the dog's eyes stared glassily gave Tallulah the creeps. As they angled the stretcher through the hallway, Tallulah saw someone had closed the back door. In all the commotion, Ellen must have left.

In the treatment room, they slid the stretcher onto the exam table. "Set a catheter," Poteet said to Jolene. "Tallulah, get a liter of Lactated Ringer's and an IV set and bring them over here. Do you know where they are? Good. Hurry up."

Tallulah grabbed the items from the cabinet and carried them to the table. Jolene had already shaved a patch of fur from the dog's right front leg and was scrubbing the bare spot with antiseptic when Ruth came into the treatment room. In one hand she held up a clipboard.

"I'm not believing this," she said. "Since when does Loren Castleberry let you do surgery on his dog?"

Poteet was ripping the plastic cover off the fluid bag. He

nodded at the clipboard. "Since I got his signature on that consent form," he said.

Jolene's head snapped up. "How'd you do that?"

"Shouldn't think I'd have to explain that to you," Poteet said coolly. Jolene drew back her heavy shoulders, as if gearing for battle. Without looking at her, Poteet jostled her aside. "Get surgery ready," he said. "The big pack and two large drapes. And the Balfour retractors."

Jolene flicked a soapy gauze into the trash and marched out of the room. When she was gone, Ruth said, "You sure he understood what he was signing?"

"That's for his lawyer to figure out." Poteet picked up another gauze and continued scrubbing Arabella's leg. "I've explained this dog's condition until I'm blue in the face. We don't do surgery today, the only thing left to explain will be does he want the body buried or cremated."

Ruth tucked the clipboard under her arm. "Way she looks, you might be explaining that anyway."

"That's where the lawyer'll come in, I'm sure." To Tallulah, he said, "Hold that vein off." She strapped her thumb over the front of the leg, just below the crook of the elbow, the way Jolene had shown her. From the corner of her eye, she saw Ruth shake her head and turn back into the hallway.

Arabella didn't react when the catheter went in. Poteet hooked up the IV and wrapped a bandage around the catheter. "Stay with her until Jolene comes back," he said, then strode away, shoulders bent forward, rubbing one eyebrow with his thumb.

A minute later, Jolene returned. "I wonder should we start prepping her," she said, just as Ruth's voice came over the intercom.

"Jolene, Dr. Poteet said to tell you Mr. Castleberry wants to sit with Arabella till the surgery. We've got two critters already here and everybody else we got pushed back to after ten. Say a half hour."

"Uh-uh," Jolene muttered. "I ain't having that old drunk in my way back here." She stepped to the wall panel and mashed the Talk button with her thumb. "Ruth? You let Dr. Poteet know that's just fine." She let up on the button and turned to Tallulah. "Dr. Poteet wants him to sit with Arabella, we'll just stick him in Dr. Poteet's office. Help me move her. Then go on get Mr. Castleberry."

Castleberry was standing in the middle of the lobby, shifting his weight from foot to foot, hands clasping their opposite elbows, muttering. An older woman in a brilliant pink nylon jogging suit sat rigidly in a chair across the room. The tiny white dog in her lap leaned into her bosom and shivered.

"Mr. Castleberry?" Tallulah said. She hesitated, then touched his sleeve. "Mr. Castleberry? Arabella's in the back. I'll take you."

Castleberry started. "Huhn," he said. As he began shuffling toward the hallway, the woman in the pink suit stared at his back, her lips pinched tight. It reminded Tallulah of the look the apricot-haired woman had given her in the truck stop parking lot, the look Ruth had given Maeve. She slapped the reception counter; the woman jumped. Tallulah narrowed her eyes at her. The woman had the grace to blush.

In Poteet's office, Tallulah pointed to the chair. Castleberry ignored her, instead lowering himself to the floor. It took him a long time to bend his knees. Jolene had laid a thick terry cloth towel over Arabella; Castleberry dragged the towel off and began stroking the dull coat over the dog's ribs. From underneath the filthy bill of the baseball cap, a sibilant murmur began and rolled on without breaking. Arabella flicked an ear back toward the sound. It was the first movement Tallulah had seen her make.

Tallulah watched him for a moment. Then she walked into the kitchen, poured a mug of Jolene's coffee, and carried it back.

"Mr. Castleberry," she said. The baseball cap twisted to one side, then the other, as if he was unsure where the voice was coming from. She knelt next to him, holding out the mug. The whiskey smell was strong today, rising off him like sour hard-edged steam.

"Do you want any milk?" she asked. "Or sugar?"

He cupped the mug in one hand. It wavered and Tallulah steadied it, setting it more firmly in his palm. He drew the mug close to his chest, then began petting Arabella again.

"OK, then," Tallulah said. She patted Arabella's hip—she could feel the bone jutting under the skin—and rose to her feet. With every pass of Castleberry's hand over Arabella's ribs, red hair drifted, like solid rain, to the floor.

Half an hour later, she led Castleberry back to the lobby while Poteet and Jolene anesthetized the dog in the treatment room. Jolene shaved Arabella's belly and scrubbed it; then she and Tallulah carried her into surgery, sidestepping in broken rhythm, careful not to touch the clipped cleaned mound of her abdomen. Upside down, Arabella's lips hung like sagging platters, exposing the pink arch of gum, the heavy yellow teeth.

Poteet came into the surgery room, cap and mask and gown on, hands clasped in front of him as though in prayer. "Ready?" he asked.

Arabella's bare belly gleamed like a basted turkey, gold brown from antiseptic spray. "Stick a fork in her, she's done," Jolene said. Poteet turned around. Jolene reached up and tied first the strings at the back of his gown collar, then the strings at his waist.

"You're done, too," she said. In the past half hour, Jolene had acted more cheerful than Tallulah had ever seen her. Practically chirpy. Maybe she'd decided her best course of action was to pretend nothing had happened; as if she'd never been angry with Poteet, had never threatened to quit, hadn't daily devised a half-dozen ways to irritate him. As if she hadn't just helped Poteet's ex-wife take his horse. Too little too late, Tallulah guessed. Because Poteet wasn't buying it; his own voice was tight, the drawl clipped short.

"Get Tallulah scrubbed in," he said.

"What?" Jolene and Tallulah said together.

"I'll need another pair of hands. You have to monitor anesthesia. She's it."

Jolene's chirpiness slipped. "All right," she said, with the same inflection she might have used to say *Crazy bastard*. She flipped a wall switch, and the lights over the surgery table flared. Whether it was the effect of their white glare, or the aftermath of Ellen, the exposed skin around Poteet's eyes seemed gray, the creases harsher, the hazel of his eyes muddy and flat. The rest of him was hidden behind blue paper cloth and the green cotton of his gown.

Jolene ushered Tallulah outside surgery to the prep sink, helped her on with the cap and mask, then handed her a sponge soaked on one side in brown soap. The other side was a stiff plastic brush. With Jolene hovering at her elbow, Tallulah began to scrub.

"Harder with that brush," Jolene said. "You want to give that dog a fatal infection? You skipped your thumb."

"I have a scratch there."

"I don't care if you got fifteen stitches. Scrub it."

From inside the surgery room, Poteet called, "This dog's not getting any younger and neither am I. Hurry up."

It took perhaps ten minutes and by the end Tallulah was a jumpy mess. Jolene would tell her what to do, Tallulah would do it, and Jolene would hiss and snap and make her do it again. They went through three glove packs before Tallulah managed to don a pair and keep them sterile. Finally, gowned and gloved, hands folded in front of her chest, Tallulah shuffled back into surgery.

"Stand there," Jolene said, pointing. Tallulah inched close to the table, facing Poteet across Arabella's ballooning abdomen. When Poteet didn't look up, Tallulah said, "I'm ready."

"I'm not blind yet," Poteet said. "Just stand there and don't touch a blessed thing until I tell you."

While Tallulah had scrubbed, both Arabella and the table had disappeared under a sea of blue paper. In the middle of the sea an elliptical hole, perhaps eight inches long and three across, exposed a solitary island of brown-stained skin. Next to her, Jolene bent under the table, laying bath towels two deep over the floor, around the base of the surgery table, over Poteet's feet, over Tallulah's.

"All right," Poteet said. He laid a scalpel on the brown island and drew his hand across. Where the scalpel had been, the skin fell open. Tallulah could feel it, her own skin sliding apart, yielding to the man-in-the-moon dagger. She didn't realize she was swaying until she felt the pressure of Jolene's hand on her back.

"She ain't gonna make it, Dr. Poteet," Jolene said.

"Yes, she will," Poteet said. "Tallulah! Don't look at the blood. Look," he pointed with an ivory-gloved finger to the drape over Arabella's chest, "right there. Keep looking there until I tell you to look somewhere else."

Tallulah swiveled her eyes from the brown island, now parted like curtains and oozing blood, to the blue paper sea covering Arabella's chest. It moved up and down, gently, long pauses in between. With each breath, the anesthesia machine clicked and fluttered. It isn't half as bad as the baby, Tallulah thought, repeating this to herself like a mantra—*not as bad, not as bad, not as bad*—as Poteet's hands floated at the corner of her vision. She was even starting to believe it when he said, "This'll get messy, now." His hand dipped low. Yellowish fluid flooded over the banks of skin and cascaded down, picking up blood as it went, freefalling off the drape, splashing onto her blue gown and onto the towels over her feet. Most of it ran on his side, but some came on hers. She jumped back, pushing out her hands. Behind her, Jolene snapped, "Get those hands up! Get 'em up!" and to her own surprise she obeyed.

"I'm going to be sick," she said.

"Puke in the mask, not the incision," Poteet said. She glared at him. He shook his head.

"You're all right," he said. "Nobody who looks that mad is about to throw up."

Under the drape Arabella's belly had deflated, like a beach ball with the air partly gone. After the drama of the flood, the incision wasn't nearly as gory as Tallulah had feared; nothing more than a narrow swath of red, like a rough stripe of lipstick drawn on the skin. The bleeding had already stopped. Then Poteet's hand slipped inside, like a seal diving off an ice floe. It disappeared up to the wrist and Tallulah closed her eyes and conjured up Kyle's wildflowers. Then Kyle himself. The smooth skin of his chest. She'd always imagined a hairless chest would be boyish, uninteresting, but she was wrong. She remembered the faint thud of his heart, the wiry strength of his arms around her, and the fluttering of nausea under her own ribs began to subside.

"Ovarian tumor," Poteet said. "I thought maybe it was. Twenty-two years, and this is only the third one I've seen." He lifted his gaze to the cabinets behind Tallulah, his torso pivoting a little as he explored inside Arabella. Then he removed his hand and turned to the instrument tray. "Ten years I've been telling Loren to spay his damn dog," he said. "Figures he waits until this."

"Is it big?" Jolene asked.

"Mother of all tumors," Poteet said.

"Can you get it out?"

"Hell if I know." He hooked one end of a blunt instrument under one side of the incision, then handed the other end to Tallulah, showing her how to hold it so that the incision yawed wide. Through the metal, she could feel his hands moving inside the dog.

"Let go," he said. She released the instrument and he laid it on the tray stand next to him. "OK. Now take hold here." She looked down. A pair of what looked like steel scissor handles jutted from the incision; he swiveled them toward her. She laid her fingers over the bright metal, mimicking his grip. When she had it secured, his hand slipped down and disappeared again.

"Pull up," he told her.

She grimaced under the mask and curled her fingers tight and pulled. It felt like hauling on a tight rubber band.

"More," Poteet said.

There was a sudden tearing noise—not so much a noise, but a *feel* that vibrated up the polished metal. Her hand jerked abruptly upward and she was staring at the ends of the instrument. They weren't scissors; instead of blades, they had jaws, wide and blunt and curved. A bit of yellow tissue quivered between the closed tips.

"Dammit," Poteet muttered. "Give me those." He opened the jaws and wiped off the tissue, then sank the instrument back into the depths of the incision. "OK. Hold it again. Pull when I say." She did. Both Poteet's hands were inside the dog now. The sight started the fluttering again under her ribs so she shut her eyes and this time she saw her mother's kitchen: red and white tablecloth, sun slanting through yellow curtains. Sharing a slice of angel food cake late at night, her mother laughing, telling funny real estate stories. The one where . . .

Tallulah felt Poteet pull: another vibration up the instrument handles. "Got you now, you son-of-a-gun," Poteet muttered. The tension on the instrument eased. Tallulah opened her eyes. Poteet's hands were still deep in Arabella but his elbows were cocked outward and he was lifting. At the lips of the incision appeared a shining dome of tissue. Its surface was irregular, studded with what looked like translucent bubbles, streaked with something else resembling lace.

"Godalmighty," Jolene said. "Thing's big as a grapefruit."

Tallulah shifted her feet on the sodden towels. She wanted to lean in to get a better look and at the same time leap away in case the thing proved capable of independent movement. The room suddenly seemed to have grown warmer by several degrees; she was sweating under the gown. The fluttering graduated to a long lazy back flip that took up the entire space between her solar plexus and her spine.

"Look at that drape and breathe deep," Poteet said. "If you start seeing white stars on black, let go of whatever you've got and get the hell away. I don't need you fainting in my sterile field."

Tallulah bit her lip until a narrow bolt of pain shot down to her chin. She focused on it, remembering Crystal-Amber, little puffs, the tiny rises of the baby's chest under her hand. She continued to bite down until the flipping in her belly receded, reluctantly, like a party-crasher turned back at the door.

It wasn't all OK after that, but when it started getting to her—the heat rising through the incision, the coppery smell of blood—she concentrated on Crystal-Amber. And on Kyle. The strength of his arms pulling her close, the look in his eyes when he'd said he loved her. Like he was drowning, and she was the lifeboat.

Soon enough—*tomorrow night*—they'd be together in a motel room. And then . . .

Poteet made a last tie and cut and pull. He lifted the tumor out of Arabella. For an instant he held it over the gashed belly, as if he'd taken it as a sacrifice to be offered; then Jolene stepped around the end of the table with a metal tray and he swiveled sideways and plopped it in. Tallulah stared at it. The moment he'd held it up her queasiness vanished as if, detached, the tumor lost any power to affect her. It lay on the tray, inert and awkward, a lumpy pink-and-white-streaked and bloodied thing.

"That wasn't so bad," she said, half in wonderment at herself.

"We're not done yet," Poteet said. He reached back into the incision.

"Remember that one assistant fainted on you during a surgery?" Jolene said. When Poteet didn't answer, she explained to Tallulah, "Hit the back of her head on the sink. Dr. Poteet was in the middle of a splenectomy and there was more blood on the floor than on the table." She turned to Poteet. "How many stitches she end up getting? Six? Eight?"

Poteet didn't answer. Now that the tumor was out, he'd sunk into a grim silence. Jolene gave up all pretense at camaraderie and joined him, speaking only to report a heart rate or blood pressure in a flat staccato. There came a long stretch of holding more retractors and clamps. Tallulah was bored. Her legs ached from standing. The sweat in the crooks of her thumbs had dissolved the powder inside her gloves; where her skin stuck to the latex, the gloves were almost transparent. She longed to pull them off, to soak her hands in cool water.

Abruptly, Poteet said, "Got that tumor sectioned into the formalin?"

"Yessir," Jolene said.

"She doing all right?"

"Stable. Heart's good. Pulse ox's steady as a highway."

"Go on, then. I'm wrapping up here. I'll holler if I need anything."

"Yessir. You want the surgery door open now, or shut?"

"Keep it shut. Oh, and Jolene." She paused in the doorway. "You let anyone—*anyone*—in this hospital again without my OK and it'll be the last thing you do in my employ. Got that?"

"Yessir."

"Go tell Loren he's got a live dog."

Jolene went. Poteet turned to the instrument tray and gathered a length of suture in his hands. "I understand from Ruth your friend's been and gone," he said.

Tallulah watched Poteet pull up a red streak of tissue with a pair of forceps and drive a curved needle through it to the other side. Another two stitches, then he said, "You going home?"

"I don't know. I haven't thought about it."

"Thinking of staying on here?"

"No," she said, perhaps a shade too quickly. Poteet's eyes flicked up to her face then back down. After a moment, she asked, "What time do we get paid tomorrow?"

"Why? Planning on skipping town?" He whipped the suture up and around the jaws of his instrument, pulled the knot tight. "You're not going to Florida, you're not stay-ing here. Not sure if you're going home. Where are you in such an all-fired hurry to get to?"

"I don't know."

"Don't know much, do you?" He wrapped the suture in a neat figure eight around his fingers and thumb. "I imagine you don't know Kyle has a fiancée." His face, what Tallulah could see of it between the cap and mask, looked no partic-ular way. He might have been discussing the weather, or the tobacco crop.

The dishes stacked by Kyle's sink. *What'd you have last night, a party?*

"As a rule," Poteet continued, "I don't involve myself in my employees' concerns. I only mention it because I swung by early this morning and Lacey was just going home. Then I come back and there you are. Coming down the same stairs." Over the incision, his hands seemed to move of their own will. Like blind twins, playing an old game. "Nice girl, Lacey. Her folks own the Pack 'n' Post in Greeley Hill."

Hibiscus flower crème rinse. Kyle's cat nestled deep in rumpled-up sheets.

Tallulah stepped back from the surgery table. "You're lying."

With his forceps, Poteet pinched up a layer of tissue translucent as pink chiffon. "Go ask him. Last I saw, he was outside messing with that fool motorcycle."

Her gloves were drawing stiff with blood. Blood was everywhere here. The middle of a road. A metal table, a horse's neck. Tallulah stripped the gloves off, dropped them to the floor. The air hit her skin in a blessed cool shock. Tallulah fumbled at the gown, trying to rip it free. Her fingers found the tie behind her neck: two pulls and the gown was off. She balled up the green cotton, stifling the urge to fling it in Poteet's face, to stop the thoughts he was surely thinking: *What an idiot. What a moron.*

Instead she said, "You think your daughter was brave. Riding that horse. Trying to jump that train."

His hands stopped. He didn't lift his head but from under his brows his eyes glared into hers and they were like a pair of hammers raised.

"I'll bet she was scared out of her mind," Tallulah said. "I'll bet she was—" she tried to draw breath, but her chest felt suddenly knocked flat, as if an invisible Leopard had struck her.

Knock it off and get in the car. Stop making such a goddamn racket.

Tallulah threw the gown onto the floor. The air came in a wrenching gasp, and she cried, "I'll bet she was thinking, *Maybe now he'll notice me.*"

Poteet swept the drape off Arabella. The yawing incision had been reduced to a red line, laddered by black stitches. It appeared far too ordinary for what had come out of it.

"Get out," he said.

She should have stopped. Later, she wished she had. But rage shimmered in her like a hot hot light, and, as Jolene swung open the door, she said, "At least your ex-wife gets another chance." She pushed her bangs out of her eyes, smeared tears sideways across her temple. "Too bad you don't."

She elbowed Jolene aside and ran out of the room.

Chapter 25

Tallulah found Kyle where Poteet said she would, by the shed, cross-legged on the ground next to his motorcycle, probing somewhere in the bike's innards with a wrench. He rotated his arm to reach up farther, and caught sight of her. "Hey," he said. "How's it going in there? I hear Castleberry's giving Ruth fits."

Take me somewhere, Tallulah wanted to say. Anywhere. Please.

Instead she asked, "Who's Lacey?"

Kyle put down the wrench and got to his feet, brushing one palm across his thigh. His eyes flitted across her face; he raised one shoulder, let it fall.

Tallulah chewed her lip. Behind her lay the hospital; ahead, the barn. To her left, the highway. She turned left and started walking.

Kyle ran ahead, pivoting to face her, blocking her way. "Let's go," he said. "Right now."

"Get out of my way."

"We'll ride over to my brother's and get his car and

blow this place." He held his hand out to her. "Come on."

His urgency pulled at her. The craziness of it. *When you love someone you just do it.* On the highway, a blue pickup towing a U-Haul trailer clipped past. Tallulah glimpsed the driver's arm on the windowsill, a cell phone to his ear. She looked at Kyle's hand, the long brown fingers. He loved her. One movement and his hand would be in hers and she could forget everything else.

"Who's Lacey?" she asked again.

He let the hand fall to his side. His eyes seemed to take a step back from hers. "Lacey ain't nobody," he said. "I ain't even seen her around."

"Since when?"

"I don't know. Maybe a week." His voice rose a little at the end, as if it was a question. The breath went out of her. Not all at once, like it had with Poteet, but slowly, leaking, as though someone had stuck pins all through her.

"Liar," she said, and in her voice she heard the echo of Maeve's: *You couldn't tell the truth if it was stenciled on your forehead.* At the memory of Kyle's rumpled sheets, the shimmering rage returned, a sun behind her eyes. She shoved him hard, making him stumble backward.

"I ain't in love with her anymore," he said, putting up his hands, fending her off. "Listen to me, will you? I ain't in love with her!"

"When I said you could come with me, I was joking," Tallulah said. "Who knew you'd be stupid enough to believe me? *God,* what a moron!"

331

He stared at her, his hands still half-raised. The stunned look on his face gave her a small mean feeling in her chest. He was the one who deserved to feel stupid. Betrayed. Not her. She pushed past him and darted across the highway. Right or left? She chose right, for the sole reason that she wouldn't have to cross in front of the hospital, with the graceful arch of Poteet's orchids in the big front windows, where anyone could look out and see her crying.

There was a Dairy Queen up ahead. She'd walk there and sit for a while on a bench and figure out what she was going to do. Just like when I got here, she thought. Except then I had ninety-three cents. Now I can't even buy myself a goddamn Tastee-Freez.

She hadn't gone more than ten yards when a car passed her on the opposite side of the road. It pulled a U-turn, and as it came toward her, drifting onto the shoulder, Tallulah was somehow not surprised to see it was an olive green sedan.

Dust washed around LUVLY1's tires. Sun glared off the windshield. Tallulah wiped her eyes hastily. She waited, but still Maeve didn't get out. The car sat idling, growling like a crouched-down dog.

Maeve had been right. Maeve was always right.

Slowly, Tallulah walked to the open passenger window. She leaned down. Maeve turned her way and for a moment, Tallulah saw blurs of herself in Maeve's sunglasses: a bright streak of platinum hair, a smudge of purple scrub top.

"I was waiting for you," Maeve said. She held her hand toward Tallulah. "Forgive me?"

Despite the heat, Maeve's fingers felt clammy and chill in Tallulah's grasp. "It was my fault," Tallulah said. "I'm the one who's sorry."

Maeve glanced sideways out the windshield. Ducking farther down, Tallulah followed her gaze. Kyle still stood at the edge of the highway, watching them. The look on his face the same as when he'd watched Tallulah and Poteet walking up the hill at the picnic. Like he'd run as fast as he could, but still the plane had taken off without him.

Tallulah let go of Maeve's hand and opened LUVLY1's door. More maps lay open on the seat; she tossed them into the back, then slipped into the car. The slam of the door was like an exclamation point. New chapter beginning. As LUVLY1 accelerated onto the highway, Tallulah let the brick and white of the hospital and the blue of Kyle's jeans slide from the corner of her vision. When all that remained was the gray asphalt ahead, she settled back in her seat.

That should have been the ending. Neat and simple, like the movies: two pals reunited, roaring down the highway. But of course Tallulah couldn't just drive off. Not without the rest of her clothes, and definitely not without the four hundred dollars she had coming to her.

Getting into Ruth's doublewide was no problem; Tallulah still had the key. She changed out of her scrubs into shorts and a tank top, surveying as she did the mess she'd made of the living room. Next to the sofa, a jumble of dirty socks and jeans and T-shirts sprawled like a fungus over the gold shag rug. Her leopard-print bra peeked out from under the coffee table.

Would Ruth miss her? Or would she just be happy to have her house back again? No more chaos. No more beer bottles hidden in the trash. Everything simple and straight and neat, the way it had been before Tallulah arrived.

Tallulah paused from sorting through the muddle of clothes on the floor and sat back on her heels. If the doublewide had never felt exactly like home, still she'd always felt safe here, and welcome.

Maybe Ruth wouldn't miss her. But she would miss Ruth.

She plucked hospital scrubs out of the pile and set them aside. Everything else she shoved into her duffel. Maeve, meanwhile, wandered from room to room. She picked things up as though to look at them, then moved on, putting them down again with barely a glance.

"Do you want your notebooks on the backseat or in the trunk?" Tallulah called to her.

"Keep them," Maeve said.

Maybe she was afraid they'd get all bent up, riding loose. "I'll put them on top, then," Tallulah said, tucking them into the duffel. "Just let me know when you want them." Maeve didn't answer. Tallulah wondered again if she'd managed to sleep, decided not to ask. The air of reconciliation in the car had lasted just until the truck stop, where Tallulah had persuaded Maeve to turn around and take her to Ruth's. After that, a crackle of irritability seemed to hover over her, and Tallulah was trying hard not to rouse it further. Anyway, if Maeve had slept, it must have been in LUVLY1. She wore the same clothes as yesterday, the yellow skirt now a mass of wrinkles all down the back.

Maeve went outside and started the car. Tallulah hurried through the doublewide, trying to see it through Ruth's eyes. She straightened doilies, wiped down the bathroom sink, loaded sheets and towels and scrubs into the washer. She waffled on leaving a note, finally decided not to. She'd see Ruth at the hospital and say good-bye in person. She couldn't write what she wanted to say, anyway. It needed a long hug, and as for words, Tallulah only hoped she could come up with something—anything—close to what she felt in her heart.

At the front door, duffel hoisted onto her shoulder, she paused. From his perch on top of the television, Tripod the cat extended his one front paw toward her in a toe-spreading stretch.

"Quit trying to run outside," Tallulah said. "It worries her." The cat blinked, yawned, then curled his head back down to sleep.

As soon as Tallulah slid onto LUVLY1's seat, Maeve said, "I have plenty of money. We can just leave. You don't need to go back there."

"Damn right I'm going back there," Tallulah said. "Two weeks' worth of cleaning shit is in that paycheck."

"But it's getting late. We need to go."

"Go where? Besides, it's only . . ." Tallulah looked at the dashboard clock, "eleven fifteen. It'll take like five minutes."

"I'm telling you, I have plenty of—"

"I know. I believe you," Tallulah said. By now they were at the intersection of Ruth's road and the highway. She pointed. "That way."

Maeve gunned LUVLY1 across the highway and swung a hard left, in the direction of the hospital. Her body telegraphed tension, as potent as the whiskey fumes that seeped through Castleberry's skin. Running her fingers ceaselessly through her stunted hair. Short sharp fidgets of her arms and shoulders and hips. Even yesterday's torrent of words, Tallulah thought, would be preferable to this silence. She was tempted to change her mind and give in, but the fact of the four hundred dollars kept her quiet. If Maeve was angry, well, she'd just have to be angry. Tallulah was going to get her money.

She hoped Poteet would be busy somewhere. In an exam room, or in the back. She didn't want to see him. Not now. Not ever again. Kyle, she could handle. He was a jerk and a coward; he'd hurt her, and she'd hurt him back. It was simple and she understood it.

But the look in Poteet's eyes, at the end, when she'd said those things to him. There had been something horrible in that look. She couldn't put her finger on it, and at the same time she couldn't get it out of her head.

LUVLY1 glided into the parking lot. "I'll be right back," Tallulah said, and got out of the car. She walked to the front door. Not the back door; she'd decided that while she was packing at Ruth's. Back doors were informal. She was here on business.

Stepping into the pool-shock of cold air, it seemed to Tallulah barely a day since the first time she'd done so, so vivid was the memory of rain-soaked exhaustion, the blood and wet-fur smell of Diesel, the ease with which Kyle had scooped up the dog in his arms. The lobby had been empty then, and it was empty now, except for Ruth, sitting behind the computer at the reception counter. She looked up when Tallulah came in.

"There you are," she said. "What happened to you? Kyle said you'd left but he couldn't say where." She peered over the counter at Tallulah's shorts. "You better not plan to work in that. Jolene'll have a fit."

"I'm leaving," Tallulah said. "I came to get my pay."

"Leaving? But—" Ruth glanced out the window. Her lips tightened.

"She's my friend, Ruth," Tallulah said.

Ruth picked up a loose pile of invoices and rapped it into order on the desk. "Honey," she said, "I grew up with a cousin loonier than a three-legged duck. I love her to death and I always will. But if she ever decides to jump off a bridge, I'm not going to hold her hand and count to three with her."

"You don't understand," Tallulah said. From outside she heard the click and thud of LUVLY1's door. No, don't come in, Tallulah pleaded silently. That was all she needed, Ruth seeing Maeve in the same clothes as yesterday, unwashed, the hair standing upright all over one side of her head. "Look, can you just give me my check? Please?"

Rummaging in her tray for a paper clip, Ruth shook her head. "Check's aren't cut yet. And with everything we got going on, probably won't be until closing tonight. He was hardly done with Arabella when one of the Wallace horses up and caught its foot in a barbed—"

"How long could it take to write one check?" Tallulah broke in. Ruth flashed a look up at her. It was the eyebrow-raised, lips-pursed look she gave to pickup truck drivers who tailgated her. To snippy grocery store clerks, to rude clients. *Hateful,* that look said. "Look, I'm sorry," Tallulah said. "But Ruth, please. Can't you just ask him?"

"That's what I'm trying to tell you. He's not here. He's gone on out to the Wallaces' place." Ruth dropped the invoices into a folder, banged the folder closed.

"But—" The phone rang. Ruth held up a finger—*hang on a sec*—and answered it.

Tallulah gripped the edge of the reception counter. The back of her neck felt like an iron band was slowly, inexorably clamping around it. No paycheck. Poteet gone. Behind her, the front door opened in a burst of warm moist air. *Please, let it be a client . . .* But Ruth, hanging up the phone, was staring past her, her sunrise eyes wide.

Tallulah stepped into Ruth's line of sight and leaned her upper body over the reception counter. "I need my money, Ruth. I earned it. I want it."

"Tallulah, come on," Maeve said from the doorway.

Ruth stood up. She walked around the counter, tugging the hem of her blue-striped top. "Honey, believe me," she said. "I'd help you if I could." Her voice, always dry, was a low, tired scrape. Even the gold filigree of her hair seemed dull. She laid a hand on Tallulah's arm. "Tell you what, how about you stay one more night?" She nodded at Maeve. "Both of you. Tomorrow, we'll see what you-all want to do."

"I already know what I'm going to do," Tallulah said. "Tell Poteet I'm coming back for my money." She backed out from under the warm weight of Ruth's hand. For a moment it hung, suspended, as though waiting for her to change her mind; in that moment, Tallulah turned away and, shoulder to shoulder with Maeve, stepped into the blinding heat of the sun.

A racket of birdsong raised Tallulah through layers of sleep, but it was the tickle on the back of her wrist that finally woke her. She flipped her hand and blinked. Wherever she was, was bright and hot. How long had she slept?

Close by, something buzzed. She reared her head, wincing at the crick in her neck. Less than two inches from her face, a yellow jacket beat its wings against a pane of glass. She scrambled upright.

"Jesus!" she said. Her voice cracked on phlegm; she cleared her throat. "Christ," she finished. She was sitting in the front seat of LUVLY1. The driver's door hung open: keys were still in the ignition. She peered at the dashboard clock. Quarter to five. She'd fallen asleep just outside Knoxville. Almost four hours ago. And this was . . . where?

Careful, mindful of the yellow jacket, she slid across to the open door. The seat vinyl pulled away from the backs of her legs with a tearing sound, like Band-Aids. She eased out of the car, stood up, and looked around.

She was in a small clearing. A campsite, it looked like;

behind the car stood a picnic table and a dusty barbecue grill. Two or three more yellow jackets cruised close over the ground, weaving in and out between the table legs, hovering over dead ashes in a fire pit. The air was thick and muggy and smelled of the woods that pressed all around. There was no sign of Maeve.

Tallulah stretched and then, massaging the back of her neck, she walked around the clearing, stepping into the brush a little ways to search. Nothing.

"Maeve!" she called. "Maeve! Where are you?"

No answer. Where had Maeve brought them to?

After leaving the veterinary hospital, Maeve had aimed the car down the highway toward Interstate 40 and hit the gas. Refused to turn around. Refused even to talk about it.

"I can't wait anymore," she kept saying.

"Can't wait for what? Where are we going?"

Maeve wouldn't elaborate. By the time Tallulah had given up, they'd already reached Knoxville, LUVLY1 cruising seventy miles an hour amid the midday traffic.

"Name anywhere you'd like to go," Maeve said.

Tallulah sighed. Her paycheck had dwindled to an invisible, irretrievable point miles behind them. Her bluff to Ruth about coming back for it had been just that: a bluff. Even as she'd said it, she'd known she didn't have the guts to face Poteet again.

Besides, she thought, Maeve was undoubtedly right, as always. Don't look back. Still, she felt an arrow of regret for Ruth. She'd wanted that last hug so badly. And to tell her thank you. As inadequate as it had seemed before, now it meant everything. And she hadn't said it.

"Anywhere you want to go," Maeve repeated.

Tallulah sighed. "I don't know . . . Paris."

"I take it back. Anywhere in the United States." Maeve's voice was warm, teasing. She sounded more like the old Maeve than at any time since she'd arrived in Clark Station. Once they'd gotten on the interstate, Tallulah noticed, Maeve's tension seemed to have eased; she'd stopped running her hand through her hair, and the rigidity between her eyes had softened.

"Elko, Nevada," Tallulah said.

"Too easy. I-75 north to Lexington. Then I-80 west to Elko."

Tallulah stared at her. "What'd you do, memorize the entire map of the United States?"

"Not Hawaii."

"Damn, Maeve." Tallulah chewed a hangnail, looking out the window. After a few minutes she said, "Why did you let the cows out?"

"That place was too small for them," Maeve said. She shrugged, as if this were self-evident. "I was sad to see them penned back in. I wonder if they'll miss it, now. Being free."

Tallulah didn't answer. She was remembering that first evening, on the roof of the Belinda. The first—and last—time Maeve had mentioned being bipolar.

I don't know what that is, Tallulah had admitted.

Maeve had spread her arms wide, taking a breath like

she was tasting all the possibilities in the night air. It means, she'd said, that the world is too small to contain me.

Unexpectedly, Maeve reached over and pressed Tallulah's arm. "I'm sorry it didn't work out with your hillbilly," she said. "I could see why you liked him. He was cute. Awful grammar. But cute."

"Yeah," Tallulah said. "He was." She squeezed Maeve's hand. "Thanks."

A month ago, if Maeve had invited her to hit the road in LUVLY1, Tallulah would have jumped in the car without a backward glance. She wouldn't even have cared which direction they took out of Portland, just so long as they were leaving. Just so long as she was escaping her life.

Let's do it. Let's go. When he barely knew her. When he didn't even know what direction they'd be headed. *When you're in love with a person, you just do it.*

They were in the thick of the city now, the interstate five lanes wide. LUVLY1 plunged along in shadow, deep in a crater ringed by eighteen-wheelers.

Kyle didn't love her. She was his escape. Nothing more. As Maeve had been Tallulah's.

"I meant what I said yesterday," Tallulah said. She had to raise her voice to be heard above the roar of the trucks. "About things changing." She kept her eyes on the truck in front of them (bright orange bumper stickers, GO VOLS), and pressed her hands together in her lap. "Wherever you're going, I can't go with you. I'm sorry."

"I know," Maeve said. Surprised, Tallulah looked at her.

She seemed grave, as she'd used to when discussing something serious; sadder maybe, but, Tallulah was thankful to see, nothing like the lashing despair of yesterday. "Just do me a favor, will you?" Maeve said. She gestured at the pile of maps in the backseat. "I found this place."

"What place?"

"You'll see. Just come with me there. After that you can take off wherever you want. Elko. Portland. Anywhere."

They hadn't said much else, not then. Tallulah felt sleep overtaking her. She'd intended to stay awake, to figure out with Maeve where they would part, how much money she would need, and, most important, where she ought to go. But she'd barely slept the night before, and then, what with Arabella, and Poteet, and Kyle, and the heat, plus laid over everything, the relief of Maeve's understanding, soothing and warm as goosedown . . . She'd take a nap, that was all. Just a catnap and then she and Maeve would sort out everything. Tallulah slid down in the seat until her neck nestled on the backrest and she closed her eyes.

She vaguely remembered the car stopping—once? Twice? She remembered mumbling questions to Maeve. But she couldn't recall what she'd asked, or if Maeve had answered.

And now she was here. Wherever *here* was. She walked back around the front of the car, where a short lane curved uphill to a larger dirt road. Trees hid the sun overhead; the air was soft, thick, bright, the shadows a steamy velvet.

Across the road, a Winnebago lay parked. A little way away were a red Honda and a large gray tent.

The day was still sweltering, maybe just a tinge cooler than before. Tallulah wondered how far they'd come, and if this was just a rest stop, or where they'd been headed all along.

She walked back to the car and peered inside. The yellow jacket was gone. She slipped into the driver's seat and cranked the keys in the ignition, then turned on the radio. Static. She rotated the dial, pausing and listening and moving on. Snatches of music, mostly country. Commercials. Then the energized voice of a DJ.

". . . a cool ninety-eight degrees here in WALHALLA. Up next, for our buddy Mark over in Lakemont, Georgia, we've got the Doobies with . . ."

The maps lay like collapsed tents on the backseat, where Tallulah had thrown them earlier. She rooted through them until she found one titled *Southeastern United States: Florida Georgia South Carolina Tennessee.* She shook it free of the others and spread it against the steering wheel. A chunk of the lower right hand corner had been torn away, but the rest was intact.

There was Knoxville. She had to hunt for Walhalla, finding it, finally, in South Carolina, near the Georgia border.

She fiddled some more with the radio. This time she had to switch to AM before she found a voice willing to give up its location. WRBN. Out of Clayton, Georgia.

Tallulah went back to the map. Walhalla. She marked the spot with a finger. There was Clayton, northeast across the border. What other town had that DJ said? Lakemont. There it was, due south of Clayton, near the same highway. Tallulah traced the highway's winding line north. Tennessee. Great Smoky Mountains. Gatlinburg, Pigeon Forge. Interstate 40, and, a hop and a skip away, Knoxville.

Tallulah frowned. She bent over the map, following the route again, this time from Knoxville down: Pigeon Forge. Gatlinburg. Dillard. Clayton. Lakemont. Tallulah Falls. Turnerville.

Tallulah blinked and leaned closer. Tiny letters, a tinier dot. But it was there. Black on white, serious as an obituary.

Tallulah Falls.

"My God," she said. She laid the map down on the passenger seat, and that was when she saw the scrap of paper, the missing corner of the map, on the gearshift between the seats. It had been folded in half, with a line of Maeve's scrawl on the outside, as if Maeve had set it up somewhere for her to find it. Tallulah must have knocked it over scrambling away from the yellow jacket.

I kept it for you. Take care of it.

Kept what? Tallulah searched the front seat. Nothing. She got out and rummaged through the back. Nothing but what had already been there: junk food trash and maps. Her glance fell on the glove compartment. She slipped back into the driver's seat and opened it. Blinked, and leaned closer. Then reached into the compartment and drew out the cash.

She counted only about half of it. She stopped at sixteen hundred, then, holding the wad in her lap with one hand as though it might disappear, rummaged deep in the compartment with the other. There was Maeve's favorite Guatemalan cloth wallet, the one she always took when she didn't want to carry a purse. Behind that, Tallulah's fingers scrabbled against something narrow and hard. A tire gauge? No, too rough. And too flat. She groped for it, pulled it out, and for a moment forgot the cash entirely. From the delicate bone handle, sized just to the length of her palm, the man in the moon looked down on the robed lady.

That first night, on the roof of the Belinda. *That bozo dropped it . . . of course I gave it back.*

Only she hadn't. She'd stolen it. It must have been easy, with everyone yelling, everyone staring at the blood on Tallulah's belly.

You can lay your life on one thing . . . from this moment on, I will never lie to you.

Maeve had lied.

Tallulah put everything back the way she'd found it: dagger, wallet, money. Then she took the keys out of the ignition and got out of the car. Several more yellow jackets had joined the party, darting low over the ground, searching for whatever it was that yellow jackets crave. One of them charged her ankles and Tallulah kicked at it. She locked LUVLY1 and set out from the campsite. Perhaps there was a store Maeve had gone to, or a coffeehouse. Time to find her. Time to find out what the hell was going on.

Just around the first bend of road was a flat-roofed, dark brown building, panels shielding the doors. A restroom. Tallulah went inside. She peed, then, discreetly as she could, she searched the other stalls and the showers. Three little girls in bathing suits, and a fortyish woman who glared at her before turning her back. No Maeve. Back outside, Tallulah broke into a jog. A glimpse of a red head stopped her, but it was only a boy lifting a bicycle off a car rack. The boy was thirteen or fourteen, tall, bare-chested, his shoulder blades sharp-edged as plywood, shadowing the knobs of his spine. The boy caught her staring; even from a distance, she could see him blush. She turned and kept going.

She searched the campground twice before she saw the sign. It stood, white letters on brown, at the intersection of the dirt road and a narrow trail obscured by brush. To TALLULAH GORGE TRAILS.

Somehow she didn't think Maeve had gone sightseeing. And yet she wasn't in the campground.

Nothing to do but go back to LUVLY1 and wait. Surely Maeve would return soon. After all, she'd left practically her whole life in the car—her ID, her money, her notebooks, the car itself. Tallulah began walking back to the campsite.

And stopped. She pulled the note from her pocket, read it again. She looked back at the trailhead and she wasn't thinking about Maeve, but about the expression on Poteet's face, the look in his eyes when he'd discovered his ex-wife's pregnancy, and again when Tallulah had yelled at him in surgery, and suddenly she grasped what it was that had eluded her before. The mare's eye had held the same look, just before she died.

Despair.

Sweat beaded in the hollows of Tallulah's armpits, her temples. Maeve had left practically her entire life in LUVLY1. Because she wasn't coming back. Tallulah was sure of it. As sure as she was that she had Maeve's permission to go. More than permission. A directive.

I kept it for you. Take care of it.

Tallulah dropped the paper. She ran back to the trail-head and plunged into the shadows. Brush whipped her bare legs. Another sign, this one white letters on scarlet: DANGER. CLIFFS WITHOUT RAILING. SEVERE VERTICAL DROPS. Tallulah ran on. A small clearing opened to her right; she skidded into it. Panting, hand pressed to the stitch in her side, she shambled to the railing and looked out into the gorge.

The cliff opposite seemed absurdly close, almost as if she could stretch and brush with her fingertips the bushes growing from its face. Then she spotted a tiny wrought iron railing, identical to the one under her hands, and she realized that what she had taken for bushes were in fact full-sized fir trees. Nausea fluttered under her ribs, as it had when she'd seen Poteet's hands slip into Arabella's abdomen. She closed her eyes. Then she forced herself to lean over the railing, into the vast empty air, and look down.

Dizziness lightened her head and her feet. She gripped

the rail hard until it passed. Then her eyes found their focus, and she stared down the cliff face. Nothing except rocks and trees and, far below, a bird—there was something about its long, tense glide that made Tallulah think of a hawk—and, farther below that, the river. This river was narrower than the Willamette in Portland, but where the Willamette was smooth, as untroubled as mud, this river thrashed into foam across the backs of the rocks and then reformed, lustrous and muscular as a snake.

No blood on the rocks. No scraps of clothing.

Her bangs were stuck to her forehead, glued with sweat. Tallulah skimmed them free, her breath working hard in the sticky air. She was overreacting. Jumpy as hell from being in this strange place. Better just go back to the car and wait.

A movement by the river's opposite bank caught her eye. A person was clambering over the rocks. The bottom of the gorge was mostly in shadow, but the person lifted her head and even in the dim gorge light Tallulah could see the spark of red. Maeve. Tallulah screamed but Maeve didn't look up, of course she didn't, no one could hear from this distance. Tallulah pushed herself away from the wrought iron and sprinted back to the trail.

As she ran the shadows grew deeper, the trees denser, their trunks slim and straight as matchsticks on cliffs too sheer to scramble down. Yet Maeve had somehow made it to the river. Tallulah pushed harder, her legs pumping, not in the steady rhythm of exercise but in flailing panic.

Please, God, don't let her do it. Don't let her do it before I get there.

Stairs on the cliff edge. Another scarlet sign. Tallulah didn't stop to read it. She plunged down the steps, her feet clattering on the metal grating.

After the twelfth flight she was sure every landing would open onto the river, only to find another precipitous drop. The bottom of the stairs was hidden by trees; she felt suspended in silent forest. Just as she was sure she couldn't run anymore, she began to hear the rush of water over rock. More flights, more drops, until at last, breath coming in whooping gasps, she thudded onto a wooden platform. The river boiled at its edge.

Tallulah's legs wobbled like old rubber bands, brittle, threatening to split. She staggered across the platform, searched the bank. There was no trail. Upstream or down? On the upstream side, the river churned to whitewater over an array of boulders, breaking against the cliff face with nowhere to pass between. Maeve must have gone downstream.

Tallulah stepped onto the rocks. Her foot slipped, and she grabbed at the platform railing. She was wearing the ancient Nikes, worn smooth across the bottom. The rocks were slick with water and algae and mud. They teetered under her weight. She hung on to branches, scrambled on all fours. Her left foot kept slipping into the water. After a few minutes, her toes were numb from cold.

Just ahead, the cliff jagged out into the water, blocking

her view of the river beyond. Tallulah edged her way around it. There, just beyond the jag, was Maeve.

She was sitting barefoot on a slab-topped boulder in the middle of the river. Her face was lifted to the sun; her eyes were closed. She looked as though she was dreaming. The yellow skirt was hiked up above her knees, her legs V'd open on the rock.

Maeve wasn't dead. She wasn't dying. She was sunbathing on a rock.

Tallulah crept along the narrow spill of stones and mud until she was a little ahead of the boulder. She and Maeve were separated now by only ten feet of rushing water.

"Maeve!" she yelled. She waved her arms. "Maeve!"

Her voice was swept away by the river. Maeve's eyes remained closed. Tallulah sank back down onto the rocks; she could think of nothing else to do. Water stole through the fabric of her jeans, and she shivered.

Then Maeve stood up. She stretched, her toes curled over the edge of the boulder, her arms curving high. Tallulah got to her feet, the rocks shifting beneath her. Just as she drew breath to yell again, Maeve fell in the water.

She didn't jump; Tallulah remembered that later, because if Maeve had bent her knees, or stuck out her arms, Tallulah would have known what she was about to do. Instead, Maeve simply twisted her feet off the boulder's edge and fell. It was so undramatic that for an instant, Tallulah could only blink at the empty air where Maeve had been.

Then she leaped into the river. The water picked her up

as though she were a doll, boneless, sweeping her backward. She twisted until she faced downstream and kicked hard, straining to swim faster than the current—there, ahead of her, a bobbing flash of yellow. She grabbed and missed. Then the water lifted her and slammed her sideways against rock. She gasped, her mouth filled with water and she sputtered, choking. She launched herself back into the current, tumbling, belly down. There—yellow. She struck out at it. Her fingers, numb almost beyond feeling, gripped something. An arm. The arm twisted, thrashing, and then the other hand joined it, beating at Tallulah's face. Tallulah seized a handful of hair; it slipped through her fingers, but not before she managed to noose her elbow around Maeve's neck and heave her chin above the surface. Tallulah angled backward toward the riverbank. Maeve flailed against her, her feet drumming Tallulah's shins. Tallulah felt herself sinking. Water closed over her head. Blood and rain, mingling on the dead face of the girl in the road . . .

Panicked, she lunged upward. When her head cleared the water, she bashed Maeve twice, hard, the heel of her hand into the side of Maeve's face. The flailing subsided.

Tallulah's shoulder struck rock; she kicked, found more slippery rock underneath. Maeve must have, too, because she began to struggle again, and this time her body seemed to have leverage. Tallulah battered her again, then thrashed backward out of the current to the water's edge. On the riverbank—not a bank, really, no sand or dirt, simply a jag of low flat stones—Tallulah let go and dragged herself, coughing, out of the water. Over the noise the river, she heard Maeve retching.

Tallulah rolled on her side. Maeve lay across a rock on her stomach, propped on one arm. Her legs were still in the river. The current nipped at her skirt. As Tallulah watched, she sagged back, letting the water rush up over her hips.

It hurt to breathe. Tallulah's throat was raw, her nose clogged with water. She pushed herself to her knees and lurched to where Maeve lay.

"Leave me alone," Maeve whispered. Her voice broke in the middle of *alone;* her breath whooped, and she retched again.

"Make me," Tallulah croaked. She wedged her hands under Maeve's armpits and dragged her a few more inches up the rock. Then her thighs gave way, and she thumped down on one hip. Her nose was running, and she was shaking with cold. Maeve coughed and spat thin blood. She drew her legs up onto the rock, bit by tiny bit, as though she were a toy on its last spark of battery. Once she was out of the water entirely, Tallulah sank down flat onto the stone, and shut her eyes against the radiant cliff-bound sky.

Chapter 27

Tallulah had awakened at four a.m. short of breath from a silver, water-thrashing dream. Afraid to go back to sleep, she'd left the bustle and noise of the emergency room for one of the hospital's smaller, out of the way waiting areas. She was watching cartoons on the wall television, arms wrapped around her knees, when Mr. Connelly found her.

The Connellys had arrived from Orlando the night before, a bare six hours after Tallulah had torn through LUVLY1 looking for anything that might have Maeve's real name, or any clue that might lead to a relative, anyone, no matter how distant. In the cloth Guatemalan wallet, tucked in a pocket behind three library cards and a video rental card from San Antonio, Texas, she'd found a smudged, dog-eared business card. Marianne E. Connelly, Systems Analyst, a cell phone number written in Maeve's handwriting on the back. Tallulah called the number collect. Marianne Connelly picked up on the first ring.

"I'm a friend of Maeve MacRae's," Tallulah said.

"Where is she? Is she all right?"

Tallulah hesitated.

"I'm her mother," the woman said. "Tell me what's happened to my daughter."

Mr. Connelly came into the waiting area, hands in his jeans pockets. "'Morning," he said. He was tall, with a hip-settled heaviness and a more rugged version of Maeve's knife-edge nose. "We thought you might like breakfast. Michelle's mother has a table for us in the cafeteria."

Who's Michelle, Tallulah almost asked; then she remembered. Since that phone call, it seemed she was always having to remember something in place of what she'd thought she already knew. Like Maeve's real name. Like the Connellys themselves. "What time is it?" she asked.

"Seven thirty," Mr. Connelly said.

It took her a while to unfold herself from the chair, feeling, as she did, that now she knew a little of what Diesel had endured. The beating the river had given her yesterday had been bad; but this morning, after a night spent scrunched in hospital chairs, she felt as though Leopard had worked over every bone she had, and some twice. Her left knee, which apparently she'd bashed against a rock, was the tenderest. Standing up, she winced. Mr. Connelly took her duffel and offered her his arm.

The cafeteria was a long, wan green room with pale linoleum, empty except for a cluster of white-coated people in the far corner and Mrs. Connelly seated at a table near the door. She rose when they came in. She was shorter than Maeve, with cropped hair faded several shades lighter than her daughter's, and a rounder face. Lines fine as spiderweb netted her cheeks.

"They have omelets," she told Tallulah. "Or French toast." Maeve's parents, Tallulah had already learned, wasted no time on unnecessaries. Last night, after they'd seen Maeve and spoken with the doctor, they had taken Tallulah to this same cafeteria. Over coffee and pie, which none of them ate, they asked her about Maeve. What she'd done in Portland. Where she'd lived, where she'd worked; what she'd talked about, what possessions she'd had. If Tallulah's answers wandered, Mrs. Connelly cut her short with another question. Tallulah's mother could be the same way, but in her it was due to a driving purpose, an instinct for the shortest pathway to a goal. In the Connellys, it seemed a guarding of energy. As if they'd long ago discovered the limits of their resources, and the need to ration them against future emergency.

"How is Maeve? Michelle?" Tallulah asked.

"Better," Mr. Connelly said. "Staying here last night, that was just a precaution. Doctors, you know. They're releasing her today."

No one said anything else until they sat down with their trays. Then Mrs. Connelly said to Tallulah, "We thought maybe you'd like to see Michelle first thing this morning."

"Sure," Tallulah said. "That would be great."

"And then you can be on your way," Mrs. Connelly said. She was stirring a packet of sugar into her coffee; before Tallulah could react, she set the spoon down and reached across the table, resting her hand on Tallulah's arm. "You have to understand," she said. "We've been through this before. Right now, after the mania, is the worst time. We've found it's best if she's just with family."

Tallulah broke her Danish in half, then half again. She would decide whether she stayed or left, and that would depend on Maeve.

When they arrived at Maeve's room, her parents went in first. Tallulah leaned against the wall, fighting down the nerves that suddenly roiled her stomach. She tried closing her eyes, but that only brought back flashes of the silver water. She opened them again hurriedly to see Mrs. Connelly standing in the doorway.

"She's still sleeping," Mrs. Connelly said. "But you can sit with her a few minutes, if you'd like."

They let her go in alone, for which she was grateful. Her first impression of the hospital room was of clutter, too brightly lit; the bed itself seemed unimportant, crowded as it was by stands of equipment trailing cords across sun-brilliant sheets. Under the blanket, Maeve seemed small. She had never seemed small before.

Tallulah walked to the foot of the bed, laying her heels down gently, careful not to make noise. Maeve's face was turned toward the window. Despite the bandage shielding her nose, her face in the sunlight reminded Tallulah of a painting she'd seen once of someone holy: Jesus maybe, or Mary. The way her skin seemed to throw the light back.

Someone—Mrs. Connelly, probably—had trimmed her hair, to make it even. It still spiked over her ear and forehead.

Tallulah set her duffel bag on the floor. There was a plastic chair by the bed, and she eased into it. Maeve didn't look asleep, not exactly. There was a subtle tension in her face, as though she was dreaming. Or maybe it was the way the oxygen tubing ran across her cheeks, dividing her mouth and chin from all that came above.

Maeve drew a deep breath. "Close those drapes, will you?" she said. Her voice cut out in the middle, like an engine that wouldn't turn over. She finished the words in a hoarse whisper and cleared her throat.

Tallulah got up and drew the window curtain, snuffing out the glare of sun that fell across the bed. Slowly, grimacing, Maeve hitched herself higher on her pillows. The bandage on her face lay like an angel's wing. Protective. And accusing.

Tallulah still wasn't sure how long they'd remained at the edge of the river, Maeve slumped and shuddering on the rock, Tallulah lying by her, too exhausted to move, let alone to think what to do next. When the last of the sun lifted from the water, though, Tallulah reached out and touched Maeve's shoulder.

"We need to go," she said. "We can't stay here."

Maeve remained hunched, unmoving, hands cupped over her face. Tallulah had to haul her up, and because she didn't have the strength to do that and still walk, she bullied and threatened until finally Maeve got to her feet. That was when Tallulah saw the blood drying in rivulets over her upper lip, her mouth, her chin, Maeve's nose a vile purplish black and swollen four times its size.

"I hurt," Maeve whispered, swaying. "I hurt."

The fight in the river. Tallulah bashing Maeve's face with the heel of her hand.

"I'm sorry," Tallulah said. "I'm so sorry. I didn't mean it." She snugged her arm around Maeve's waist, laid Maeve's arm over her shoulders. "It'll be OK," she said, and half-supporting Maeve, half-dragging her, she'd led them from rock to rock, headed upriver to the cliff stairs.

With the drapes closed, the only source of light in the hospital room was the fluorescent strip on the wall above the bed. Under it, the pale walls and banks of equipment seemed to have no color of their own but picked up shadings from whatever was around them: the red of Maeve's hair, the aqua trim of her hospital gown. In the dimmer light, though, the green and purple bruises edging out from under Maeve's bandage appeared less livid, less hurtful.

"How are you?" Tallulah asked.

Maeve blew her breath out and grimaced. "I'm sorry," she said. Her voice sounded muffled and nasal. After a moment, she added, "That's two sorries down. About five hundred more to go. I've found it takes about six months to say them all. I'll think I'm done, then I'll run into somebody, and it's 'I'm sorry' all over again."

Silence. Tallulah beat the corners of her brain for something to say. "LUVLY1 is here. In the parking lot, right downstairs. Waiting for you." She strived for a cheerful tone, but it came out high-pitched and harsh. As though she was bribing a two-year-old to do something unpleasant. If their situations were reversed . . . but no, she couldn't say anymore what Maeve might do in her place.

"It's yours," Maeve said.

"But you're getting out today. I mean, you'll need her."

"I don't want it. I told my dad already, he'll write something to make it legal. They don't want it. So take it."

"But you've had her so many years—"

"Eight months." A smile—a thin-lipped, scrawny cousin to her old smile—flitted across Maeve's mouth. "Poor Tallulah. Never believe a bipolar on a manic high. They're liable to tell you anything." Her fingers felt along the edge of the bandage, as if to ascertain that nothing could creep underneath. Then she lay back on the pillow, draping the crook of one elbow over her eyes.

Tallulah waited. But Maeve said nothing else.

"I had to call them," Tallulah said. "I'm sorry. But I didn't know what else to do."

When the cliff stairs had come into sight, Tallulah had thought the worst was over. They'd started up them, Maeve supported on one side by the railing, the other by Tallulah. And they climbed. Over five hundred steps to the top,

Tallulah found out later from the ranger who gave her directions to the hospital, and every time Maeve sank down to rest on a landing—and she rested on every landing—Tallulah was terrified that she would have to beat and bully her again to get her up. If they hadn't met the tourists coming the other way, Tallulah knew they would not have made it. The tourists—two couples, Tallulah remembered that much, but other than that she seemed to have wiped all details about them from her mind—gave them water and helped them the rest of the way up the stairs, then along the trails to LUVLY1, the two men carrying Maeve in a chairlift between them, Tallulah reeling behind, supported by one of the women, while the other ran in the opposite direction for the ranger.

Tallulah wondered how much of it Maeve remembered. Or if, like herself, the ordeal was already melding into one long surreal nightmare of green foliage and the warm honey-colored wood of the stairs, suffocating heat, and always, always, the roar of the river below.

"Was it me?" she asked.

Maeve didn't lift her arm from her eyes. After a long moment, she said, "Was what you?"

Did I make you do it? How did you ask someone such a thing? But through the long night, the if-onlies had tortured Tallulah: if only she'd gotten to Florida on time. If only she'd agreed to go with Maeve that evening on the hill above the graveyard. If only.

Tallulah traced a line in the blanket with her finger. "Tallulah Falls," she whispered.

Maeve dragged her arm above her head, let it sink into the pillow. "Michael kicked me out. So I bought the maps. To see where I should go. I found your name. . . ." She stared at the ceiling, her lips moving a little, as if she were trying to fit pieces together that didn't match. "I thought it was a sign to find you. And I did, but that wasn't it. It wasn't enough." She draped the arm again over her eyes. "I'm tired."

"I can come back if you want me to," Tallulah said. "Do you want me to come back?"

A minute passed on the bedside clock. The silence seemed to crawl over Tallulah's skin. When two minutes had gone by, she started to speak but her voice stuck. She cleared her throat and tried again. "I brought you your notebooks," she said. She pulled them out of the duffel and laid them on the bedside stand, next to an uneaten bowl of cut-up melon. "I gave your wallet and the money to your folks. But I kept the man-in-the-moon. Is that OK?"

Under the slack pale weight of her arm, Maeve was silent. A knock sounded on the door. Unsure what to do, Tallulah stood. Maeve's other hand lay inert on the blanket, and Tallulah laid her fingers lightly on the wrist. She'd intended just a touch, but Maeve's hand curled upward and gripped hers. Tallulah started in surprise.

"I'm sorry," Maeve whispered. Two tears trickled down the curve of her cheek.

Tallulah sobbed; she pressed her other hand hard against her mouth, then swooped low and kissed Maeve's forehead. The skin was cool and damp under Tallulah's lips. As if the warmth that used to radiate from Maeve, like a small sun, had somehow been doused in the river.

"Just be well," Tallulah said. She squeezed Maeve's fingers, hard, as though she could press all that was in her heart into Maeve's flesh. "Be happy. Promise me." Maeve's grip tightened in response. Another knock on the door, louder. Tallulah lifted Maeve's hand, kissed the bruised knuckles. "I'll see you sometime," she said. "I will." She picked up her duffel, swung it to her shoulder, and walked out of the room. She didn't look back.

The Connellys were standing just outside the door. They led Tallulah a little way down the hall, waiting, politely, while she wiped her eyes on the back of her hand. Mrs. Connelly dug a tissue out of her purse and gave it to Tallulah.

"Did Michelle tell you about the car?" Mr. Connelly asked. When Tallulah nodded, he reached into his shirt pocket and pulled out a folded piece of paper. "This says it's yours. No way of knowing where the pink slip is, unfortunately. You'll have to apply for a new one."

"Is she going to be OK?" Tallulah asked.

Mr. Connelly looked away down the hall; but Mrs. Connelly met Tallulah's eyes straight on. Her face was worn, threadbare as old jeans. It was the same look she'd had last night, when she'd told Tallulah some of what Maeve had been through, what they'd been through with her. She'd recited years and episodes like a familiar prayer, without emotion, her thoughts seeming to slip elsewhere.

"You want me to say yes," she said now. "It would be nice to say yes. So. Yes. She'll be fine."

"If she was a diabetic," Mr. Connelly said, "she'd take her insulin. Right?" He lowered his voice to a harsh whisper, as if afraid Maeve would hear him. "In the old days," he said, "they'd have blamed it on how we toilet-trained her or some damn thing. They'd have called her crazy and locked her up. Now they understand, they have medicines, but she just won't . . ."

"Everett," his wife said.

I am Maeve Anaïs MacRae. I renounce the culture of What and I reclaim the culture of Who.

"She just wanted to be Maeve," Tallulah said. She spoke slowly. Feeling her way ahead, trying to puzzle out the *how.* "And she was. It came off her, this incredible energy, like perfume. Everyone loved her. Everyone wanted to be her friend."

Both the Connellys were looking at her intently, Mr. Connelly's pale eyebrows drawn down, his mouth open a little, as if trying to absorb her words directly into himself. Then Mrs. Connelly reached for Tallulah and pulled her close. It was the kind of unexpected gesture that Tallulah had always associated with Maeve. She felt the tears rise again, hovering hot under her eyelids.

"You saved her life," Mrs. Connelly said. "Thank you for

that." She hugged Tallulah hard. Then, as abruptly as she'd embraced her, she let her go. "Everyone always wants to be her friend, when things are good. You were the only one who ever stuck through the hell."

You were. Already Tallulah had been placed in the past.

"Do you need anything?" Mr. Connelly asked. He pulled out his wallet, began riffling through it.

"No, I've got a paycheck coming. Really."

He folded a few bills in his palm and held them out. "Gas money," he said. "Take it."

Reluctantly, she did. She gripped the money in one fist, shook their hands with the other. After a few steps down the hall, Tallulah glanced back; but the Connellys had already gone in to their daughter.

In the gift shop, Tallulah bought a candy bar, breaking a dollar of her change into coins. There were pay phones by the front entrance; she'd seen them last night. Tallulah dropped the coins into the slot, listened to them fall.

"Debbie," she said, when the automated menu asked for her name. *About five hundred sorries to go.*

It was almost three o'clock by the time she made it to Clark Station. The client parking lot in front of the veterinary hospital was empty. The front door was locked. Standing under the awning, hand on the door handle, Tallulah wondered for a moment if something terrible had happened. Then she remembered it was Saturday.

She walked around the back of the hospital. No cars there, either. Poteet's truck was gone. Kyle's motorcycle was in the shed, though. Tallulah studied the door of his apartment, blank at the top of the stairs.

She went back to LUVLY1, got in, and swung the car onto the highway.

Finding the lake wasn't difficult; amid the church signs nailed to telephone poles and erected on posts (ASHBURY PIKE BAPTIST CHURCH, 0.2 MI; UNITED METHODIST CHURCH, 0.4 MI), were arrows directing the way. Finding Poteet's house, though, took almost two hours. The last and only time she'd been there had been for the hospital picnic, just after the accident, Tallulah and the baby in the ditch, little breaths shared between them. Of the ride to Poteet's that day, she remembered only a gravel driveway winding uphill, the flicker of sunlight through green leaves.

It was a bigger lake than she'd thought, and half the driveways wound uphill through stands of trees. By the time Poteet's expanse of lawn unfolded in front of her, with its six greenhouses standing catty-corner to each other, it seemed to Tallulah she'd tried every gravel track in the county. Her arms ached from hauling LUVLY1 through three-point turns.

Luck was with her in one way, at least. The white truck was parked in the carport.

Tallulah pulled in behind it and got out of the car. Flies milled and darted in the carport's shade; one buzzed by her face and she waved a hand, shooing it off. She heard a faint thump-thump from across the lawn; there, under a pair of twisted oaks, lay Diesel. He picked up his head as she approached, his tail raising puffs of dust where it beat the ground.

"Hey, goofball," she said. "What are you doing here?" He rolled onto his side and raised a front leg. *Scratch my chest.* She was bending down to oblige him when the door to one of the greenhouses swung open. She straightened up. Poteet stepped out in dirt-smudged jeans and a blue work shirt, wiping his hands on a rag.

"This is a surprise," he said.

What she'd planned had seemed simple. Now, seeing him, and the wariness on his face, she found she couldn't say anything.

Poteet half-turned toward the open door and gestured to it. "You never did see my orchids," he said.

She slipped across the threshold, ducking her head a little as she passed him. Inside, fans whirred on either side of the door. It was cool, the air barely sweet. Not cloying like roses, or overwhelming like the gardenias her mother loved. Even the light was a cool, faint green, as though the plants by their sheer mass tinted the sunlight filtering inside.

Studying the orchids was easier than facing him. She wandered down the aisle, pausing to brush a finger along a row of spiky, yellow green petals. The centers of the flowers were fleshy triangles, a creamier, pale green, with dark speckles. More spikes angled up from the flower tops.

Behind her, Poteet said, "That one's a *Brassia verrucosa*."

"It looks like a daddy longlegs," she said.

"Actually you're right. People call them spider orchids. Now that one over there—"

"I'm sorry about what I said." Tallulah dug her hands into her pockets, her elbows stiff. She kept her eyes fixed on the flowers. "I was angry. If I could take it back, I would."

When he didn't answer, she turned to look at him. He was staring at the ground, hands on his hips. She couldn't see his face. "You come here just to tell me that?" he said.

"And to get my pay." Tallulah added, "But I didn't apologize just for that, if that's what you're thinking."

Poteet looked up at her then. Sharp, but not angry. To her relief, no sign of that terrible brittleness. "I wasn't thinking anything of the kind," he said. He hooked a hand around the back of his neck, wincing, as if easing a knotted muscle. "Wait here," he said, and left.

He returned a few minutes later with an envelope and a book. He held them out to Tallulah. The book was tiny, smaller than her palm, but thick, with an old-fashioned black-and-white photograph of a man's bearded face on the creased tan cover. *The Song of Myself.* Walt Whitman.

"That was Emily's favorite," Poteet said.

He'd already lost his daughter's horse. She couldn't take his daughter's book. Tallulah shook her head and tried to give it back to him, but he walked past her, ignoring her outstretched hand.

"I told you she was the bravest person I ever knew," he said. "Of course she was scared. Everyone's scared. She never let it stop her, that's all." He stooped to examine a plant. "Ruth mentioned you might be going for an EMT. Or a paramedic. You like the idea of saving lives?"

Tallulah rubbed the side of her thumb along the book's edges. The pages were so worn, they felt like velvet against her skin. "I'm not sure," she said. "Maybe."

"You'll lose lives, too. Nobody ever thinks of that, ahead of time." He rotated a pot a few inches clockwise. "Think you could handle that? Someone dying on you?"

A girl crumpled in the road. The life flicking out of a horse's eye. The flutter of a baby's heart under her fingertips.

Maeve falling in the river, Tallulah leaping in after her. Damn lucky, the doctor had said. You ought to have both drowned. At the memory, gooseflesh rose across Tallulah's arms.

"Guess I'll find out," she said.

Poteet nodded. "Honest answer." He peered closely at a spray of blooms. He slid a penknife out of his pocket and carefully cut one free. "You remind me of her. The way you get mad and be damned." He held the flower toward Tallulah: a brilliant orange star, at its center a scalloped funnel, red-speckled and narrow as a throat. She reached for it, but he didn't let go; so that for a moment, both of them grasped it, her fingers above his on the slender stem. "Anybody doesn't notice you," he said, "they haven't eyes to see." His own eyes were shadowed, deep as pools. He let go of the flower. "Remember that." He took a step back, turned, and walked out the greenhouse door.

Tallulah waited in the cool green light, holding the flower in both hands. When he didn't come back, she went out onto the lawn. Poteet wasn't there. Not in the carport, not on the hill sloping down to the lake. For a long moment, she looked at the little silent house. Then she crossed the lawn to LUVLY1.

The envelope she slid in the glove compartment under the man-in-the-moon dagger. She nestled the book into a side pocket of her duffel, by itself, where it wouldn't get damaged.

The orchid she tucked behind one ear.

Maps were still strewn over the backseat. She rummaged among them, until she found one with a corner entirely blue with ocean. She tore the corner off, and, using an armrest as a desk, she wrote: *Thank you. Thank Ruth, give her a big hug from me.* She hesitated, chewing on the cap of the pen. She'd wanted to ask Poteet how Arabella was, and Mr. Castleberry. She'd wanted to ask him about Kyle, if only to say Kyle's name one last time to someone who knew him. Dammit, she'd wanted to ask him which way to the interstate.

She bent over the armrest and scribbled, *Make sure Jolene gets home on time.*

Tallulah carried the note back to the greenhouse and anchored it under the nearest pot. When she came back out, Diesel got up from his spot under the oaks and lumbered over to her. Where he'd been shaved for tubes and catheters, on his side and down his legs, the fur was already growing back. No more than a fine black fuzz, glossier than the rest of him. Tallulah reached down and scratched the hollow at the base of his throat. He thumped a hind leg on the ground. Kick-starting his motorcycle.

"You take care of him now," she said. She kissed the top of his head—the fur was hot and smelled of clean dust—then walked away. At the car, she looked back to see Diesel ambling onto the porch. He scratched at the door—one bold swipe of his paw—and waited, tail waving, as if in perfect faith that the door would open.

Tallulah kicked off her huaraches and tossed them onto the backseat. Even though she'd left the windows open, the inside of the car was blistering. Palms dancing on the steering wheel, she backed LUVLY1 around in a lovely, sweeping arc until its hood pointed down the driveway. There was a gas station on the highway between the lake and Clark Station. She would ask for directions there. Knoxville tonight, easy. Then ten hours of driving a day. Maybe twelve, if she wasn't tired. By Wednesday, she'd be home.

Acknowledgments

My sincere gratitude to my writing teachers: Verlena Orr, who taught me that writing is worth turning one's life upside down for; and Karen Karbo, who never settled for less than my best and never gave less than hers. Many thanks to Choi Marquardt, Connie McDowell, Dan Berne, Jerry Isom, Laura Wood, Dave Thomas, Karen Holland, Valerie Hashizume, Kathleen Leatham, and all the Writers of Renown, past and present, for their honest and invaluable critique. To Jill Schoolman of Archipelago Books, for her friendship, encouragement, and wanton passion for literature. To Don and Melinda McCoy and everyone at North Portland Veterinary Hospital: your affectionate support of this oddball in your midst means more than you will ever know. To Renee Meronek, DVM, for providing information regarding colic in horses (any inaccuracies are mine alone); and to Ed Ramsay, DVM, for fine conversation and boating on the lake. And to all my friends and colleagues in Tennessee, for your generous hospitality and patience with a young Californian: you taught me so much, and I thank you.

To the late Judith Joyce, for her loving heart and her fierce, magical writing: I will never forget.

Many thanks to Literary Arts, Inc., which supported this work through an Oregon Writers Fellowship.

To Dorian Karchmar, my deepest gratitude; I can neither imagine nor wish for a finer agent. Thanks also to Mercedes Marx and everyone at Lowenstein-Yost Associates for their zealous support.

Melanie Cecka is a writer's dream, an incisive and passionate editor; thank you for taking on Tallulah's story, and for giving me the tools to make her shine. And for their enthusiastic welcome and care, my thanks to the staff of Bloomsbury Children's Books.

Thanks to my family, with love.

To Mitch—no words can express my heart.